MENTAL CASE

MENTAL CASE

JAMES NEAL HARVEY

ST. MARTIN'S PRESS
NEW YORK

A THOMAS DUNNE BOOK.
An imprint of St. Martin's Press.

MENTAL CASE. Copyright © 1996 by James Neal Harvey. All rights reserved. Printed in
the United States of America. No part of this book may be used or reproduced in any
manner whatsoever without written permission except in the case of brief quotations
embodied in critical articles or reviews. For information, address St. Martin's Press, 175
Fifth Avenue, New York, N.Y. 10010.

Library of Congress Cataloging-in-Publication Data

Harvey, James Neal.
    Mental case / by James Neal Harvey. — 1st ed.
       p.   cm.
    "A Thomas Dunne book."
    ISBN 0-312-14014-2
    I. Title.
PS3558.A7183M46   1996
813'.54 — dc20   95-40422
                                          CIP

First Edition: April 1996

10 9 8 7 6 5 4 3 2 1

This book is for Grant

MENTAL
CASE

1

The young woman strode down the west side of Fifth Avenue at a steady pace. She was tall and slender, and in the bright spring sunlight her blond hair reflected glints of gold. Although her features were partly obscured by large, gradient-density sunglasses, it was apparent to anyone who looked at her that she was beautiful; she had a model's high cheekbones and short, slim nose, and her full-lipped mouth was wide and sensuous.

Smartly dressed in a gray coat and medium-heeled pumps, she carried a large black leather handbag, its strap slung over her left shoulder. Except for her extraordinary good looks, she seemed to be just one more of the countless pedestrians enjoying pleasant weather on this Saturday afternoon, after a winter that had dumped tons of snow on New York.

As she walked, men glanced at her admiringly, but she paid no attention to them; she held her head high, and behind the glasses, her eyes were unreadable. She passed the Channel Gardens promenade at Rockefeller Center, and then at 47th Street, she turned right, entering the city's diamond district.

A few steps in from Fifth Avenue was a store that appeared more decorous than its neighbors. Its facade was beige limestone, and in its show windows were items of precious jewelry. The prices were very high, and perhaps for that reason the shop was not as busy as some of the others. A sign over the entrance said PAUL SERENBETZ JEWELERS. The young woman opened the brass-mounted glass door and went into the store.

Inside were three customers: a middle-aged man and woman who were looking at gold bangles, and another woman in a cashmere coat who was buying a ring. The gray-haired jeweler was waiting on the couple, and a female clerk was serving the other customer. A uniformed guard was standing in a corner.

The young woman waited her turn patiently, her arms at her sides, looking straight ahead. Only the clerk acknowledged her, smiling and saying she'd be with her shortly. The young woman nodded briefly and the clerk resumed dealing with her customer.

Meantime, the couple seemed unable to make a choice. Finally, the woman said she thought they ought to look around, and her companion nudged her toward the door. As they left the shop, the jeweler went about putting the bangles back into the showcase.

The customer in the cashmere coat wrote out a check and handed it to the salesclerk, asking her to gift wrap the ring. The clerk said she'd be happy to, then took the ring and the check into the back room.

The jeweler then looked up at the young blond woman and smiled. "Yes, may I help you?"

"I want to buy a diamond necklace," she said. Her tone was low-pitched, revealing no emotion.

"Of course. Did you have any particular style in mind?"

"I want one with a lot of stones—large stones."

He was looking her over, gauging her. "I see. Can you give me a minute, please? I have some that are really outstanding, but they're not in the case. Something like that, I don't keep on display. I'll get them for you."

She nodded briefly.

"I'll be right back." He turned and went through the door behind him, where the clerk had gone a moment earlier.

The young woman remained motionless. Beside her, the woman in the cashmere coat said, "Lovely day outside, isn't it?"

"Yes." She didn't look at the other customer.

The woman seemed about to make another remark, but then apparently changed her mind. Something about the younger shopper's manner, and what she could see of the stony expression, was offputting. She looked away and tapped long red fingernails on the glass surface of the display case.

The jeweler returned from the back room, carrying a stack of three flat black grosgrain boxes. Placing the boxes on the counter, he opened them and took out strings of gems, which he laid side by side on the black velvet pad.

The necklaces were breathtaking. All three were heavily worked with diamonds that were mounted in platinum settings. In the light from the overhead fluorescent bars, the gems glittered against the black velvet like stars in the night sky.

"These are very special," the jeweler said. "I buy the stones myself and design the necklaces. Each one is unique."

The other customer couldn't help peering over at the display. "Say, those are fantastic."

"Yes, they are," the jeweler said proudly. "Every diamond is very high quality, at least a VS, and with G color. And none of them are smaller than a half a carat." He indicated the center stone in one of the necklaces. "That one is three carats."

The young woman made no comment. Taking the bag from her shoulder, she set it on the counter.

"They're all beautiful," the jeweler said. "Just a matter of what you like. You care to try one on?"

"Yes." She pointed at the piece that contained the largest diamonds. "That one."

"Fine, let me help you."

"No, I'll do it." She picked up the necklace and draped it around her neck, fastening the clasp at the back.

The jeweler's smile widened. "Ah, that's lovely on you."

She looked at him.

"I mean it. Absolutely wonderful." He stepped aside and gestured toward the mirror that covered the wall behind him. "Here, look for yourself."

The young woman glanced at her reflection and then returned her attention to the jeweler.

"I can make you a special price," he said.

She made no reply, but opened her bag and reached inside.

And took out a heavy stainless-steel revolver.

The jeweler's eyes bulged at the sight of the weapon. He raised his hands, and as he did, she shot him in the chest.

The bullet knocked the man backward, his pupils wide and his mouth locked open in astonishment, a bright red blossom spreading on his white shirt. He stumbled against the wall and began to slide down it.

The young woman turned to her left, training the pistol on the guard. For an instant, he gaped at her as if unable to grasp what had happened, and then his hand snatched at his own gun in the holster on his hip.

She shot him next, the slug slamming into his belly and doubling him over but not taking him down. His cap fell off and a second shot struck him in the top of the head. He collapsed in a heap on the floor of the shop.

The other customer found her voice then. She let out a piercing shriek that ended abruptly when the young woman put a bullet between her eyes. Her head snapped back from the impact and she fell against the display case, rolling downward onto her side, dead before she landed on the terrazzo surface. Her hands and feet quivered for a moment and then she was still.

The young woman looked at the door to the back room and saw that the clerk had opened it a crack and was peering in horror at the bloody scene. As the muzzle of the pistol swung toward her, the clerk slammed the door. The young woman fired again, the bullet punching a hole in the wooden panel where the clerk's head had been a split second earlier.

Mounted high on a wall in the corner of the store was a small video camera. The young woman looked up at it and saw that it was staring back at her.

She raised the pistol, and as she did, her pulse raced faster and faster. Her head throbbed as the pounding of her heartbeat reached a deafening climax, and above the sound, she could hear a voice calling to her.

"Horrible!" the voice screamed. "Vile! Hideous! Filthy . . ."

For a moment, she stood stock-still, listening. Then she realized the voice was her own.

Still gazing at the TV lens far above her, she shoved the barrel of the pistol into her mouth and pulled the trigger.

2

At his desk in the Special Investigation Unit of the Manhattan District Attorney's Office, Detective Lt. Ben Tolliver sat back in his chair and sipped coffee from a Styrofoam cup.

Tolliver was bored. The case he was working on involved racketeering in the city's construction unions, which was like trying to pin the tail on not one but an endless line of donkeys. Make an arrest, and ten other guys popped up to take the place of the accused—which led to more arrests and more indictments, but few convictions. As a result, the courts were clogged to choking and defense attorneys got rich and it cost more and took longer to build in the city than it ever had.

To some detectives, an assignment like this would be a coveted prize. Shuffle papers; work nine to five. Kiss a few asses to move up in grade; live the good life until it was pension time. And along the way, if you were smart, some of the money that greased the trades would come your way as well.

Ben hated it. The slow-moving, grind-it-out procedures of gathering evidence were enough to make him loathe going to work, and to put him to sleep when he got there. Sure as hell this wasn't why he'd joined the NYPD.

Although exactly why he had, those many years ago when he'd been a starry-eyed kid just out of the Marine Corps, it was hard to remember. Probably because at the time he thought he'd be dedicating his life to winning the battle against the forces of evil, not growing calluses on his butt.

Ironically, getting this assignment had been his own fault. Back when he was in charge of the Sixth Precinct detective squad, he'd run up an impressive record, breaking a number of high-profile cases. That had brought him to the DA's attention, and had led to his being here now, spending most of his time chained to a desk.

A tall, rangy man, he wasn't physically suited to working indoors, either. With his burly shoulders and his cap of dark curly hair, his ice blue eyes and brush mustache, he looked as if he might be a construction worker himself, instead of a plainclothes cop. After an hour or two in his tiny glass-enclosed office, he got itchy, longing to stretch his legs, get out in the air. Even the noxious exhaust-laden fumes of the city were preferable to the atmosphere in here.

"Hey, Ben."

He looked up, to see Capt. Fred Logan enter the room.

Logan was the commander of the unit, and in looks and temperament, the opposite of Tolliver. He was ten years older, with thinning reddish brown hair and round features, his manner that of a shrewd old pol. While Ben loathed wearing a tie and sometimes didn't, the captain was a natty dresser, favoring dark suits and bright foulards. Today he had on a navy double-breasted, and the tie was red and yellow.

"Hello, Cap. Surprised to see you here on a Saturday," Tolliver said. "Thought you'd be playing golf."

Logan smiled. "Just came in to clean up a few things."

That figured. There was never more than a handful of the dozen men and women in the unit working on a weekend; today Ben could see three of them at their desks out in the open area, and what they seemed to be doing mostly was swapping gossip. In another hour, they'd all be gone, and on Monday they'd put in for overtime.

"Got something I want you to look into," the captain said.

Inwardly, Tolliver groaned, envisioning yet another paper trail— more fake receipts to hunt for, more inflated invoices, more canceled checks made out to ghosts and phony corporations.

But Logan surprised him. "There was a shooting a little while ago. I picked up the dispatcher's call on the scanner in my office. A woman went in a jewelry store on West Forty-seventh Street and blew away three people. Then she killed herself."

Ben whistled softly. "What was her problem?"

"No word on that. I called Midtown North and spoke to Terry McGrath. They caught the case."

"Sounds like she had a grudge."

"Either that or she just went crazy and started shooting. Although a female mass murderer is a new one on me."

"Who was she?"

"That was another shocker. McGrath told me she had ID in her wallet that said she was Beth Whitacre. Her father's an investment banker who raised a lot of money for the mayor's campaign."

"Oh, Christ."

"What is it—you know those people?"

"I've known Linc Whitacre for years—ever since I came on the job. Never met his daughter, though."

"The media will go batshit," Logan said. "And so will the mayor and the PC."

"You have any more on what happened?"

"No, that's it. McGrath has a couple of his men on the scene and he said he'll be going over himself. I want you to get up there and find out what you can, write a report. The old man'll want to know."

That was true. An incident of this kind would have far-reaching implications, and DA Henry Oppenheimer was above all politically astute. He'd want to have the facts in hand as quickly as possible.

Tolliver gestured toward the pile of papers on his desk. "I'm supposed to get this ready by Monday. We're trying to make a case against August Rafella, one of the Gambinos' lawyers."

"Yeah, I know. But don't worry about it. You got Grady and Melnick working with you, right?"

"Yes."

"So let them handle it. Who's the ADA?"

"Norman Krantz."

"I'll speak to him on Monday. For now, you get into this other thing, okay?"

"Sure." Tolliver rose to his feet, picking his blazer off the back of his chair and shrugging into it. "Where on Forty-seventh?"

"Near Fifth. Cops'll have the street blocked off at that end."

As he rode down in the elevator, Ben thought about what Logan had told him. Lincoln Whitacre's daughter had killed three people and then herself? What the hell could have possessed her?

3

The fastest route from the Criminal Justice Building to midtown was the FDR Drive. Tolliver drove his Ford Taurus up Centre Street to Houston, turning right and heading for the FDR. Going north, the East River Park was on his right, and beyond it the swift, roiling waters of the river. He picked up speed, squinting into the bright sunshine.

He had the right machine for hurrying. The Ford appeared innocent enough on the outside, a plain blue sedan, but on the inside it was something else. Specially prepared by the factory for police work, the car was powered by a beefed-up 32-valve V-8 with an intercooler and high-lift cams. The car could top 150 mph, and to hold it on the road, the suspension featured antisway bars and heavy-duty shocks.

But the Taurus's charms didn't stop there. The NYPD's Motor Transport people had added a few additional touches, such as bullet-resistant glass all around and armor plate in the front door panels and behind the driver's seat. Under the dash was a sawed-off 12-gauge shotgun in a quick-release scabbard, and the car's trunk held extra ammunition along with a coil of nylon rope and a complete set of burglar's tools.

Experience had taught Tolliver it was wise to be prepared, even if you didn't know what it was you were preparing for. As proof of the adage, the Taurus was the second he'd owned. The first had been wrecked after a high-speed chase in another case. In that one, the armor had saved his life—not once, but twice.

He got off the FDR at the UN exit. Going across town, the traffic abruptly slowed to a crawl. Ahead of him for as far as he could see, the stream of vehicles was barely moving. Reaching under his seat, he picked the portable flasher off the floor and leaned out the window, slapping the device onto the roof of the car. Then he hit the hammer, activating both the red light and the siren.

As the unholy wail rent the air, other vehicles reluctantly pulled over to let the Taurus go by. In this town, people thought they were doing you a big favor by giving way to a police car or even an ambulance. One asshole in a Cadillac just went on inching along in the middle of the street, staring straight ahead and ignoring the flasher and the *oo-ee-oo-ee* behind him. Finally, Ben tapped his bumper against the rear of the other car. The Caddy gave ground and he whipped past.

When he reached Sixth Avenue, he again headed north. The traffic was a little lighter here, but thick, nevertheless. At 47th Street, he turned right again, going east on the westbound street. He was able to race along it because, as Logan had said, cops had sealed off the Fifth Avenue end.

Spotting the crime scene was no problem; there were three patrol cars there now and two ambulances, along with a CSU van. Flashing lights were throwing bright beams in all directions.

Tolliver pulled to a stop and turned off the ignition, then shut down the flasher and the siren. He dropped a police placard on the dash before getting out of the vehicle.

As he approached the store, he saw that cops had put yellow tape across the sidewalk in front of the place. They'd also set up blue-painted wooden barricades and were holding back a large crowd of rubberneckers. The media had arrived, as well; they monitored police radio channels around the clock, and now reporters and photographers were pushing their way to the forefront, among them at least two TV cameramen.

Ben was relieved to see that his girlfriend wasn't among the reporters. She was Shelley Drake, a newscaster for WPIC-TV, and she had a bad habit of bugging him for information on cases he was working. That had caused friction between them, and he often wished she'd gone into another line of work.

After clipping his shield and ID to the breast pocket of his blazer, he checked in with the uniform who was recording the log and then went into the store.

What he found inside looked like a battlefield after a firefight. Blood was everywhere, splattered on the walls and the display case and standing in viscous pools on the floor. As Logan had told him, there were four dead. The ME hadn't arrived yet, so the ambulance attendants hadn't taken out the bodies; they lay as they'd fallen, in the grotesque postures imposed by sudden death. The place was swarming with police officers and forensic technicians.

The detective heading the Crime Scene Unit was Sgt. Jack Weber, a guy Ben had worked with on a number of occasions. Rumpled and jowly, Weber was chewing a cigar stub and looking harassed. Tolliver couldn't blame him. Whatever chance the techs had of finding anything of value was gone by now.

"Hello, Ben," Weber said. "Welcome to bedlam."

Tolliver nodded. "Quite a party, Jack."

"Isn't it? Fucking clowns stomped all over the place before we got here. I don't know how they train these shitbirds nowadays."

A young cop was staring at the dead security guard. He glanced up, looking sheepish on hearing the detective's remark.

Weber seemed not to notice, or to care. "The broad that did it really shot up the place. Looks like she took 'em out one, two, three before she popped herself off. That's her in the middle of the floor."

Ben stepped over to the body Weber had indicated. The young woman was sprawled on her back, arms flung out on either side. The slug she'd fired into her mouth had driven pieces of her palate, brains, and skull through the top of her head, leaving a gory hole in its wake. Despite the expression of shock on her face, Ben could see that she'd been beautiful. Her features were cleanly sculptured, and the ends of her blood-soaked hair were a pale silky blond.

Looking down at the remains, Ben showed no reaction. But his gut was churning. No matter how many times he'd seen shattered bodies, the faces contorted in agony and the life gone out of them in a crimson stream, the sight always had the same impact. The fact that she'd fired the fatal bullet herself made it no less tragic; she'd be dead forever. He thought of her father, then wondered again what could have driven her to do this.

Curiously, an ornate diamond necklace was draped around the young woman's neck. Except for that, she was dressed well but conservatively, in a gray coat and black shoes. A large-lensed pair of sunglasses lay next to her body; presumably, she'd been wearing them when she pulled the trigger the final time.

The pistol was also nearby on the floor. Ben saw that it was a .357 Magnum Colt Python. The type of weapon was no surprise; a female shooter almost invariably favored a double-action revolver, because it was simpler to operate. Like a cheap camera—just point and shoot.

As Tolliver watched, a technician outlined the pistol in chalk, then stuck a pencil into the barrel. He picked up the weapon and dropped it into an evidence bag.

Ben turned to Weber. "How many rounds did she fire altogether?"

"Six. She put an extra one in the guard. Maybe she was a feminist and he gave her some shit."

"That's five. Where'd the other one go?"

"She took a shot at the clerk and missed. The clerk was in the back room and opened the door when the shooting started. This one shot at her, and the clerk ducked back in again. She's in there now, with two guys from Midtown North. The owner was her uncle."

Tolliver noticed a large black leather shoulder bag standing on the counter. Beside the bag was a velvet jeweler's pad with two more dia- mond necklaces laid out on it. Apparently the young woman had been trying on the jewelry when she started shooting; that would explain the necklace around her neck.

"The bag hers?" he asked.

"That's where we got her ID," Weber said. "You hear who she was?"

"Yeah, I did."

"Crazy, isn't it? Her father's rich, got all kinds of political con- nections. She must've just flipped out."

"That could be. You find the slugs?"

Weber held up a small plastic envelope. "Just one so far, but we'll keep looking. Probably some are still in the bodies. I'll run this through ballistics and check the serial numbers on the gun, see if we can trace it."

Ben studied the body of the guard next, lying facedown in a pud- dle of blood. The top of the man's head was covered with wisps of gray hair and there was a blackish hole in the center of it. This puncture was much smaller than the one in the blonde, because it was an entry wound. It was apparent that the other bullet had hit the guard in the midsection; more blood had spread from under that part of his body.

Stepping closer to the counter, Tolliver looked over at the remains of the jeweler. The man was slumped against the wall, the front of his white shirt stained red. A pair of rimless glasses had fallen from their perch and hung from one of his ears. His eyes were glazed and half- closed, his teeth clenched in a grimace of pain. The appearance of his face was characteristic of somebody who'd been shot in the heart; they had just enough time to hurt terribly before dying.

Ben's gaze swung back to the second woman. The look on this one's countenance was altogether different. Her features were locked in a look of astonishment that might have been funny if the circumstances hadn't been what they were.

"Apparently this was a customer," Weber said. "We don't know who was shot first, or if the shooter knew any of them."

Tolliver thrust his jaw toward the fallen guard. "My guess is, she would've taken him out either first or second, because he was armed. And his pistol's partway out of the holster. Most likely the customer just had the bad luck to be here. That leaves the jeweler."

"The camera will tell us."

Ben glanced up at the tiny TV camera mounted high in a corner, its wide-angle lens ogling the scene in the showroom. The tape would be black-and-white, blurry and indistinct, but it would provide a record of the action.

He turned back to the CSU detective. "Be sure to send me a copy of the videotape right away, will you, Jack?"

"Sure thing."

"Hey, gimme a break," somebody said. Tolliver looked around and saw that the CSU photographer was trying to move officers aside so that he could continue taking pictures.

Weber yelled, "Anybody who hasn't got a job to do in here, get out now."

Several of the cops shuffled out the door of the shop. After they'd gone, the detective said to Ben, "Too late, but what the hell. At least we'll be able to move around now. You wonder why I got an ulcer?"

The photographer's flashgun illuminated the confined space with brilliant bursts of light. Tolliver waited until the man had taken about two dozen exposures, then made his way around the counter. He looked again at the body of the jeweler and stepped past it, going to the door that led into the back room.

There was a bullet hole in the wooden panel, about five and a half feet up from the floor and perhaps three inches from the edge. Ben studied it for a moment, then opened the door.

4

The salesclerk was sitting in a chair, flanked by the two detectives from Midtown North. The small room was cluttered, boxes and cartons everywhere. On one side was a table with wrapping paper on it, and above that were shelves that went to the ceiling. A large gray steel door with a flush-mounted combination lock was set into the rear wall.

The clerk was dabbing at her eyes with a sodden handkerchief. Her round face was tear-streaked and puffy, but she was trying to put up a brave front. She had on a blouse, with a cardigan sweater over it, her mousy hair hanging in lank strands. Every few seconds she'd draw a deep breath and then shudder as she exhaled.

Tolliver didn't recognize either of the detectives. Both were younger men, wearing suits and solemn expressions. One of them got to his feet as Ben entered, frowning as he looked at him and then catching sight of the gold shield and ID. "Oh, Lieutenant. I didn't know—"

"That's okay. I'm from the DA's Office. I need to file a report on this."

"Sure. I'm Joe Novotny. This is my partner, Mike Cooper. The young lady here was the only witness."

"If you don't mind," Ben said, "I want to talk to her." Even though he outranked them, he was making an effort to be courteous. He knew how detectives felt about having an outsider stick his nose into a case they were on. He'd had the same experience himself.

"No problem," Novotny said. He and Cooper moved back to let Tolliver get closer to her. "This is Marcia Geller," Cooper said.

"I'm Lieutenant Tolliver," Ben said to her. "I know this has been terrible for you, but I have to ask a few questions."

The young woman shuddered again. In a small voice, she said, "I've already told these officers everything I could."

"I'm sure you have, but I'd appreciate it if you'd go over it again. Besides, you might remember something you hadn't thought of earlier."

She nodded resignedly. "I'll try."

The chair she was sitting in had been pulled back from the desk, and there were also a couple of straight-back ones the detectives had been using. Ben dragged one of the chairs nearer to hers and sat down.

"I understand you were related to the owner," he said.

"Yes. He's my uncle, Paul Serenbetz. I mean, he was my uncle. Oh, God." She clapped a hand to her mouth and shut her eyes. Ben thought she might break down, but after a moment, she pulled herself together.

"Take your time," he said. "Can we get you some water?"

She blew her nose into the handkerchief and then drew another deep breath. The skin around her nostrils had become red and irritated. "No, I'll be all right."

"Have you worked here long?"

"Since I got out of college last year. I used to be part-time while I was in school. Sometimes my aunt Ethel's here, too."

"Anyone else?"

"No. Just the security guard."

"What happened here today? Tell me everything you saw."

"It was a little before three o'clock. We weren't very busy then. We were busy in the morning and right after lunch, but then it quieted down."

"Go on."

"There were only three customers in the store. I was waiting on one of them and my uncle was waiting on the others. Then this woman walked in. The one who . . . did the shooting."

"Did you know her?"

"No, I'd never seen her before. But I remember thinking how attractive she was, and well dressed. Classy. You work in a store like this, you can tell."

"Did you get the impression your uncle knew her?"

"No. At least he didn't act like he did."

"She say anything?"

"No, she was very quiet. I told her I'd be right with her, and she just nodded."

"So you didn't hear her voice."

"No."

"Then what?"

"Then the other two customers left and my uncle took care of the woman. I went back to waiting on my customer. She bought a ring for her daughter and asked me to gift wrap it for her. I came in here to do that."

"Who were the other customers? Did you know them?"

"No, I'm pretty sure I'd never seen them, either. It was a couple— man and a woman—around the same age as Uncle Paul."

"Did they buy anything? If they used a credit card, we could locate them."

She shook her head. "They just looked at some gold bracelets and then they left."

"Okay, go on."

"My uncle came in here then, and he went into the vault. When he came out, he was carrying jewelry boxes. He said the customer wanted to see diamond necklaces."

"He didn't keep them in the window, or in the display case?"

"Oh no. We have necklaces on display, but not like these. These were very special. Even with a guard in the store, he always wanted to be extra careful. The crime around here the past couple years, you wouldn't believe it."

Tolliver would believe it. "Did he say anything else?"

"No. He went back out then, carrying the boxes."

"What was the value of the necklaces?" Tolliver asked.

"I'm not sure. My uncle was the only one who handled anything on them."

"Can you give us an idea?"

"I think he was asking around a hundred thousand apiece."

"What happened next?"

"After he left, I went on gift wrapping the package, and a minute later, I heard this loud noise, like an explosion. At first I didn't know what it was. I went to the door, and then I heard the noise again, two more times. I was, like, what is this—were those shots? I opened the door a little, and . . . Jesus."

"What did you see?"

"My uncle was on the floor, by the door, with blood all over the front of him. The woman was holding a gun. She shot Mrs. Halloran, and when she saw me, I slammed the door and locked it. Then a bullet came right through the door." She pointed to the hole in the door panel, the wood splintered on this side.

"Where was the guard?"

"He was on the floor, but I couldn't see him. I didn't know he'd been shot, too, until after."

"And then?"

"And then there was another shot. I was so scared, I could hardly move." Suddenly, she sat bolt upright. "Oh, here's something. I just thought of it."

"Yes?"

"The woman with the gun? When I opened the door, I saw she had on one of the necklaces. I was thinking just now about how she looked when she shot at me, and I remember she had on the necklace."

And she's still wearing it, Ben thought. Aloud he said, "What did you do next?"

"I grabbed the phone and called nine-one-one, and after that, I heard people yelling. Then the police came in the store. When they called out to me, I opened the door." She bit her lip, looking as if she might cry again. "It was so awful."

"Tell me about your uncle, Miss Geller. Is it Miss?"

"Yes."

"He owned this place?"

"That's right. He was in the business all his life. He was a messenger first, and then he worked for Brenner's, down the street aways. That was before he opened this shop."

"How old was he?"

"Fifty-one, his last birthday."

"Did he have children, he and your aunt?"

"Two. Natalie's married, lives in Chicago with her husband. Jeff is nineteen. He's a junior at Columbia."

"Where does the family live?"

"West Eighty-fifth Street."

"About the young woman—are you quite sure you'd never seen her before?"

"Yes. I mean, as sure as I can be."

"And you don't believe she was someone your uncle knew?"

"No, I don't. He would've said something to her when she came in."

"All right, you've been very helpful. But now think hard. Is there anything else you saw that you haven't mentioned?"

"No. Except . . ."

"Except what?"

"The whole time, when she first came in and later when she was shooting the gun, she was the same."

"The same?"

"I mean, she didn't seem excited or anything. She was just, like, calm. It was weird, now that I think about it. Really weird."

5

Tolliver went back out into the front of the store, beckoning Novotny to follow. As he stepped into the showroom, he saw that a medical examiner had arrived and was looking at the bodies. This was another guy Ben had worked with on previous cases, a carrottop with a beak nose and a nervous, twitchy manner. His name was Edgar Feldman, but behind his back, cops called him "Dr. Woodpecker."

At the moment, Feldman was crouched over the corpse of the guard, his black satchel lying open on the floor beside him. The ME was dressed incongruously, wearing a tan zippered jacket over a white lab coat and white pants, his hands encased in a pair of yellow rubber gloves. He was taking the body's temperature. Rigor mortis had not yet set in, so he had no trouble performing the task. The purpose was to fix the time of death, which in this instance wasn't open to question, but the process was one of several routine steps.

Feldman looked up and grinned. "Where there's smoke, there's Tolliver. How've you been, Lieutenant?"

"Great. But I thought they were going to send a doctor."

"And what you got is a Hall of Fame pathologist. Lucky you."

"This is Detective Novotny," Ben said. "The PC assigned him, to make sure you don't screw up."

"Then he can take the day off. I never make a mistake."

"Yeah, I know. And when you do, you smooth it over."

"You need new material," Feldman said. "Besides, that's a mortician's joke. I'm in a different business."

"You think you can tell us if this guy's dead?"

"He is, definitely. The first bullet hit him in the belly, but the one in the top of his head is what killed him."

"Uh-huh. When you're finished there, we'll have a look."

Tolliver then moved to the counter, where the black shoulder bag was resting next to the pair of diamond necklaces. He asked Novotny what else was in the bag.

"Just ordinary stuff," the detective said.

"Show me."

Novotny took out the contents: a wallet of alligator hide, a hairbrush, a lipstick and a compact, a partly depleted roll of mints, a pair of ticket stubs from the Vivian Beaumont Theater, a small book of phone numbers, a blue Mont Blanc fountain pen, a woolen cap, and a receipt from Bergdorf Goodman that said she'd spent $268.33 on lingerie.

"What's in the wallet?" Ben asked.

Novotny carefully laid out each item. Among them were a New York State driver's license and an embossed security pass from the Metropolitan Museum of Art, each bearing the dead woman's photograph. The license gave her home address as on East 89th Street, and the date of birth put her not quite four months past her twenty-sixth birthday. An insurance card said to notify her father in case of emergency.

In addition, the wallet held a Citibank card, as well as credit cards from AmEx, Saks Fifth Avenue, Bergdorf, Ann Taylor, and Tiffany. Seeing the Tiffany card made Ben wonder again whether she'd picked the Serenbetz store at random or had chosen it deliberately.

Lastly, there was a sheaf of bills; they totaled $140. A change compartment in the wallet contained a few coins.

Tolliver got out a pocket notebook and a ballpoint and jotted down notes on what he'd seen so far. When he finished, he said to Novotny, "Go through the sales records here. I want to know if she ever did business in this shop before. The clerk says she was a stranger, but I want to be sure."

"Okay, I will."

"Have you notified her father?"

"Yes. I called him right after I spoke to Lieutenant McGrath. I would have had somebody go up there in person, but I was afraid he might get wind of it from the media first. I don't know how they got her ID so fast, but they did."

"How did he take it?"

"Like you'd expect. He didn't believe it. Kept saying there had to be some mistake, that his daughter couldn't kill anybody. When I convinced him it was true, he wanted to rush right down here. I told him absolutely not, to stay away. I said we'd get back to him later, that he'd have to identify the body. Finally, he agreed."

"And that was it?"

"Pretty much."

At that point, the ME moved away from the body of the guard, saying, "Okay, Lieutenant, he's all yours."

"Be right there, Doc."

The detectives then stepped to the remains, taking care to avoid the pools of drying blood.

Technically, they weren't supposed to touch a body until a medical doctor had declared the subject dead, a formality Ben often ignored because he thought it was silly. He'd once gone to the site of a bomb blast in SoHo, a house where the guy who built the device had set it off prematurely. The house was a shambles, and the only piece of the bomber the cops found was his left leg. They'd waited for an ME to tell them he'd expired before they picked up the leg.

"You can do the honors," Ben said.

"Sure thing, Lieutenant." Novotny expertly tossed the guard's body, coming up with nothing unusual. The contents of his wallet revealed that he'd been a retired police officer living in Queens.

They checked out the corpse of the female customer next, moving behind Feldman. None of the objects found in her purse or in the pockets of the cashmere coat suggested her life had been anything out of the ordinary. Her name was Ruth Halloran and she'd lived in Mamaroneck, was forty-four at the time of her death, single, with one child. Probably divorced, Tolliver thought.

So far, there was nothing to indicate a connection had existed between her and the woman who killed her, but Ben knew the detectives would run down the possibility anyway. He continued to feel that Halloran had simply been in the wrong place at the wrong time.

They already knew the jeweler's background. Lying half-slumped against the wall with a bullet in his chest seemed an unfair way for a life of hard work to end. The contents of his pockets were as common as what had been found on the others. In his wallet were snapshots of a dark-haired woman and two kids.

The possessions of all the dead would go into evidence bags and be turned over to a property clerk. When the police investigation was completed, the items would be returned to the victims' families.

Again, Tolliver looked at the scene around him, shaking his head at the senselessness of what had occurred here. He considered motives, trying to find some logic behind the slaughter of these people. But there didn't seem to be any. Even the idea that Beth Whitacre had simply been unbalanced didn't hold up—not altogether, anyway. There were too many unanswered questions.

Feldman examined her body last. Ben stood by and watched, saying nothing until the ME finished. When Feldman finally rose to his feet, Tolliver said, "What about drugs, Doc—you think she was high when she did this?"

"Can't say. I looked for tracks and couldn't find any."

"Maybe she was popping something."

"Maybe. Only indication would've been her eyes, but the bullet shattered the optic nerves and burst most of the blood vessels. The pupils are dilated, but shock could've caused that. After they do the post, the lab'll put out a toxicology report. That'll tell you."

At that point, ambulance attendents came into the store and went about trussing up the bodies while Jack Weber's men chalked outlines of the corpses' positions and began making a grid of the site. Another technician was collecting samples of bone, tissue, and blood and putting them into plastic sacks, then tagging the sacks.

Feldman waved cheerfully. "Have a nice weekend, everybody." He left the store, satchel in hand.

Mike Cooper came out of the back room and spoke to Tolliver.

"We're gonna send the girl home in a patrol car now, Lieutenant, unless you want to talk to her some more."

"No, go ahead. I'm about through."

"Well, well," a voice said.

Ben turned, to find Lt. Terry McGrath approaching, the head of the Midtown North detective squad. McGrath was sandy-haired and had freckles sprinkled across his pug nose. He looked dapper in his glen plaid suit. With him was another guy Tolliver recognized—the zone commander. This one was red-faced and beefy and wore a black raincoat. Neither man seemed overjoyed to see him.

"Hiya, Terry," Tolliver said. "Fred Logan asked me to have a look at this."

"Yeah, I figured. This is Captain Jarvis. Captain, Ben Tolliver. From the DA's unit." He made the last part sound as if he'd bitten into something sour.

They exchanged hellos, and then the men moved past him, staring at the carnage.

"Jesus," Jarvis said. "What a fucking mess."

Jack Weber came over then and began giving them a rundown of what his unit had found. They ignored Tolliver.

Their coolness toward Ben didn't surprise him; he knew there were two reasons for it. The first was that, like Novotny and Cooper, they resented someone from another jurisdiction getting into their case—especially a case of this magnitude. Intradepartmental rivalry, cops protecting their domain, was as old as the department.

The second reason was Tolliver's attachment to the Manhattan District Attorney's Office. That made other cops, from the PC on down, automatically suspicious of where his loyalties lay and where his report might end up, what repercussions it might cause.

But so what? He had a job to do, and he would do it no matter what they thought. Anyway, he'd learned all he could here. He turned and went out the door.

Out on the street, cops had put up additional barricades to keep the civilians back. The media swarm had also grown larger, and several of the reporters recognized him, shouting questions as he emerged from the store entrance.

He saw that Shelley was now among them, a good-looking blonde in a trench coat. He took care not to acknowledge her. Having a personal relationship with a newscaster could cause problems, and for that reason, he kept the connection as quiet as possible.

He pushed his way through the pack.

"Hey, Lieutenant," a guy from the *Post* called out. "What made Whitacre go nuts? Why'd she kill three people and then shoot herself?"

Somebody else yelled, "Is it true she couldn't stand her father's politics and that's why she went crazy?"

Tolliver reached his car and opened the door. "There'll be a statement for you later, as soon as the investigation is further along."

To his annoyance, Shelley elbowed her way forward. Her cameraman was close behind, focusing on Ben. She shoved her face into the shot and spoke into a handheld mike. "With me here at the scene of the shooting is Detective Lieutenant Ben Tolliver. Lieutenant, do you think the police can get the answers as to why she did this?"

Through clenched teeth, he said, "I'm sure we'll bring the case to a satisfactory conclusion."

"Do you think she was out to murder those people, and her own death was an accident?"

"I don't know, but I intend to find out."

She tried to say something else, but he turned away and climbed into the driver's seat, slamming the door.

A shout went up as an ambulance crew was spotted wheeling a gurney out of the store. A green vinyl body bag was strapped to the gurney and another attendant was opening the door of an ambulance. The reporters turned away from Tolliver and surged en masse toward the scene, flashes winking, camcorders rolling.

Meantime, the civilians were oohing and aahing, some of them taking pictures, as well. He could hear it now: Look at this, Belinda—I was right there when they were bringing out the bodies.

Ben started the engine and began turning around on the narrow street. Coming here had been bad enough, but what he was about to do next would be worse.

6

The Whitacres lived on Park Avenue at 73rd Street. The building was typical of the ones built along here in the twenties, solid and imposing, its pale stone face decorated with frescoes and fluted half columns. As Ben had expected, a group of reporters had already gathered on the sidewalk outside the entrance. This time, he paid no attention to their questions, stepping past them on his way inside.

The maroon-uniformed doorman examined his credentials carefully before deigning to call up to the apartment. When he put the phone down, he said to go to 32C.

The elevator was old and slow. When he stepped out, Tolliver went to the Whitacres' door and rang the buzzer. The corridor was deserted, and not the slightest sound from neighboring apartments or from the street penetrated the thick walls; the structure was as quiet as a mausoleum.

A maid opened the door. She led him into the foyer, and moments later, Lincoln Whitacre appeared. He was a tall man, about the same height as Tolliver but not as husky, wearing a tweed jacket and flannels, and a blue shirt open at the collar. His face was drawn and pale.

"Hello, Ben," Whitacre said as they shook hands. "I wasn't expecting to see you."

"I'm very sorry about your daughter, Linc. I'm sure you know that."

"Thank you. But I gather you're here officially, is that right?"

"Partly, yes. I have to make a report for the district attorney, and I wanted to talk with you and your wife first."

"I understand."

Ben looked at him. He'd first met Whitacre when the banker was young and eager, working at a fund-raiser for a congressional candidate's campaign. At the time, Tolliver was a rookie cop assigned to a detail at the event. The two had become friends, and Ben had seen him a number of times over the years since then. Whitacre had once put in a good word for him with the police commissioner, and that was the kind of favor you didn't forget. It made coming here now just that much harder.

This evening, Whitacre seemed weary and a lot older. There were patches of gray at his temples and deep lines in his face, and it was apparent that he was trying to keep his emotions under control. "You'll have to bear with us," he said. "We're in a state of shock, as you can imagine."

Ben could; he'd had this task more than once, and it was an aspect of police work every investigator hated. Talking to a family member about a loved one who'd died suddenly and violently was a miserable part of the job. "I'll make this as brief as possible."

"Sure. Please come on inside."

He led Tolliver down a hallway, past a curved staircase leading to a second floor, and then into a sitting room that was decorated with a combination of English and American antiques.

It occurred to Ben that this area looked more like what you'd expect to see in a house in the country than in a duplex in Manhattan. The chairs and sofas were covered in brightly printed chintz, and there were old oil paintings of sporting scenes on the walls, men and horses and dogs, the riders in red-coated hunting regalia. Vases held sprays of spring flowers: yellow daffodils, white jonquils, scarlet tulips.

A door opened at the far end of the room, and a woman entered. She had the same high cheekbones and wide jaw, the same slender body as her daughter. And her hair was the identical shade of blond. Only a network of tiny lines at the corners of her eyes and the edges of her mouth revealed her age. She had on a dark skirt and a simple white blouse.

"You know Enid," Lincoln said to Ben.

Tolliver mumbled condolences as she stepped toward him, noting that her blue eyes were steady, her manner calm. She seemed as much in control of her emotions as her husband, but outward appearances could be deceptive.

"Hello, Lieutenant. Sorry we have to meet again under such circumstances."

"So am I," Ben said. "Very sorry." It occurred to him that this was what Beth undoubtedly would have looked like twenty-five years from now, if she'd lived.

"Ben has to ask us some questions," her husband said. "For a report."

She nodded.

"Please sit down," Lincoln said to Ben. "Can we offer you something to drink?"

"No, thank you." Tolliver deliberately chose a straight-backed chair, preferring not to be overly comfortable in such a situation. Whitacre and his wife took positions on a sofa facing him.

"I'm going to have one," Enid said. She shook her head slowly. "I still can't believe this has happened."

"Scotch?" her husband asked. He pulled a bell cord.

"Please." She directed her attention to Ben. "It's already been on the news, on television. The whole thing is just so ghastly. Did you ever meet Beth, Lieutenant?"

"No, I never did."

"She was a lovely girl. Or young woman, I should say. She was always correcting me on that. A lovely young woman."

"I'm sure she was." Ben thought of her lying in the middle of the carnage she'd created, with her brains spattered all over the store. He was glad her mother hadn't seen her then.

The maid appeared and Whitacre asked her to bring them the drinks, nothing for their visitor. She left the room.

"The doorman told us some of those ghouls from the media are prowling around the building," Whitacre said. "They've also been calling here every few minutes, but I won't talk to any of them."

"You'd think they might have some feeling for what this has done to us," his wife said. "Beth was our daughter and we loved her. This is shattering to us."

Whitacre rubbed the bridge of his nose between two fingers. "It's a terrible loss. She had the best part of her life ahead of her. And now it's all gone, wiped out."

Tolliver saw that Enid's expression had changed; she seemed close to pleading. "Lieutenant, is it possible that this was somehow jumbled—that the detective who telephoned us earlier got it wrong? I mean, that perhaps Beth didn't . . ."

"No, it's true. I was at the scene not long afterward. She did it, without question."

"My God. Poor, poor Beth."

"And the other people as well," Lincoln said.

Enid's voice broke. "They must have had families, too. I'm sure everyone's . . . devastated."

"I know this is hard for you," Ben said. "But there are things I do have to ask."

Whitacre exhaled. "All right, but I'd appreciate it if you could keep whatever we tell you as confidential as possible."

"I'll do that, Linc."

"I have a good many enemies, I'm afraid, because of my political activities. The media would love to drag our name through the mud."

"They're already doing it," his wife said.

The maid was back, bearing a silver tray with two glasses of amber liquid over ice. She served the drinks to the couple and then left once more.

"So let's get to the point," Whitacre said. "I'm sure the first question you want to ask is what impelled our daughter to do such a thing. And the answer is, we have no idea. She seemed reasonably content, had a good job and was enjoying it. We were totally stunned when the detective called us."

"Was Beth under unusual stress lately?"

"Not that we were aware of."

"Did she have a history of emotional problems?"

"She had some difficulties," Enid said. "Starting when she was a teenager. But no worse than what a lot of others go through."

"What kind of difficulties?"

"When she was away at school, she became sort of listless and withdrawn for a while. We kept her out for a semester and had her counseled. After that, she was much better."

"Was the counselor a psychotherapist?"

"No, just a guidance counselor."

"What were the other times?"

"Every now and then, she'd get down on herself. She'd become very unhappy and depressed. But she always came out of it, and then she'd be okay until the next time."

"It seemed to go in cycles," Whitacre said.

"Was she ever treated by a psychiatrist?"

"Not while she was living at home. At least, we never sent her to one."

"What about recently?"

"I suppose it's possible that she was seeing someone. But if she was, she didn't tell us about it."

"Any drug use, do you know?"

"I think she may have experimented with pot, when she was younger."

"Would you know if she used cocaine?"

Enid shook her head and spoke emphatically. "That would have been totally out of character."

"How about alcohol?"

"Now and then a glass of wine, but that was all. She didn't like hard liquor."

"The jewelry store where it happened was named after its owner, Paul Serenbetz. He was one of the people she shot. Had she ever bought anything there, to your knowledge?"

"I don't ever recall hearing anything about that," Whitacre said. He looked at his wife. "Do you, Enid?"

"No, I don't."

"Have either of you done business in that store?"

Both shook their heads.

"Another victim was a woman named Ruth Halloran. Did Beth ever mention that name to you?"

Again they looked blank and gave negative answers.

"Where did Beth work?"

"At the Metropolitan Museum of Art," Whitacre said. "She was an assistant curator."

That explained the security card from the Met in the young woman's wallet, Ben thought. "And you say she liked her job?"

"Yes, very much. Honestly, for her to have snapped this way is just incomprehensible to us. She was never in any trouble, before this."

"Had you seen much of her recently?"

"The last time was a few weeks ago," Enid said, "and she was perfectly normal. In fact, she was quite cheerful."

"Were you living here while she was growing up?"

"Yes, we were," Whitacre said. "We bought this apartment before she was born."

"You have other children as well, don't you?"

"One son. Scott is five years older. He's a lawyer, with Webley, Blake and Dinsmore, in Boston."

"How did he and Beth get along?"

"Very well," Enid said. "There was enough of a difference in their ages that they didn't compete. He was terribly upset when we called him."

"Where did Beth go to college?"

"Cornell. She majored in history and graduated magna cum laude, which tells you something about how bright she was."

"She also had a great interest in art," Whitacre added. There was a note of pride in his voice. "After Cornell, she did graduate work and then spent a year studying in Florence."

"And that's what led her to go to work at the Met?"

"That's correct. As I said, she liked her job very much."

"What about her personal life—she must have had men friends?"

"She was engaged," Enid said. "That is—"

"Who was her fiancé?" Ben pressed.

Whitacre answered. "His name is Ken Patterson. They weren't formally engaged, but they were going together."

"And were planning to be married?"

"Yes."

Tolliver was an old hand at interrogating people. He sensed something was amiss there. "But there was trouble between them?"

"Nothing serious. They shared an apartment, and then Beth moved out a while back—to a place of her own. She just needed some breathing room, some time to think things over."

"There was nothing to it, actually," Enid said. "I'm sure they would have been together again before long."

"What does Patterson do?"

"He's a financial adviser," Whitacre said. "With Branford Sylvester, here in Manhattan."

"Where does he live?"

"East Fifty-third Street."

"Have you spoken to him about this?"

"No, we haven't. I hope the media won't climb all over him, too, but they probably will. You know what reporters are like."

Enid said, "It's just awful, the way they can attack you. And the only thing you can do about it is to keep quiet and just take whatever they hand out. If you protest, that only makes it worse."

"How true," Whitacre said. "We were scheduled to attend a very important dinner tonight. The national party chairman will be there. But that all seems so trivial now. We'll be keeping a low profile for some time."

The next question was a rough one, but Ben had to ask it. "The gun she used was a Colt revolver. A three-fifty-seven Magnum. Do you know where she might have gotten such a weapon?"

"Good lord, no."

"You weren't aware of her having a gun?"

"No, definitely not."

He saw no reason to push them further; they'd answered every question he'd asked. He stood up. "Thank you both for your patience."

"I'll walk out with you," Whitacre said.

Ben said good night to Enid and followed her husband back to the foyer.

When they reached it, Whitacre turned to him, saying, "I was told it will be necessary for me to identify Beth's body."

"That's right, Linc. Other officers will be in touch with you about that."

"Then what?"

"Then there'll be an autopsy, and after that, her body will be released to whatever funeral home you designate."

"Why does there have to be an autopsy?"

"Because New York State law requires it in a homicide case."

Whitacre winced but said nothing. He opened the door and escorted Tolliver to the elevator. "Ben?"

"Yes?"

"There's something I'd like you to do for me. And not just for me, but for Enid and Scott, too. And most of all, for Beth."

"Name it."

The lines in Whitacre's face looked as if they'd been carved into his flesh. "I loved my daughter. I don't know what happened, what made her do what she did. But I have to know. I have to know it, or I'll go crazy myself. Can you understand that?"

"Yes, I can."

"Find out, Ben. Find out. Even if the answer is something horrible, I have to know, no matter how much it hurts. I keep thinking that maybe somehow it . . . wasn't her fault. You see?"

"Yes."

Whitacre held out his hand. "Will you promise to do that? For an old friend?"

Tolliver shook his hand. "You know I will, Linc."

They waited in silence until the elevator came. Then Ben stepped into the car and pressed the button for the lobby.

7

Philip Harkness wanted to kill somebody.

He didn't care who the victim might be. Male or female, young or old, it didn't matter. What mattered was that he drive his knife into a living human being, and that he do it tonight. The only question was which one would give him the best opportunity.

To look at him, you'd never guess he could harbor such thoughts. Of medium height and build, there was nothing remarkable about his appearance. His face was open and bland, and a lock of his longish brown hair flopped down onto his forehead. Wearing an old tweed jacket and jeans, he moved through the crowds on the sidewalk at an easy, almost casual pace. Just another guy going for a stroll on a Saturday night in the springtime.

But inside, he was wound tight enough to explode. Tension was making him tremble, and his pulse was pounding. The knife was concealed in the left sleeve of his jacket, blade up, his fingers curled over the handle.

The area where he was walking was in the West Village, bordering the Hudson River. It was called the meat market, because of the dozens of packing plants in the vicinity. It was also called that because of the bars: straight, gay, lesbian, and variations of all three. Whatever your preference, you could find it here, for hire or for free.

He went up Greenwich Street to Gansevoort and then turned toward the crumbling docks that extended into the river. Most of the people he passed were young and boisterous, out for a good time. A lot of them seemed high, either on alcohol or drugs, and the air was laced with the acrid odor of marijuana smoke. The sound of their chatter and their vacuous laughter rose above the recorded rock that drifted from the bars.

To Harkness, they were candidates, and he looked each of them over carefully.

The fat one there, in the Mets sweatshirt. Holding hands with the short, ugly girl. Be nice to ram the knife into that bag of suet, hear him squeal like a stuck pig.

Or the two characters with the spiked hair and the pins through their noses, the ones wearing tight black rags. God only knew what they might be, or what they thought they were. A good way to find out would be to open them up, cut into whatever he found there.

And how about the foursome coming toward him. Probably blue-collar workers of some kind, cruising the neighborhood looking for fun or trouble, whichever came first. They had red faces and were drinking out of bottles contained in paper bags. And they were braying at each other's raunchy jokes. One of them was singing off-key in a boozy voice. Harkness would love to see what color that one's blood was. He stepped aside to let them pass.

The problem was, none of these dipshits were alone. They were all walking with someone else, and besides, there were too many of them. It would be impossible to use the knife and then slip away unseen, even if he did spot a suitable prey.

What he needed to find was one person, someone walking by himself. Or herself. In fact, a street whore would do just fine. And yet at the moment, he didn't see a single one. It occurred to him that hookers were like cops: They were never around when you needed them.

But damn it, he had to do this. He *had* to.

He kept going, wandering a random course, his frustration heating to full-blown anger. It was getting late, and he'd been out here for hours. Was he going to waste the whole fucking night?

He was closer to the river now, and he could smell the stink coming off the oily waters. Just ahead of him was the West Side Highway, and there weren't as many pedestrians in the vicinity. He slowed his gait and looked toward Horatio Street.

And there was his man.

The guy was alone, oblivious, and coming in Harkness's direction. Shuffling along, in no hurry. He might be drunk; it was hard to tell. Also, he was wearing a suit and tie, which made him a kook in this locale. Not too tall, a little fleshy, certainly no athlete.

Perfect.

Harkness stepped into the shadows of a building that had wooden boards nailed over the windows. He glanced back and forth anxiously, checking whether he'd be observed when he made his move. He could see a cluster of people farther up the street, but they seemed to be having an argument of some kind, waving their arms and yelling at one another. That would keep them occupied; they'd never notice what he was up to.

Steady now. Stay cool.

Ducking back into the darkness, he flattened himself against the wall of the building. He rubbed the palm of his right hand on his jeans to get rid of the sweat and then drew the knife from his sleeve. The hard wooden handle felt good in his fist.

Despite his resolve, it was hard to remain still. He was aware that his heart was hammering, that his mouth was dry and his breathing rapid and shallow. He tried to force himself to relax, to concentrate on what he was going to do.

The sound of the steps grew closer. Gripping the knife tightly, he raised it over his head.

And then there was the target, no more than three feet away.
Now!

Harkness stepped out of the shadows and plunged the knife into his quarry's chest.

The force of the blow buckled the man's knees. He staggered but didn't go down, looking at Harkness with eyes wide and mouth hanging open, as if he couldn't believe what was happening to him. A gurgling sound came from his throat, and he raised his hands in a feeble gesture.

To Harkness, the thrill was like an electric shock. He shuddered, an incredible warmth enveloping him, his cock pulsing as it pumped semen. The spasm seemed to go on forever, but in fact, it lasted only a few seconds.

He withdrew the knife and jumped back as a geyser of blood spurted from the wound. The man's eyes glazed, and he collapsed onto the sidewalk.

Harkness bent down and wiped the blade on the leg of his victim's pants. He returned the knife to its hiding place in his left sleeve and walked away, not looking back.

Never in his life had he felt so alive.

8

Tolliver found a parking space for the Ford just off Third Avenue in the mid-Fifties, which on a Saturday night was no small feat. He jockeyed the car into it and then went looking for a phone.

There were a number of restaurants in the area and many of the stores were still open. As a result, people thronged the sidewalks. The air had grown colder; after the sun had gone down, it no longer felt as much like springtime.

He went into a bar and grill and asked for the public telephone. The bartender told him it was in the rear, and when he got there, he found some guy holding a glass of booze while he spoke into the phone, arguing with a woman about why she wouldn't meet him that night.

Ben waited several minutes for the call to end, and when it didn't, he stepped closer and stared at the caller. The guy glanced at him, looking pissed off, but finally he banged the instrument down and stomped away.

A Manhattan directory was chained to the wall next to the phone. Tolliver pored over it. There were dozens of Pattersons listed, including one on 53rd Street—a Kenneth M. He made a note of the number, then called it.

What he reached was a recording that said, "Hi, this is Ken. I'm out right now, but please leave your name and number after the beep."

Ben was about to hang up when a male voice overrode the answering machine. "Hello?"

"Ken Patterson?"

"Who's this?"

"Detective Lieutenant Tolliver, NYPD. Are you aware of the shooting incident this afternoon involving a friend of yours?"

There was a pause, and then the voice said, "How do I know you're who you say you are?"

"I've just come from the Whitacres' apartment on Park Avenue," Ben said. "They gave me your name. If you want to check on me, I'll give you my shield number and you can call police headquarters."

Another pause. "All right, Lieutenant, I'm Ken Patterson. What do you want?"

"I asked if you were aware of what happened earlier today."

"Yes, I saw it on TV. I've been out on the island and just got back. I was going to call the Whitacres myself."

"It's important that I talk with you."

"Listen, I know absolutely nothing about—"

"I need to ask you some questions. You want me to come to your place?"

". . . No, I'll meet you somewhere."

"Okay, where?"

"You know Billy's?"

"Yes."

"That's right around the corner from me. I'll be waiting for you."

After hanging up, Ben went back out onto the sidewalk and started walking. Traffic in the streets was dense, and the pedestrians he passed had the air of revelers out on the town. He left his car where it was, hoping some cowboy in an NYPD tow truck wouldn't ignore the placard and haul the vehicle away.

Billy's was an old-style saloon, on the east side of First Avenue at 51st Street. The owners claimed its mahogany bar and dark paneling and converted gaslight fixtures dated back to the time of its opening in 1870, and they might have been telling the truth. At least the interior looked it.

Genuine relic or not, business was thriving when Tolliver walked in. People were standing three-deep at the bar, talking and laughing in loud voices. He pushed his way through them, and when he got a bartender's attention, he ordered a draft beer and then looked around.

"Right here, Lieutenant."

He turned, to see a young man with clean-cut features and short brown hair. The guy was wearing a windbreaker and holding a half-empty glass.

Ben smiled. "Am I that obvious?"

The young man's face was grim; he didn't return the smile. "I've been watching for you. I'm Ken Patterson."

"Hello, Ken. Let's see if we can find someplace to talk."

"I've already got a table for us. In the back."

The bartender served Tolliver his beer in a frosted mug. Ben paid for it, and, carrying the mug, followed Patterson to the rear of the room, where they sat facing each other across a red-checkered tablecloth.

A waitress came by with menus, but Tolliver told her they wouldn't be ordering food. She said that was no problem and moved away. The table was in a corner, and although Billy's was crowded, they could talk without being overheard.

Patterson stared at him and shook his head. "What a hell of a thing."

"Yes, it was that."

"Of all the people in the world, Beth was the last person you'd ever expect to do something like this. I mean, you just couldn't imagine her killing somebody."

Tolliver watched him carefully, weighing Patterson's words and the way he was saying them. "But that's what happened."

"On the news, it said there were three dead, besides herself. Is that true?"

"Yes."

"For God's sake, why? Why did she do it?"

"That's what I'm trying to find out. You were pretty close to her, weren't you?"

"Yeah, I was. And that's the only reason I agreed to talk with you. I thought maybe there'd be some way to, I don't know, explain it."

Ben understood what he was groping for, even if Patterson didn't realize it himself. His reaction was the same as Linc Whitacre's. He was hoping to find an interpretation that might lessen Beth's responsibility for the apparently wanton massacre.

"Maybe we can work it out together," Tolliver said.

Patterson looked at him. "Did she just, like, go in there and start shooting?"

"More or less."

"God. Those poor people. And poor Beth."

"Do you know if she'd ever been in that place before—Serenbetz Jewelers?"

"I have no idea."

"She never mentioned it to you?"

"Not that I remember."

"Do you know the store?"

"No. I've been in the neighborhood, in the diamond district, but I don't recall that specific store. I'm pretty sure I never heard the name before this happened."

"Was Beth fond of jewelry?"

"Not overly, I don't think. That is, she never made much of a fuss about it."

"Did she have a lot of it?"

He thought about that. "No, I wouldn't say so—not from what I saw. She had a few things—some pearls, and an opal ring. Couple of gold bracelets. And a Cartier watch. But what she had wasn't much out of the ordinary for someone like her. Nothing you'd call extremely valuable, or ostentatious."

"Did she own a gun?"

"No. Or if she did, I never knew about it. I can't even picture her with one. She detested violence."

"How about you—do you have a gun?"

"No."

"Ever own one?"

"No, never."

"When did you see her last?"

"About a month ago."

"Her parents said you'd lived together for a while."

"Yeah, we did. She moved into my apartment late last summer. And then moved out a month ago."

Ben wanted to ask why she had, but not yet. Better to let Patterson talk, get him to loosen up as much as possible. "How long had you known her, before you started living together?"

"About three months. I met her at a party, and then I called her a few days after that."

"And then you started going with her?"

"Not right away. We dated a few times on and off, but it wasn't anything serious. At first, she seemed kind of flaky, but then when I got to know her, I realized that wasn't so at all. In fact, she was quite sensitive. And shy. She was always leery of people she didn't know well."

"Was she working at the Met then?"

"Yes. She had a title, something like assistant curator, but it was really a nothing job. And that bothered her. She was very bright, and yet she had all these self-doubts. Most of the time, she felt she was somehow inferior, not as able as other people. She knew she was intelligent, but she couldn't make it work for her."

"And that troubled her?"

"Yeah, it did." He seemed hesitant. "Look, Lieutenant. Can this be off the record, the things I say?"

"Sure, that's understood. Whatever you tell me will be held in confidence." For good reason, Ben thought. There was nothing to compel Patterson to talk to him at all. If the young man wanted to, he could walk out of here and never say another word on the subject.

"Okay," Patterson said. "You want my opinion, I think her emotional problems were much deeper than anyone realized. I know that may sound obvious now, but I wouldn't want her parents to know I said it. See, I think they should have recognized it years ago, gotten some help for her."

"Maybe the need wasn't so apparent."

"Maybe not. But I remember her telling me the others in her family were all strong, well-adjusted people. She felt like she was some kind of a freak or something. She'd go into these terrible fits of depression, and when that happened, she'd be so far down, she wasn't the same person."

"She talk about that often?"

"No, not often. But a couple of times, it just poured out of her. Once or twice, we stayed up all night long, smoking pot and talking."

He suddenly seemed to realize what he'd said. "Hey, I hope that part won't get to be public. I wouldn't want her folks—"

Ben waved a hand. "I told you, this is all confidential. You think those problems were bad enough to make her snap the way she did?"

That stopped him. He looked startled, then said, "No. That is, I doubt it. It just doesn't fit."

"Why doesn't it?"

"I don't know . . . it just seems like the opposite of what I would have expected from her. When she was at her worst, feeling really down and the most troubled, she'd kind of withdraw into herself. Like she was shutting out the world. It was unusual even to see her get mad."

"But sometimes she did?"

"Oh, sure. Although it never lasted more than a few minutes. And she didn't hold grudges, either. Once it was over, that was the end of it."

"She ever get angry at you?"

"Yeah, now and then. But like I said, it didn't last. And I sure as hell never saw her do anything violent. She wasn't one of these people who'd throw things or whatever. She might say something, or yell even, but she'd be more likely to cry than anything else."

"So there never was a hint of some hidden explosiveness."

"No. In fact, she was a very gentle person. And concerned about a lot of issues. Like the homeless, and cruelty to animals, things like that. She could get all weepy over a stray dog."

"You said she moved out of your apartment about a month ago. Was that because of a fight?"

"No. Definitely not. We had a good relationship at the time, I thought. Although—"

"Yes?"

"This might seem strange, in light of what I've been telling you."

"That's okay. Go ahead."

Patterson swallowed some of his drink. "In the last few weeks before she left, she seemed to change. And for the better. I remember thinking, She's finally getting it together. Starting to feel good about herself. I was very happy about it."

"Did you tell her so, discuss it with her?"

"No. I didn't want to say anything that would call attention to the way she was acting. She was so fragile, I suppose I thought it could upset her, send her in the other direction. That was the last thing I wanted to happen."

"So you were getting along fine at the time you split up."

"Yeah, we were."

"Then what made her move out?"

"I'll be damned if I know. It was a total surprise to me."

"She say anything when she left?"

"No, nothing. I came home one night and she was gone. I always got home later than she did; it's not unusual for me to get stuck in the office until seven or eight, or even later. But this night, there was no Beth. Just a note on the fridge."

"What was in the note?"

"That she was leaving and she thought it would be best for both of us. Said not to try to contact her."

"And that was it?"

"That was it. I was knocked over." He drained his glass.

"You want another drink?"

"No, I've had enough."

"So what happened next—did you try to get in touch with her?"

"Yeah, I did. I called her at work, but she wouldn't talk to me. And then on a hunch, I called her old apartment. Sure enough, she'd kept it while we were together."

His tone became wry. "Kind of a safety factor, I guess. In case it didn't work out with me. But when she answered and I tried to talk to her, she hung up. Then when I called a couple of days later, the number'd been changed."

"Was that the last contact you had with her?"

"Yes. That was the last time I heard her voice." He bit his lip.

"Tell me something," Ben said. "Did she ever try to get professional help on her own?"

"I don't know."

"She ever say she was considering it?"

"No. I'm pretty sure I'd remember if she had."

Ben drank the last of his beer. "Okay, Ken. It was good for us to have this talk."

Patterson shifted in his chair, obviously agitated. "But Lieutenant, what do *you* think? Do you have any idea what could have caused her to do such a thing?"

"Not at this point. It's what I'm trying to find out."

"You think we'll ever know?"

"Hard to say. Too bad she didn't try to get help, though. Might have prevented this from happening. It's possible that she'd still be alive. And so would three other people."

The young man clenched his hands and stared down at them. "If only she'd talked to a doctor before she flipped out."

9

In the fourth-floor study of his house on East 80th Street, Dr. Jonas Drang poured cognac into a snifter. Then he settled into his leather wing chair and sipped the fiery liquid.

This was the room where he always felt most comfortable. He'd built a fire, and the glow from the logs crackling on the hearth created long shadows that danced on the walls. The brass-bound mahogany desk with his computer on it stood in one corner, and nearby was the Pennsylvania dry sink he used as a bar. At right angles to where he sat was the chesterfield sofa he'd bought at an auction in London, and covering the floor was an antique Persian rug.

The television was in a cupboard under one of the bookcases. He used the remote to flip through the channels and finally settled on WPIC-TV. There was some inane movie on at the moment, a romantic comedy that had nothing whatever to do with the way people interacted in real life, and he paid no attention to it. The late news would be on soon, and that was what he wanted to see.

Crossing his legs, he held up his snifter and looked at its distorted reflection of his face. Above his prominent nose, his eyes were dark and piercing, and his square jaw gave him a look of determination. There wasn't a single strand of gray in his thick black hair.

Drang was proud of his appearance. Powerfully built, he felt the image he projected was that of a highly intelligent man, strong but scholarly. Perfect for one who possessed knowledge about the working of the human brain that few others could comprehend.

More than once, patients had remarked to him that they felt he could look directly into their minds and see the secrets that were hidden there. He'd pretended to be amused and had brushed away the compliments. In fact, he was deeply gratified, although certainly not surprised.

The movie droned on. He glanced away from the TV set and stared into the flames. The cognac he was drinking was his favorite, Rémy Martin XO. Together with the fire, it produced a warmth that made him feel pleasantly snug.

Another thing he liked about this room was the privacy it afforded. No one else was allowed in here—not the housekeeper, who had long ago given up trying to come in to dust and clean, and not even Anna, his assistant. This was his inner sanctum, where he could think and write and dream.

He could also relax here, physically. Instead of the black suits he wore at all other times, winter and summer, in this room he could put on the baggy corduroy trousers and the cardigan sweater he had on now. The suede slippers on his feet were as soft as gloves.

He swallowed more of the brandy, the alcohol further easing the tension he'd felt earlier. This had been more than a trying day; it had been a disaster. To have put in so much effort, only to see his work come to nothing, was humiliating.

Not that the incident had been totally unexpected. He'd even agree that it could have been prevented, but that was an admission he'd make only to himself. Drang could not stand to be mocked, not even by forces beyond his control. And when the mistake was his own, it was almost impossible for him to accept the responsibility.

And yet, where *had* he gone wrong? The woman had been bright, personable, pretty. While she'd also been filled with repressed doubts and self-loathing. Given to wide mood swings. Poised on the outside, with a maelstrom of conflicting emotions within. A superb subject.

Fortunately, finding someone that well suited to his work was not difficult. Next week, another young woman would be coming in for evaluation. She might turn out to be a candidate; you never knew.

Then there was the young man he'd been treating, Philip Harkness. That one had been showing excellent response. The doctor would have to be more careful in the future, however, not to allow the work to go awry again. His long-range plans were much too important. Hereafter, he'd monitor his patients even more closely.

What he always looked for was a weak personality, a mind that was completely malleable. Basically, the patient should be suffering from what Freud had called the etiological process, in which unconscious conflict aroused anxiety and led to the maladaptive use of defense mechanisms. That, in turn, would result in the subject experiencing severe depression—ideal, for Drang's purposes.

Harkness, on the other hand, obviously had deeper problems. Yet Drang was not deterred by that; in many ways, his condition merely made the patient more useful. How well was Harkness responding? The supreme test would come sometime tonight, when the young man went hunting in Greenwich Village. If he succeeded, that would be splendid. And if he didn't, Drang would adjust his treatment accordingly.

But the doctor also wanted a *female* mind. That was what had been so disappointing about losing the patient today. She'd shown so much promise, and he'd been so sure he could achieve positive results with her.

And now? Now she was nothing but a lifeless mass of tissue and bone and hair and fluid, occupying a drawer in the morgue. Lying cold and useless, all her promise locked forever in an agglomeration of cells that would soon begin to shrivel and rot. What a waste.

The news came on, and his attention snapped back to the television set. A blond woman wearing a trench coat was speaking on camera; he turned up the volume.

The reporter was standing in front of the exterior of a jewelry shop, talking into a handheld microphone in a segment that had been taped at the scene. Police cars and an ambulance were parked nearby, and officers swarmed about the entrance to the store. A large crowd of onlookers was straining against blue-painted wooden barriers, threatening to topple them.

"... this afternoon in a blaze of gunfire," the reporter was saying. "The killer has been identified as Beth Whitacre, twenty-six years old, of Manhattan. All three of her victims died at the scene. After that, she turned the gun on herself. Beth Whitacre's father, Lincoln Whitacre, was well known for his fund-raising efforts on behalf of the mayor's successful election campaign."

Drang listened closely to the breathless description of the shootings. He'd already heard a news flash on the radio, and this reporter didn't seem to have much to add.

But then the camera followed a detective who emerged from the store, and reporters began yelling questions at him as he went to his car. The detective looked annoyed, answering tersely that he intended to find out what had led to the shootings.

Drang blew air out from between his lips. Only one man would ever have the answers: the doctor himself. Certainly not some ignorant cop.

The next shot showed a gurney with a body strapped to it being wheeled out of the shop and loaded into the ambulance.

The camera then cut back to the reporter, who said, "Beth Whitacre had everything to live for. She was beautiful, she had a great family and a fine career. We may never know what caused her to carry out today's apparently senseless slayings. However, Lieutenant Tolliver is a noted homicide detective, and as you heard, he is confident he can get to the bottom of it. This is Shelley Drake, WPIC-TV, New York."

Dr. Drang hit the off button and the picture imploded. He sat back and sipped his brandy.

The authorities had none of the answers, of course. Nor would they have. Already such vapid phrases as "We may never know what caused" were being used in accounts of the killings.

But who was this insolent police detective? There was no possibility that he'd get anywhere with his investigation, and yet it might be wise to take special precautions. An overzealous policeman could be a nuisance.

Getting up from his chair, Drang stepped to the dry sink and replenished the cognac in his snifter. Then he went to his desk and sat down. Seeing the report had given him a slight headache.

Opening the lower right-hand drawer in the desk, he rummaged around for a bottle of aspirin. It was hard to find; there were a number of containers in here, most of them filled with compounds he thought of as mementos or curiosities he'd collected over the years.

There was Darvon, for example, once considered a miracle pain-killer but now known to have caused many deaths; thalidomide, infamous for the hideously malformed babies produced by pregnant women taking it back in the fifties; imipramine, a monoamine-oxidase inhibitor responsible for countless brain hemorrhages; and a number of others, including several exotic poisons.

There was even a vial of cyanide capsules, exactly like the one that had enabled Hermann Goering to escape justice at Nuremberg. One of the tiny golden spheres held enough of the substance to kill ten men. It would be wise not to take one of those by mistake.

Drang found the aspirin and opened the bottle, shaking two tablets into his hand and popping them into his mouth. He washed them down with a swallow of cognac and then put the bottle away. Almost immediately, he felt better as the aspirin took effect; acetylsalicylic acid was still one of the most effective analgesics known to man.

Rising from his desk, he returned to the leather chair before the fire. The headache subsided further, and once more he felt at ease.

As he stared into the flames, he thought about the patients he'd be seeing in the week ahead. There would be Harkness, of course. And later the new one, the woman. With luck, she'd be just what he was hoping for.

Then everything he'd learned from the experience with Whitacre would be put to good use. He'd begin anew, and this time, he'd achieve his goals.

10

The alarm jarred Tolliver out of a deep sleep. Half-awake, he slapped the button that turned the thing off and then fell back again. It took several seconds for him to get his bearings.

This was Sunday morning. And he was in his own bed, alone. Usually, he spent Saturday nights with Shelley, but yesterday's developments had blown that. Mental pictures of the crime scene and his subsequent actions came flooding back into his consciousness.

He swung his legs over the side of the bed and stood up, feeling a little rocky after having slept only a couple of hours. There was also a lousy taste in his mouth, a reminder of the bourbon he'd drunk before he'd finally packed it in.

Yawning, he stretched and looked through the skylight in the vaulted ceiling. Judging from the direction the clouds were moving, the wind was out of the east, threatening rain. That was not much to complain about; almost anything would be welcome after the past winter. He went into the bathroom, and by the time he'd brushed his teeth and showered and shaved, he was in considerably better shape.

Returning to the bedroom, he put on his standard work clothes: blue button-down shirt and gray pants, black socks and loafers, a striped tie. Small change and a sheaf of bills went into his left front trouser pocket, keys into the right. The leather case containing his shield and ID he put into the right rear, wallet into the left.

Next he strapped the custom-made Gaylord holster onto the small of his back. The pistol it held was a 7.65 Mauser semiautomatic. Built largely of alloys, the gun weighed even less than his old standby, the Smith Airweight he sometimes carried as a backup.

The Mauser's cartridges were smaller than the 9mms that were regulation in the NYPD these days, but the projectiles were 60-grain Black Talon hollowpoints. The slugs were capable of penetrating armor, and they also mushroomed once inside whatever they hit. They weren't authorized for police use, but knowing he might come up against guys carrying Uzis and AK-47's and 12-gauge street-sweepers made Tolliver see the rules in a different light. If the brass didn't care for his choice of ordnance, that was tough shit. It was his life that was on the line, not theirs.

Lastly, he put on his blazer and tucked his notebook into the inside pocket.

From there he went into the kitchen, where he fixed himself his usual five-minute breakfast: orange juice, two halves of an English muffin smeared with blueberry jam, a mug of black coffee.

There was a tiny Sony TV on the counter; he turned it on and flipped channels while he ate. The story of the Whitacre murders and suicide was all over the tube, yesterday's tapes fleshed out with backgrounders on the young woman and her family. He was irritated to see that WPIC-TV's coverage included the exchange he'd had with Shelley outside the store. That was followed by the inevitable shot of a body being loaded into the meat wagon.

After the piece on Whitacre, a different reporter appeared. This one was a male, speaking from a desk in the studio. "We have a breaking story just in," he said. "Another homicide took place in Manhattan last night, hours after the mass murders at Serenbetz Jewelers. This latest killing occurred in Greenwich Village. A man who was visiting the city from upstate was stabbed to death by an unknown assailant, and there was no apparent motive for that murder, either. Detectives were questioning a witness who saw the attack. Identity of the victim has been withheld, pending notification of his family. We have no further details at this time, but we'll bring you updates as they come in. Stay tuned to—"

Ben turned off the set and went into the living room, carrying his coffee mug. For a few moments, he stood before the window, staring out at the panoramic view. His apartment was on the top floor of a converted loft building that overlooked the South Street Seaport. From here, he could see the old sailing ships tied up at the docks, and near them the shops and restaurants. The neighborhood was quiet at the moment, but only because it was early. Later on, the area would be swarming with tourists, as it was on any day of the year.

He sipped coffee, continuing to look out the oversized panel of glass as he thought about the Whitacre case, going over what he'd learned, and what he hadn't. So far, the negatives were way ahead; the shootings were as puzzling to him now as when he'd first heard about them.

It was also interesting that another apparently senseless murder had taken place on the same day. The Village was in the Sixth Precinct, where he'd once headed the detective squad.

Curious, Tolliver stepped to a telephone and called the squad room, asking for Lieutenant Flynn. In Ben's time there, Flynn had been a sergeant, the number two in the unit. After Tolliver was assigned to the DA's Office, Flynn had been moved up and given command. Ordinarily, he wouldn't be in on a Sunday, but today there was a homicide to deal with.

When Flynn picked up the call, Ben asked him about the stabbing.

"Victim's name was George Merola," Flynn said. "White male, forty-nine years old. Owner of a small company in Utica that fabricates metal parts. Witness said the killer was also white, and seemed like a young guy. But he only got a glimpse of him before he took off."

"What time was it?"

"Little past eleven. Say, Ben? What's your interest in this? I heard you were working the thing in the jewelry store. It was on TV."

"I'm looking into that for the DA. Case belongs to Midtown North."

"You don't think there's a connection, do you? Between that case and this one?"

"No. It just struck me as odd."

"You kidding me? This is psycho city. What's odd about some nutball running around loose?"

"Who was the witness in your case?"

"Derrick Taylor, black male, twenty-eight. He told us he was with three of his friends, cruising the bars around the meat market. The others got in an argument and so he left them, went off by himself. Then he noticed the victim walking alone, about a block away. At that point, the perp jumped out from behind a building and stabbed the guy. Taylor called his friends and they all ran down there, but the perp was gone. The ME said Merola had a single wound, in the heart. He was dead when he hit the ground."

"Taylor the one who reported it?"

"No. Somebody drove by and called nine-one-one on a cellular. Patrol car responded and Taylor's buddies split when they saw the cops. He stayed with the victim, though. Gave us what I just told you."

"You buy his story?"

"Yeah, I do. Merola had five hundred and forty bucks on him and a diamond pinkie ring, plus a bunch of credit cards. Nothing was touched."

"Taylor have a sheet?"

"We checked on that. All it showed was one arrest, loitering for drugs. Charge was knocked down to a dis con and dismissed."

"Anything else on the victim?"

"We had the police in Utica inform his wife and question her. She told them he was here on a business deal, staying at the Hilton. She was surprised he had that much cash on him, and she had no idea what he was doing in that neighborhood. He had no enemies, as far as she knew."

"And that's it?"

"So far. No robbery, not motive, no nothing. We're checking his contacts."

Ben said to let him know if they got anything new on it, then hung up. He left the apartment, his mind again focusing on what he had to do this morning.

Because of the politics, the Whitacre case would generate a firestorm. The media were already fanning the flames.

11

The streets were nearly deserted at this hour on a Sunday, and consequently the trip to the Criminal Justice Building took only ten minutes. When Tolliver walked into the unit's offices in the huge old building at 100 Centre Street, Fred Logan was already there. The captain was wearing what for him was a casual outfit, a plaid sport jacket and a knit tie. He waved Ben into his office.

"I was on the phone half the night," Logan said.

"Yeah, I know."

"Must've been around two when I called you, wasn't it?"

"Thereabouts."

Logan filled Styrofoam cups from the electric pot he kept on a table behind his desk and handed one of the cups to Tolliver. "Hope you didn't have company."

"No such luck." The captain sometimes rode him about how it must be wonderful being single in a town full of hungry women, and Ben suspected it was because he was jealous. Logan's wife reminded Tolliver of a DI he'd had in boot camp.

But this morning, the unit commander was not in the mood for by-play. He sat at his desk and swallowed some of his coffee. "Not only did I get calls from Galupo and the PC; I also got one from the old man."

"They want to know why we didn't have all the answers yet?"

"That was the gist of it, sure. And on top of that, Galupo had another little problem." Anthony Galupo was chief of detectives in the borough of Manhattan, a man not known for his patience.

"Which was?"

"Which was Jarvis and McGrath bitching to him about how you messed up their investigation. I think their noses were bent because you told a TV reporter you were taking over the case."

"That's bullshit. I didn't say that at all."

"Yeah, but that's what it sounded like. I saw it myself, on the news. And by the way, the reporter's a friend of yours, right?"

"I know her, yes."

"You want to be careful with that. Could put your nuts in a vise if it got out you were giving her information."

"I'm not. She asked me questions, like a lot of the others. What I said was that I intended to find out what made Whitacre do the shooting."

"Well, anyway, that remark is what lit the fuse."

Tolliver sat in one of the visitor's chairs and tried the steaming black liquid in his cup. It was bitter enough to curl his tongue. "What did the DA have to say?"

"Told me how this was a very sensitive situation and that it was important we handle our end of the investigation with great care. Said the mayor was upset because he had a personal relationship with the Whitacres as well as a professional one. He wants a thorough report on what happened yesterday, and then he's to be kept completely up-to-date until the case is closed. You can see why, right?"

"Yeah, sure."

"Commissioner said about the same thing, although he put it a little different."

"I'll bet he did."

"You know what's going on there. He and the mayor have been bragging about how they're making the streets safe again. And now here's the daughter of one of the mayor's friends committing wholesale murder. Media's having a field day with that."

"So I've seen."

"The PC also said he expects full cooperation between us and the precinct squad assigned to the case. We're not to forget our first responsibility is to the department, even though we're assigned to the DA."

Ben made no reply. He despised the politics that kept the department churning.

"I also got another call, from that bitch Alice Kovala." Kovala was the PC's deputy for public relations. Cops at every level considered her a royal pain in the ass.

"She want to organize a press conference?"

"She already did. It's scheduled for tomorrow morning at headquarters, and she said we should be prepared to attend it."

"That'll get Midtown North even more pissed," Tolliver said.

"Hey, what'd you expect? The minute I heard that call on the scanner, I knew the shit would hit the fan. I told you that, didn't I? Talk about a high-profile case. It's the big story on TV, and Kovala says all the tabloid shows are sure to do features on it."

Tolliver thought of his visit to the Whitacres the previous afternoon. How right they'd been about the mauling the media would give the case, and them personally. If anything, the exposure would be even worse than what they expected.

Logan drank more coffee. "You said the Whitacre woman didn't know any of the people she shot?"

"Apparently not. The store clerk told me she'd never seen her before. She didn't think her uncle knew her, either."

"What'd you find out from Whitacre's family? You went to see them, right?"

"Yeah, I did. It's like I told you last night. They have no idea what made her do it."

"You believe that?"

"Sure, why wouldn't I?"

"Because somebody doesn't just go crazy and start killing people right out of the blue. There're always signs along the way. That guy Ferguson, the one who shot all those people on the train on Long Island? Or the one that killed the lawyers in San Francisco? Every mass murderer is a creep that gives off signals. They brood about how everybody hates them, or how they hate everybody else. By the time they blow up, it's been cooking for a long time."

"That may be. But with her, nobody knew the problems were anywhere near that serious. I interviewed her boyfriend as well, and he said she got depressed from time to time. But there was never any indication she was capable of violence."

"Her boyfriend. They live together?"

"They did, but then she moved out a month ago."

"Okay, so there's an indication right there."

Ben said nothing. Logal seemed to be grasping at straws.

But the captain kept after it. "Who is he, the boyfriend?"

Tolliver gave him a rundown on Ken Patterson and told him about the conversation they'd had in Billy's the night before.

When Ben finished, Logan said, "Be sure you put that in your report. She split with her boyfriend and it made her despondent."

"I don't know whether it did or not."

"Hey, look. We need to come up with something here. The victims are dead, and so is the perpetrator. In a week or two, it'll blow over. But for right now, it's a hot potato, and I don't want us to get our fingers burnt. You follow me, Lieutenant?"

"Yeah, I understand."

"Good. So let's hear some positive suggestions, okay?"

Ben again tried to drink his coffee and then gave up on it. One positive suggestion would be for Logan to learn to make a decent pot of the stuff. Instead he said, "I had the CSU send me a copy of the videotape from the store camera."

"I want to see that. Bring it in and we'll look at it."

Tolliver left the office and went across the open area to his own cubicle, where he dropped the cup of coffee into the wastebasket. A videocassette lay among the piles of paper on his desk. He returned with it to Logan's office and handed the tape to the captain.

Alongside the scanner that sat atop the bookcase was a small TV and a VCR. Logan shoved the cassette into the machine and turned it on. A moment later, a grainy black-and-white image appeared on the screen.

There was no sound on the tape, which made the action seem all the more bizarre. The young woman walked into the store and waited patiently to be waited on, standing motionless while three other customers held the attention of the jeweler and the female clerk.

When at last her turn came, she spoke briefly with the jeweler and waited again while he went into the back room. When he emerged and placed the necklaces on the counter, she chose one and put it around her neck. Then she reached into her handbag and pulled out the pistol.

The gun recoiled, jerking in her hand as flashes and puffs of smoke appeared at the muzzle. The jeweler fell, then the guard and the female customer. The next shot hit the door leading into the back room just after the clerk ducked back and shut it.

And then the most grotesque action in the entire episode took place. The young woman turned and looked up, staring directly into the lens of the camera. Before this, she'd shown no emotion whatever, but now her expression changed. Her eyes bulged and her lips pulled back from her teeth in horror, as if she'd discovered some awful truth.

She shoved the barrel of the pistol into her mouth and an instant later the top of her head burst open, the force of the shot lifting her up onto her toes and causing her arms to fly out from her sides as she went over backward onto the floor. After that, the only movement in the picture was that of the slowly widening dark pools surrounding the bodies. Seconds later, the tape ended.

Logan was silent for a moment. Then he said, "I'll be goddamned."

"Yeah, very strange."

"I mean, it doesn't add up. She couldn't have been trying to rob the place, or after she shot them all, she would've run out of there with the necklaces. You get a value on them, by the way?"

"Around a hundred thousand apiece."

"Not surprised, all that ice. But she didn't even start to leave. Just stood there and blew her head off."

"Yes."

"And she was so calm. Not a twitch, until right there at the end."

"So I saw."

Logan rubbed his jaw. "You think she was on drugs?"

"Anything's possible. The toxicology report will tell us that. We'll have it in a few days."

"No clue from the ME?"

"No. He said her eyes were too badly damaged for him to tell when he looked at her. We'll have to wait until the post, and then hear what the lab says."

"Might be the answer, that she was on something."

"I don't think so."

"Why not?"

"You saw that tape. She was like a statue through the whole thing. Compare that with what you usually see in a robbery where the perpetrator's high. The guy's so wired, he's ready to jump out of his skin."

"So maybe it was a different kind of substance."

"Maybe. But like what? If somebody takes drugs before doing what she did, they want to be pumped up. They go for speed, or crystal meth, right?"

"Yeah, that's true."

"Yet she was totally cool."

"How about tranquilizers?"

"Come on, Cap. She'd need something that would give her an edge, not put her to sleep."

"I suppose. You pick up anything from her parents or the boyfriend that tells you she was a user?"

"From what I could learn, the only thing she touched was an occasional joint."

"Maybe they were trying to cover it up."

"Also possible, but I doubt it."

Logan was silent for a moment. Then he retrieved the cassette from the VCR and handed it to Tolliver. "Okay, see what else you can get, and then write your report for Oppenheimer. Cover every possibility, including drugs. Even if you don't believe it, put it in there. I don't want anybody saying we did a half-assed job. You follow me?"

"Yeah, I do. By the way, you hear about that other homicide last night, the one in the Village?"

"No, what was that?"

"Victim was knifed in the street. I called the Sixth and talked to Ed Flynn. He told me the guy was a businessman from upstate. There didn't seem to be a reason for that one, either."

"Any witnesses?"

"One. He said the killer stabbed the victim and then just walked away. The witness and some friends ran over there, but the guy was already dead. Cops found over five hundred bucks in his wallet, and he had on a diamond ring."

"Maybe the perp had a grudge against the guy," Logan said. "Or else it was a hit."

"Didn't sound like it. Flynn said they called the victim's wife in Utica and she told them her husband was here on business and staying at the Hilton."

"So what was he doing in the Village?"

"Nobody can say. Might have been lost, or maybe he was looking for a hooker. It was near the meat market, over by the river. You know what that neighborhood's like."

"Yeah, I do."

"And a hit man wouldn't use a knife."

"No, you got a point there. Sixth have any leads?"

"None. What struck me was that here was another one that didn't seem to make any sense at all. Two homicide cases, with no motive in either one of them."

Logan shrugged. "All it says to me is, there are a lot of wackos around. There are times when I think the whole city's gone crazy."

"Yeah, but still—"

"But still what? You're not telling me there's some link between them, are you?"

"No, I suppose not."

The phone rang, and Logan answered it. Tolliver picked up the videocassette and went back to his own office.

Logan was right about one thing: Beth Whitacre's killing spree didn't add up—especially when you tried to explain how such violence could be produced by a shy young woman whose emotional problems had surfaced only in occasional bouts of depression.

Furthermore, the one place where the reasons might be found no longer existed. That was in the mass of brain cells she'd caused to erupt in a bloody spray through the top of her head.

Ben wondered if there was a way to reconstruct what had been going on there before she pulled the trigger. He got out his notes and began going through them.

12

One of the jottings in the notebook caught Tolliver's attention; he'd made it after his meeting with Ken Patterson. The young man had said that before Beth had moved out, she seemed to have changed for the better, emotionally.

Ben wondered again whether she'd been seeing a shrink. Although Patterson claimed he didn't know, that might have accounted for the difference in her demeanor. Maybe she'd made some progress and then come apart.

If that turned out to be true, if she had been getting treatment, it stood to reason that the doctor could supply a lot of the answers Tolliver was looking for.

He chewed his pencil, thinking about it. The first problem would be to locate the shrink. There were several thousand of them in New York, ranging from so-called psychological counselors to full-fledged psychiatrists with medical degrees.

But even if he succeeded in finding a doctor who'd treated her, then what? A bigger problem would be getting the guy to divulge what he might have learned about his patient's emotional state. All the ones Ben had run into tended to be secretive about their practices.

The whole thing was a long shot, but worth a try; at this point, Tolliver had nothing. He looked in his directory for the telephone number of the American Psychiatric Association and wrote it down. No one would be there today; he'd call tomorrow. How far he'd get would probably be another story.

Going back to his notes, he looked at what he'd scribbled at the crime scene. Among them was a reminder to talk to the people Beth had worked with at the Met. Her boss might be able to give him something; he'd make that contact as soon as he could.

Another reminder was to ask about the possibility of drugs in her bloodstream at the time of the killings. He called the medical examiner's office and spoke to an assistant ME, who told him the Whitacre postmortem was scheduled for Tuesday. That meant a rush had been put on it; the system was so jammed that an autopsy often didn't take place until weeks after death.

Tolliver knew why this one was being given precedence. If you were prominent enough, even after you died you were moved to the head of the line. And besides, a lot of people were interested in the case, on both sides of the political issues.

Next he telephoned Midtown North and said he wanted to speak to Joe Novotny. When the detective came on, Tolliver asked him if he'd checked to see whether Beth Whitacre had ever done business in the Serenbetz store prior to the shootings.

"Sorry, Lieutenant," Novotny said. "I got orders that if you want anything, you have to talk to Lieutenant McGrath."

"Put him on."

"He isn't in right now."

"Have him contact me at the DA's Office," Tolliver growled, and hung up. This was the kind of chickenshit that drove him crazy. It would do no good to unload on McGrath; if Ben complained, the squad commander would feign innocence and put out double-talk about the need to stay in channels.

Tolliver took a deep breath and went on laying out his investigation. He'd made a promise, and he'd do his best. But this one sure as hell wouldn't be easy.

13

On Sunday morning, Dr. Drang rose early and began his daily routine: thirty minutes of vigorous calisthenics, followed by a shower and a shave. After that, he brushed his thick raven hair and put on a black suit, starched white shirt, pin-dot gray tie, black shoes. Then he inspected himself in the full-length mirror on the wall of his bedroom.

Impressive, he thought as he struck poses for himself. Obviously a man of intellect and purpose, one a stranger would think was the leader of some important organization. The head of a multinational corporation, perhaps, or a diplomat. Or better than any of those, an eminent psychiatrist. Satisfied, he went down to breakfast in the dining room on the second floor.

Like all the private rooms in the house, this one was furnished with antiques. The table and chairs were Queen Anne, mahogany and dark green leather, and there was a Hepplewhite hunt board with slender, tapering legs and a rosette motif. Heavy plum-colored drapes covered the windows, which faced the street. Drang opened them a crack and peered out, observing that the weather appeared to be clearing. No matter; he'd be busy inside the entire day.

He sat at the table and began reading the Sunday edition of the *Times*. The story was on the front page, under the headline MURDERS ON 47TH ST., and a subhead that read: *Lincoln Whitacre's Daughter Kills 3, Then Self.* There were also photographs of Beth and her father, as well as of the three victims.

The doctor read through the article quickly. It detailed the murders and the suicide that had taken place in the jeweler's store, then went into the backgrounds of the killer and the people she shot. There were also the predictable bromides by the police commissioner about the need for more officers to combat escalating violent crime in the city, and a statement by the mayor expressing sympathy for the victims and their families.

In addition, the story contained comments by someone the *Times* described as an expert criminologist, a Ph.D. named William Metrusky, who was on the faculty of the John Jay College of Criminal Justice. Metrusky said Whitacre's actions were similar to those in other cases of mass murder, in which the perpetrator suffered from delusions of persecution and gave vent to repressed anger. In his opinion, Whitacre had felt the world was against her. He theorized she might also have resented people who spent large sums of money on jewelry.

Reading that made Drang laugh out loud. William Metrusky, he decided, was an asshole—about on the same level as the investigator who'd been quoted on TV last night.

Lastly, the story referred to Lt. Ben Tolliver working on the case, on special assignment from the Manhattan District Attorney's Office. Upon reading that part, Drang didn't laugh at all. The *Times* said the detective was well known for having solved a number of important homicide cases, and the article implied that if anyone could uncover the reasons for the seemingly mindless shootings, Tolliver could.

Drang thought about that for several minutes and then went on leafing through the paper. He certainly would not be intimidated by some bumptious cop, no matter what the man's reputation might be. Nevertheless, the article was troubling.

At that point, his housekeeper served him his usual breakfast of poached eggs on dry toast. She was Jamaican, overweight and ungainly, but efficient enough for him to put up with her. She didn't live in, but arrived early each morning to begin the day's cooking and cleaning chores. He went on reading as he ate.

The story of a second homicide was buried at the bottom of a page much further on, and it took up only a few inches of space. It said the victim, a businessman visiting the city, had been stabbed to death on one of the grimy streets in Greenwich Village, not far from the Hudson River. There was no suspect, and no valuables had been taken. The police speculated that was because the perpetrator had been scared off before he could loot the dead man's body. Drang read that piece carefully also.

After a second cup of coffee, he left the dining room and went downstairs to the hallway leading to the rear of the house. He unlocked a door, stepped through, and turned on the lights, closing and locking the door behind him. Then he went down the long flight of stairs into the cellar.

Immediately, he was greeted by a high-pitched chirping and chittering as the rats sensed his presence. He took a lab coat from its hook and put it on over his suit jacket, and as he approached the cages, the animals' cries increased in volume.

These were not the small white rats favored by most researchers. Drang had long ago concluded that such animals were too weak and timid for his work. What he favored were the fierce and highly intelligent Norway brown rats, members of the family Muridae, species *Rattus norvegicus,* the most aggressive creatures of their kind on earth.

Many of the specimens here were over a foot long, not including their naked scaly tails, and weighed several pounds. Pity the unsuspecting cat that pounced on one of these.

So long had he worked with animals of this type, so well did he know them, Drang felt he could almost understand the sounds they made, as if they spoke a language he could comprehend.

Some of the rats jumped up against the wire mesh of their cages when they saw him, noses twitching, tiny high-pitched voices calling out to him. Some of the others ignored him, and some glared at him defiantly and hissed. While still others cowered silently in corners, fearful even of looking his way.

He knew why. A portion of them were being tested with a regimen of good food and antidepressants, while most of the rest were subjects in his wide-ranging experiments with the neurotransmissions of pain. Others were numb from ingesting heavy doses of powerful inhibitors.

And some were part of his own newly developed procedures, with which he'd made the most astonishing discoveries of his career. It was easy to tell at a glance which group was which.

He walked along the cages, spending a few moments looking into some, a longer time with others. Each of them bore a chart listing the formula being given its inhabitant and detailing the results.

Among the rats being treated with antidepressants were a number that were sleek, inquisitive, almost playful. These were on fluoxetine, and they displayed well-balanced, even-tempered dispositions. Drang liked to think of them as constantly upbeat.

Then there were others that were on more esoteric compounds, such as amitriptyline, amoxapine, and doximil, and these were less happy. In fact, as their charts indicated, they suffered from a range of negative reactions, including arrhythmia, hypotension, and seizures.

Still worse were the rats on hallucinogens. They were zonked on lysergamides and indolealkylamines, bombed on cholinergics, flying over the moon on cannabinoids.

Finally, there were the animals that the drugs had driven quite mad. These looked out at him with wild red eyes as they sucked oxygen into their lungs in short, feverish gasps.

Even for the rats in this group, Drang felt a certain empathy. He knew exactly what they were going through, understood just what dreadful impact the chemicals were having on their brains.

But results were what counted, and he was deeply gratified by the progress he'd been making. Occasional failures, such as the incident with Beth Whitacre, were to be expected. It was impossible to do bold exploratory work in uncharted areas, seeking to prove theories that at one time would have been thought fantasy, without stumbling now and then. What one had to do in such circumstances was to learn from mistakes, not dwell on them.

A long white laboratory table stood on the side of the room opposite from the cages. He stepped over to it and began preparing the different doses of drugs that would be administered to the animals. As he worked, he made notations in a notebook he kept on the table.

When he finished, he mixed the compounds with the animals' food, which also varied according to the tests he was running, and then made additional notes on what he'd observed of the condition of the rats in the various groups. After that, he fed them the mixtures, cautiously funneling the concoctions into their cages.

Some of the rats attacked their rations voraciously, and some seemed indifferent but ate anyway. Others approached the blend of food and drugs warily, and a few continued to cringe in the corners, refusing to eat any of it. No matter; they'd all consume the mixtures eventually. It was either that or die.

He watched them for several minutes, and then he sat at his table once more and leafed through his notes.

He was so close, so very close. Merely thinking about reaching his goals was thrilling to him. In a relatively short time from now, he would achieve his ultimate triumph, the crown jewel in his life's work. When that happened, he would become rich beyond his fondest dreams.

And along the way, he'd also gain the revenge he longed for, something he wanted almost as much as the money.

Opening a drawer in the table, he took out a yellowing clip from the *LA Times*. It featured a photograph of a group of men, and the caption identified them as psychiatrists attending a conference in Los Angeles. The conference had taken place many years ago, but Drang would never forget it. It had been there that he had first made public his theories on psychopharmacology, nervously reading the paper he'd written on the subject. When he finished, he'd been pleased, even exultant.

And then, to his surprise—and horror—one of the members of the group attacked his theories, denouncing him as a fraud and saying his ideas were dangerous. And he'd done it in the most humiliating way possible: by ridiculing his paper and Drang along with it. The audience laughed uproariously, while Drang wanted to die.

It wasn't until later that he'd come up with a better idea. He looked at the group photo now, feeling his rage as hot and acidulous as ever as he picked out his tormentor.

There stood Dr. Arthur McKenzie. He was wearing his customary expression of contempt, the look of superiority that was so much a part of him. His weak mouth was twisted in a smirk, and his eyebrows were lifted slightly, implying he knew so much more than any of the others.

Well now, Drang thought. You're not aware of it, Arthur, but the day of reckoning is coming. I can't say when it will arrive, exactly, but arrive it will. And soon. I promise you that.

After a moment, he put the clip back into the drawer and closed it. Then he took off the lab coat and went back upstairs, locking the door behind him.

One of his patients was due to arrive a few minutes from now. Ordinarily, Drang did not treat patients on a Sunday. But this one was special.

14

Drang's office didn't look like an office at all. There was no desk, no computer or fax machine. The furnishings were comfortable chairs and tables with tall lamps, mostly done in muted tones of brown and beige. The carpet and the wallpaper were of soothing shades of green, and oil paintings of vague abstract shapes hung on the walls.

A leather couch stood at the far side of the room, with a pair of chairs nearby. Next to one of the chairs was a cherry-wood cabinet, and beyond that were bookcases that rose to the ceiling. The windows were covered by draperies of umber wool.

Drang stepped to the bookcases and took down a notebook, then sat in one of the chairs and began looking through the pages. The jottings on them concerned the patient he was about to see.

He'd been reading for several minutes when a knock sounded at the door. "Yes?"

Anna, his assistant, thrust her head into the room. She was a ponderous woman, unattractive but dependable, like his housekeeper. She wore a white uniform and had her dark hair tied back in a bun. An illegal alien from Bulgaria, she cost him less in wages than someone of comparable skills, and her unlawful presence in this country gave him an advantage. He liked holding her illegality over her head.

"Mr. Harkness is here, Doctor," she said.

He got up and put the notebook back into the bookcase, then returned to his chair. "Show him in, please."

She stepped aside, and a young man entered the room. Anna then closed the door.

"Good morning, Philip," Drang said. He sat with his arms folded over his chest.

"Good morning, Doctor."

Drang indicated a chair facing the one he occupied. "You may sit down."

Harkness dropped into the chair, and for a moment Drang studied him appraisingly. As usual, the patient was sloppily dressed, wearing a battered jacket, jeans, and a pair of scuffed loafers. With his youthfulness and casual appearance, it would be hard to guess he was a prosperous graphic designer. This morning exuberance was showing in his open face, in his large hazel eyes.

"So," Drang said. "You were successful."

Harkness nodded. "Very successful, Doctor."

"And how does that make you feel?"

He sat up straight, clasping his hands together. "Fantastic. Better than I've ever felt in my life. I never thought I could actually do it."

"But you did do it."

"Yes, I did it."

"Were you nervous?"

"A little. Although more tense than nervous, I'd say."

"And excited?"

"God, yes. So excited, I was shaking. It was like—"

"Well?"

"Like the first time I had sex. I wanted it more than anything, but I wasn't sure I'd get what I was after. You know what I'm saying?"

"Of course I do. Tell me, did you have an erection?"

"Yes. How did you know that?"

"A normal reaction, Philip, under the circumstances."

"I see."

"And then how did it feel, when you were actually doing it?"

"It was marvelous."

"Thrilling?"

"Very. I had this incredible warmth, all over."

"Did you have an orgasm?"

The boyish features reddened. "Yes, I did. Right at that moment, right when I swung the knife and felt it go in."

"Also quite normal. Nothing for you to be embarrassed about, I assure you. Was there anything else about the experience, about the way it affected you?"

"Just that I felt like, I don't know, like I could do anything."

"Good. Very good. Because you can, you know."

"I know I can. I know it now. I can do *anything*."

"I have no doubt of that, Philip. But let me ask about a few important details. First, did anyone see you do it?"

"No, positively not. I made sure of that."

"No one was anywhere near?"

"There were some people farther up the street, but they didn't see what happened. They were arguing among themselves and not paying attention to anything else. Besides, it was pretty dark."

"Excellent. And when you left, no one saw you then, either?"

"No."

"Very good. Where did you go after that?"

"Home. I went straight home. It's funny, but that was like sex, too. Afterward, I mean. I felt drained, physically."

"Did you sleep well?"

"No, not really. I kept waking up. Even though I was tired, I was too excited to sleep."

"That's understandable. But today you can rest, lie around and relax. Then tomorrow, it's back to work. Are you looking forward to it?"

"Yeah, I am. Very much so."

"Because you have a brand-new sense of confidence, is that it?"

"That's it exactly. It's like I told you. There's nothing I can't do."

"Quite true. Just so long as you take your medicine regularly. You've been careful about that, haven't you?"

"Yes, of course."

"It's vital that you not forget."

"Don't worry, I won't. I'd never forget. And speaking of the medicine, I was wondering."

"Yes?"

"Would it be possible to increase the dosage?"

"Not right away. At the moment, you're on eighty milligrams a day, correct? Plus the booster?"

"That's right."

"We'll see about adding to it later on."

"Good. I don't know what I'd do without it. What's happened to me is almost like a miracle."

"Tell me about that. I want to hear it in your own words."

Harkness took a deep breath. "When I first came here, you know what I was like. I was doing good work, had a fine job and made plenty of money. And yet I was ready to jump out the window. I couldn't believe how fucking down I was."

"Go on."

"I was half-nuts, to be blunt about it. And the part about being suicidal is no bullshit. I used to think about doing it—cutting my wrists or something."

"And now?"

Harkness looked at the doctor and blinked. He licked his lips and his voice grew soft. "Now there is absolutely nothing in the world I can't accomplish."

"And is that gratifying to you?"

"It's the greatest thing that's ever happened."

"Yes, I'm sure it is."

The expression on the patient's face was almost worshipful. "All due to you, Doctor. And the medicine."

Drang smiled. "I'm glad you've made so much progress. And I assure you, you'll continue to improve, just so long as you do as I tell you and continue to take your medicine regularly. That's clear, isn't it?"

"Entirely clear."

"All right, then. Now if you'll push up your sleeve, I'll give you the booster."

Drang turned to the cabinet beside his chair and opened a drawer. Inside was a hypodermic syringe. He took it out and uncapped the needle, then tested it by squirting a few drops onto the carpet.

It took only a moment for him to locate the radial ulnar vein on the underside of Harkness's arm. He slipped the point of the needle into the vessel and depressed the plunger, sending the contents of the barrel into the young man's bloodstream.

"Ah-h-h." Harkness let out his breath. "That's wonderful."

Drang withdrew the needle and put the syringe back into the drawer. Then he leaned forward and gripped the young man's wrists. He brought his face close to Harkness's and stared deep into his eyes. "You wouldn't want me to stop giving you the medicine, would you, Philip?"

"No, Doctor. I'd die if you did that."

"Then listen carefully. As I told you when we began, you must never reveal to anyone that you're taking it, or where you're getting it.

In fact, no one is to know that I'm treating you at all. Do you remember agreeing to that?"

"Yes."

"You'd never go back on your word, would you, Philip?"

"No, never. I swear it. I've never told anyone. Not Cathy, not anyone."

"Cathy is your girlfriend, isn't she?"

"Yes."

"You must be careful not to mention any of this to her. Not ever."

"I won't. I promised you I wouldn't, and I never will."

"Very well. You must always do exactly what I instruct you to do. You understand, don't you?"

Harkness's eyes glazed, as if he were a rabbit that had been cornered by a snake. His tone dropped still lower, until it was barely audible. "I'll always do exactly what you instruct me to do."

"That's fine, Philip. You enjoyed last night, didn't you?"

"I loved it."

"You'd like to do it again, wouldn't you?"

"Yes. I want to very much."

"I'll tell you when, Philip."

"Will it be soon?"

"Very soon."

Drang released his grip and sat back in his chair. "You may go now. Have a pleasant day. I'll see you tomorrow."

15

Ben got home a few minutes before the late news was due to go on. After checking the answering machine and finding there were no messages, he took off his tie and jacket and the holster containing the Mauser and deposited them in the bedroom. From there, he went into the kitchen and dropped ice cubes into a glass, then opened a bottle and poured bourbon over the ice.

Back in the living room, he settled into an overstuffed chair and switched on the box, tuning to WPIC-TV. He kicked off his shoes and swallowed some of the whiskey, grateful for the relaxing warmth that spread through him.

The world news was on first, a potpourri of disasters taking place around the globe. Then came clips showing floods in California and politicians telling lies in Washington, followed by reports on the local scene. There'd been a fire in Queens and a drive-by shooting in the Brownsville section of Brooklyn that had killed two, stories unlikely to stir more than a yawn among members of the TV audience.

Finally, Shelley appeared, sitting at a desk in the studio. She had on one of her power suits, a dark gray one that looked great, he thought, with her honey-blond hair and blue eyes.

But her opening startled him: "This just in. We have exclusive information on the mass murders committed yesterday by Beth Whitacre."

Tolliver leaned forward.

"An investigator now believes," Shelley said, "that Miss Whitacre may have gone to that store for the express purpose of carrying out the brutal execution of the jeweler, Paul Serenbetz. Ruth Halloran, the customer who was also killed, was simply an innocent bystander. Apparently, the security guard tried bravely to stop the mayhem, but as he was reaching for his own pistol, he too was shot down in cold blood. According to the investigator, Serenbetz was the primary target. Why was he? At this point, the police can only speculate."

Ben stared at the tube. What was this shit, and where had she been getting it?

"Speaking on the condition he wouldn't be identified," Shelley went on, "one officer said Miss Whitacre may have turned the gun on herself because she thought police were about to enter the store to arrest her. Rather than allow that to happen, she chose to die. Stay tuned to this station for further information as it comes in. This is Shelley Drake, WPIC-TV, New York."

Ben gulped down the rest of his bourbon. For the love of Christ, who could she have been talking to?

He zapped the set and went back into the kitchen, where he poured himself another drink. Whoever her source was, the cop would get his balls chopped off if his identity got out. The PC was rabid about leaks in a high-profile case. Woe to the guy who was stupid enough to get caught running his mouth to the media.

Tolliver stood there musing for several minutes, sipping whiskey and staring out the window at the lights in the South Street Seaport. He suddenly realized he was hungry. Lunch had been a pastrami sandwich and a beer, and he hadn't eaten anything since. Maybe he should call for a pizza.

The wall phone rang.

He picked it off the hook. "Yeah?"

Shelley said, "Hi, it's me. How was I?"

"Insane. Who the hell were these unnamed sources you were quoting?"

"Hey, don't bite my head off. You know I can't reveal that. It'd be unethical."

"It would, huh? Let me tell you what *I* think. First, it's twenty to one the unnamed investigator was you. Second, the anonymous cop was probably some uniform at the scene, and you conned him into telling you the guard was trying to draw his gun. Am I right?"

"Ben, be reasonable, will you? I didn't say anything that wasn't true."

"Maybe, maybe not. But most of it was conjecture."

"What are you so ticked off about? I have to be competitive. This is a big story."

"And you're out to make it bigger."

"You know why I was calling? To tell you I'd been hoping to come down and spend the night with you and that I was sorry I couldn't make it."

"That so?"

"Yes, that's so. My editor wants me to put together a feature on mass murders, with Whitacre as the centerpiece. I'm going to start working on it right away."

"Wonderful."

"You don't have to be sarcastic. I think it's great, even if you don't. I'll call you again when I can. Maybe you'll be in a better mood by then."

A sharp click sounded in his ear, followed by the hum of the dial tone. He hung up the phone.

At that point, the full import of what was going on here struck home. Unfortunately, the fact that Shelley Drake was his girlfriend was much too well known. And while her slickly cobbled-up story hadn't fooled him, it would a lot of other people.

So who would cops and rival members of the media surmise was the anonymous source who'd been feeding her inside information?

"Goddamn it," Ben said aloud.

He poured himself another bourbon. Tomorrow would be some bitch of a day. Count on it.

16

In the morning, Tolliver drove uptown to the Metropolitan Museum of Art. The largest institution of its kind in the United States, the museum was a gargantuan sprawl of white limestone on the eastern edge of Central Park. He parked on a cross street, then walked back to the main entrance on Fifth Avenue at 82nd.

Since the museum was always closed to the public on Mondays, he had called ahead to make an appointment to interview Beth Whitacre's boss. He went up the wide flight of steps to the front doors, and once inside, he explained to the attendant that he had an appointment, then asked for directions to the administration offices.

Beth Whitacre's boss turned out to be a pleasant surprise. She was dark-haired and trim and wore a white blouse and a checked skirt. Her name was Judy Corelli, and Ben guessed she was only a few years older than Beth had been. He realized he'd been expecting an old crone, which was preconditioned thinking, a practice he tried to avoid. Her office was an inside space, small and cluttered. He showed her his credentials and she offered him a seat.

"I know you have to do this," she said, "but I don't think my nerves can stand much more."

"I'll try to make it as easy for you as I can."

"We were just stunned by what happened on Saturday. It's all anybody's been talking about all morning."

"That's to be expected."

"I've already told the police everything about Beth I could. Wouldn't you rather speak with our director, Mr. Cromwell?"

"Other investigators are doing that," Ben said. "I wanted to see you because you and Miss Whitacre worked together. You probably knew her better than anyone else here did, right?"

"Yes, I suppose that's true."

"Then I'd appreciate it if you'd answer a few questions. I'm trying to find out what led her to do what she did."

"I wish I could tell you," Corelli said. "But I don't have any idea. I was completely incredulous when I heard the news."

"Must have been quite a blow to you."

"It was." Her eyes misted. "Beth was like a kid sister."

"I'm sorry."

She looked at him. "That's kind of you. The other detectives were so . . . callous, I guess I'd have to say. They acted as if it was all cut-and-dried. Just another case."

"They're only doing their job. No matter what was troubling her, she did kill three other people. It was bad for everybody, all the way around."

"Yes. It was."

"How long had she worked here?"

"Not quite two years. It would have been two years in July." Her eyes again filled with tears, and she wiped them with a tissue.

"How were her work habits? Was she dependable?"

"Oh yes. She was always on time, did everything I asked her to do. Most of my work has to do with certifying the evaluation of consignments and pieces that are donated. We do that partly for insurance purposes and partly to verify tax claims a donor would make to the IRS. To an outsider, it would seem deadly dull, and to be honest, I suppose it is. But Beth never complained."

"Did she seem happy to you?"

"She had her ups and downs. I didn't know much about her personal life. Except that I knew who her father was, of course. Everyone here did."

"Ever meet her boyfriend, Ken Patterson?"

"Yes, once or twice. He seemed like a nice guy."

"Did she ever talk to you about that relationship?"

"Not really. She might have referred to him now and then. But that was all."

Ben realized Corelli was hesitant about saying too much, probably out of a sense of loyalty. It was a reaction he'd seen before, in other cases.

"Tell me this," he said. "Were there ever any signs that she might have been having emotional problems?"

She looked away and took a deep breath before turning back to him. "Lieutenant, I'll tell you what I can, but I'm uncomfortable making judgments about someone I knew and liked who's now dead. What she did was dreadful, but I don't know that I'm in any way qualified to analyze her."

"I'm not asking you to. All I want you to do is answer my questions as fully and as truthfully as you can."

"All right. I'll do my best."

"Ever see her lose her temper?"

"Heavens no."

"You said she had her ups and downs. Tell me about the downs."

"She'd get depressed. Here you had this bright, beautiful person, and yet she seemed to think she wasn't as good as other people. Not as smart, not as attractive. Sometimes when she was like that, it was hard for her to do even the simplest things—writing or typing, talking on the phone. It was as if everything frightened her."

"How did you feel about that?"

"I tried to be as patient as possible, telling myself she'd get over it."

"You weren't tempted to let her go?"

"Oh no. I felt sorry for her. And sure enough, when she got into one of these things, after awhile she'd come out of it. Then she'd be all right until the next time."

"Did you ever talk to her about the problem?"

"In a roundabout way. I mean, I didn't sit down with her and say, Look here, you're depressed and you have to do something about it. I just tried to convey to her that I understood and that I thought it might be good to get some help."

"How did she respond?"

"She just kind of brushed it aside. Then this past winter—it might have been sometime in February or early March—she had this haggard look, as if she wasn't eating or sleeping. I was worried about her, and I suggested she see somebody."

"How did she take that?"

"The same way. But not long afterward, she started to change. Became more happy and outgoing. And more confident."

"How did she show it?"

"Mostly by the way she reacted to other people. Once when one of the administrators said we'd made a mistake on recording an appraisal, she stood right up to him. And then she showed him it wasn't our mistake, that we'd been given the wrong information in the first place. She was quite aggressive about it."

"And did that stay with her?"

"It certainly did. She was like that from then on."

"You must have been surprised."

"I was, believe me. I don't think I've ever seen anyone's personality change so fast. She made a few remarks about it herself, too."

"Such as?"

"Such as saying how great she felt. She actually began attacking the job. I was even thinking that maybe I ought to talk to our human resources people about promoting her into a more important position."

"And all that began after you suggested she get some help for her depression."

"That's right."

"So you think that's what she did?"

"Lieutenant, I'd be willing to bet she was seeing a psychiatrist. She started taking long lunches, and I had a hunch that's what she was doing."

"You never asked if she was getting treatment, or who the doctor was?"

"No, I didn't want to be nosy."

"Can you think of anything else that was unusual about her?"

"Not offhand."

"I'd like to see her office."

"Certainly." She got up and left the room, leading him into another enclosure across the way.

This space was even smaller than Corelli's, with barely enough room to turn around. It contained a desk and a chair and a table with a computer terminal. On the desk were a Rolodex, a calendar, a leather-bound appointment book, and two framed photographs. One photo showed Beth with her parents and a young man Ben surmised was her brother. The other photo was of Ken Patterson.

Tolliver leafed through the appointment book first, going over the pages for the previous six months. He found many scribbled notations, but no mention of Serenbetz Jewelers. He did find one for a "Dr.," however, on a weekday in January. No name, just the two letters. Many of the other entries were simply initials with no explanation, and some were illegible.

Next he checked the Rolodex. No Serenbetz there, either, and nothing on a doctor. From what he could see, the listings were all devoted to the Met's business.

He then asked if Beth might have stored personal files in the computer.

"No, because she couldn't have kept them private," Corelli said. "The terminal's linked to our mainframe, so anyone here can call up the files."

There was also a small bulletin board on the wall. Tolliver squinted at it, but the pieces of paper tacked to the board all seemed to be staff memos and the like. The only nonbusiness items were a concert schedule from Lincoln Center and a birthday card signed "Mom and Dad."

Judy saw him looking at the card. "I want to write to her parents. They must be feeling terrible."

"Yes." He returned his attention to the desk, opening the drawers and poring over the contents. The top one was filled with an assortment of pens, paper clips, and other odds and ends, including a pocket calculator and a subway map. The few personal items were credit-card receipts from clothing stores and restaurants. There were more papers in the other drawers, but all of them pertained to Beth Whitacre's job.

He poked around the tiny office for another few minutes, finding nothing that would shed further light on her personal contacts or activities. Finally, he picked up the appointment book. "I want to look through this again," he said. "I'll return it later." He had no right to take it, but Corelli didn't object. Probably she was just glad to be getting rid of him. He thanked her for her help, then left the building.

Walking back to his car, he thought about what she'd told him. She'd be willing to bet, she said, that Beth Whitacre had been seeing a psychiatrist. So there it was again.

Glancing at his watch, he realized he barely had time to make it down to headquarters for the press conference.

He had a feeling he'd be stepping into a hornet's nest.

17

The conference was held outside the front entrance of One Police Plaza. It featured an assortment of brass along with lesser ranks, stationed behind a battery of microphones.

The PC was there, and Chief of Detectives Galupo, along with Lt. Terry McGrath and his boss, Capt. Michael Jarvis, the zone commander who oversaw the Midtown North Precinct. Tolliver and Fred Logan were at the end of the lineup, where they'd been placed by Alice Kovala, the commissioner's deputy for PR. Kovala herself flanked the other end, looking like a mother hen watching over her chicks. A phalanx of uniforms was also on hand.

Although the weather had cleared, portable lights were glaring in the cops' faces, put there by Kovala's crew so that the TV cameras would get the best-possible pictures. Reporters jammed the steps leading to the entrance, looking up at the row of police officers.

Tolliver stood blinking into the sunshine and the blazing lights, wishing he was somewhere else. He'd spotted Shelley among the media crowd, and he wished she was somewhere else, as well. He was careful to avoid making eye contact with her.

Chief Galupo spoke first, mouthing platitudes about the police conducting a thorough investigation into the shootings. He then tossed the ball to the man he said was in charge of the case, Lieutenant McGrath.

Looking uncomfortable, McGrath stepped to the microphones and said it appeared the young woman had experienced severe emotional problems, which had caused her to become violent. To Tolliver, this was like observing that the sky was blue.

McGrath then added that Miss Whitacre apparently had been having difficulties in her work and her personal life and that the pressure might have become too much for her—which was yet another declaration of the obvious. When he finished saying nothing, the ladies and gentlemen of the media began pelting him with questions.

One reporter asked whether there was any connection between the killer and her victims. McGrath said that a probe by his squad had revealed none. He said the fact that she picked them at random was another indication that she was mentally unbalanced at the time.

The next question was whether her parents had had any indication she was crazy before she went off the deep end. McGrath said they hadn't. As if he hadn't been paying attention, another guy wanted to know if she'd ever been a patient in a mental hospital.

McGrath kept his cool as he fielded the inquiries, many of them totally asinine, and Tolliver was relieved when at last the conference seemed to be about over. The plain fact was that the cops had little to add to what the reporters already knew, and everyone was aware that this performance was largely for show, anyway. The media vultures were simply picking over the bones of Saturday's slaughter, hoping to find a few morsels to spice up the evening news.

But then a guy from NBC-TV yelled, "Lieutenant Tolliver, you said you'd get the truth about why the Whitacre woman shot those people and then herself. What've you come up with?"

Oh shit, Ben thought. He'd been apprehensive that the media might focus on him; it was the main reason he'd wanted to duck this exercise. "We're continuing our investigation," he said.

"So what's the real reason why she did it?"

"We're working on that." It was out of his mouth before he realized he'd made a gaffe.

The reporters smelled blood. One of them shouted, "That mean the officers on the case have made mistakes? Or is there more to it than you're letting on?"

"That's not what I said."

"But that's what you meant, right? You got another angle?"

"The investigation is still going on."

"But no progress?"

"I'm making plenty of progress," Tolliver grated. He was damned if he'd let these characters push him around. "Whatever it was that caused her to do what she did, I will find the answers."

Other reporters began shouting more questions at that point, and then Deputy PC Kovala pushed her way to a mike. "That's all we have time for today. There'll be a bulletin for you if more information comes to light. Thank you very much." She signaled to her crew and the lights went out.

The reporters went right on firing queries anyway, complaining that the police weren't giving them all the facts. Meantime, the cops ignored their shouts, turning and going back into the building. Some of the more aggressive among the media tried to follow them, but the squad of uniforms blocked the way.

Inside, Terry McGrath shot a glance at Tolliver that could have scorched paint off the wall. Ben paid no attention. If his rejoinders had ruffled feathers, that was too damn bad. He continued walking down the hall.

A voice said, "Tolliver."

Ben turned, to see Chief Galupo approaching. Despite his gray suit and dark tie, Galupo still looked like the army major he'd once been. His black-olive eyes were snapping with anger.

"Yes, sir?"

"Come with me. I want to talk to you."

They got into an elevator and went up to the twenty-seventh floor. The car was crowded with other cops, and nothing was said until Tolliver followed the chief into his office.

The room was a reflection of the man. It was sparsely furnished, with a desk and a few straight-backed chairs, along with a pole bearing an American flag. Photographs of the PC and the mayor were hanging on the walls, and the single window looked out on the spidery cables of the Brooklyn Bridge.

Galupo shut the door and sat at his desk, indicating a chair across from it.

When Ben was seated, the chief said, "Can you tell me just what the fuck has gotten into you?"

"Sir?"

"First you butt in on a case that doesn't belong to you, and then you take it upon yourself to run your mouth about it in that press conference. Telling the world you'll come up with information that other cops can't get. Only you can do that, right? Because nobody else is as smart as you, is that it?"

"I didn't realize how it would sound." The excuse seemed lame, even to Tolliver.

Galupo's eyebrows lifted. "You didn't realize? Not only did you embarrass Lieutenant McGrath and Captain Jarvis; you made the whole department look bad. Including the commissioner, and me, too, not that it matters to you."

"Chief, I was told to write a report—"

"Report, shit. You think because you're assigned to the DA's Office that gives you special privileges?"

"No, I don't."

"I'm glad to hear that, Lieutenant. I really am. I thought maybe you forgot you're a member of the police force. That you figured you were now on Mr. Oppenheimer's staff."

Ben knew better than to argue. He kept his mouth shut.

"The fact is, your unit is responsible for investigating mob activity, not homicides being handled by a precinct squad. The work of the unit is a service we provide to the DA. There is a chain of command in this department, and you will respect it."

Galupo's swarthy features grew darker. "It's also come to my attention that you may be giving information to a reporter who's a personal friend of yours."

That one he couldn't let go by. "Sir, that's just not true."

"Are you sure?"

"Positive."

"You goddamn well better be. Or I guarantee you'll be facing disciplinary action. Is that clear?"

"Yes, that's clear."

The chief was quiet for a moment. Then he said, "Let me explain something to you, Tolliver. The Whitacre case is a black eye on New York. Innocent people were killed, and the perpetrator was a member of one of our leading families. But you know what? They're all dead, and nothing'll bring them back. What the city needs now is to heal, to put this mess behind us. You follow what I'm saying?"

"I think so."

"I'm glad you do. So you go finish your report for the district attorney, and that will be the end of it. But don't you ever step on the toes of your fellow officers again. Understand?"

"Yes, sir."

"Good. That's all, Lieutenant."

Tolliver left the office and took the elevator down to the first floor, anxious to get out of the building and away from there.

On his way back to 100 Centre Street, it occurred to him that while he'd been getting reamed, Captain Logan had stayed conveniently out of sight.

But the hell with it. Political pressure or not, there was no way Ben would back off now.

18

You arrogant prick," Drang said. He hit the button that turned off the TV, and Tolliver's face disappeared.

Drang had been sure the story would have begun to fade by now; after all, what else was there? The officers who spoke first at the press conference had as much as admitted they knew no more at this point than they had directly after the incident occurred. The Whitacre woman snapped emotionally and committed three random killings and then destroyed herself.

As far as the world was concerned, there was nothing more to the case. A regrettable tragedy, but unfortunately, things like that happened often in America. Now it was all over but the funerals, three of which were scheduled for tomorrow, according to what Drang had read in the *New York Times.*

So why was this loathesome shit of a cop staying after it? He was like a dog worrying a dead rabbit, refusing to let go. Even after the other detectives had obviously been ready to mark the case closed, there this Tolliver was, implying that the investigation hadn't been handled properly and that he was the one who would uncover the truth.

What was the man's motive—was he doing this to call attention to himself? Was he so hungry for publicity? Or was it possible that he might actually find a way to trace Beth Whitacre to the psychiatrist who had been treating her?

But even if he did, as unlikely as that was, what difference would it make? Obviously the young woman had been emotionally disturbed, or she wouldn't have needed psychotherapy in the first place. If her illness had led her to carry out an unexpected act of violence, that could not have been the doctor's fault.

And yet, having a policeman rooting around in the situation would be highly unwelcome. Drang was too close to attaining his goals to countenance interference at this point. Damn it, why couldn't the fool leave well enough alone?

Relax, he told himself. This is no different from any other problem. To solve it, begin by gathering the facts. Then examine them— coolly, dispassionately, objectively. Who is this man, and what is he?

Going to his desk, he switched on his computer and the modem, then called up the Dun & Bradstreet credit-rating service he subscribed to. The database provided information on anyone Drang wished to check on, revealing the individual's finances and personal history. The doctor frequently used the service to get comprehensive reports on patients he was treating.

He typed in his password, and when he was admitted, he entered the subject's name and then New York City. Within seconds, a list of Tollivers flashed onto the screen. There were a eighteen of them living here, but only one with the first name Ben. Drang keyed that one.

What popped on next was the detective's life in a nutshell.

Tolliver had been born in the Bronx and attended schools there, then spent four years in the Marine Corps. Upon discharge, he joined the NYPD. Moved up the ranks to detective lieutenant, commanding the squad in the Sixth Precinct. Earned a bachelor's degree in political science via night classes at NYU. At present, he was a member of the Special Investigation Unit in the Manhattan District Attorney's Office. Decorated six times for bravery. Single, never married. The report also listed his home address—a rented apartment—and his telephone number.

Reading the data, Drang blew air through his lips in an expression of contempt. For all his bluster, the detective had to be an idiot to work for the miserable salary the city was paying him. As proof of that, Tolliver had accumulated only a handful of assets, chief among them a car and a few dollars in the bank.

Perhaps, Drang thought, he'd been assuming the cop was more capable than he actually was. Maybe all this bold talk of his was nothing more than braggadocio—in which case, his investigation would go nowhere.

But then again, the personality type often attracted to police work was anal-compulsive, and frequently narcissistic. Typically, a zealot who thought he was doing something noble. That could make Tolliver dangerous. He was already claiming he wouldn't stop until he knew what had motivated Beth Whitacre.

Drang resolved to weigh the problem carefully before deciding on a course of action. For the moment, he'd let the information simmer in the back of his mind. He shut down the computer and began reviewing the correspondence on his desk.

First, he glanced through the checks that had been sent by various of his patients. In the morning, Anna would stamp them for deposit and send them to his bank. By and large, the patients were a bunch of dullards who interested him very little—whiny matrons and acne-faced teenagers, a motley collection of neurotics. Useful only in that they paid their bills. Not nearly so fascinating as someone he might involve in his experiments—a Harkness, for example, who paid in cash so that there would be no record.

Next, he looked at the fax he'd received earlier from his lawyer in Zurich, telling him the offer on the villa he wanted to buy had been accepted. That was good news; he'd seen the place back in February and had known at once it would be perfect for his work. Since then, negotiations had gone on, and now the place would soon be his.

The move was a key part of his plans. There were many important advantages to setting up the new laboratory in Switzerland, and living there would be far better than New York. He was excited about making the change.

Lastly, he looked through the letter and brochure that had been sent to him by the American Psychiatric Association, an organization he detested. Although he'd read the materials several times, he got them out and studied them again.

The mailing was an invitation to the association's upcoming convention, to be held in New York, at the Waldorf. The brochure outlined the program, listing the lecturers and their subjects. As well as individual speakers, there would be a number of panel discussions. Each of the talks and speeches would feature noted authorities in the profession, men whose reputations were well known to him.

One photograph in the brochure leapt out at him. It had been years since Drang had seen those weak features, but looking at the photo made it seem like yesterday. What he beheld was the soft face of Dr. Arthur McKenzie.

Of all the people Drang had encountered in his work, none inspired greater animosity than what he felt for this man. Staring at the photo, he could hear McKenzie's thin, scratchy voice demeaning Drang's work, damning him with scorn and derision. He could see the disdain in the small piglike eyes, the flick of his fingers as he dismissed Drang's ideas as those of a pretender, a medical fraud.

And now McKenzie was to be a featured speaker at the convention? How outrageous. It was McKenzie who was the imposter, if only the boobs who belonged to that pompous organization had the sense to realize the truth. The man had no talent of his own, and he bitterly resented those who did. Jealousy was what had motivated him to attack Drang, nothing but pure, unbridled jealousy.

Yet here McKenzie was, about to be honored by his colleagues. It was ironic, but at the same time propitious, because this was precisely the opportunity Drang had been looking for. The response he'd planned was ingenious, typical of his thinking.

He put the materials into a desk drawer and again thought of the detective who'd appeared in that TV newscast. What had the man meant when he said he was making progress? It wouldn't do to have him or anyone else upset Drang's plans now. Not when he was at last on the brink of success.

So Tolliver wanted to challenge a mind that was far superior to his own? That would be a bad mistake on his part. It might be amusing for Drang to show him what it was like to be the hunted, rather than the hunter.

The doctor had already created the mechanism. He'd shaped and sharpened it, made certain adjustments. Tonight he would test it again.

19

Dr. Alan Stein lived in one of the old row houses near Tompkins Square Park. Tolliver went up the steps and rang the bell, carrying the videocassette. A minute later, he heard locks being undone, and then the door swung open and Stein's massive frame filled the doorway.

With his spray of wiry hair and short gray beard, the doctor put Tolliver in mind of a lumberjack. Especially wearing his usual work clothes, a denim shirt and khaki pants. He thrust out his hand, blinking owlishly behind black horn-rims. "Hello, Lieutenant. Good to see you."

Ben shook the hand. "I appreciate your giving me some time, Doc."

"My pleasure. Come on in. I just made a fresh pot of coffee."

Tolliver followed him to the back of the house, where his study was. Although Stein was on retainer as a consultant to the NYPD, his services weren't often utilized. Most cops held a dim view of psychiatrists, trusting them even less than they did defense lawyers, which was going some.

Ben, on the other hand, often found this man's help to be invaluable. Before setting up his private practice, the doctor had been on staff at the Fairlawn Hospital for the Criminally Insane, as well as at St. Elizabeth's. He had no illusions about the motivations of the killers, rapists, con artists, and assorted other malefactors he'd dealt with over the years.

The study was where Stein saw patients and where he sometimes wrote articles for psychiatric journals. Books were crammed into over-flowing bookcases and stacked haphazardly on the desk, and still other volumes lay on the floor. A table held a computer and a printer, plus a TV set with VCR. There were worn leather chairs across from the desk, and the inevitable Freudian couch against the far wall. A bar stood in one corner.

Stein filled two china mugs with coffee and handed one to Ben. "So, you brought the tape?"

Tolliver held up the cassette. "Yeah, but don't expect too much—the quality's pretty poor. The techs tried to enhance the original, but this was the best they could do."

"At least it's something." Stein put the cassette into the machine, and a few seconds later, the images appeared on the screen.

Once again, Ben was fascinated by the macabre show in the jewelry store. Even though he knew what was coming, it was eerie to watch the young woman stand there with all the calm of a professional executioner. When she reached into her bag and drew out the pistol, he wanted to shout, Don't do it!

But what happened next was as inevitable as nightfall.

Stein watched the sequence without comment, and when the tape ended, he rewound it and ran it again. Then he turned off the machine and waved Ben to one of the leather chairs, taking the other one himself.

The doctor sipped coffee. "Interesting. And quite an atypical behavior pattern in such a situation. She seemed extraordinarily calm, right up until the last moment."

"Didn't she, though."

"What have you learned about her?"

Ben recounted his interview with Lincoln and Enid Whitacre, as well as the ones with Ken Patterson and Judy Corelli. As he spoke, Stein sat silent and motionless, fixing him with the magnified owl eyes.

"What about the value of those necklaces?" the doctor asked. "The media said a million dollars, although that sounds like an exaggeration."

"It was. They're worth around a hundred grand apiece."

"I see. Valuable enough."

"Sure. You think that's relevant?"

"I think the necklaces may have had some significance, apart from their value. But just what that was, I have no way of knowing."

"The way she acted is what gets me. You ever come across a case like this?"

"No, never," Stein said. "We had female murderers at the hospitals I worked in, but none of them had killed in the course of a robbery. The only woman I can think of who did was the prostitute in Florida who robbed and shot her johns."

"Aileen Wuornos."

"Right. Wuornos was also one of the few female serial killers I've ever heard of. As you know, it's unusual for women to commit violent crimes, compared with the number carried out by men. In fact, it's far less common for them to commit crimes of any kind. For example, of the entire prison population in the state of New York, less than five percent are female. But I'm sure you're aware of that."

"Yeah, I am. Although this one seemed cooler than most men would have been. Some of us thought she might have been on drugs."

"That's conceivable."

"And yet I couldn't think what she might have been using. Uppers would have had her juiced, and she didn't act like that. Or do you think it's a possibility?"

"No. She was too steady, too deliberate. And above all, too composed."

"And tranquilizers would have had her too far down, right?"

"Yes. Valium, Librium, Halcion—any one of them would have slowed her reflexes, made her drowsy. And she was hardly that."

"Go back to the uppers for a minute. Is there anything that might fit?"

Stein thought about it. "Not I that I can think of, offhand. Phencyclidine or any of the hallucinogens or psychedelics would have produced noticeable reactions. She would have been visibly agitated, sweating heavily, highly excited. LSD, proscaline, psilocybin—any of them would had that effect. Same thing would have been true if she'd been on amphetamines. Racemic, for example, or D-isomer. Or phentermine. They're all related to mescaline, and they stimulate the central nervous system. If she'd been high on one of those, you would have seen plenty of signs."

"What, then?"

"At this point, impossible to say."

"What about the new drugs? Prozac, for instance. That would have kept her calm, wouldn't it?"

"I don't believe it would. Not under those circumstances, anyway. Prozac is fluoxetine hydrochloride, a nontricyclic antidepressant. People take it because it helps them feel upbeat and confident, keeps them buoyant. That's not to say it doesn't produce some unwanted side effects, or that there haven't been some incidents involving patients who were taking it."

"Including murder and suicide?"

"A number of suicides, and there was a case in Kentucky where a man killed eight people. The defense claimed it was because he was on Prozac, but the jury didn't buy it."

"Any other substance come to mind?"

"Not at the moment. What did the lab have to say?"

"I'll have a toxicology report from them in a couple of days."

"That should tell us something."

"Yeah, but suppose she wasn't on drugs. Suppose she just went crazy—like somebody who kills strangers because he's pissed off at the world. That's possible, too, isn't it?"

"Yes, it is. Although that doesn't fit her behavior, either. The mental disorder you're describing is paranoid schizophrenia, of course. The killer is projecting his or her own hostilities and conflicts onto others."

"So I understand."

"That's what happened in all those mass murders we've heard about lately. But in most of them, the killer is anything but quiet. He's usually the opposite—consumed by rage, shouting curses, howling about revenge. He wants to settle the score with his boss, for example. Or his fellow workers."

"Or his neighbors," Ben said.

"Right. Or even all other human beings, because his sick mind is telling him he's been wronged. He's externalizing blame."

"Sure. It's somebody else's fault."

"Exactly. Therefore, he wants to inflict pain, wants to make his victims suffer the way he thinks they made him suffer. He's filled with hatred, so he goes out and kills people. But he's certainly not serene while he's doing it."

"What drugs are used to treat that type of sickness? Is there anything that would keep somebody calm, like she was?"

"The most effective medication is haloperidol. But no one taking it would do what this young woman did."

"Which brings us back to square one."

"Yes, but don't misunderstand me," Stein said. "What I'm giving you is little more than conjecture. Neither I nor anyone else can draw a psychological profile of someone after seeing them for a few seconds on videotape."

"I realize that."

"You say both her boyfriend and her boss thought she was seeing a psychiatrist?"

"Her boss thought so, but the boyfriend wasn't sure."

"If she was, it would help if you could talk to whoever was treating her."

"I know," Tolliver said. "I'm trying to find out who she saw."

"Good. The doctor might surprise you and cooperate."

20

The following morning, Tolliver telephoned the American Psychiatric Association. He identified himself as a police officer and asked for the director. When the guy came on, he was civil enough, until Ben began asking questions. Then it was as if a steel door had clanged shut.

Sorry, the director said, the APA had no information concerning what doctor was treating whom. Such a relationship was a private matter between psychiatrist and patient. And even if the association had such records, they certainly would not release them. That, he sniffed, would be against APA policies.

Ben put the phone down in disgust. This was a problem cops ran into all the time. Physicians, dentists, ophthalmologists—anybody connected with a field of medicine—acted as if they were on a holy mission. He'd probably get the same reaction from a vet.

Nevertheless, there had to be a way for him to get what he wanted. Opening a drawer in his desk, he took out Beth Whitacre's appointment book and began going through it for the third time.

Most of the entries appeared to involve the Met's business. There was one on a collection of paintings due in from an estate in Florida, another on additions to the Rockefeller collection of primitive art. But only a few were spelled out, and many he was unable to decipher at all. The majority had been written in a kind of shorthand: "J re Myer Galleries"; "Euro TL"; "Call BP"; "Ltr Goodman"; and so on. Still others were simply a string of letters or digits. He had no idea what the significance of those might be.

The ones he thought could be personal were equally hard to translate—"K 4 Seas 6," for example. It might indicate she'd planned to meet Ken Patterson in the Four Seasons restaurant at six o'clock, but that was only a guess. And anyway, the notation had no bearing on what he was hoping to find.

The "Dr." scribble on a Thursday in January was the one he found tantalizing. Did that mean she had an appointment with a doctor—or a psychiatrist? Or was Ben's interpretation merely wishful thinking?

But even if he'd guessed correctly, so what? There was no name, just the letters. He was still wrestling with it when the phone rang.

He picked it up. "Lieutenant Tolliver."

"Ed Flynn, Ben. We had another homicide last night, same MO. A stabbing with no apparent motive. I thought you'd want to know."

"What happened?"

"Victim owned a boutique on Hudson Street. He worked late, taking inventory. Left a little after one o'clock. He was on his way home when somebody came along the sidewalk and stuck a knife in his chest."

"Witnesses?"

"Yeah, we got one of them here now. He was a short distance away when it happened."

"I'd like to hear what he has to say."

"Sure, come ahead."

Ben left the office and went down to his car. As he drove through Little Italy and Chinatown on his way to the Sixth Precinct headquarters, he thought about what Flynn had told him. Another unexplainable murder? Maybe committed by a demented killer? It couldn't have anything to do with the Whitacre case, and yet there were just too many unexplainable things going on here. Maybe Logan was right; the whole town had gone crazy.

The station house was a gray brick building that straddled the block between West Tenth and Charles streets. Tolliver nosed his Ford in among the blue-and-whites and scooters in the parking lot and left the plate on the dash.

When he walked in, cops at the desk were supporting a bearded man in a T-shirt who was too drunk to stand on his own. A thick white bandage covered the top of his head, and the T-shirt was encrusted with dried vomit. Other officers were restraining a burly black youth who was calling them dumb-ass motherfuckers. Across the way, three young women wearing miniskirts and spike heels were arguing with a uniform and a civilian who probably was an undercover vice cop. Seeing the goings-on gave Ben a twinge of nostalgia.

The squad room was on the second floor. He trotted up the stairs, and when he stepped inside, the scene there was familiar, as well. Detectives at the battered gray metal desks were typing reports, talking on the phones. At the far end of the area, Ed Flynn and two others were questioning a man who was sitting beside one of the desks. Tolliver stepped over to where they were gathered.

Flynn was in shirtsleeves, his collar open and his tie pulled down. He was long and lanky, with dark wavy hair and a lean face. Judging from the chin stubble and the shadows under his eyes, he'd been on the case straight through the night. The others also looked as if they'd gone sleepless. They were Frank Petrusky and Carlos Rodriguez, both members of the squad back when Ben was running it. The man they were interviewing was wearing a blue warm-up jacket and a Yankees cap. A straggly mustache decorated his upper lip.

The detectives greeted Tolliver as he approached, and then Flynn introduced him to the man sitting beside the desk. His name was Arturo Sanchez.

"Tell us again what you saw," Flynn said to Sanchez. "From the beginning."

Arturo seemed pleased to have an audience. "Yeah, okay. Like I said, after I got done work, I went in Molly's for a beer. I come out of there and I'm going to the subway, and there's a guy walking ahead of me on the sidewalk."

"Going in the same direction you were?" Ben asked.

"Yeah, I'm like thirty feet in back of him. I walk along aways, and then I see this other guy coming toward us. All of a sudden, he stabs the one in front of me. No warning, nothing. He just pulls out a knife and sticks him. Then the one who got stabbed, he grabs the guy who did it."

"So they fought?"

"No, it wasn't no fight. The guy who's cut, he's going down, but he's holding on to the other one's coat." Sanchez gesticulated, waving his hands. "Then he lets go and falls on his face."

"And the stabber?"

"He straightens up and I think, Shit, man, I don't want nothing to do with this fucker. But then he turns around and takes off."

"After that, what?"

"After that, I go up to the guy who's down and turn him over, and there's blood all over him. Some other people come by, and they start yelling for help."

"Did you get a good look at the man with the knife?"

"Sure, I seen his face under a streetlight. He was a young white guy."

"What else do you remember about him?"

"Uh, he was kind of skinny, not too tall."

"What color hair?"

"I think it was brown."

"Did he give any sign he knew the one he stabbed?"

"No. He just come along and kaboom, like that. It was weird, man."

"You work in that neighborhood?"

"Yeah, I do sanitation."

"You do what?"

"I'm a janitor."

"Where?"

"Office building on Seventh Avenue."

"Okay. About the two men. Had you ever seen either of them before?"

"No, I'm pretty sure I never did."

"All right," Tolliver said. "That's all I have." He motioned to Flynn he wanted to talk in private.

While the other detectives went on questioning Sanchez, Flynn led the way into his tiny office, just off the squad room.

"Arturo's story hold up?" Ben asked.

"Yeah, the other witnesses told us more or less the same thing. Man and his wife, waiting for a cab. It was late, so there weren't many people around. We talked to Arturo last night and showed him mug shots, but he said no to all of them. Then we pulled him in again this morning and went over it all again. The couple's coming back in, too, later on."

"You get anything else?"

"Just these." Flynn opened a drawer and took out a glassine bag. He opened it and shook out three yellow capsules onto the surface of his desk. Each was about five-eighths of an inch in length, the type of gelatin cylinder any number of drugs were packed in.

Ben looked at them. "Where did these come from?"

"They were on the sidewalk, beside the body. Could have belonged to the victim, or maybe the perp."

"Or neither one."

"True."

"How about Arturo?"

"Says he has no idea, never saw them before, even at the scene. Anyhow, I'll get them analyzed."

"You have photos?"

"Yeah, right here." Flynn opened a manila envelope and took out a set of eight-by-ten black-and-white glossies. He handed them to Tolliver. "CSU sent them over, just before I called you."

Ben studied the photographs. A number of them showed a slender dark-haired man lying on his back on the sidewalk. His mouth was open, and he was staring back at the camera with half-lidded, sightless eyes. Blood had soaked the front of his shirt, and there was more of it underneath him. He was wearing a light-colored jacket, and that was bloodstained, as well.

Other photos had been taken in the morgue. In those, the victim was naked, lying on a table with a linear gauge set beside the vertical puncture in the center of his chest. Close-ups revealed that the wound was three and a half centimeters in length.

"ME told us the knife went through his sternum and straight into the heart," Flynn said.

Tolliver peered at one of the close-ups. "Good-sized blade."

"Yeah, a butcher knife, probably. Hell of a wallop, to penetrate the bone like that."

"How does this wound compare with the one in the other homicide?"

"Almost identical. We're pretty sure it was made with the same knife. Postmortem should confirm that."

"How about the description the witness gave you in the first one?"

"It fits. That witness said the stabber was slim and had quick moves. Arturo got a much better look at him, though."

Ben again glanced at the photograph of the dead man. "Who was this one?"

"Name was Harold Speiser. Lived on Christopher Street. His boyfriend told us about him working late. He owned the boutique for three years. No known enemies, according to the friend. And there was sixty bucks in his pants pocket."

"You check for a sheet?"

"Yeah. Nothing on him here or in Albany."

"Huh."

"You really think there could be some kind of a tie to the Whitacre case? I mean, that's a real stretch, isn't it?"

"On the face of it, yes. But it's damn strange that all of a sudden we've got people killing other people for no reason. Let me know, will you, if his friend gives you anything that could connect Speiser to Whitacre? Or her victims? Any kind of a link anyplace."

"Sure, Ben. Will do."

"Thanks, Ed. I'll see you later." He started out of the office and then turned back. "One other thing. Call me when you get word from the lab on what's in those capsules, okay?"

"Yeah, I'll do that."

21

Jonas Drang listened intently as Harkness recounted the previous night's event. The young man's face was radiant, his hazel eyes bright with excitement. It had gone well, he reported; the victim had struggled a little, but only for a moment.

"Struggled a little?" Drang asked.

"Yeah, he tore my jacket, the dickhead."

"And you fought back?"

"No, there was no fight. He just kind of grabbed me, and then he died. I was watching his eyes and I saw it happen." Harkness sniggered. "Like somebody turned out the lights."

"I hope you made sure no one was nearby."

"There was one guy, but he wasn't close enough to see my face."

Drang didn't like the way that sounded. "Who was this?"

"Just some jerk who was on the street. I only got a glimpse of him, but he looked like a spic. Had on a baseball cap."

"You're sure he couldn't see you clearly?"

"Uh-huh. Nothing to worry about. Really."

"All right. Then what?"

"Then I was gone. Ducked over to Eighth Avenue and caught the C train. Got off at Twenty-third Street and went home."

This was fascinating, Drang thought. A few weeks ago, the patient had been a sniveling cur, afraid of being kicked. And now look at him. Listen to the expressions of self-assurance, the aggressiveness coming through.

If anything, Harkness sounded a little *too* self-assured. Even somewhat cocky. The doctor would have to deal with that before it got out of hand. "Tell me, Philip, was this as thrilling to you as the first time?"

"Oh, yes. I'll say it was. I came again, too. Right when I stuck him."

No inhibitions now, Drang noted. Harkness was actually boasting. It was time to rein him in a bit. "Well now, you're making some nice gains, aren't you?"

"Yeah, I feel fine."

"Then I think it would be wise to increase your dosage. From now on, you're to take five capsules a day. That will move you up to a hundred milligrams."

"Hey, great."

"Yes, I believe it will be helpful to you. Also, I want you to take it easy for a time. No more adventures until I tell you otherwise. Is that understood?"

"Yes, of course. Whatever you say, Doctor."

"Good. And now we'll give you your booster." Opening the drawer in the cabinet beside his chair, Drang took out the hypodermic syringe.

After giving Harkness the shot, Drang sent him on his way. Then he got his notebook from the shelf and jotted down his observations. Even though Harkness continued to display somewhat erratic behavior, not hewing to orders as closely as Drang would have liked, the changes in him were nothing less than amazing.

The doctor wondered what the pioneers of his profession would have thought. Freud and Jung and Adler and the rest of them, a gaggle of jealous practitioners who'd snarled like dogs over a bone, each arguing that he knew more than the others about the workings of the human mind.

But in fact, they'd known next to nothing.

With his bold experiments in psychopharmacology, Drang had outdistanced them all. Not only had he probed uncharted areas of the brain, territories the others never dreamed existed, but, far more important, he'd learned how the brain could be *transformed*—reprogrammed chemically. Harkness was living proof of his success.

Drang closed the notebook and put it away, then glanced at his watch. He had over an hour before the next patient was due—the new one, the female.

He left his office and went down the cellar steps into his laboratory.

22

The rats greeted him with their squeaking and chirping, many of the livelier animals jumping up at the bars of the cages as Drang entered the lab. Glancing over at them, he took a long white coat from its hook.

The doctor was in a good mood. After the fiasco with Whitacre, his work was going well again, and he was pleased by the progress he was making. The few wrinkles in his treatment of Harkness could be ironed out with little trouble. The increased dosage of the medication would ensure that.

After putting on the coat, he approached the cages. The specimen he wanted would be one of those he'd injected yesterday, in preparation for today's work. He took his time making a selection, spending several minutes watching the creatures milling about in the wire enclosures.

Choosing one wouldn't be difficult; all of them were robust animals—which was typical of Norway rats, and one of the reasons they were so well suited to his needs. By nature hale and vigorous, they adapted readily to any environment, subsisted on any diet. Although he kept these clean and well fed, they would have been quite at home living in filth and eating anything from decaying vegetation to maggots and rotting flesh.

Yet as hardy as they were, that was but one of their attributes. Far more important to the doctor was their mental capacity. By nature, rats were also extremely intelligent. They were much brighter than dogs, for example, ranking with pigs and porpoises on the mammalian intellectual scale.

For that matter, the only creatures smarter than rats were monkeys, which weren't nearly as rugged physically and hence weren't as suitable for experiments to do with the human brain. In fact, monkeys were prone to a wide variety of illnesses and could die from the slightest infection, even a common cold. They were also hard to come by and cost a fortune. Still another drawback was that they were benign, friendly creatures; they actually had a sense of humor, an aspect that was rare among animals and not at all one that Drang wanted.

Rats, on the other hand, were invariably both cunning and sly.

They did their stealing and looting in the dark, befouling the areas they infested and spreading diseases to which they themselves were immune. And although devious and furtive, they could be ferocious when threatened. Rats were the criminals of the animal kingdom.

This morning, Drang decided on a sturdy male with a large head and a long, scaly tail. The rat constantly twitched its whiskers, an indication of alertness, and its greenish brown coat was thick and sleek. It was apparent that the animal was in excellent health.

As Drang watched it, the rat returned his stare with fearless dark eyes tinged with red. That was another thing he liked about this particular creature: it obviously hated him.

Pulling on a pair of rubber gloves, he stepped closer to the cage. From a shelf, he took a metal rod with a wire loop on the end, and then he opened the top of the enclosure. The rat looked up at him and for a moment tried to scurry away, but it had no place to run. Realizing it couldn't escape, the beast reared up on its haunches and snarled at him.

"Ah," Drang said. "You're quite a brave fellow, aren't you? I admire you for that." With a quick, deft move, he dropped the snare over the animal's neck and tightened the loop. The rat struggled and kicked, but to no avail.

"Come with me now," the psychiatrist said affectionately. "I have a surprise for you."

He lifted the squealing rodent out of its cage and carried it over to the lab table. Holding the rat down on the white porcelain surface, he picked up a cleaver with his free hand.

Oddly, he almost regretted what he was about to do. Not because he felt the slightest twinge of pity, or because he regarded such actions as cruel. In that respect, there was a kind of mutual understanding between the rodent and himself. The rat would have done the same—or worse—to him, and without a second thought.

Rather, it was because deep in his psyche, Drang felt a primeval empathy with his enemy. Here was a creature in many ways much like himself. The rat was highly astute, and it lived according to a singularity of purpose Drang found admirable. There was no foolishness about fairness or equal treatment, no attempt to contrive justice as a salve for an abraded conscience.

In fact, there was no conscience. And hence, no guilt. That meant that neither were there any of the endless self-deceptions with which weak men tortured themselves. Instead, the rat lived entirely by its instincts and its intellect, thinking of nothing but how to gratify its own needs. It was a creature that Sigmund Freud would have described as driven only by a pure, undifferentiated id.

But business was business.

"So now," Drang said to the rat, "you will serve my needs, just as I would have served yours." He raised the cleaver and chopped off the animal's head.

Blood squirted from the severed arteries, and for several seconds, the decapitated body went on scrabbling, claws scratching the tabletop, before it grew still.

The head was what Drang wanted. Sweeping the body into a plastic bag, he carried it over to the large open vat on the far side of the room and dropped it, bag and all, into the yellow liquid in the vat, a mixture of nitric and hydrochloric acids. He knew that in a short time nothing of the corpse would remain, not even its skeleton. Then he put away the snare and wiped the blood from the table with alcohol and a paper towel.

After adjusting the overhead light, he set the rat's head upright between the jaws of a small stainless-steel vise, tightening the device just enough to hold the head firmly in place. With a sure touch, he trimmed away the pelt with a scalpel.

Next, he used a thin-bladed electric surgical saw to cut a circular path horizontally through the frontal, parietal, interparietal, and supraoccipital sections of the rat's skull.

It was like opening a soft-boiled egg. He lifted off the tiny cap of bone, and there was his prize: a teaspoonful of gray cells, moist and shining. With the same careful, deliberate touch, he scooped out the creature's brain and placed the collection of cells in a blender.

There was a small refrigerator among the pieces of equipment on the table. He retrieved a container from it, in which were the brains of four other rats he'd killed earlier. He added them to this one and turned on the blender, letting it run for a few seconds, until the contents had been reduced to a putty-colored mush. Finally, he turned off the machine and ladled the material into a centrifuge.

Drang enjoyed this procedure; invariably, it filled him with a sense of anticipation and excitement. It was like exploring a part of the universe never seen before, like visiting some remote planet hitherto unknown. The satisfaction was enormous, and he never tired of the effort. Even his mistakes were stimulating.

The techniques he was using now had first been developed by Solomon Snyder, the doctor whom Drang most revered. Snyder was considered by many authorities to be the father of modern biological psychiatry, and he was regarded as a surefire bet for a Nobel prize. Nearly all major developments in the field depended to a large extent on this aspect of his work.

What Snyder had done was to pioneer in the isolation of nerve endings that transmit biogenic amines. He discovered he could inject a rat with a dose of an amine and then wait for the compound to bind to the animal's nerve endings. When that had taken place, the rat could be killed and its brain ground up, and then the nerve endings could be centrifuged and separated out. Astonishingly, the extract would still be active, and it would function like living nerve cells.

The resulting material, Snyder labeled a synapstome. When exposed to a neurotransmitter, the effects could be measured and projected. For testing purposes, the method had proven to be invaluable. After blending and binding, rats' brains could help a scientist to predict the effect of various drugs on the living brains not merely of other rats but also on the brains of human subjects.

This discovery was what had enabled the doctors who developed Prozac to learn how the basic compound—fluoxetine hydrochloride— could inhibit serotonin uptake in humans. That, of course, was the secret of how the new antidepressants helped patients to overcome depression while also promoting an overall sense of happiness and well-being.

The same process was used by Drang to conduct his experiments in the alteration of human brain chemistry through the use of drugs. He owed a great deal to Solomon Snyder, and thus far he'd made great strides in his experiments.

But as successful as he'd been to date, he'd also run into problems. The trouble was, it was difficult to predict with certainty just what effect different drug doses would have on his patients when his experiments were carried out with bound extract of rats' brains. To his surprise, the results on the cells of rats were sometimes quite different from those achieved when the drugs were administered to a human subject.

As a consequence, Drang's experiments occasionally produced reactions that were not only disappointing but also catastrophic. And whereas he was thrilled with the progress he'd made in the years since he'd begun his work, he nevertheless longed for a more predictable method, one that would give him the results he sought, not merely often but every time.

The answer to this problem, of course, was obvious. What he needed were not the brains of rats, but those of humans. Yet following through on the solution would present a whole new set of difficulties.

One was the unavailability of suitable cadavers. Even as a licensed MD, it would be next to impossible for him to arrange legally to come into possession of newly dead bodies. He'd looked into the idea of representing himself as a small medical school, but that hadn't worked out; such schools had to be licensed and were regulated by state authorities. The subterfuge would be seen in an instant.

And even if his scheme had been successful, the cadavers would have been of no use to him. They had to be virtually pickled in formaldahyde to satisfy state requirements, and what he needed were fresh, healthy brain cells, free of any type of contaminant.

So what to do? He'd also considered picking up whores and bringing them back here on the promise of doing business. He would use them, then remove their brains afterward.

But that wasn't practical, either, because he could be certain that a prostitute's body would already be full of drugs by the time he came into possession of it. And so-called dirty drugs at that, ranging from heroin and crack cocaine to phencyclidine, which would make the brain cells useless.

He'd then thought about coaxing a derelict into his car and injecting him with propoxyphene, which would cause instant death from respiratory failure but would not damage the tissues. Same problem, however: a large portion of the bum's brain cells would already have been destroyed by alcohol.

Nevertheless, finding a way to acquire human brains was something to think about. And think about it Drang did, often. He was wrestling with the question now, as he placed some of the amine-treated rat brain extract into a lab dish and prepared to test it with a neurotransmitter that had been laced with Zymatine.

He knew he'd come up with a solution eventually, just as he was sure that sooner or later he'd reach his ultimate goals. He hadn't the slightest doubt of that. The stakes were too high for him even to consider any other possibility.

When he did succeed, the reward that would be coming to him would be unlike any a scientist such as Snyder could even imagine.

That one was money.

Drang was positive he would realize riches from his work that would enable him to live on a scale enjoyed only by Arabian princes. And wasn't *that* something to contemplate!

At the moment, however, he needed to concentrate on the task at hand. He reached for a test tube containing the synapstome required for the test, and as he did, the telephone buzzed.

Annoyed, Drang was tempted not to answer it. But then he looked at his watch and saw that it was time for his next appointment.

Ordinarily, he hated to be pulled away when he was working down here. This interruption, however, he could tolerate. In fact, he'd been looking forward to it.

He turned and picked up the telephone. "Yes, Anna?"

"The new patient is here, Doctor."

"Tell her I'll be right there," he said.

23

The morgue at Bellevue was in the basement. Tolliver went down the steps and through swinging doors, his footsteps echoing as he walked along the corridor. The area was refrigerated, and the smell of disinfectants bit his nostrils. Unlike the upper floors of the old hospital, it was quiet down here, and no one was in a hurry. He shivered a little in the chill, dank air.

Turning a corner, he saw two attendants lifting bodies off gurneys and depositing them in drawers that the men slid out from the walls. The corpses were male and female and of all ages, wearing nothing but toe tags. Rigor mortis had long since disappeared, and some of the heavier ones were hard to handle. A few were badly decomposed, and not even the cold could hide the stench coming from them. The attendants were nonchalant, however, as offhand as if they were loading sacks of flour. After putting a body inside, they slammed the drawer shut and went on to the next one.

Ben walked by, going to the end of the hallway, where there was another set of doors. A uniformed officer was standing beside them.

Tolliver hated coming here. He wasn't sure how many autopsies he'd attended during his twenty-odd years on the job—probably somewhere around three hundred. Yet watching the procedure always drove home the frailty—and the brevity—of human life. He'd seen bodies of people who'd been shot, stabbed, strangled, chopped, gassed, hanged, drowned, poisoned, and killed by a range of more exotic methods. Their deaths had been terrible, and then in this place they'd suffered a final indignity, their naked carcasses dissected and pawed over.

He showed the cop his ID and stepped through the doors. The room was large, painted a sickly shade of yellow. In the center was a row of six stainless-steel tables, all of them occupied and with pathologists at work. Several of the tables were surrounded by an audience of detectives; the cadavers on those were people who had died in the course of violent crimes. Some were victims, some perpetrators, but at this juncture, there was no way to tell who had been which.

The table bearing Beth Whitacre's remains was easy to pick out. Ben saw her nude body lying on it faceup, with Midtown North's Novotny and Cooper watching the efforts of the pathologist and his assistant. As Tolliver approached, the detectives greeted him with nods, their expressions guarded.

The pathologist was David Farricker, a sad-faced man wearing a baggy green surgical uniform. Tolliver had seen him perform postmortems a number of times in the past. Farricker looked up and smiled, his cheerful demeanor at odds with his appearance. "Ah, Lieutenant. You're just in time for the grand opening."

"Hello, Dave."

"I think you know my helper, Joel Bassett. And of course you're familiar with the young lady."

Tolliver looked at Beth's corpse. The blue eyes that had been ruined by the fatal bullet were open and staring upward, and her long blond hair was streaming in the water than ran constantly down the surface of the slightly tilted table. Her flesh had been cleansed of bloodstains and was bluish white, except where it had been darkened by lividity. Again he was reminded of how much she'd resembled her mother. Her face had been beautiful before she fired that last shot.

"Well now," Farricker said. "Let's not keep her waiting. You know how women are."

He bent over the body and quickly made three incisions, one from each shoulder diagonally down to a point just below the ribs, the third from there down to the pubic bone. Next he peeled back the flaps of skin, and using heavy shears, clipped open the ribs. After that, he cut and tied off the carotid arteries and the colon, then the trachea and pharynx. Bassett drew out the dark red abdominal fluid with a suction hose and measured it in a bottle. It showed three quarts, which meant she'd lost about half her blood.

As he worked, Farricker kept up a running line of chatter into a microphone that was suspended from overhead, describing his observations. His comments were being recorded, and later they would be transcribed for inclusion in the autopsy report. From what Ben was hearing, Beth's organs appeared to have been normal, and she'd been in generally good health prior to her death.

While Farricker was so occupied, his assistant cut open her scalp and removed the shattered top of her skull with an electric saw. He took out the brain and placed it in a pan, which he set on a nearby counter, next to a sink. The damage that had been done by the bullet was horrendous.

In one deft move, Farricker then lifted out the entire viscera—heart, lungs, kidneys, liver, and intestines. He deposited the organs in another, larger pan and carried them over to the sink, where he washed them. As he did, Bassett returned to the table and began sewing shut the eviscerated body.

The pathologist glanced over at the detectives. "That's it, gentlemen. At least as far as the dramatic part goes. After this, I'll be slicing up the goodies here and examining them under a microscope. Everything I see will be in the report."

"No surprises up to now?" Ben asked.

"Just one. I found it before you got here. Come on, I'll show you." Farricker stepped back to the body and waited for a moment, until his assistant finished his stitching.

When Bassett moved away, Farricker picked up Beth's left arm. He pointed to the flesh on the inside, just below the elbow. "What do you see, Lieutenant?"

Tolliver moved closer. A small brownish dot was visible on her skin, but just barely. "What is it?"

"A puncture wound. There's one on the other arm, too. Care to guess what made them?"

"Not a needle?"

"Ah, very good. Your powers of perception are as sharp as ever. They were made by a hypodermic syringe, in my opinion."

"So she was on drugs after all?"

"I won't know that until I send a sample of her blood to the lab and hear what they have to say. But let me ask you another question. Does this look like an ordinary track to you, the kind you find on a junkie?"

"No," Ben said. "Those are usually scabby, and there are bruises. I can hardly see this one."

"Exactly. If this was caused by an injection, then whoever gave it to the lady knew what he was doing. Interesting, huh?"

Cooper spoke up. "Could've been routine, couldn't it? Like maybe a doctor gave her a flu shot or something?"

"Entirely possible," Farricker said. "Until you consider that she has them in both arms. But once again, we'll have to wait and see what the lab says. I'll send a list of specifics for them to look for when I ask for the toxicology report."

"Let me know," Tolliver said. He noticed Cooper and Novotny exchange glances on hearing that, but he didn't much care what they thought. "I'll see you all later." He left the room, anxious to get out of this grim place.

As he walked back along the icy corridor, he wondered if the pathologist had picked up one of the answers he'd been looking for. Needle punctures, made by a professional? Could that be a lead, pointing toward what had gone on with Beth Whitacre before her furious outburst?

Or was it just one more imaginary piece of evidence, appearing important but taking him nowhere? As Farricker had said, he'd have to wait and see what the lab reported.

When he rounded the corner, Ben noticed that the men loading corpses into the drawers had finished their work. They'd left the gurneys standing unoccupied in the hallway, awaiting the next batch of customers.

He stepped past the gurneys and picked up his pace as he headed for the stairway.

24

The woman was stunning, Drang thought. When Anna brought her in, he sensed a strong animal attraction about her. In fact, he almost smelled it the instant she walked into his office.

She was in her early thirties. He knew this from the patient-information form she'd filled out. Her hair was dark blond, and her large violet eyes were set far apart above a slightly upturned nose and a ripe-lipped mouth. Best of all, she had a lush body that practically called out to be stroked and fondled and fulfilled sexually.

She was also beautifully groomed. She wore a beige box-cut jacket, open in front so that it didn't hide the curve of her breasts, and a skirt cut fashionably short, revealing her finely shaped legs. And she was carrying a quilted leather handbag that he recognized as a Chanel.

Lovely, and moneyed. The perfect patient, at least insofar as the initial impression was concerned. He'd been hoping for something offering promise, and this one appeared to be all that and more.

He was careful to reveal none of what he was thinking. Instead, he kept his features totally impassive when she approached, not rising from his chair and merely nodding slightly, saying, "Good morning, Mrs. Dallure."

"Hello, Doctor." Her voice was small and soft and rather shy, in sharp contrast to her appearance—which was a good sign.

"Please sit down." He indicated a chair opposite his, watching appreciatively as she sank into it and crossed her elegant legs.

"Your first name is Florence," he said. "Is that correct?"

"Yes, but my friends call me Flo."

"Flo it is, then."

"My maiden name was Maybury. I'm divorced, and I may start using it again."

"The form she'd filled out contained all her personal data, but he'd only glanced at it before she came in. He wanted to ask her questions directly, for a number of reasons. "Was the divorce recent?"

"Very recent. I went to Mexico. Just got back a couple of weeks ago."

"Was that your first marriage?"

"Yes, it was."

"How long were you married?"

"Six years."

"Do you have children?"

"No."

Good, he thought. Brats were an encumbrance, and they could produce unwelcome complications. He already had a fairly good idea of what her problems would turn out to be, once she began telling him about them. At the moment, she was somewhat reticent, which was to be expected.

"What does your former husband do?"

"He's president of a company that imports computer parts from the Orient."

"Was he in favor of getting a divorce?"

"No."

"But you were?"

She looked down and fiddled with the strap of her handbag for several seconds. When at last she lifted her gaze to meet his, she said, "I was, at first. And when I think about it objectively, it was the best thing that could have happened, under the circumstances. But now I guess I'm just . . . terribly depressed."

"And that's why you came to me."

"Yes. At least, it's one of the reasons."

"What were the others?"

"It's hard to describe them. I simply feel miserable. I don't want to see people, or be seen by them. It's a great effort for me even to go out of the apartment. Most of the time, I just want to be by myself. I know that's not good for me, but I can't help it."

"It's quite understandable. Divorce is one of the worst traumas a human being can experience. Often crushing, emotionally."

Her expression instantly turned into one of gratitude. "I'm so glad to hear you say that. Sometimes I feel like I'm abnormal or something."

"Why is that?"

"Mostly because of the way my family reacted when they heard we were getting divorced. They sounded as if it was all my fault, as if I'd let them down. And with my friends, it was worse." A note of bitterness edged into her voice. "If I could call them friends."

"What did they do?"

"They made me feel like a loser. Said I'd been a fool, that Gary had taken advantage of me. That's my ex-husband, Gary Dallure. And now they're laughing about it behind my back."

"How do you know that?"

"I've picked up things. Remarks have come back to me. And when I think about it, I have to admit they're right. I *was* a fool. A total fool."

"Suppose you tell me what led to the divorce."

She blinked back tears. "He was screwing around. There's a lot more to it than that, but that's what it comes down to."

"And how about you, Flo—were you faithful?"

She seemed taken aback. "Absolutely. I never stepped out of line once, the whole time we were married."

"But he was unfaithful to you."

"Yes. Practically from the start. And I was too dumb to know what was going on, right up till the end."

He decided to feed her anger a little. "That's dreadful. No wonder you're having problems now, in light of the way he treated you."

She took a Kleenex from the pocket of her jacket and touched her eyes with it. "He's a bastard. A real bastard."

"Did you know any of the other women?"

"Oh yes. Some of them, anyway. Some of them were friends of mine. I told you I was a fool, didn't I?"

"You're not a fool. Trusting people doesn't make you a fool. How did you finally learn what he'd been doing?"

"I began to see things. Lipstick that I knew wasn't mine on a shirt collar. I'd answer the phone and the caller would hang up. Things like that. Then there were nights when he said he had to be away on business, and on one of them, an executive in the company called our apartment, wanting to speak to him. The more suspicious I got, the more I began to see. Pretty soon it was so obvious, I couldn't believe how blind I'd been."

"Did you confront him?"

"Not right away. I just kept my eyes open, and there it was. We'd go to a party, or to our club, and I'd see the way he acted."

"With your friends."

"Yes. With my friends."

"Where was that, the club?"

"In Connecticut. We had a weekend house there. We were members of the New Canaan Country Club."

"And eventually you did confront him?"

"Eventually, yes. At first, he denied it, but then when I started to name names, he finally admitted it. Begged me to forgive him, said he'd never do it again. Which was just another lie."

"But you refused?"

"No. I actually said I'd give him another chance. Can you believe it?"

"Of course I can. But I gather he didn't keep his word?"

"No, not at all. A tomcat doesn't change, Doctor. I learned that the hard way. One afternoon about a month after our big blowup, I called his office and he wasn't there. So then I started watching him again. Once when he went out, I followed him. He went to Chantilly and had lunch with Betty Dobson."

"Another friend?"

"My best friend. Or so I thought."

"Was she married?"

"Divorced. I guess she couldn't wait to get her hooks into him. I went into the restaurant and saw them together and then I ducked out before they saw me. I got a cab and sat waiting in it until they came out. I had the cab follow them, and guess where they went?"

The answer was obvious, but he wanted her to say it. "Where was that?"

"To her apartment, of course. The bitch."

"And then you started proceedings?"

"Not exactly. We had still another huge scene, and this time he knew I had him. So he finally agreed to a divorce, but he asked if we could agree to a settlement and then I'd go to Mexico. Like an idiot, I said okay. I hate it that I'm so stupid."

The fact that she despised herself was encouraging. "Why does that make you stupid?"

"Because I could have had a much better settlement. My lawyer warned me, but I let Gary convince me it would be a fairer way to do it."

"And now you don't think so?"

"I think he screwed me. Again."

"Why did you agree to such an arrangement?"

"I don't know. Maybe because in the back of my head I thought someday we'd get back together. I know that sounds childish, but that's what I thought."

What Drang asked next was an important question. "Have you been seeing other men, now that you're divorced?"

"No. That's one of my problems. I can't even imagine going out. Just the idea of it scares me to death."

"Why is that?"

"Because men can't be trusted—not any of them."

He wanted to probe a little further into the chances she might have for a new relationship and her attitude toward such a possibility. "Has anyone approached you? Has some man shown an interest?"

"Oh yes. My lawyer, the snake. And the husband of one of my friends. My former friends."

"How did you respond?"

"I didn't want anything to do with them. I was horrified, and disgusted."

"Because you thought they just wanted to use you?"

"Yes. And also because I could see what had become of me."

"What did you think had become of you?"

Once more her eyes filled, and she dabbed at them with the tissue. "That I'm, you know, a worn-out bag. Somebody to go to bed with and that's it. Both of them acted as if they'd be doing me a favor."

"Tell me, Flo. Before your marriage, had you ever had a serious relationship?"

"Yes. I had my first big love affair when I was in high school, and then a few others in college. Men were always attracted to me."

Drang could see why. "And that was all?" It hardly seemed possible.

"No. There were people I was involved with after I came to New York, but only one that was really serious before I was married."

"And who was he?"

"A man I worked for. I had a job in a company that remodeled offices. That was how I met Gary, by the way, but that was much later on. He was one of our clients. Anyway, the head of the company started taking me to lunch, supposedly to talk business. Said I showed great promise, that I had a fine future with them. I was sap enough to fall for it, and you know what happened next. After awhile instead of lunch, it got to be dinner, and then one night, he'd rented a hotel room."

"So he misled you."

"Yes. He was married, with a couple of kids. Our affair went on for two years, with him stringing me along the entire time. Told me he wanted to leave his wife and marry me. Which wasn't true, of course. That wasn't what he wanted."

Drang knew very well what the man had wanted. And he didn't blame him. "But you finally realized he wasn't being honest?"

"I finally realized he'd been deceiving me, from the beginning. I was crushed, when I caught on. And then there was Gary. We dated for about six months, and at Christmas he took me to St. Croix and proposed."

"I assume the marriage was happy, for a time?"

"Very happy. At least, I was very happy. And I guess he was, too. He had a wife to take care of him, and plenty of girlfriends to have fun with. I can't tell you how it affected me when I learned the truth."

You don't have to tell me, Drang thought. I already know, and I'm delighted. "You said that after the divorce, when other men approached you, that was when you began to feel worthless?"

"No, before that. I guess from the time I realized Gary had decided I wasn't good enough for him. I felt as if I was less than worthless. As if I was nothing but dirt. A stupid nothing."

Excellent, Drang thought. She hadn't been all that secure to begin with, and now she'd convinced herself she had no value as a human being. "Very interesting," he said. "And most understandable."

She glanced at him and chewed her lip. "There've been times when I couldn't even get out of bed. Just stayed there the whole day, wishing I were dead."

"That's very sad, Flo. A lovely young woman like you."

"Do you think you can help me, Doctor?"

He steepled his fingers and studied them for several seconds before answering. When he looked up, he said, "In all probability, I can. Although I must warn you, it will be difficult. We'll have to explore your present emotional condition much further, of course. Although I already see what many of your problems are, and I'll tell you now that the scarring is quite deep."

She opened her bag and got out a fresh Kleenex, touching her eyes with it. "I know that."

"Nevertheless, I believe I can help."

"I'd be very grateful if you could."

"First, there are some things you'd have to understand. And agree to."

"What are they?"

"For one, you're in need of a complete psychological makeover. You've been badly battered emotionally, probably even worse than you realize. What I'd have to do is give you a new start."

"A new start?"

"In terms of your personality. By using the latest techniques in psychotherapy, many of which I've personally developed, I could help you to build a new, stronger self. It would be hard work for both of us, but the rewards would be great. You'd become secure and confident, and in time you'd see yourself in an entirely new light."

"Is that really possible?"

"Of course it is. There's no reason for you to go on suffering as you have. If you're willing to put the effort into it, I can practically guarantee success."

"What would it entail?"

"A program of intense psychiatric care. Daily visits, at least in the beginning."

"How much would that cost?"

"My fee is two hundred dollars an hour."

"I see. Would the payments qualify as a medical expense?"

"For insurance reasons, you mean?"

"No, for my divorce settlement with Gary. It calls for him to pay all my medical expenses, if I have any."

Again Drang was delighted. And then he could have kicked himself for not quoting a higher rate. But this arrangement was splendid nonetheless. Many insurance companies balked at paying claims for psychotherapy, and now he wouldn't have to deal with that at all.

"It certainly would," he said. "Moreover, it's quite just, don't you think? The person who caused your problems is the one who'll be paying for your recovery."

For the first time, she smiled. Her full lips curved upward, and that enhanced her animal attractiveness, making her even more exciting to him. "I never thought of that," she said. "But you're right, of course. When would you want to begin?"

"The sooner the better. I'm sure you don't want to go on feeling miserable for a moment longer than necessary. It's apparent to me that you're in an acute state of depression. Which can be dangerous."

The violet eyes widened. "Dangerous?"

"Indeed. It's possible for your pain to become locked into your subconscious, so that experiencing it is a permanent part of your psychological state."

"Oh God. I couldn't stand that. I'd kill myself first."

"You see? Even in this discussion, you're revealing that in your subconscious mind, you've been toying with suicide. Which is extremely destructive, of course."

She was silent for a moment, looking down at her lap. When she again lifted her gaze, the expression on her face would have been pitiful, if Drang had been capable of feeling pity. She swallowed. "So when should I come back?"

"Check with Anna when you leave. Tell her I said to find a spot for you tomorrow, even if she has to cancel someone else. I don't want to alarm you, but I think it's vital that we begin at once."

"All right, Doctor. I'll do that."

"In the meantime, I'm going to put you on a mild antidepressant."

He opened a drawer in the cabinet next to his chair and took out a plastic vial. Handing it to her, he said, "Take four of these capsules a day."

"What are they?"

"A new compound. Similar to Prozac, but more effective."

"Ah. I've heard of Prozac. Aren't quite a number of people taking it these days?"

"They certainly are. Millions of people, in fact. It's being hailed as a miracle drug, but I think that's hyperbole."

She looked at the vial. "What does this one do?"

"Calms you down, reduces anxiety. Helps you to be more accepting of yourself and your situation."

"Lord knows I could use that."

"It's only a beginning, of course. Merely something to smooth the way, as it were, while we get into the root causes of your problems and start the real work. I'm also going to give you an injection, which will increase the effectiveness of the antidepressant."

"An injection? Ugh, I hate needles."

"You'll hardly feel this. Push up your right sleeve, please."

He again reached into a drawer in the cabinet, this time taking out the syringe. Turning back to her, he grasped her bare arm with one hand while with the other he slipped the point of the needle into the faint blue ridge on the inside of her elbow.

Her skin was exquisite, he thought. And thrilling to touch. As smooth as ivory, but excitingly warm.

He finished injecting the drug, then put the syringe back into the cabinet, saying, "There now, nothing to it, was there?"

"No, I guess not." She adjusted her sleeve. "I hope I'm not expecting too much. But you know, I'm encouraged. Just by seeing how quickly you were able to size up my situation and how you knew right away what had to be done."

He flicked his fingers in a gesture of modesty. "That's what I'm here for, Flo. I'll see you tomorrow. Oh, and one other thing."

"Yes?"

"It's very important for you not to discuss the treatment with anyone. In fact, you shouldn't even mention that you're seeing me. It could turn around and have an upsetting effect on you, because people would begin to pry. That's human nature, unfortunately."

"Don't worry, there's no one I confide in these days. No one. I've learned my lesson."

"Good."

She rose from her chair and took a deep breath—which in itself was rewarding, as her chest swelled under the open jacket. Drang pretended not to notice, taking care to keep his professorial expression firmly in place.

"I'll look forward to it," she said. "And Doctor?"

"Yes?"

"I really appreciate your understanding."

"My pleasure," he said. "I always welcome an opportunity to help someone. Especially someone who so obviously needs me."

25

I just got the tox report on Whitacre," Farricker said.

Ben cradled the telephone between his collarbone and his jaw and picked up a ballpoint, flipping to a fresh sheet of the yellow pad on his desk. "Okay, go ahead."

"The lady was clean. I had the lab run tests for every substance abused by man, and they came up negative on all of them. No lysergamides, no phenylalkylamines, no—"

"Hey, come on," Ben said. "What are we talking about here?"

"None of the mind expanders. No LSD, no PCP, no mist."

"That's better."

"No hallucinogens whatever. No amphetamines, either. No bennies, speed, or meth. And no THC, which is the ingredient that makes marijuana fun."

"What about crack, or heroin?"

"Not so much as a single milligram in her dainty blood. And she hadn't drunk any alcohol."

"So she'd taken no drugs whatever."

"The only thing they found was a compound that's like fluoxetine, and that's harmless. It's nothing more than a mood enhancer."

"Would that explain the needle marks on her arms?"

"I doubt it. This stuff, she would've taken orally."

Ben thought back to his discussion with Dr. Stein. "Fluoxetine is Prozac, right?"

"Right. Everybody's favorite antidepressant. Fluoxetine is the actual compound. Prozac is the brand name. Eli Lilly makes it."

"But that's not what this was?"

"The lab just said it was similar. There are a whole bunch of drugs out now that're in the same category. Paxil is one; Zoloft is another. They're called SSRIs, which stands for selective serotonin reuptake inhibitors. All they do is give the patient a positive outlook. People taking them feel optimistic, and don't get down on themselves."

"How much was in her system?"

"There was a fairly high level in her blood, but it would've made her happy, not like she wanted to go out and kill people."

"But that's what she did. And the store's videotape showed she was completely calm when she started shooting. Couldn't it have been this drug that kept her that way?"

"I don't think so. Although I'll admit, some people have had bad reactions to it. You'd have to talk to a psychiatrist to get the answer. But from what I know, you can't blame what she did on an antidepressant."

"What if she overdosed?" Tolliver was aware of what Stein had said about that as well, but double-checking couldn't hurt. "Could that have turned her aggressive?"

"An overdose would've made her sick to her tummy, or put her to sleep. But it wouldn't have turned her mean."

"You're sure."

"I'm not a pharmacologist, but I'm reasonably sure, yes."

"Okay, thanks."

"Anytime, Lieutenant. I'll send a copy of this over to you."

Ben put the phone down and scribbled notes on what he'd been told, then doodled on the pad for a time. He made two circles, and after that he turned them into bulging eyes, surrounding them with an ugly face that had warts on its nose.

He'd heard plenty about the new antidepressants, of course. You couldn't live on this planet and not be aware of them. There had been cover stories in *Time* and *Newsweek,* TV features, long articles in the newspapers. All hailed them as a great discovery that had helped countless people overcome depression, as well as various other emotional problems. Now there were many such drugs on the market, according to Farricker.

And Whitacre had been taking one of them.

Was that why she'd seemed so cool when she began committing murder? And was it possible the drug had produced a bad reaction, causing her to flip out, regardless of what either Farricker or Stein had said?

Was it also possible that neither of them knew enough about the drug to be certain? After all, Farricker was a pathologist, not an authority on drugs. And would a psychiatrist know that much about the actual chemical reaction the drug would have?

Tolliver went on thinking about it, adding large floppy ears to the doodled features. Then he spun the Rolodex. He found Stein's number, picked up the phone, and called it.

Stein answered on the third ring.

"Tolliver, Doc. The pathologist who did the post on Beth Whitacre just called me. The toxicology report says the lab found an antidepressant in her blood. High levels of it."

There was a moment's silence, and then Stein said, "What was the compound?"

Ben glanced at his notes. "The lab said it was an SSRI, but they couldn't pin it down."

"Interesting. And surprising. I wouldn't have expected that."

"I was surprised, too, after what you told me. Makes it all the more important to find out who her doctor was."

"It certainly does."

"At the autopsy, I was shown needle marks on her arms. But the pathologist said the drug they found in her blood would've been taken orally."

"That's correct; an antidepressant would have been."

"Let me ask you something. Do you know how these drugs actually work—what their chemical effect is?"

"Yes, I do. I've read the clinical studies, and I know quite a bit about them."

"Then how about filling me in?"

"Certainly. Whenever you say."

"I'd also like you to think some more about how Beth Whitacre could have been on an antidepressant and still have gone berserk. Are you positive the drug couldn't have caused her to flip out?"

"As much as I can be. Although what you've told me does raise a troubling question."

"Which is?"

"If the subject showed evidence of psychosis—and I'm guessing that Whitacre might have before the incident—then putting her on an antidepressant would've been a serious procedural error. What a doctor is supposed to do in such circumstances is to hospitalize the patient at once, not disguise the problem with a drug. So why did he prescribe this medication, whatever it was?"

"I'm wondering that, too, Doc. I'll get down to see you as soon as I can."

"Anytime, Lieutenant."

Ben hung up. And drew a long, drooping mustache on the doodled face.

26

Philip Harkness opened his eyes and winced as the morning light hit them. He felt as if he'd been on a long acid trip, or maybe stoned on hash and bennies for days. He'd done that with his friends from time to time, when he was a student at Pratt. They'd get high and stay that way until either the money or the junk ran out, whichever happened first.

There was the summer he and another guy had driven an old wreck to Mexico and fried their brains with mescaline and peyote and mushroom caps and anything else they could scrounge, eating only an occasional meal of frijoles and beans, washed down with tequila. By the time they got back to New York, he couldn't remember half the things they'd done, the places they'd been. They joked about it afterward, calling it the "lost summer."

But this was worse. His stomach was queasy and his nerves were like hot wires. When he climbed out of bed, his legs trembled, and for the first few steps, he was barely able to navigate. He took his time in the bathroom, and when he came out, he was steadier, although not much.

Judging from the rattle of dishes and the aroma of coffee coming from the kitchen, Cathy was busy making breakfast. He hoped she wouldn't nag him again this morning; lately, she'd been getting under his skin.

Besides, he had more important things to think about. There were the package designs he'd done for General Brands, the studio's most important client. The designs were for a new cigarette brand, and the client was paying a hefty fee for the project. Today, Ray Mercer, the head of the studio, was to present the revised concepts for final approval.

As he got dressed, putting on his customary chambray shirt, jeans, and an old sport jacket, he thought about the presentation. He was reasonably sure the people at General would like what he'd done, but what if they didn't? The mere thought that his designs might be rejected was enough to induce a panic attack; he pushed the idea out of his mind. After slipping on his loafers, he went into the kitchen.

Cathy was standing at the stove. She was dressed for work, wearing a blouse and skirt and heels, her hair carefully brushed. Little Miss Prim and Proper, all set to go to her crappy-ass job as a statistical analyst in an insurance company. Harkness couldn't imagine anything more boring.

She turned to him. "Good morning."

He grunted a reply and sat at the table.

She placed a cup of coffee in front of him. "Phil?"

"What is it?"

"Who's Dr. Drang?"

He stared at her. "Where did you get that name?"

"You were shouting it, in your sleep."

"And you were listening to me?"

"How could I help it? People could hear you a block away. Who is he, and what's this medicine you were yelling about? Is that the stuff you've been taking? Those capsules?"

He made no reply, just sat glaring at her, suspicion turning to hot anger. He had it now; she'd been eavesdropping, trying to put together information on him.

"Who's Dr. Drang, Phil?"

Still he said nothing.

She wouldn't leave it alone. "You said some really crazy stuff—about how you'd taken your medicine and you had a knife. You said you killed somebody."

"It was nothing," he snapped. "Just a dream."

"No, it wasn't just a dream. It was a terrible nightmare, like a lot of others you've been having lately. I know you don't like me saying this, but there's something very wrong, Phil. I'm worried about you."

"I'm telling you I'm fine, goddamn it. And anyway, it's none of your fucking business."

Hurt showed in her eyes. "It *is* my business. I care about you, and I want this to stop."

The heat was building, threatening to burn a hole in his belly. "Get the hell away from me."

But she kept on. "Is the medicine causing it? I don't know who this Dr. Drang is, but he's not doing you any good. The medicine is harming you, Phil. Can't you see that?"

He jumped up and punched her in the face, knocking her backward onto the floor. She sat there, her eyes wide with disbelief. A drop of blood appeared at the corner of her mouth and trickled down her chin.

It was as if a red haze had descended over his vision. "You stupid cunt!"

She scuttled away, the expression in her eyes turning instantly to one of fear as she saw what rage was doing to him.

"Stupid cunt!" he snarled again.

There was a straight-backed chair standing against the wall. She grabbed it, trying to pull herself to her feet.

Harkness looked at his hand, expecting the knife to be there, but it wasn't. He'd deal with her anyway—he'd break her fucking neck. He leapt toward her.

Cathy flung the chair at him. It hit him in the knees and he fell over it, crashing facedown onto the floor. He cursed, the coppery taste of blood filling his mouth as he untangled himself from the chair and went for her once more.

She was too quick for him. Already on her feet, she turned and dashed to the front door of the apartment, opening it and rushing into the hallway.

Harkness darted after her. Just as she got to the stairway and began clattering down it, a door opened at the end of the hall, and a neighbor poked her head out.

It was the nosy old bitch who lived in the rear apartment, scowling disapproval.

Harkness stopped. The woman glowered at him and he gave her the finger. Then he turned and walked back to his apartment, going inside and slamming the door behind him.

He took his time cooling out, spitting blood into the bathroom sink and then leaning his back against the wall until his breathing was again under control. After that he got out the vial of capsules. He took two, washing them down with coffee. And then, just to be sure, he took two more.

Forget his medicine? No, Doctor. He'd never do that.

27

What I want to know," Ben said, "is how these antidepressants work. I'm told SSRI means selective serotonin reuptake inhibitor, but what the hell does *that* mean? Just what effect do the drugs have, and why are so many people taking them?"

Alan Stein adjusted his horn-rims. He and Tolliver were in his study and it was late afternoon, an hour after he'd seen his last patient of the day.

"Let's begin with how they work," the psychiatrist said. "Inside the brain, every memory, every emotion—in fact, everything that has to do with temperament—starts with chemicals that are produced in the neurons. These chemicals function as neurotransmitters, carrying messages between brain cells. The messages they carry determine our various moods and our emotional outlook. One of the key neurotransmitters is serotonin, which acts as a censor on unwanted behavior."

"A censor, how?"

"It keeps people from doing things they don't want to do, or shouldn't do. If the amount of serotonin the brain is able to utilize is too little, a person can suffer from a number of personality disorders. People who have the condition may be painfully shy, or have difficulty focusing on important matters. They can be compulsive eaters. Or they might become anorexic and starve themselves. They may be terrified of speaking in public, or have any of various other emotional difficulties. As a result, they become depressed."

"So how do the drugs change that?"

"They correct the chemical imbalance by increasing the amount of serotonin the brain can make use of. As the acronym indicates, they inhibit reuptake, which simply means the drugs enable the brain to keep the serotonin in steady supply. So when people take such a drug, they're able to overcome their behavioral problems, which in turn helps pull them out of their depression. They become more confident and are generally happier, because now they can control whatever it is that's troubling them."

"Then the drugs are more than just antidepressants."

"Yes. Although depression is the only condition they're licensed for. Despite that, doctors have been prescribing them for everything from obsessive gambling to obesity. Even for premenstrual syndrome. Got a problem you can't cope with? Don't worry—here's a little pill that'll fix everything in a jiffy."

"That sounds like quackery to me."

"Many authorities would agree with you. Take the way Prozac is handed out. At the present time, doctors write more than a million prescriptions a month for it. Yet most of those doctors are not psychiatrists. They seem to think they've discovered the ideal all-purpose cure for emotional distress."

"And Prozac is just one of these drugs, right?"

"Yes, but it's by far the leader. Eli Lilly got it on the market first, and it dominates the field. After you called, I did some research on the business these products are doing. So far, the other important entries are Paxil, from SmithKline Beecham, and the Pfizer entry, which is Zoloft."

"Yeah, the pathologist mentioned those. How big is the market?"

Stein picked up his notes from the table beside his chair and read from them. "At the present time, it represents just over four billion dollars in annual sales. Of that, Prozac's share is two billion a year and rising. Zoloft has eight hundred fifty million in sales and is growing at nearly the same rate. Paxil runs third, with five hundred fifty million. Lump all the dozens of others together and you have the remaining half a billion and change."

"Do they all work the same way?"

"More or less. As I've told you, Prozac is fluoxetine hydrochloride. Zoloft is sertraline; Paxil is paroxetine. Chemically, they're all related, and they all perform the same function. Fundamentally, what the drugs do is help people to stop behaving in ways that are undesirable."

"And when that happens, they're no longer depressed."

"Correct. They become more cheerful, and some are even euphoric."

"No wonder they buy billions of dollars' worth a year. People must love the stuff."

"They do. Prozac is by far Eli Lilly's largest-selling product, as well as the world's leading antidepressant. Nearly seven million people now take it regularly, in the United States alone."

"When I talked to the pathologist about it, he mentioned unwanted side effects."

"Yes. In certain people, the drugs produce chronic stomach upset, or diarrhea. In others, they cause insomnia and weight loss. And they can also reduce the sex drive. In fact, the libido often disappears altogether."

"That last one sounds like a lousy trade-off."

"I would think so. But some patients claim they're so glad to be relieved of their former symptoms, they don't care whether they have sex or not."

"Do you prescribe the drugs yourself?"

"I have, but rarely. There is a danger, I believe, in simply doling them out willy-nilly. And yet that's just what many doctors do. Which is not only irresponsible; it could also cause great harm."

"How so?"

"Drugs of this type should only be taken when the patient's difficulties are relatively mild. But unfortunately, many of the prescribers aren't qualified to diagnose emotional problems. They might be perfectly well-trained medical doctors, but they're not equipped to deal with mental illness, and they often fail to recognize the symptoms. Yet they go right on prescribing the drugs, virtually for any complaint. Sometimes for patients who have a serious disorder."

"And what happens then?"

"Instead of improving, the problem can become exacerbated, or obscured. The patients think they're better, and they go on gulping the drugs. Then suddenly, it all comes crashing down around them. They might end up in mental hospitals."

Tolliver thought about it. When we talked earlier, you said a few commit suicide, and maybe even murder. Couldn't something like that have happened to Beth Whitacre? The toxicology report showed drugs of that type in her system when she died, so isn't it possible that they were prescribed by a doctor who didn't know what he was doing?"

"They might have been, yes."

"Then from what you've told me, isn't it also possible, or even likely, that she was psychotic before she ever took the stuff?"

The owl eyes fixed on Tolliver. "I have no way of knowing that. But to prescribe such drugs under those circumstances would have been criminal."

"Exactly."

Stein was quiet for several moments. Then he said, "Can you get me a sample of her blood?"

"I don't know, but I can try. What do you want to do with it?"

"Send it to my friends at St. Elizabeth's. No offense, but the lab there may be quite a bit more sophisticated when it comes to analyzing blood for foreign substances."

"Okay, I'll ask the pathologist to send some of it to you. Any other ideas?"

"Just one. Find her doctor, Lieutenant."

28

There were high levels of an antidepressant in Beth's system," Tolliver said.

Lincoln and Enid Whitacre looked at each other. They were with Ben in the living room of their apartment. He'd called and asked to see them, knowing it would be painful for them to hear the news he had. Their daughter's body had at last been released by the morgue, and a private funeral was scheduled for the next day.

"I had no idea she was taking medication," Enid said. "Did you, Linc?"

Whitacre shook his head. "That's a total surprise to me. She never said anything about it."

Enid turned to Ben. "What was it?"

"Apparently, the lab couldn't pin it down. They said it was a compound similar to Prozac, or Paxil. Or one called Zoloft."

"You need a prescription for those drugs, don't you?"

"Yes, you do," Tolliver said. "That's why I'm here. I'm trying to locate her doctor. Can you tell me who that was?"

"Not offhand," Enid said. "She used to see Crandall Barnes, who's our GP. But that was years ago. After college, she made her own choices about things like that. I recall her saying something to me once about going to a gynecologist, but I don't know who it was. All part of being independent, I guess."

"Are you sure she never mentioned seeing a doctor because she was depressed? Or a psychiatrist?"

"No. I would have remembered if she had."

Whitacre said, "I think we told you she had some emotional problems from time to time when she was growing up, but we didn't think they amounted to much. Obviously we were wrong, or she wouldn't have broken down the way she did."

"She did have spells of depression, though," Enid said. She looked at Tolliver. "And of course that's what those drugs you mentioned are for. Isn't that true?"

"Yes, that's what they're for."

"I've read about them. Aren't a lot of people taking them these days?"

"They are, yes."

Whitacre frowned. "I don't get it. It's one thing for someone to be suffering from depression and taking medicine for it. But it's quite another thing for them to commit a terrible act of violence. It's obvious now that Beth was severely ill. That's not the kind of disorder that could be treated with drugs like the ones you're talking about, is it?"

"No," Ben said, "not from what I've been told. That's why I want to find the doctor who prescribed them."

"Yes, of course."

"I wish we could help you," Enid said.

"Did she have health insurance? That might give me a lead."

"I don't know," Whitacre said. "She went off our policy some years ago, when she became an adult."

"At the time of the incident, she was no longer living with Ken Patterson, but was back in her own apartment. Is that true?"

"Yes."

"Did you collect her things . . . afterward?"

"We did, yes," Whitacre said.

"Do you have them now?"

"No. That is, we sent her clothes to a charity. The only things we kept are keepsakes—some old photos, a few pieces of jewelry, things like that."

"What about her personal records—a diary, or checkbooks, or bank statements?"

"She didn't keep a diary," Enid said.

"And we turned over her financial records to our lawyers,"

Whitacre added. "At her age, she didn't have a will, and the estate has tax obligations."

"What's in the estate?"

"We set up a trust fund for her when she was a baby. The money was invested in securities, and they've done rather well. She came into the principal when she graduated from Cornell."

"I'd like to have a look at those records."

"Sure, I'll have a set of copies sent to you."

Ben got up to leave. "Good. I'll keep you posted."

29

Copies of Beth Whitacre's financial records were hand-delivered by a messenger from the law firm that represented her family. Tolliver opened the bundle on his desk and started with her bank statements, poring over a list of checks she'd written during the year prior to her death. They showed payments to her landlord and NYNEX and VISA and AmEx and department store charge accounts and to dozens of other vendors.

As he'd hoped, they also showed that one payment had been made to a doctor, back in January. So he'd been right about the entry in her appointment book after all. According to the record, the doctor's name was Susan Roth.

Ben looked in his directory and found an S. Roth, MD, on East 72nd Street. He telephoned her, giving her his shield number and explaining why he was calling. There was no way of knowing whether she'd be willing to help, and on the basis of past experience, he fully expected her to refuse.

But Dr. Roth was sympathetic. She told him she had been Miss Whitacre's gynecologist and said that she was horrified when she learned of the tragedy involving her patient. She said Miss Whitacre had been coming in for checkups at six-month intervals, and the visit in January was routine—pelvic and breast examination, a Pap smear. Patient had been in good health.

Ben asked about Beth's emotional state. Seemed all right, Dr. Roth said. Nothing unusual. Although the doctor hadn't been looking for anything of that nature. Had the doctor prescribed drugs of any kind for her? No, never.

Tolliver thanked her and hung up.

So if Beth Whitacre hadn't seen a doctor about depression, or anything else to do with her mental health, where had she gotten the drugs that were in her bloodstream when she died?

Ben thought about it for a time, frustration chewing at him. Like so many aspects of the young woman's life and sudden death, the answer was hidden from him, out of reach. He loosened his tie, then went on studying the papers.

There was no reference to health insurance in any of them. Could she have had coverage through her job?

He telephoned the Met and spoke to Judy Corelli, who told him yes, Beth would have been covered by the institution's group policy. He asked her if she could find out whether Beth had made any claims during the past year. Judy said she'd try but that he shouldn't count on it; such information was almost sure to be considered private. He said he'd appreciate whatever she could give him and then hung up.

Next, he looked at copies of Beth's income-tax returns to the federal, state, and city governments. She'd never taken more than the standard medical deduction, which didn't require a breakdown of specifics. So that was another strikeout. He went on digging.

As Lincoln Whitacre had said, the trust fund he'd set up for his daughter had done well. The portfolio consisted mainly of shares of common stock in blue-chip companies, and the growth in market value over the twenty-six years since the inception of the fund had been remarkable. Up nearly 500 percent, in fact.

But aside from indicating that the young woman had been well-off financially, the records revealed no information that would help Tolliver with his investigation.

He was about to push the papers aside when something caught his eye. According to reports from the brokerage, Beth had begun making cash withdrawals of several thousand dollars each, beginning in March of this year. The withdrawals had been made every two or three weeks and had gone on until a few days before her death. Why had she wanted all that cash?

He went back over the bank records and saw that she'd also regularly transferred smaller amounts from the fund into her checking account throughout the year, apparently to bolster her modest salary from the Met. That made the cash withdrawals all the more curious. Could she have been using the money to pay for psychotherapy and had wanted to keep that a secret? If in fact that's what she had been doing, it would make locating the doctor just that much harder. Nevertheless, there had to be a way.

Ben then called each of the city's psychiatric agencies. There were more than fifty of them, and the task took hours. All of them gave him more or less the same reply: They acted as if he was crazy himself even to make such an inquiry. After the last such call, he slammed the phone down in disgust.

Following that, he went at it from every angle he could think of, contacting clinics, hospitals, even ambulance services. But he got nowhere. As he knew all too well, the medical community had long surrounded itself with a great white wall.

An idea struck him: Maybe it was the doctor himself who didn't want to be identified. If that was the case, the reason for it would be obvious. He called NYPD Records and had them fax him printouts of complaints against psychotherapists over the past three years.

There was a surprising number of them, the majority resulting from accusations of sexual abuse made by female patients. Nearly all the cases had been settled out of court. Only one had led to a prison sentence; the convicted therapist was serving eighteen months in the Green Haven facility in Stormville.

Some of the other doctors had left the city, but most were still in practice. The ones who remained in New York would be worth talking to; he made a note to contact them.

There was still another possibility, of course—which was that the drugs had not been prescribed by a psychotherapist at all, but by an MD other than Susan Roth. Alan Stein had talked about how general practitioners were dispensing antidepressants as if they were aspirin. But there were several thousand licensed doctors in New York. Checking them out would take forever, even if Tolliver had a team of detectives to do the work, which he didn't.

In addition, there was little chance that the doctors would choose to cooperate.

And yet, somewhere in this city was the doctor who had prescribed those drugs for Beth Whitacre. Who was he, and how could Ben find him? Who else might he be treating? What was he doing now?

30

When Drang entered the lab, the rats filled the musty air with shrill cries. Some of the animals leapt up against the thin steel bars in excitement at the sight of him, while as usual others cringed in the farthest corners.

This morning he would conduct an interesting experiment. But first he wanted to inspect the occupants of the cages. He put on a lab coat and began making the rounds.

The rats on antidepressants were quite frisky, he noted, even though he'd increased their daily dosage to a point far above what he would have considered tolerable. While the makers of the compounds contended they were safe, their lawyers were constantly defending them in lawsuits brought by people claiming one or another of them had caused great harm. Drang had wanted to see for himself what effects extreme doses of the drugs could bring about.

Thus far, only one of the test animals had been unable to ingest the heavy doses and remain healthy. That one was having a seizure even as Drang watched. He studied the creature with interest as it shuddered and shook and finally went into convulsions. A moment later, it flopped onto its back and lay still, eyes glazed, paws in the air.

The doctor jotted a few lines in his notebook and put the book aside. Then he opened the top of the cage, and using the metal rod with a wire loop on the end, he grasped the carcass by the neck. Lifting the dead rat out of the cage, he carried it over to the large open acid vat on the far side of the room. He released the loop and the corpse plopped into the yellow liquid, sinking below the surface.

After that, Drang went on with his tour, checking on the animals' reactions to the various drugs he was using in his experiments. To his satisfaction, all the rats were exhibiting what he considered normal responses, although to a uninformed observer, many of the rodents would appear to be in strangely unnatural states.

Those on phenmetrazine, for example, were racing nonstop in circles around the floor of their cages, while the ones he'd fed alprozolam appeared to be asleep on their feet. Some of the others were showing signs of ventricular hypoxia, and still others were obviously dying from cardiovascular toxicity. But all of that was what the doctor had expected.

When he finished his inspection, Drang sat down at the lab table and again opened his notebook. Leafing through the pages, he thought about the mistakes he'd made with Beth Whitacre. He was quite sure that Zymatine, one of the primary compounds in the mixture he'd been giving her, was not the culprit, as powerful as it was. Nor was doxevil, the tricyclic. Instead, he reasoned, the problem lay with the relative amounts in the combination of the two.

Adding to his difficulty was that to achieve the results he wanted, it was necessary to vary the amounts from patient to patient, and there was no way of telling beforehand what the precise dosage should be. Too small an amount tended to produce a conflicting set of signals between the prefrontal cortex and the amygdala, and thence to the hypothalamus, which controlled motivational states. If the dose was too great, the patient would die as surely and as swiftly as the rat Drang had disposed of in the acid vat.

The problem was exasperating, he thought, as he had so many times. And then in the next moment, he considered the rewards that would soon be his, and his enthusiasm returned, stronger than ever. On the positive side, there was the progress he was making with Flo Dallure, who was showing signs of becoming his best patient ever. Harkness was also responding well, despite the fact that he'd obviously been psychotic long before Drang had begun treating him.

But that was of no concern to the doctor. He had achieved a near-total breakdown and rebuilding of the young man's personality, and that was what counted.

But what about the major problem? he asked himself. It was still not possible to predetermine the precise mixture of drugs needed for optimum results in each new patient. He'd have to do still more experiments with the rats, in the hope of finding the answers he wanted. Over the next few days, he'd resume his work in grinding and blending extracts of the animals' brain cells. That had given him the best predictive information to date.

But now it was time for this morning's experiment. Returning to the cages, he checked the two specimens he'd set aside for it. When he looked into those cages, the reactions he saw were more interesting to him than those displayed by any of the others in the room.

In one cage, the rat was fat and healthy, the picture of contentment. As Drang approached, the creature barely glanced at him, showing neither excitement nor anxiety. For several weeks, he'd been feeding it liberal amounts of maprotiline, along with double rations of grain and chopped raw beef.

In marked contrast, the rat in the second cage was gaunt and feverish, its red eyes flashing. When he came near that one, the animal looked up at him with utter fearlessness. And then it moved closer, hunching its shoulders, setting itself.

To Drang's delight, he saw that the rat was not merely being observant; it was *measuring* him. It lifted its head and opened its mouth, exposing the two long yellow incisors in its upper jaw, obviously hoping for an opportunity to attack. It wasn't wasting energy on ineffectual lunges at the bars, despite its obvious rage. Instead, the rat was seeking an opening, looking for a chink in its enemy's armor. It was trying to find a way to kill him. And that was very gratifying.

He smiled, staring back into the feral red eyes. This creature was the latest in a long line of animals he'd used to test the compounds he'd been developing, the same compounds he'd been using to treat Whitacre and Harkness and Dallure and some of the others. As with those subjects, he'd also given the rat boosters of the tricyclic by injection. With this animal, however, the injections had been massive.

Carrying the cages one at a time, he took them over to his lab table and placed them on it side by side. The rat on maprotiline paid no attention to what Drang was doing, nor to its new surroundings. But the other rat now turned its attention to its sleek neighbor. It slowly crept closer to the bars that separated the two, never taking its feverish eyes off the first.

In addition to the doors in the top, all the cages had side gates that could be opened electronically or by hand. For this test, Drang would open them manually. He pushed the two enclosures tight against each other and then slid the gates upward, creating an opening between the cages. The placid rat seemed not to notice, didn't move beyond twitching its whiskers.

The second rat did not hesitate. It leapt into the other's cage and sprang onto the fat, docile rodent. The victim squeaked once in fear and tried to scramble out of the way, but it was too late; there was no chance for it to escape.

The attacker tore open its quarry's hide, ripping and slashing with its fearsome incisors, disemboweling the victim and devouring its guts while it was still alive. Within seconds, there was nothing left of the first animal but tufts of fur and scraps of flesh and bone.

When it had consumed everything but the other's tail, the killer crouched on the floor of the cage and licked the crimson puddles with its flickering tongue. All the while it drank, it kept its gaze fixed on Drang.

Excellent, he thought. Not perfect yet, perhaps, but very good indeed. He watched for a while longer, then closed the gate of the cage containing the survivor.

The buzzer sounded, and he was pleased to hear the sound, knowing what the message would be. He picked up the telephone. "Yes, Anna?"

"Mrs. Dallure is here, Doctor."

"Fine. I'll be right up."

31

As she stepped into his office, Drang thought Flo Dallure looked especially lovely today. Although he thought that every time he saw her. She had on a lacy blouse that teased him with glimpses of her wonderful breasts, its pale green color contrasting beautifully with her dark blond hair and her violet eyes. After Anna had shut the door behind her, Flo stepped over to the couch and lay down—without being told.

But of course, she had been told. For some time now, he'd been telling her exactly what he expected of her, and her response had been flawless. He went to the door and locked it, then followed her to the couch. Drawing a chair close, he sat down beside her.

"How are you today, Flo dear?"

Her voice was a soft monotone, little more than a murmur. "I'm fine, Doctor."

He opened the drawer in the cabinet at the head of the couch and took out the hypodermic syringe. "Are you feeling relaxed, and happy?"

"Very relaxed. And very happy."

He pushed back her sleeve and inserted the needle into the median basilic vein on the inside of her left arm. "And you looked forward to seeing me today?"

"Yes, I did."

Exerting steady pressure with his thumb, he sent the contents of the barrel coursing into her bloodstream. "You think of me often, don't you, Flo?"

She sighed as she felt the effect of the chemicals. "Yes. I think of you often."

He withdrew the needle and returned the syringe to its place in the cabinet. "And is that exciting to you, thinking about me?"

"Yes, it is."

"What about last night, Flo? When you were in bed, did you think about me?"

"Yes, I thought about you."

"In a sexual fantasy?"

"Yes."

"Did you masturbate?"

"Yes, I did."

"And did you enjoy it?"

"Very much."

"In your fantasy, what did you see us doing together?"

"I saw you kissing my breasts, and then my belly and my thighs, and then you were between my legs."

"And then what?"

"And then you were on top of me and we were making love."

"Did you have an orgasm?"

"Yes, Doctor."

"More than one?"

"Yes. I had several."

"Good. And is it exciting for you now, to tell me about these things?"

"Yes, it is."

"Then it would be good to masturbate again, wouldn't it?"

"Yes, Doctor."

"So go ahead and do that, Flo."

Obediently, she pulled up her skirt and put her hand down into her panties.

Watching her was making Drang's pulse race. "Are you dreaming about it again, Flo? Seeing the things we did together?"

"Yes, I am."

"And are you very excited now?"

"Very excited."

"Then it's time for me to help you reach another level."

"Whatever you say, Doctor."

He bent over her and unbuttoned her blouse, then unhooked her bra and pulled the garments aside, freeing her breasts. His fingers were trembling, and he could hear his breath rasping. He brought his face down and buried it in the warm flesh, kissing her nipples and taking them into his mouth. Beneath him, Flo moved her body and moaned.

Quickly, he undressed her. She helped him, arching her back and raising her legs as he peeled the clothing from her. Next he stood and took off his own clothes, tossing them over the chair, and then he lay down on the couch with her and took her into his arms.

The experience was glorious—not only because she was a beautiful, passionate woman but also because she carried out his wishes without question, no matter how bizarre, all the while responding exactly as she'd been ordered. Whatever he could imagine having her do, whatever act he wanted, she performed perfectly. And begged for more.

It was like having his own exquisite love toy. In fact, that was exactly what she'd become.

She spoke to him constantly. "You're wonderful, Doctor. I love the things you do to me. No other man could ever satisfy me the way you do. Ah, ah, that's fantastic. Don't stop. Please don't. Keep on doing that to me; it's so good."

His orgasm was like an explosion, thrilling as it burst inside her and drained him. When at last he was sated, he lay beside her, happily exhausted. Never in his life, he thought, had he enjoyed a more satisfying sexual adventure.

He realized, of course, that he was using her to fulfill fantasies of his own, and that was amusing to him. How many generations of men had dreamed of a relationship like this one? Wherein a stunning woman could be molded into a virtual slave, her brain and personality reformulated to his specifications?

And best of all, there were no strings attached.

If Drang tired of her, or for any reason decided to end the relationship, he could do so with ease. He could leave her with only pleasant memories of him, having excised anything that might be incriminating.

Marvelous, wasn't it? Not even she herself would be able to make a complaint against him. Nor would she have any desire to do so. In fact, he could leave her with no memory of him at all, if he chose, wiping the impressions from her brain cells as simply as he would erase data from his computer.

Eventually, he would also be able to load into her mind information that had nothing to do with reality. Then he could introduce recollections of events that had never occurred, imprint them on her memory in such a way that to her dying day she would believe absolutely that she had experienced them.

That was a goal he hadn't quite reached yet, but he would in time; he was sure of it. Just as he was sure that his research and his experiments were leading him into an understanding of the brain and its functions on a level far beyond any that other scientists had ever imagined, let alone realized.

For the first time in the history of the world, man would have unlocked the secrets of mind control. He, Jonas Drang, would have achieved that long-sought prize, and the effectiveness of his methods would make the efforts of others over the past half a century seem childish by comparison.

Best of all, the monetary value would be enormous.

But he wasn't there yet. Not quite, no matter how satisfying his experiments with Flo had become. She was by far his greatest success to date, but he still had a way to go, even with her.

It was also important not to forget that the results he'd attained with other subjects had not been nearly as gratifying—the work with Beth Whitacre, for example.

Beside him, Flo stirred. "What would you like me to do now, Doctor?"

He smiled to himself. That was another attractive feature he'd devised. She was insatiable, but only as long as he wished her to be. When he was satisfied, he could turn her off instantly, as if there were a switch in her head that he could flick whenever he wished.

"That's enough for today," he said. The release of his sexual tension had left him affable and relaxed. He watched as she got dressed, her manner as calm as if she'd been for a walk in the country.

After that, he rose from the couch and went into the bathroom. When he returned, he put his own clothing back on, then stepped to a mirror that hung on the wall nearby and knotted his tie. When it was adjusted to his liking, he pulled on his jacket and saw that she was standing quietly, waiting for his instruction.

"You may leave now, Flo. I'll see you tomorrow, at the same time. Be sure to take your medicine."

"Yes, Doctor, I will." She picked up her purse and left the room.

When he was again alone, Drang thought about his other prize patient, Philip Harkness. The young man wasn't nearly as stable as Flo. He'd have to watch Harkness carefully, until it was time for him to carry out the task Drang had devised for him.

That assignment was too important even to consider the possibility of failure.

32

Over the following week, Tolliver visited the offices of each of the psychiatrists who had been charged with misconduct and attempted to question them.

The results were mixed.

Most of the doctors screamed harassment and refused to divulge any information whatever about their patients. Their protests followed more or less the same line: The fact that they'd made one small mistake in their distinguished careers gave the police no right to bother them. It was outrageous, they said, for them to be singled out. They would refer the matter to their lawyers and would complain to the district attorney, or the chief of police, or the commissioner, or the mayor. One claimed to be a personal friend of the governor and said he'd see to it that Tolliver was thoroughly reprimanded.

In the end, Ben had no choice but to back down. The records he'd been sent showed that these guys had settled the charges out of court, paying off their accusers in exchange for silence. The women had taken sums of money and agreed to forget about the abuses they'd suffered.

Why had the victims knuckled under? Because the alternative would have been for them to go to trial. And that would have meant revealing to their families and friends and the rest of the world what had gone on while they lay on the psychiatrist's couch.

Most of the women couldn't face that. Appearing in court would be bad enough, with defense lawyers drawing verbal pictures of them as wanton sluts who'd practically begged the doctors to have sex with them. Tell me, Mrs. Smith—isn't it true that you went to the doctor because you weren't getting enough from your husband to satisfy you? Isn't it true that you've never gotten enough? When you went to your appointments with the doctor, how were you dressed? Short skirt? Low-cut blouse? Isn't it true that having sex with him was entirely your idea? How many other extramarital affairs have you had?

And as demanding as that would be, she'd know the husband or the boyfriend would also be asking questions. How did it get started,

Helen? Did you egg the guy on? Did you like it? Was it better than with me? You were actually paying the doctor to do it with you? What the hell kind of tramp are you, anyway?

Then to top it all off, there would be the newspaper reports. The *Daily News* and the *Post* loved stories like that. Mother of three carries on wild affair with psychiatrist. Society matron is red-hot mama behind doctor's locked doors.

The papers might even run her photograph, list her address, and write about her husband's job.

And what about her kids? They'd have to face their friends in school, have to take the jeers and taunts. Have to listen to the dirty jokes that featured their mother.

Still another factor would be her own friends—the women she went to lunch with, or worked with, or shopped with—and the people she and her husband saw socially. Some would be genuinely sympathetic, but others would only pretend to be, while actually talking about her behind her back.

Until she would wish to God she'd never opened her mouth, never gone to the police, never agreed to press charges.

And so she wouldn't. Instead, she'd give up, take the money, and call off the dogs—all the while despising herself for having been used, for allowing her self-esteem to be crushed because she hadn't had the guts to see that the lousy bastard of a doctor got what he deserved.

Ben understood that. He'd seen a sufficient number of those cases to understand it completely.

Unfortunately, the shrinks understood it, too. They knew that not only had they gotten away with penalties no more painful than writing checks to their lawyers and the women they'd abused but that, in addition, they could go right on closing the door in the face of any cop who tried to question them. From a legal standpoint, if not a moral one, their slates were clean.

A few of the doctors Tolliver talked to, however, were moderately cooperative—perhaps out of guilt over past sins. They contended they'd never treated Beth Whitacre. Had never met her, knew her only through the onerous publicity generated by the murders she'd committed. And of course, they were familiar with her father's reputation. Thank you very much, Lieutenant, and good-bye.

By the end of the week, Ben was ready to chew nails. Except for having learned from the toxicologist's report that Beth Whitacre's blood had contained a substance that should not have caused her to go on a homicidal rampage, he had nothing.

But then he again got a call from Ed Flynn.

"How you doing, Ben?"

"Lousy. How about you?"

"The same. Ice-cold on both my homicides. I did get word from the lab, though, on what was in those capsules that were found near the second victim."

"What was it?"

"Lab wasn't sure. The report said it was an antidepressant, but they couldn't pin it down."

Tolliver sat up straight, gripping the phone. "Say again?"

"It was an antidepressant. You know, like Prozac, or Zoloft. Not them, but a similar compound. I spoke to one of the techs and he said it was just a feel-good drug, nonaddictive and harmless."

"Could he tell you anything else about it?"

"No, that was it. But anyhow, like we discussed, there's no way of knowing whether the capsules were dropped by the victim or the perp or by somebody else."

"Listen, Ed. I'm going to let you in on something, but you've got to keep it under your hat."

"Sure, what is it?"

"The tox report on Beth Whitacre showed high levels of an antidepressant in her blood."

There was a pause, and then Flynn said, "Holy shit."

"Right."

"So maybe there's a link between your cases and mine after all. You thought there could be, right from the beginning."

"I wasn't sure, and I'm still not. From what I've learned, a hell of a lot of people are taking those drugs. So it might mean something, but then again, it might mean nothing."

"Yeah, of course. It does seem strange, though, doesn't it? Especially when drugs like that are supposed to be so mild."

"That bothers me, too. Anyway, I want to push the possibility of a link. And if there is one, I wouldn't want the word to get out."

"Christ no. The media'd blow it into a big deal and that could spook the guy."

"Exactly. Send me down a copy of that lab analysis, will you?"

"Yeah, I'll fax it right away."

"And be sure to let me know if you get anything else. I'll do the same from my end." Tolliver hung up.

Maybe things were starting to come his way.

33

It was past midnight when Tolliver got home. He took a shower and put on a robe, then poured himself a bourbon on the rocks. He gulped that one and refilled his glass, then went into the living room and slumped in the easy chair in front of the TV. After surfing channels, he finally settled on an old John Wayne. His nerves were jumpy, and he was having trouble unwinding.

The whiskey wasn't helping much. As he watched, Wayne fanned the hammer of his Colt and sent three Indians to the big wigwam in the sky. That didn't help much, either.

The buzzer sounded.

Ben cocked his head. Somebody calling him from the street entrance at this hour? Or was it a drunk who'd wandered over from the South Street Seaport and was pushing a few buttons just for the hell of it? That happened sometimes.

For a moment, he was tempted to ignore the call, but then the buzzer sounded again. Finally he pulled himself upright and stepped to the intercom, which was on the wall next to the front door.

He flipped the switch. "Yeah?"

"Hi. Are you there?"

He groaned. "No, I'm in bed asleep, where you should be."

"Hey, let me in, will you? It's dangerous down here. Somebody might make off with me."

"I should be so lucky." But he pressed the door release, then went back to the box and turned off John Wayne.

Two minutes later, there was a soft knock at the door. He undid the locks and opened it.

Shelley stepped inside, and he shut the door and relocked it. When he turned back, he found her holding her mouth up to be kissed. He gave her a halfhearted peck on the lips.

She pouted. "You don't seem very glad to see me."

"It's late."

"Aw, come on. I'm sorry if what I did caused you trouble. I didn't mean to." She took off her trench coat and put it in the closet beside the door. Already making herself at home.

"Besides," she went on, "I've come with a peace offering."

"What is it?"

"Make me a drink and I'll tell you about it."

"Yeah, all right. Bourbon?"

"Fine."

She followed him into the kitchen, where he filled a squat glass with ice and whiskey and topped off his own.

He handed her the fresh glass.

She touched it against his. "It's nice to be with you again. I've missed you."

"Uh-huh. Cheers."

They drank, and then she said, "Did you see the feature I did on mass murderers?"

"No, I was spared that."

"Too bad, it was great. We got a nine share, and for a local station in this market, that's terrific."

He looked at her. She had on a light tan dress that was cut low enough to make him notice. With her blond hair, the effect was wonderful. But even more than her physical charms, it was her outlook that invariably impressed him. She was always up, always optimistic—which had to be a basic requirement for survival, in her business.

He swallowed more of his bourbon. "So what is it you were going to tell me?"

"It's about two other cases—two homicides, both in the Village."

Alarm bells went off in his head. He put his glass down on the kitchen counter. "Shelley, what are you getting at?"

"My sources tell me there could be a connection between those and Whitacre."

"Goddamn it."

"Then it's true, isn't it?"

"Who's been talking to you?"

"You know I can't reveal that."

"You can't, huh? The first—"

"Listen, will you? I swear I won't use it. I owe you that. But if it got to me, there's a good chance some other reporter'll pick it up, too, isn't that so?"

She had a point. Police officers were notorious for slipping information to the media, sometimes in return for favors owed and sometimes for payoffs. But Ed Flynn, never. Tolliver knew the lanky Irishman too well. Flynn had a fondness for booze, broads, and horses, but he was a dead-honest cop. Nonetheless, some ass-wipe in the Sixth had been shooting off his mouth.

"So why are you telling me?"

Shelley put her own glass down and stepped close, opening his robe and slipping her arms around his waist as she pressed her body against him. She brought her mouth to within an inch of his and said, "I told you why. It's a peace offering. And I've missed you."

He couldn't help himself. He could smell her perfume and he was aware of the warmth as she pushed tighter and ground her hips. He gripped her buttocks in his hands and mashed his mouth on hers.

She opened her mouth and they stood locked that way for several moments, probing each other's tongues. When they came up for air, she whispered, "Now then, aren't you glad I'm here?"

"Some."

"Sure you are. I can feel it."

"So can I."

"I'll make you a deal."

A deal? Now? That was Shelley for you. "What is it?"

"If I pick up anything else that could help you," she said, "I'll handle it the same way. I'll pass it on to you, and I won't use it."

"And?"

"And when you get this thing sorted out, you give me an exclusive."

"You know I can't—"

"Yes you can. I never reveal my sources, remember?"

"So you said."

"Then it's a deal?"

"Yeah, it's a deal."

She went on grinding her hips against him. "Promise?"

"Sure." He picked her up and carried her into the bedroom. At that point, he would have promised her anything.

34

In the morning, Shelley was still asleep when Ben got up. He showered and dressed as quietly as possible, then slipped out of the apartment. As soon as he reached his office, he called Ed Flynn and let him know about the leak.

Flynn's reaction was what Tolliver had expected: "Son of a bitch."

"You got any idea who it was?"

"Probably somebody on the squad. But not Frank or Carlos. I'll nose around, see if I can find out."

"If you do, kick his head in."

"Don't worry, I'll do more than that." Flynn hung up.

Ten minutes later, Fred Logan came into Tolliver's office and perched on the edge of the desk. "What's going on with the Whitacre thing? You got your report finished?"

Ben exhaled. "Not yet."

"What's taking so long?"

"I don't have all the answers." That was the understatement of the century.

"What do you mean? I'm told McGrath's squad wrapped their investigation. What else are you looking for?"

"That's the trouble. I don't know."

Logan's eyebrows hunkered down. "Hey, listen, Lieutenant. Everybody in the case is not only dead but buried. It's over. Past. Now the DA's waiting for a report, and you better give him one. Also there's a lot of other things we got to contend with around here."

"Yeah, I realize that."

"Norman Krantz was in my office a few minutes ago. He's bitching about how he doesn't have enough investigators on Rafella."

"He's got Grady and Melnick," Ben said. "Plus a half a dozen of his ADAs."

"He wants you. Says he's ready to go to Oppenheimer and complain we're holding him up."

"Oh shit. I'll talk to him."

"Fine, you do that. And by the way, I want you to fill me in on everything you've been doing on Whitacre. In case the old man asks me, okay?"

"Yeah, sure."

"Right now, I've got to go to a meeting on another case. Some broker at Smith Barney's been peddling inside information on an acquisition. The feds are involved with that one. But get together with me on Whitacre as soon as you can."

"I will."

The captain got off the desk and left the office.

Ben threw his pencil down on the pile of notes in front of him. Maybe Logan was right. Maybe the connection between the Whitacre case and the ones Flynn was working was a pipe dream. Maybe the thing to do was to tell Linc Whitacre he'd done all he could, that it was time for everyone to get on with their lives. Then he'd write his report and turn it in, go back to chasing paper on the mob lawyer. And yet—

The phone rang. He answered it.

"Lieutenant, this is Judy Corelli. I have some information for you. Beth made a claim on her insurance at the end of February."

"What was it?"

"The person I spoke to is a friend of mine who works in accounting, and she was nervous about saying much. All she told me was that Beth made a claim for treatment by a Dr. Mark Rainsford. The amount was two hundred dollars."

"And that was it?"

"That was it. I hope this won't cause any trouble for my friend."

"It won't, I promise you."

After hanging up, Ben jotted down the name Corelli had given him. He was reasonably sure he'd never heard it before, and yet somehow it seemed familiar. Why?

Judy said Beth Whitacre had made the claim at the end of February. Tolliver got out her appointment book and scanned the pages. And there it was: "Mark R."

But the entry still didn't explain why the doctor's name had rung a bell. There were plenty of guys with the first name Mark. Why did—

Ah. He had it. Flipping through his notes, he looked at the list of psychiatric agencies he'd called in an effort to learn whether Beth had gone to any of them. Sure enough, there was a Mark Rainsford among them, on West 62nd Street.

Telephoning the agency again would be a waste of time. He grabbed his blazer and headed for the elevator.

35

When Ben entered the waiting room, he found three people sitting there: the receptionist, a teen-aged boy, and a woman who probably was the kid's mother.

The receptionist had a round, pleasant face. She looked up from her desk and smiled. "Yes, sir, may I help you?"

He displayed his shield and ID. "Lieutenant Tolliver, NYPD. I want to speak with Dr. Rainsford."

Her smiled stayed in place. "The doctor is with a patient just now. May I ask what this is in reference to?"

"It's in reference to a homicide investigation. It's important that I see him."

The affability faded. She picked up a phone and touched the intercom button, then whispered into the mouthpiece. When she put the instrument down, she said, "It'll be a few minutes, if you'd care to wait."

Tolliver would. The few minutes became fifteen, and then twenty. Meanwhile, he stood with his arms folded, the teenager and his mother staring at him.

Finally, the buzzer sounded, and after another whispered telephone conversation, the receptionist said, "Doctor can see you now." She indicated a door to her left, and Ben went through it.

Rainsford was alone, sitting at his desk. Apparently, patients left via a side door, which would obviate their going back through the waiting room when it was time to leave.

The doctor was doing his best to look like Sigmund Freud—right down to the gray hair and black spectacles and short spade beard. Apparently his office had also been designed to fit the image; the walls were paneled in dark wood, and rows of framed diplomas were hanging behind him.

Ben again flashed the tin, and Rainsford glanced at it briefly.

"Sorry to interrupt your schedule, Doctor, but I need some information."

"What kind of information?"

"Back in February, you treated a young woman named Beth Whitacre. Is that correct?"

Rainsford frowned. "I'm sorry, but I can't give out any information concerning my patients. I'm surprised, frankly, to find you even asking me to."

"Doctor, let me explain. By the way, you're familiar with the case, aren't you? You know about the incident in the jewelry store?"

"Of course I know about it. The media exploited the story endlessly. So?"

"So obviously Miss Whitacre had severe problems, to do what she did. All I want is to gather whatever facts I can about what led up to the event. I'm not trying to embarrass anyone, and anything you tell me will be kept in strict confidence."

The bearded man considered this, then cleared his throat. "Lieutenant, ordinarily I wouldn't speak to you at all about such a matter. The relationship between doctor and patient regarding the patient's mental health is one in which privacy is not only important but vital. I'm sure you realize that. However, it's also true that Miss Whitacre's death was a great tragedy, as it was for the other unfortunate people involved."

"Yes, it was."

"Therefore, I'm willing to relax the rules a bit. I can tell you that Miss Whitacre came here once, and spent exactly fifty minutes with me. She complained of being depressed, and I used most of our time together to acquaint myself with her history. In that brief period, I gained no more than a superficial knowledge of her situation."

"Would you have a theory as to what caused her to become violent?"

"No, I would not. I was shocked, frankly, when I heard the news."

"I see. Tell me this. During that session, did you give her any drugs, or prescribe them?"

"Absolutely not."

"And when you had this talk, that was the only time you saw her?"

"Yes."

"Did you make notes on your discussion with her?"

"Yes, I did."

"And then you wrote up an evaluation?"

"Of course. But as I said, it was only preliminary."

"Would you mind showing that to me?"

"I certainly would mind. In fact, it's out of the question."

"You realize I could have the evaluation subpoenaed."

"I doubt that you'd succeed, but if you wish to try, go right ahead."

The doctor had him there, but Ben did his best not to show it. "I may just do that."

One corner of Rainsford's mouth lifted in a supercilious smile. "Have a nice day, Lieutenant."

"You too, Doc."

Once back on the street, Tolliver stifled his anger. Being frustrated 90 percent of the time was part of the job. And yet, there was something about what Dr. Mark Rainsford had told him that didn't ring true.

Whatever it was, Ben intended to find out.

36

Drang spent a delicious hour with Flo Dallure. He had progressed with her now to the point that he could use her to act out all his own fantasies, some of them going back to his boyhood. The ancient dreams were hot and feverish, and in those long-ago days, they'd left him breathless. He would summon them from his memory and then order her to bring them to life.

It was wildly exciting when he did that—like going into a secret location that was known only to him, a hidden place that was dark and secluded and where he could do anything he wished with a beautiful woman. She would be totally compliant, and he could contrive any situation, satisfy any lustful desire. It was fantastic.

He knew the sessions with Flo were very much like masturbating. Except that with her, his couplings were a thousand times more satisfying than his fist had ever been. She was so bound by his demands that she herself was similar to a figment of his imagination. Whatever he wanted, she did. Whatever he could conceive, she performed. And she carried out his orders with exactly the degree of passion he directed.

Strangely, he'd never had very good relationships with women, and that had always been a source of bitter disappointment to him. It wasn't that females had failed to find him attractive; he was sure they had. After all, he was quite good-looking, he felt, in a distinguished, rather aristocratic way. And he was physically strong and appealing, as well.

But from the time he was a very young man, they'd shied away from him. The pattern had always been the same: He'd meet someone and become friendly with her, but then when an opportunity for intimacy arose, the woman would recoil, as if she'd turned over a stone and seen something crawling there. Something disgusting and, at the same time, frightening. She would flee from him, and no amount of cajoling could bring her back.

As a result, he'd sometimes taken out his resentment on whores—cheap ones, preferably. Not because money was a consideration, but because he liked the air of degradation that surrounded the kind of pig you found wandering through the streets at night.

Eighth Avenue was a good place to look for them, and so was Eleventh. Or you could pick them up near the entrance to the Lincoln Tunnel. Foul, stinking creatures, sometimes drunk, but more often stoned on crack or heroin, trolling for johns who'd pay them enough so that they could buy more drugs after they'd given most of what they earned to their pimps.

Drang understood that about himself as well, of course. To buy such a miserable wreck was to degrade all women, including the one who'd given birth to him.

Beautiful women, on the other hand, desirable women, existed for him only in the mental images he created during masturbation. Which was something else he understood, long before he began his formal training in psychiatry. The desirable beauties he conjured up in his mind could never recoil from his advances, could never reject him. They were his, to do with as he wished.

Today, he made Flo act out a scene he'd first invented during the painful days of his adolescence. He stood in the center of the room, fully dressed, while she slowly took off her clothes in front of him. He watched her, not moving a muscle as she attempted to arouse him, stroking herself and moving sensuously, slowing licking her lips while she kept her eyes locked on his.

Drang all but ignored her. He stood as upright and still as a statue while she posed provocatively. And he remained that way as she got down on all fours and crawled toward him, moaning with desire. When she reached him, she slithered up his body and kissed his mouth, pressing herself against him and working her pelvis. Still he refused to respond.

She undressed him then, one small step at a time. Unbuttoning, unzipping, her fingers moving over him as lightly as butterfly wings as she constantly caressed him and whispered filthy invitations in his ear.

Then at last, when he too was nude, red-faced with desire and with his breath coming in short gasps, when he couldn't stand not having her for another second, he slapped her hard across the jaw, knocking her to the floor.

After that, he made her get up and assume one position after another as he took her roughly, almost savagely. Leaning backward against a bookcase, from behind as he bent her over the couch, sitting on his lap in a chair, straddling him as he lay on the floor. On and on, with her supple body twisted into every attitude he could think of.

By the time the hour was up, he was drenched in sweat and puffing hard, as slack and weak as if his joints were made of rubber. Leaving her on the couch, he went to the bathroom at the end of the room, entering it and closing the door.

There he washed quickly and then dried himself with a towel. Catching sight of his image in the multiple mirrors that lined the walls, he smiled and posed for a few moments, admiring his reflection and feeling pleased with himself.

When he came out, Flo was fully dressed and sitting in a chair, looking as coolly composed as if she'd just dropped by to say hello to a friend.

Not only had he turned her into the perfect outlet for his own sexual pleasure, as rewarding as that was, but far more important, she now represented living proof of what his work could produce. He had succeeded in virtually erasing her original personality, replacing it with a new one designed by him. That was a fabulous achievement, and he'd only begun to explore the ways the technique could be used, and the ways he could market it. He was sure his discoveries would be worth millions.

There was already plenty of evidence on that score. His lawyer in Zurich had faxed him that discreet inquiries had generated interest among political and military leaders in several countries. All Drang had to do now was to take the next steps in his plan here and then make his move to Switzerland.

He looked at Flo. She'd not only be a perfect companion for him; she'd make a wonderful demonstration of the changes that could be brought about through the use of psychopharmacology in the hands of a master.

The telephone buzzed. Drang frowned; Anna had strict orders not to disturb him when he was with a patient.

He picked up the instrument. "What is it, Anna?"

There was a note of urgency in her heavily accented voice. "Sorry to bother you, Doctor. I have Dr. Rainsford on the line."

"Did you tell him I was busy?"

"Yes, but he said it was very important."

Drang was puzzled. Rainsford was a psychological counselor who sometimes sent him patients— for a fee, of course. The man took himself quite seriously, although he wasn't even a medical doctor, merely a Ph.D. What could be so important that he'd insist on being put through?

"I'll take the call," he said.

An instant later, Rainsford's voice came into the receiver. "Dr. Drang?"

"Yes, how are you, Doctor?"

"Fine. Sorry to disturb you, but there's something I think you should be aware of. A police detective was here earlier, making inquiries about a patient I referred to you."

A chill passed through Drang as he realized the import of what he was hearing. "Is that so?"

"Yes. The patient he asked about was Beth Whitacre. The one who—"

"Yes, I know who she was. I had only a preliminary talk with her, and after that, I never saw her again." Damn it, he'd completely forgotten that the Whitacre woman had first come to him via Rainsford, back in March.

"I see. In any event, I thought I should tell you. The policeman was quite arrogant."

"They often are."

"Naturally, I told him as little as possible."

"Good. Only way to handle them. Do you recall the man's name?"

"Yes. It was Tolliver. Lieutenant Ben Tolliver."

Drang's mouth went dry. But he kept his tone even. "Did he ask about anything else?"

"No, that was it. I'm simply advising you as an act of courtesy."

"I appreciate that. It's terribly annoying, sometimes, the way these minor authorities take it upon themselves to pry into one's business. It's as if they try to make trouble, even when there isn't any."

"I feel the same way. Have a good day, Doctor."

"Thank you, Doctor. You do the same. And thank you for letting me know." He hung up.

This was incredible, and totally outrageous. The furor over the

Whitacre case had died down long ago, as the media went on to exploit other topics that would excite their witless audiences.

And yet here was this cop, the same blowhard who'd spouted off in the televised newscasts, rooting around like a hog in a garbage heap. No wonder the police were called pigs.

But the man couldn't be ignored. The fact that Tolliver had come dangerously close to connecting Beth Whitacre to the doctor who'd been treating her was highly perturbing. Perhaps the detective was more capable than he seemed.

Drang glanced over at Flo. She was sitting quietly, the picture of tranquillity. She'd sit here this way all day if he wanted her to. But he had a problem to solve.

"You can go now," he said to her. "I'll see you tomorrow."

He watched as she walked out the door, and then he slammed his hand down onto the arm of his chair.

Damn that fool cop. What if he pressed Rainsford further? Or discovered the connection through some other means? Drang couldn't permit that to happen. Not now, when he was so close to bringing all his plans to a triumphant climax.

How to handle this? He knew how. He knew exactly how.

The doctor looked at his watch. In two more hours, Philip Harkness would be coming in for his daily session.

When he did, Drang would have an assignment for him.

But first, there were preparations to be made.

37

An important question was what weapon should be used. Drang rejected the knife immediately, for several reasons. One was that Tolliver was a big man, much larger than Harkness and undoubtedly stronger. For another, the policeman would have had both training and experience in hand-to-hand combat. Also, he was likely to be more alert than the average person.

No, the knife was out. Too many chances for something to go

wrong. And besides, Drang had already laid out a different project for Harkness involving a knife, and that one was succeeding admirably. He wouldn't want to mess it up now by introducing complications. Far better to keep the two things separate.

A pistol, on the other hand, would be ideal. Firearms didn't care how big or brawny or well-trained a target might be. Aimed properly, they would kill anyone, swiftly and surely. And if the shooter didn't place the bullet precisely where it would do the most damage, Drang had a remedy for just such a contingency. Moreover, a pistol could be concealed almost as well as a knife.

The doctor kept his in a drawer of the cabinet here in his office. He got it out now and inspected it. The weapon was a Ruger Redhawk revolver, a .44 Magnum with a seven-inch barrel. Its steel surfaces were blued, and it had checkered wooden grips.

This was a formidable handgun, one of the most powerful in the world. Each of the six projectiles in the cylinder weighed three hundred grains, and the cartridge load supplied enough energy to send one of the bullets through a bus engine end to end.

Drang had paid a thousand dollars cash for the gun, no questions asked. The dealer from whom he'd purchased it was a cordial gentleman who operated from the trunk of his car in the Mott Haven section of the Bronx. Drang assumed that the dealer had bought it in some southern state a day or two earlier. The Ruger bore serial numbers, but that didn't matter; there was no way the weapon could be traced to its present owner.

The pistol was loaded. Drang removed the cartridges and put the gun back into the drawer. Then he left his office and went down into his laboratory, taking the cartridges with him.

The rats greeted him with their usual chorus, but on this occasion he paid no attention to their shrill cries. Going to the long lab table, he sat down and went to work.

First, he used a scalpel to make a crosscut in the leaden nose of each bullet. Next, he rummaged around on the shelves for the small container of tetrathion concentrate he kept there. When he found it, he placed a cartridge in the vise and with a cotton swab applied a small amount of the liquid to the cut in the end of the projectile. Using tweezers, he lifted the prepared bullet out of the vise and set it upright on the table. Then he repeated the process with each of the remaining five rounds.

In a few minutes, he knew, the tetrathion would adhere to the lead and dry to a gummy consistency. At that point, he could carry the bullets back up to his office, so long as he exercised reasonable caution.

As he waited, Drang thought about the detective. The insolent dummy would never realize he'd become the prey himself in this game he insisted on playing. Of course he might guess, before he died. And then again, he might not. That was a nice irony, another aspect of the scheme Drang found amusing.

The pistol cartridges would be transportable now. To be sure their poisoned tips wouldn't touch his skin, he wrapped the cartridges in a sheet of plastic. Then he carried them back up to his office. Once there, he reloaded them into the Ruger, then returned the pistol to the drawer in the cabinet.

A short time later, Anna announced Harkness's arrival, and Drang had her show him in.

When they were alone and the young man was seated across from him, Drang said, "Afraid I have some bad news for you, Philip."

Harkness brushed the unruly lock of brown hair back from his forehead. "What is it, Doctor?"

"A police detective has been trailing you."

His eyes widened. "Oh my God. Are you sure?"

"Unfortunately, yes. I'm quite sure."

"That's terrible. How did he find out about me? Has he come here? How did he—"

"Calm yourself. He hasn't been here, and he doesn't yet know your name. I found out about this through one of my contacts. I've learned he's been investigating the killings in Greenwich Village and that he's very close to discovering your identity."

"Christ."

"We need to think about this coolly and objectively. Can you do that?"

Harkness swallowed. "Yes, I can."

"Good. Obviously, it's important to develop a counterstrategy. You can't afford to be caught. You know what would happen if you were. Not only would you go to prison, but there's a chance that under the new laws, you could be executed."

Harkness was staring at him, his mouth hanging open.

"Even if you weren't," Drang went on, "prison life would be horrible for you. Convicts rape good-looking young inmates, as you probably know. And of course, once you were incarcerated, there's no way you could have your medicine."

The words tumbled out. "I'd kill myself. I mean, I'd really do it. I told you I was thinking about it before I started seeing you. Jesus, why did this have to happen? I was sure nobody saw me. I have to get away from here. Leave the city. I—"

"Philip, listen to me. I believe there is a solution to this problem— a very practical one. In fact, it would even give you a great amount of satisfaction."

The young man clenched his fists. "What is it, Doctor? Tell me. I'll do anything you say."

Of course you will, Drang thought. Aloud, he said, "The solution is to destroy this detective. Before he destroys you."

A light shone in the hazel eyes. "Destroy him. Yes."

"A perfect answer, don't you think?"

"Yes, it would be. Do you know who he is?"

"I know everything about him," Drang said. "His name, his rank, his background. I know where he lives, and where he works. I also have a picture of him, a photograph that was printed in the newspaper."

"Good. Very good."

"There is a way for you to do this that cannot fail. At the same time, there will be virtually no risk to you. Do it, and that will be the end of this man's attempts to ruin your life. Do you understand what I'm saying?"

"Of course I do."

Drang reached out and opened the drawer in the cabinet where he'd put the pistol. He got it out and held it up.

As Harkness caught sight of the weapon, his mouth curved in a knowing smile. "Doctor, you're wonderful."

Drang placed the heavy revolver on the surface of the cabinet.

"Listen carefully while I explain what you're to do and how you're to do it."

The young man nodded eagerly. "Go ahead. Tell me."

"I'll do that, Philip." Again Drang reached over to the cabinet, and this time, he opened a second drawer, taking out the syringe. "But first, push up your sleeve."

38

There was construction going on in the neighborhood. As a result, the streets were cluttered with barricades and heavy equipment. Harkness watched the restaurant from his parking place across the street, sitting quietly in the rented Toyota. He'd followed the cop and the other man over here from the Criminal Justice Building, then had slipped the car in between a bulldozer and a cement truck.

Crouched at the wheel in semidarkness for more than an hour while doing nothing but staring at the entrance to the restaurant would likely have given most people a fit of impatience. But Harkness was not like most people.

The heavy pistol was resting on his lap. Its weight was no problem; in fact, he found that reassuring. He liked the feel of the weapon, the slight oiliness of the cold blue steel, the way the checkered wooden grips fit his hand.

The one part he was careful not to touch was the cylinder; Dr. Drang had told him contact with the noses of the bullets should be carefully avoided, explaining that the slugs were laced with a deadly poison. The substance was so toxic that introduction into the bloodstream of even a tiny amount would result in agonizing death. Thus if the victim didn't die from the gunshot wound, the poison would surely kill him.

The restaurant was busy. People were going in and out of the place in a steady stream, and he kept a sharp eye on them. It wouldn't do to overlook the detective when he finally reappeared.

Meantime, Harkness had plenty to think about. He knew he'd

probably get only one good chance, which meant he'd have to choose his spot carefully. Then it would be up to him to make the most of it.

And make the most of it he would. He hated the cop much more than the others, the strangers he'd done with the knife. In fact, there was a special loathing he felt for this creature who was tracking him like a jackal. That would make taking him down intensely gratifying. Harkness was looking forward to it.

He glanced at his watch. What the hell was keeping him? Tolliver had been in the fucking restaurant forever. Was he ever going to come out?

Maybe it would be better to get closer, Harkness thought. That would give him a better shot. He got out of the Toyota and slipped along the driver's side. The large cement truck was parked next to the car. He moved over to it and rested his forearms on the fender, holding the heavy pistol in a two-handed grip.

Aim carefully and squeeze, Dr. Drang had told him.

Now all Harkness had to do was wait.

39

So you went to this shrink," Logan said, "And he didn't give you much."

"Next to nothing," Tolliver replied. "But my gut tells me the guy is a phony."

"They're all phony. I never met one that wasn't. You want some wine?"

"Sure, that sounds good."

Logan signaled to a waiter, who scurried over. The restaurant was Tavio's, two blocks from the Criminal Justice Building. The place was jammed, as it always was in the evening, and at midday as well. The customers were a mixture of prosecutors, defense attorneys, defendants, witnesses, and cops. With the courts in Manhattan operating twenty-four hours a day, Tavio's never had to worry about business.

"Bring us a bottle of Chianti," Logan ordered.

"Yes, sir, right away." The waiter hurried off.

Ben twirled spaghetti on his fork. There were few things he liked to eat as much as pasta, and the chef here was a near genius at making his favorite sauce, tomato with plenty of garlic and fresh clams.

"What was this guy's name?" Logan asked.

Tolliver shoved the forkful into his mouth and spoke around it. "Rainsford. Dr. Mark Rainsford."

"And he admitted seeing Whitacre?"

"Yes. Although I already knew he had from what her boss at the Met told me. Anyway, Rainsford said he saw her only once, and that was it. She never came back."

"That check out?"

"Yeah, her bank statement confirmed it. But what he said sounded odd."

"Why did it?"

"Because he claimed he spent the one session he had with her making a preliminary evaluation. Think about that. We know she was in bad shape—she had to be. That's why she went to him in the first place. And look at what she did later on in that jewelry store. So if this guy is a professional psychotherapist and he did an evaluation, he had to know there was something very wrong with her."

"Yeah, so?"

"So all he told me was that she was depressed. As if it was as simple as that. You said yourself that in a case like this, the killer had to be really sick. Does her problem sound like the kind of thing you'd go to a shrink for just once?"

Logan took a thick chunk of warm bread from the basket and began buttering it. "I don't go to one at all. Never have, never will."

"Yeah, but that's strange, isn't it?"

"Okay, so maybe he was giving you a line of shit. But what'd you expect? You think the guy's gonna open up to you? He's gonna tell you, Oh sure, she was a raving maniac and I knew she was dangerous, but I didn't do anything about it?"

The waiter returned with a straw-encased bottle of Classico. He uncorked it and poured a taste for Logan, waiting until he got a nod of approval before filling both men's glasses.

When they were again alone, Ben said, "No, I didn't expect that. In fact, he did what I thought he'd do—gave me the back of his hand. He tried to slough off whatever was really going on with her. But that doesn't mean I have to buy it."

"No, but what if you don't? You're saying she was crazy and the shrink knew it, right?"

"That's what I think, yes." The pasta was angel hair, cooked al dente. Tolliver had never tasted better.

"So therefore he should have had her committed?"

"I don't know whether he could have at that point. But I do know that if she was that sick, she should have been in a hospital. The least he could have done was to notify her parents, get some help from her family."

Logan raised his glass. "Cheers."

"Salut." The wine had the characteristic tartness Ben also liked. He drank off his glass, and Logan refilled it.

"What else?"

"I asked him if he'd prescribed drugs, and he said he hadn't."

"And yet you told me the lab said there was an antidepressant in her blood, right?"

"Yes." Tolliver decided he wouldn't mention the drugs Ed Flynn's investigation had turned up in the homicides he was working. If he did, Logan would probably tell him to keep his nose out of the Sixth Precinct's business. It wouldn't be the first time.

"You check on this guy Rainsford?" the captain asked.

"Not yet, but I intend to. I'll talk to the Office of Professional Medical Conduct about him."

"Yeah? What are you gonna tell them—you're suspicious? They'd laugh at you. You know the routine. Anybody makes a complaint, they conduct their own investigation. You remember the dentist? The one on Park Avenue that used to give women nitrous oxide, and then when they were out of it, he'd stick his cock in their mouth?"

"Yeah, I remember the case."

"After they got him, the cops who worked on it found out from the board he'd been suspended ten years before that for doing the same thing. Soon as he was reinstated, he went right back to his old tricks. If there is one thing all those guys do, it's protect each other. And that includes the members of the board."

"I realize that; I've dealt with them before. They'd still have to let me know if he'd ever been disciplined."

"Yeah, but he could have done things, whether they disciplined him or not."

"What I need is a court order that would force him to give me his records. Then I could find out what shape Whitacre was really in when she went to him."

"What do you show the judge for probable cause?"

Ben swallowed some of his wine. "That's a problem."

"I'll say it is. You'd be running around in circles, Lieutenant. You need to get into the doctor's records to find evidence to take to a judge, but you can't get into the records without a judge signing an order. The one person that could corroborate is Whitacre, and she's dead."

"Complicated, isn't it?"

"It is that. You know anything else about this Rainsford?"

"No. I called Alan Stein, and he'd never heard of him."

"Stein's the shrink who's a consultant to the department?"

"Right. He said he'd keep trying."

The waiter was back. He poured more wine for them, finishing the bottle. "How about some dessert, gentlemen? We've got nice fresh cannoli, or I could whip you up some zabaglione."

"Just coffee for me," Logan said. "Espresso."

Ben was tempted; he loved Italian pastry. And he could eat a quart of zabaglione at a sitting, no problem at all. But then he thought better of it. "Espresso for me, too."

When the table had been cleared and they were again alone, the captain said, "So what do I tell the DA?"

Tolliver shook his head. "Nothing, yet. I still think there's something the shrink's hiding."

"Whether there is or not, Oppenheimer's waiting for a report."

"I'll write one when I've got the facts. Anyway, at the moment he must have a few other things on his mind."

"That's true," Logan said. "Right now the big news is that corruption mess in the Four-one. I thought IA had that under control, but it looks like everybody'll wind up getting crunched—including the precinct captain."

"Deserves it. The stupid shit."

"Yeah, but about Whitacre."

"What about it?"

"Maybe I should tell the old man we've done everything possible, and then you can go back to work on Rafella. Grady and Melnick are busting their balls on it, but like I told you, Krantz wants you heading it up."

The waiter served them espresso, then moved off. Ben twisted a sliver of lemon peel over his and dropped it into the rich mixture, then drank from the tiny cup.

Logan looked at him. "Well?"

"I want to stick with Whitacre. The more I see of it, the more convinced I am that it wasn't what it seemed to be."

"Okay, I can give you another day or two, but that's all."

"There has to be a way," Ben said, "for me to get the truth out of that shrink."

"Fine. Get it. Just don't go pissing into the wind." The captain finished his espresso and signaled for the check.

40

Harkness wondered if somehow Tolliver had left the restaurant without being seen. Maybe he'd been hidden from sight behind some of the other customers who were going in and out of the place. Or maybe there was a side door and he'd left that way. Still another possibility was that the cars driving by on the street had obstructed Harkness's view.

In any case, he was getting goddamn tired of waiting here, draped over the dirty fender of the truck. He was also taking a hell of a chance, training the pistol on the entrance of the place. Even though it was dark and he was obscured by the big vehicle, somebody might catch sight of him and start yelling for a cop.

Harkness gritted his teeth. Where was the son of a bitch? Was this really nothing but a waste of time?

Suddenly, he snapped to attention. There was Tolliver; he was sure of it. There was no mistaking the curly black hair and the mustache. The detective was coming out the front entrance of the restaurant, accompanied by another man.

Harkness lined up the Ruger's front sight with Tolliver's head. Steady now, he told himself. Just keep applying pressure until this thing goes off and you blow his fucking head apart. Steady, steady—

Someone stepped in front of the two men—a fat woman, one of a party of several people who were going into the restaurant. They moved on by, blocking Harkness's vision.

Shit. He raised his arm, pointing the muzzle of the pistol skyward. When the sidewalk was again clear, Tolliver and the other man were gone.

Cursing his luck, Harkness's gaze swept the area. There they were—farther down the street. He again leveled the Ruger, and then he stopped. He couldn't get a shot off now. Tolliver was too far away for him to be sure of hitting his target. And besides, there were people walking past on the sidewalk.

The two men stood together talking together for a moment, and then Tolliver went in one direction, his companion in another.

Harkness kept his eye on Tolliver. The detective walked a few more paces and got into a car that was jammed in among the other vehicles. He started the engine and pulled out into the stream of traffic.

Harkness jumped back into the rented Toyota and put the pistol on the seat beside him, then turned the ignition key. When the car started, he switched on the lights and slipped away from his parking place, maintaining a position two vehicles behind Tolliver's. The detective was driving a blue Ford sedan, and following it would be easy. There was too much traffic down here for anyone to move very quickly.

The Ford drove along Worth Street and then turned down Pearl. Harkness continued to hang back, staying on the alert for any sudden turns. There weren't any, and he knew why: Tolliver was on his way home. Harkness already had the address; it was only a short stretch from here, in the vicinity of the South Street Seaport.

When they reached the area, Harkness watched as the blue Ford turned down a ramp that led into a basement garage in one of the buildings. The metal door rattled upward, the car drove inside, and the door closed again.

For several minutes, he sat looking at the building. It was one of the half-dozen or so old ones along here, all of them dwarfed by the enormous glass-and-steel business towers just to the west, at the edge of the financial district. Like its neighboring structures, this one was a mere five stories high, built of brick and with a sloping roof.

It probably had been a warehouse originally, he thought. Now it was all apartments with views of the Seaport and the river. To his left, he could see the restaurants and shops, still going strong despite the late hour, the masts of the ancient sailing ships looming from the nearby wharves.

The building also appeared to be as secure as a small fortress. Its occupants could come and go via the basement garage, without having to leave their cars on the street. The only exposure they'd have would be if they were to use the door into the small, brightly lit lobby.

Most of the windows in the place were dark now. As he studied the building, Harkness saw lights go on up on the top floor. Was that where the detective lived?

Reaching into the glove compartment, he got out the binoculars he'd brought along and trained them on the windows up there. He adjusted the focus, and after a moment, he spotted a figure looking out toward the Seaport.

He was right; that was Tolliver, and he was standing at the largest of the windows, his arms folded. After a moment, the detective moved away, and a short time after that, the lights went out.

So not tonight, Harkness thought. But there would be other opportunities. He put the Toyota in gear and pulled away, turning west on Grand Street and heading for Broadway.

41

Tolliver called the New York State Office of Professional Medical Conduct and spoke with the chief of investigations, whose name was

Mildred Michaels. He told her he wanted information on a Dr. Mark Rainsford, and she put him on hold. When she came back on a few minutes later, she said there were no complaints against the doctor.

Michaels's tone made it clear she expected that to be the end of the conversation. Ben then asked if he could drop by. She hesitated, then finally said she could see him at two o'clock that afternoon.

The department was at 5 Penn Plaza, in the complex that housed Penn Station and Madison Square Garden. Ben had lunch at his desk, ham and cheese on rye and a beer, and then drove up there. When he arrived, he thought of the good times he'd had in the Garden: Knicks games, Rangers games, and best of all, the fights. At the moment, the NBA play-offs were in full swing, but the Knicks were out of it. Maybe next year.

He left the car on the street and went into the building. According to the tenant listing in the lobby, the offices he wanted were on the tenth floor.

When he stepped off the elevator, he made his way through a labyrinth of hallways before he found the frosted glass doors with the department's name on them. Going inside, he presented his credentials to a secretary and told her the chief of investigations was expecting him. The woman called Michaels's extension, then directed him to her office.

She turned out to be about what he'd envisioned: an angular woman whose hair was tied back in a bun. She looked tight-lipped and austere in a starched white blouse, peering at him suspiciously when he walked in.

Her office matched her appearance. It was functional but drab, with only a few personal touches: a small plant, a coffee mug, a framed photo of a woman holding a small dog. And that was all. Like Michaels, no nonsense.

Ben tried charm, showing her his shield and ID and smiling as he said, "Afternoon, ma'am. I'm Ben Tolliver. We spoke on the phone. I know you're busy, and I apologize for interrupting you. But I'd like to ask you a few more questions."

It didn't work. Her face was like what you'd see on an ice sculpture. "What is it you want to know, Lieutenant?"

He kept the smile in place. "Mind if I sit down?"

"If you wish."

It wasn't hard to guess what was going through her mind. People in a job like hers didn't consider cops the enemy, exactly, but they didn't think of them as far from it. Another factor was that Michaels wouldn't be at all happy to have a detective horning in on what she undoubtedly considered her exclusive province. He'd had this reaction before often enough. It was the same old territorial imperative: this is my turf; stay off it.

He took the chair next to her desk. "I'm interested in checking further on the psychiatrist I talked to you about—Dr. Mark Rainsford."

"I believe I told you there have been no complaints against Dr. Rainsford. Not through this office, or anywhere else in the state of New York. All our records are kept in the Board of Regents' offices in Albany. They show no problems with him."

"Yes, ma'am, I understand that. But let me ask you a hypothetical question. Not about Dr. Rainsford, but in general. Okay?"

"Depends on the question."

"Sure. This is just for my own edification. Let's suppose a doctor had a complaint made against him and your office conducted an investigation. In the course of it, you found the charge was true. The board would then discipline him, is that right?"

"That's correct, yes."

"And let's say the charge wasn't serious enough to cause him to lose his license, but instead he was suspended. Okay?"

"Go on."

"What would be the duration of the suspension in a situation like that?"

"The length of time would be up to the board. It varies."

"How much does it vary, generally speaking?"

"Generally speaking, quite a bit."

Jesus, talk about pulling teeth. "What are the parameters?"

"Anywhere from a few months up to two years."

"In other words, a doctor could do something serious enough to get him suspended for two years, but then he'd be cleared to practice again?"

She stiffened. "The members of the board all have extensive expe-

rience in these matters, Lieutenant. Most of them are doctors themselves. You can be sure that in the event of a violation of the code of professional conduct, the punishment would be appropriate."

I'll bet it would, he thought. Aloud he said, "Fine. I'm sure that's
true. So let's say, in this hypothetical situation, our doctor gets a suspension that's somewhere in the midrange. We'll assume he's suspended for a year, okay?"

She crossed her arms. "So?"

"And let's suppose that many more years go by, and there is never
another complaint against him during that time. Would the earlier incident then be expunged from his record?"

"No, it would not. It would remain a permanent part of his professional history, for as long as he is alive and practicing in this state."

"So there's no possibility that the doctor's record would fail to
show it? No matter how much time had gone by?"

"Correct. It would always be there."

"I see. That's very helpful." It wasn't, but he was still hoping to
find a thread he could pursue. Although he was having no more success
than when he'd started.

"Is that all, Lieutenant?"

"Almost. On the subject of Dr. Rainsford again—can you tell me
where he went to college? And to medical school?"

"Yes, I suppose I can give you that information." There was a PC
on a table behind her. The machine was turned on, but the screen was
blank. Michaels swung her chair around and tapped the keys.

Ben tried to get a glimpse of the image that came onto the monitor, but her body blocked his vision. Which was probably intentional, he
thought.

After a few moments, she picked up a pencil and jotted notes on a
pad, then hit the keys again. The computer screen once more went
blank. She swung back to face Tolliver.

"Dr. Rainsford completed his undergraduate studies at Tolson
State College in Mississippi, and he also received his master's degree
there. He then went on to the Silverhill Institute in Nevada, where he
earned his doctorate."

Not exactly a blue-ribbon education, Ben thought. Aloud, he asked, "And where did he intern?"

"Intern? He didn't. Dr. Rainsford has a Ph.D. in psychology. He's not a physician."

"So then he's not actually a psychiatrist?"

"No. He's a psychological counselor."

That was interesting. It certainly didn't square with Rainsford's lordly manner. "Do you have anything else on him?"

"That's about it."

"How about date of birth, and where he's from, originally?"

She was keeping her irritation from showing, if he didn't look too closely. Turning back to the computer, she brought it to life once more. When she swung back, she told Tolliver that Rainsford had been born in Ocean Side, Long Island. The date of birth, Ben calculated, would make him fifty-eight years old at the present time.

"And that is all the information I can give you," Michaels said. There was a note of satisfaction in her voice. "Dr. Rainsford has been doing referrals for almost thirty years, and he has never had a problem."

Tolliver looked at her. "He's been doing what?"

"Referrals. He evaluates a patient, and then sends the person on to a psychiatrist for treatment."

"That means he doesn't treat patients himself?"

"I don't know, but probably not. And now if you'll excuse me," Michaels said, "I have work to do."

"Well, I certainly appreciate all your help."

"Good day, Lieutenant."

On the way out, Ben could have kicked himself. What he'd just learned had never occurred to him. Despite all the pretentiousness, Rainsford wasn't a shrink at all. The reason he'd seen Beth Whitacre only once was because he'd referred her to another doctor.

And that was the one Tolliver was looking for.

Now the problem was how to locate him, which was the same one he'd had all along. Nevertheless, he was now one step closer.

That made this trip worthwhile after all.

42

That evening, Tolliver went to Alan Stein's house and dropped off a sample of Beth Whitacre's blood. He apologized for having taken so long to get it, explaining that the police lab was swamped. The doctor said he understood, and that he'd send the sample down to St. Elizabeth's right away and ask his contacts there to rush an analysis.

Ben then brought Stein up-to-date on his investigation. Knowing beforehand what the answer would be, he asked if there was some way he could check on Mark Rainsford's referrals without getting a court order that would force the doctor to turn them over.

Stein shook his head. "You know the problem there, Lieutenant. Someone in Rainsford's position would guard that information as if it were solid gold—which is exactly what it is, as far as he's concerned. The doctors to whom he refers patients pay him hefty fees for doing so. If he were to disclose their identities, or anything to do with the patients he sends them, he'd be taking a chance on ruining his business."

"I suppose that's true."

"Believe me, it's quite true. If the word got around, the doctors he provides the service to would shy away from him. He'd be killing the goose, as it were."

"So how am I going to get what I need? I can't ask for a subpoena; no judge would sign one."

"I don't know, offhand, but let me think about it. Maybe I can come up with a solution. Meantime, let's see what we can find out from the blood sample. The results just might give you enough to get that order."

"Uh-huh. Pretty slim chance, though, wouldn't you say?"

The psychiatrist smiled. "Yes, but I believe in positive thinking. How about a drink?"

"Thanks, Doc, but I want to go back to my office. Call me as soon as you get word on the blood."

"I'll do that, Lieutenant."

43

Harkness sat huddled behind the wheel of the Toyota, its lights out and engine idling, watching the front of the house Tolliver had gone into. He was still bitter at having missed his chance when the detective had come out of that restaurant, but now with any luck he'd get another opportunity. He'd better not screw this one up.

Harkness had again followed the detective from the district attorney's offices on Centre Street, and now he was wondering what Tolliver was doing in the darkened structure that was nearly identical to its neighbors.

Was the cop running down a lead? Continuing to pry into corners, looking for evidence that would shed light on the killings Harkness had carried out? Was that what he was up to?

Or was this a personal matter? Maybe he was calling on a girl-friend, relaxing by getting himself laid at the end of a trying day.

Whatever, Harkness despised the bastard. Just the thought of having the detective on his trail was enough to make him break out in a sweat. What Dr. Drang had talked about was true, of course. If he was caught, going to prison would be worse than dying—much worse.

Harkness remembered a guy he'd known who was hauling van-loads of pot from Florida, making two trips a week. He was doing great until one day he came out of the Holland Tunnel and blew a tire in the middle of Canal Street. A cop got nosy and made him open the rear of the van. The judge sentenced him to five years in Attica, but he didn't last five weeks. The brothers passed him around until his insides were so badly torn he bled to death.

No, there was no way Harkness would go to prison. And besides, the doctor's solution would be a hundred times more satisfying. Harkness detested cops, on principle.

He lifted the Ruger from his lap, thrilling to the potency and the power represented by the massive pistol. It was like having the biggest dick in the world. Knowing that with what you held in your hand you could blow away your enemy whenever you wanted, just by crooking your finger. Here, asshole. Suck on this.

The poison would cause the detective to suffer horrible agony before dying, the doctor had said. But Harkness wasn't so sure that was the way he wanted this to end. Better, he thought, to plant one of the heavy slugs in the middle of the cop's head. See it fly apart like a water-filled balloon. He laughed out loud, thinking about that.

Harkness checked his watch. What the fuck was the man doing in there?

At that moment, the door of the house swung open. Instantly alert, Harkness gripped the wheel with his left hand, holding the pistol in his right. The cop's car was parked about thirty yards farther along the street, on the side opposite the house, with Harkness facing its rear.

Tolliver stood for a moment in the lighted doorway, evidently saying good-bye to someone, although Harkness couldn't make out the other person. After a moment, the detective waved and began trotting down the steps. Behind him, the door closed.

When Tolliver reached the sidewalk and stepped off the curb, Harkness put the Toyota in gear and shoved the pistol through the open window on the driver's side. He pressed his foot down on the accelerator and the car leapt forward, rapidly picking up speed as Harkness steered it straight for the figure in the street.

At the last moment, the cop turned his head. Illumination from the streetlights wasn't bright enough for Harkness to see his face clearly, but it had to be registering stunned realization as danger roared down on him. Tolliver jumped to the left of the onrushing car, scrambling to get out of the way.

Harkness took aim and fired shots from the big pistol as fast as he could pull the trigger. The weapon bucked in his fist as it threw a fusillade of poisoned slugs at its target.

44

Instinctively, Ben threw himself headfirst through the air, diving between two parked cars. Gunshots boomed, the concussive reports of a large-caliber weapon shattering the quiet of the neighborhood. He felt a bullet tug at the cloth of his blazer as he scrambled to get out of the line of fire, and other slugs punched holes in the cars and chipped concrete from the sidewalk.

The gutter was damp, and there were bits of smelly debris in it. He landed facedown in the mess, half-stunned by the impact and with his head reeling from the near miss. He pulled himself to his feet and scraped a handful of filth off his chin, tugging the Mauser from its holster and then looking to return his attacker's fire.

All he saw was a vague shape in the distance, the glow of streetlights reflecting from shiny black metal. An instant later, that too disappeared.

Lights went on in a couple of the nearby houses, but no one opened a door or looked out a window to find out what was going on. Citizens in New York had learned long ago that becoming overly curious at the sound of gunfire was a good way to get killed.

But then Alan Stein came out his front entrance. He was carrying a long flashlight in one hand, a large semiautomatic pistol in the other. He turned on the flashlight and froze Tolliver in its beam. Running down the steps, he called out, "Ben, you okay?"

"Yeah, I'm all right," Tolliver said. He put the Mauser back into its holster and brushed dirt from his clothing.

Stein crossed to where Ben was standing. "I heard shots. Sounded like a war going on."

"Did to me too, Doc. Let me have that light a minute, will you?"

Taking the flashlight, Tolliver played the beam over the cars he'd ducked between. One of them, a Chevrolet sedan, had two holes in the rear fender. He also saw places where pieces of the curb had been blown away.

"Must have been a real cannon," Stein said.

"At least."

Ben raised the beam and shined it on the cement foundation wall of the nearest house, illuminating a crater that was more than an inch across. Stepping to the wall, he squatted down and inspected the cavity.

Stein followed, kneeling beside him and peering at the hole. "Looks like there's a slug in there."

"Yeah, let's see if we can dig it out." Tolliver shoved a key into the hole and pried at the bullet for a few seconds, then stopped. "This won't do it."

"Would a screwdriver work?"

"Might. Hold on a minute. I've got one in the car." He stepped over to the Ford, opening the trunk and taking a heavy screwdriver and a hammer from his toolbox.

The task required several minutes of hacking into the cement, but finally Ben retrieved the misshapen chunk of lead. He held it up between thumb and forefinger. "Big mother."

Stein was again holding the flashlight. "What caliber, would you say?"

"Maybe a three-fifty-seven Magnum, maybe bigger."

"Someone really wanted to harm you, Lieutenant."

"I got the message." Ben brought the missile closer to his nose. "Stinks, doesn't it? Not just like cordite, either."

"Wait a second," Stein said. He got out a handkerchief and held it in the palm of his hand. "Drop it here."

Tolliver did. "What is it?"

"I'm not sure. But it smells to me like phosphoric acid."

"So?"

"So phosphoric acid is used to make some of the deadliest poisons known to man. Parathion is one, but there's an even deadlier one called tetrathion. Either one can kill you if it gets into your bloodstream."

"Good thing it missed."

"Doubly good. A bullet of that size would have done terrible damage, no matter where it hit you. And if it didn't kill you, the poison would have."

"Nice."

"Nice friends you have. Any idea who might have wanted you dead?"

"I can think of a number of people. But right now, the top candidate would be hard to pick out."

Stein closed the handkerchief around the lump of lead. "I'll have the lab look at this as well, if it's all right with you."

"Sure, be my guest." Ben stood up, and so did Stein.

"Let me know, Doc. I want to get back to my office."

"Watch yourself, Lieutenant."

"Yeah, I will." He turned and went to his car.

45

How did it go, Philip?"

The young man brushed back the lock of hair from his forehead. "It went fine, Doctor. I waited until I was sure I couldn't miss, and then I blew the scumball away."

Drang appraised his patient's appearance. Harkness's eyes were red-rimmed and slightly swollen, and there were dark circles under them. Also, there was a barely perceptible tremor in his fingers. He looked as if he hadn't slept for days. Perhaps he hadn't.

"How close were you when you fired?"

"Just a few feet. Eight, ten at the most."

"Where was this place?"

"East Tenth Street. Not far from Tompkins Square Park. He went to a house there."

"And you waited for him to come out?"

"Yes. I sat in the car, waiting for him."

Drang wondered what had drawn Tolliver to the location. Was it business? Pleasure? That would be interesting to find out. "Did you note the address?"

"No."

"Or see the person or persons who lived there?"

"No. He was in the house a while. When he came back out, somebody was at the door, but I couldn't see who it was."

"Could you make out whether it was a man or a woman?"

"No. It was dark, except for the streetlights, and there wasn't much light coming from the house when he left."

"Where was he when you shot him?"

"In the street. He was crossing to where he'd parked and I was sitting there waiting for him. I had my lights out and the engine running, and when he started across, I drove at him as fast as I could."

"Why did you do that?"

"I wanted to run over the son of a bitch. Smash him flat and then shoot him."

"Philip, that wasn't part of the plan, was it?"

"No, not exactly. I mean, I know I was supposed to kill him with the gun, but to tell you the truth, I was so fucking mad I wanted to grind him under the wheels. After that, I was going to shoot him."

"I see." This was disconcerting. And unfortunately, it was also typical. Despite all the work Drang had done with him, Harkness continued to show flashes of independence, to take actions contrary to what had been spelled out to him beforehand. He was much like an unruly child whose rebelliousness sometimes made him untrustworthy.

The patient was watching him anxiously. "But you can understand that, can't you, Doctor? I mean, this shithead was trying to do the same thing to me, wasn't he? Isn't that true?"

"Yes, Philip. That's true. So you tried to hit him with the car. But you missed?"

"By just a couple of inches. He must've heard the car coming at him, and then he dove out of the way."

"Where did he go?"

"Between a couple of parked cars. But don't worry, I could see him laying there. I hit him at least twice."

"How many times did you fire?"

"Four, I think. Maybe five."

"So half your shots missed?"

Harkness's face fell. He licked his lips. "Yeah, but so what? It was dark and he wasn't the biggest target, all scrunched down in the gutter between those cars. But I hit him, I know I did. And besides, you told me all it would take was a scratch, because of the way the bullets were fixed, isn't that right?"

"Yes, that's right. Tell me this. Did you stop when you fired?"

The patient's eyes flickered, a telltale sign. "No. I mean, I guess I slowed down a little, so I'd be sure the bullets would hit him."

"And then?"

"And then I hightailed it out of there. I'm positive nobody saw me. I didn't turn on my lights until I was near the park."

"What did you do with the pistol?"

"What you told me to do. I drove over to the West Side, to one of the piers near Perry Street. I threw the gun in the river, as far out as I could heave it."

"Very good." But it wasn't, of course. The aberrant behavior was disturbing, and so was the lack of cognition the young man was displaying.

"So it worked out okay, didn't it?"

"Yes, Philip. It worked out okay." Drang opened the drawer in the cabinet beside his chair and took out the hypodermic syringe.

Harkness pushed up his sleeve and held his arm forward. "It's a relief, I'll tell you. I was having nightmares about what could've happened if that prick kept on."

Drang inserted the needle and depressed the plunger. "I'm sure you were. Tell me, how is your job going?"

"Well. It's going well. I did some designs for a new cigarette General Brands is bringing out, and the client liked them. Mercer's going to give me a raise."

"Mercer is your boss?"

"Yes, and a real thief."

"Why is that?"

"Because he lives off me and the other designers. He has no talent of his own, just peddles our work. He's nothing but a fucking leech. I'm the one who should be running the place."

Also typical, Drang thought. Violent mood swings, ranging from depression to manic delusions. Why was it so difficult to establish a proper balance in the drugs he was giving this man?

"Perhaps someday you will be running it," he said. It was important to encourage him, to keep him believing that good things would eventually come his way. The pot of gold at the end of the rainbow.

"I'm sure I will," Harkness said. "I certainly could do a hell of a lot better job than Mercer does."

Drang withdrew the needle from the patient's arm and returned the syringe to the cabinet drawer. "What about the other things in your life? Your relationship with your girlfriend, for example."

"That's over."

"Oh? You hadn't told me that."

"Yeah, we broke up some time ago."

"Why did that happen?"

"She was giving me a lot of shit, so I threw her out."

"What kind of shit, Philip?"

"Telling me I was acting strange, and that the medicine was causing it. Fucking ridiculous."

Apprehension gathered in the back of Drang's mind like a dark cloud. "What did she know about your medicine?"

"Nothing. She just saw me taking the capsules, that's all. I never told her anything about what they were."

"And what about me, Philip? She didn't know who your doctor was, did she?"

The eyes flickered again. "No. She had no idea."

"Remember, Philip. You swore you'd never reveal to anyone that I was treating you, nor would you ever discuss the treatment. That's our agreement, isn't it?"

"Yes, of course. You know I wouldn't violate that. I'd never tell anybody anything about it."

"Good. Be sure you never do. You're going to work now, I assume?"

Harkness rose from his chair. "Yes. I'll see you tomorrow, Doctor."

"One other thing, Philip. I want you to increase the number of capsules you're taking."

Drang opened a second drawer in the cabinet and took out a package, handing it to him. "From now on, make it six of these a day, instead of five."

Harkness smiled. "Thank you, Doctor. Thank you very much."

After the patient left his office, Drang sat where he was for several minutes, thinking.

Then he went to his desk and took out the page of notes he'd put there. He glanced down them, looking for the telephone number he'd gotten from the computer report. When he found it, he called the number.

It rang twice, and then a voice answered: "Lieutenant Tolliver."
Drang quietly put the phone down, cursing under his breath.

46

Tolliver hung up, thinking the caller probably had gotten a wrong number. Then he went back to trying to figure out who had made an effort to kill him the night before.

First off, he doubted the would-be assassin was a professional. The effort had been too clumsy for that, and too ineffectual. The guy had tried to run him down with a car, and then he'd blasted away with a gun that could have stopped a bear. And he'd missed with both weapons. Very sloppy work, all the way around.

A hit man, in contrast, would never have resorted to either method. A car was almost completely unreliable for such a purpose, too easy to misdirect. Also, trying to run over an enemy was an act of rage, not one you'd call coolly objective. It was the kind of mad-dog thing a husband would do when he thought his wife was screwing around, or vice versa. Here, take that, goddamn you.

No, a car was out. And a gun? A professional would have used one, but not of that caliber. The weapon of choice with the boys was a .22 semiautomatic equipped with a silencer.

In addition, the shooter would have made a different approach. He would have waited in the shadows, stepping out when Tolliver was unlocking his car. And then, *pop, pop.* Two in the back of the head, creating no more noise than a couple of farts. After that, he'd quietly walk away. End of story.

Still another factor that ruled out a hit man was motive. Although Ben was an investigator who'd been working on mob activities for months now, he was hardly the kind of target the Gambinos or the Genoveses or any of the three other New York families would go after. They had enough trouble these days without taking out cops.

And lastly, there was the question of the poison on the slug. Alan

Stein had said the stuff was one of the deadliest substances known to man, that even a tiny bit in your bloodstream was enough to kill you. That was yet another strange wrinkle. Mob guys never messed with such high-tech innovations. At least Tolliver had never heard of them doing so.

What did that leave—somebody who'd been nursing a grievance? Maybe some mope Ben had helped put away, and who'd been sitting in the can for a few years, plotting revenge? That was a possibility, maybe even a good one.

The more Ben thought about it, the likelier the theory seemed. Wouldn't be the first time something like that had happened. There was a case in Brooklyn a while back, involving an ex-con who'd done fifteen in Ossining for armed robbery, second trip. First thing he did when he got out was to buy a shotgun. Sawed off the barrel and went looking for the judge who'd sent him up. *Blam.* Now we're even, Your Honor.

Yeah, that could fit. Without even straining his memory, Tolliver could think of a dozen guys who'd love to get square with him.

And the case he was working on now? That was the most remote possibility of all. Even though it was beginning to look as though some doctor might have overdosed the young woman with the wrong kind of medicine, Ben's probing around wasn't the kind of thing that would get somebody pissed off enough to want to kill him.

Speaking of wrong medicine, he'd been meaning to check back with Ed Flynn. He picked up the phone again and called the Sixth Precinct. When he got Flynn on the line, he asked the squad commander how he was doing with the knifing homicides.

"Still nowhere," Ed told him. "We had all four witnesses back here twice. The guy who saw the first one, in the meat market, and then the three others who saw the one on Hudson Street. We must've shown them every mug shot Records had. We got one maybe ID, but when we checked, we found out the suspect's been in Rikers for a year on a drug rap."

"You get any more on the victims?"

"Yeah, a little, for what it's worth. Turns out the businessman from Utica was busted there a month ago for soliciting a prostitute. The hooker was an undercover vice cop. April fool, right?"

"Yeah. So?"

"So that probably confirms what he was looking for down here," Flynn went on, "when he got knifed."

"Most likely. What else?"

"On him, not much. The other guy, the one who owned the boutique? He was brought up on arson two years ago. Another shop he owned had a mysterious fire. Charge was dropped for lack of evidence."

Ben had little hope of hearing a positive response to the next question, but he asked it anyway. "How about ties to Whitacre?"

"None. And no ties between the victims, either. We tried it every which way, but it comes up empty. They didn't know each other, and apparently they didn't have any contacts in common—at least, none we've been able to trace."

"And that's it?"

"That's it. How about you?"

"I'm still trying to run down the drugs that were in Whitacre's system. That's one of the things I called you about. You still have any of the capsules that were picked up at the Hudson Street scene? Or did they all go to the lab?"

"No, I still have one. Why, you want it?"

"Yeah, I do. Be interesting if we could pin the stuff down, see if there's a match between your compound and the one in Whitacre."

"Uh-huh. Although I wonder what that would prove. You said yourself it seems like everybody in New York is taking some kind of an antidepressant."

"It's the in thing to do, Ed."

"You telling me that? When I came on the job, the big wipeout was gin. Now there's so many new kinds of shit I can't keep up with them all."

"Neither can most other people, including me."

"Anyhow, I'll send the capsule down to you. Good luck."

"You too." Tolliver hung up.

47

Today's session with Flo Dallure wasn't as satisfying as usual, Drang thought.

Nor as satisfying as it should have been.

But that wasn't her fault. She did everything he demanded of her, without question or protest—even the most bizarre acts. He whipped her bare buttocks with his belt. Instead of complaining, she begged for more, just as she'd been instructed. She leered at him and flickered her tongue, like the most lecherous bitch imaginable.

No, the problem wasn't with Flo, but with Drang himself. He was distracted, which for him was an unusual mental state. One of the abilities he prided himself on was his remarkable capacity for concentration. When something was important to him, either because it was pleasurable to him or because it was a dilemma, he could shut everything else out and give the subject his undivided attention.

But this afternoon, here he was, rolling around his office with this marvelously desirable woman, and all he could think about was his failure to give that goddamn detective what he had coming to him. It was maddening.

After a time, Drang gave up in disgust. When you have a difficulty to contend with, he thought, you have to face it. Otherwise, it can fester like a boil. It must be dealt with, solved and brought to a satisfactory conclusion with a proper course of action.

He told Flo to get dressed, then went into the bathroom. When he came out, he put his own clothing back on and sent her on her way, saying he'd see her tomorrow.

After that he told Anna to cancel his appointments for the rest of the day. Leaving his office, he went down the steps into his lab.

The rats were chittering and squeaking, but he paid no attention. In fact, he didn't hear them. Putting on his lab coat, he began pacing back and forth.

The first thing to do, of course, was to analyze the problem. What had he done wrong? What were his mistakes? As distasteful as the answers to those questions might be, they also were obvious.

To begin with, the task he had given Harkness was beyond the young man's capabilities. It had required a cool, dispassionate approach, which by definition would have been impossible for him to carry out.

In fact, Harkness had done exactly what Drang had prepared him to do: He vented his fury. As a consequence, instead of performing a calm execution, he'd made a wild attempt to mete out punishment. He wanted Tolliver to suffer terribly, and merely knowing the poison on the bullets would accomplish that wasn't nearly enough to satisfy him.

The second mistake Drang had made was in choosing a pistol as the weapon. It was one thing for Harkness to dispatch someone with a knife, letting himself be driven by white-hot rage, deriving orgasmic pleasure from plunging a steel blade into his victim's heart. But it was quite another for him to aim a heavy revolver at night and hit his target.

So how had Harkness gone about his assigned task? By losing all control. He'd attempted to smash the detective with his car, and then fired wildly at him as he sped by. Missing, naturally, with both attempts.

And that, in essence, was where the plan had gone wrong. Like most ill-conceived schemes, it never had a chance of succeeding. It was a failure from conception.

As much as Drang hated to admit it, he and no one else had made the mistake. Tolliver was still alive, still pursuing his miserable little investigation, an investigation that could be ruinous to Drang and all his plans if by some fluke it succeeded.

What, then, should be done now? That was also obvious. There was no way the detective could be allowed to go on; it was now more important than ever that he be stopped. The question was, How?

An idea occurred to him.

Drang stopped his pacing then and thought about it. Like all good concepts, this one was relatively simple. And it would be extremely effective.

He glanced over at the rats that were watching him from their cages, their eyes reflecting redly from the light above his lab table.

Stepping to the table, he began assembling the ingredients he would need: first a quantity of chlorate of potash, then a generous amount of sesquisulphide of phosphorus. He had some of each on the shelves to the right of the table. Next, a small glass container, and a few ounces of HNO_3, nitric acid.

He'd also want a container. The small carton in which chemicals had been shipped to him recently would do nicely. A few other things were necessary, but they were easily obtainable. For now, he would prepare the basics.

He hummed while he worked, a melody from *Aida,* the triumphant march of the trumpeters in Act Two. It would be nice to surprise the lieutenant, he thought. After all, everyone loved to receive unexpected presents.

And this time, there would be no opportunity for Harkness to fail.

48

Detectives know that 90 percent of their work consists of grinding out details: sifting through whatever facts are known, questioning witnesses and informants and people who might have pertinent information, canvassing the vicinity of the crime, going over what they have again and again and then again. All the while hoping to find the one person who could give them a solid lead, the one strand that could tie together the pieces of the puzzle, scratching for solid evidence to make the case.

Of the remaining 10 percent, only a little amounts to clever sleuthing. The rest is luck.

The chances for success in a murder case? On average, eighteen hundred homicides take place in New York each year, and just under half are cleared. That means detectives know going in that the odds are five-four against. With rapes, robberies, and burglaries, they're much worse.

As a result, there is an underlying sense of failure that weighs heavily on those in the job. Some cops learn to live with it. They keep their sanity by becoming jaded and cynical, developing a sour attitude toward everyone whose path crosses theirs, telling themselves that nothing is forever. Others get into the bottle, or drugs.

And some eat the gun.

Tolliver had long ago made peace with himself. He'd gone

through a heavy boozing phase for a time, back when he was a detective third, and had learned that trying to work while stumbling around with a sick hangover was no answer.

Now what he did when he came to a point where he was stuck was to sweat the frustration out of his pores. This morning, he left his apartment and went to the police gym on 34th Street, instead of to his office. He spent an hour there, hitting the speed bag, skipping rope, lifting weights.

He knew he'd about run out of possible directions to go in with Whitacre. His efforts to track down her shrink, or the doctor who'd prescribed the medication, had led him smack into a brick wall. Or a white one, he reminded himself—the barrier erected and maintained by members of the medical profession.

But at any rate, he was stymied. Acknowledging that, even to himself, was a tough thing to do. Nevertheless, the session in the gym helped; by the time he'd showered and dressed, the world didn't look quite as dismal as it had.

From there, he went down to the Criminal Justice Building. The only thing new that greeted him was a package Ed Flynn had sent, containing the yellow capsule that had turned up at the crime scene on Hudson Street. Ben put that in his pocket; later on, he'd drop it off with Stein and ask the doctor to have the ingredients checked.

Then he sat at his desk and got out his notes, spreading them out before him in chronological order. He studied them for a long time, chewing on his pencil.

The weakest part of his investigation was the beginning. Not that he'd lit any fires with his brilliant efforts later on. But after Terry McGrath had whined about interference in the case and then had been backed up by Chief Galupo, Ben had failed to follow up on a number of loose ends.

He went over that phase now, reviewing what he'd jotted down in Serenbetz's jewelry store the day of the shootings.

Two of the notes jumped out at him. Both related to objects that had aroused his curiosity at the time, angles he thought might lead him somewhere. And both just might have given him a glimpse into whatever it was that had led Beth Whitacre to go there with a loaded revolver.

He swept the notes into a drawer and locked his desk. As he left his office, he hoped he wouldn't be too late, that the evidence still existed.

There was only one way to find out.

49

He's still alive, Philip."

"What? That's impossible. I shot him. I put the gun on him and shot him while he was in the street. He was right there, and I wasn't more than a few feet away. I told you, I couldn't miss. I know I hit him at least twice. Maybe more than that."

"He's still alive."

"Are you sure? How do you know that, Doctor?"

"I checked. He's alive and well, and he's tracking you."

"Jesus Christ. I can't understand it. I mean, I was so *sure.*"

"Yes, I know you were. But it's true. He's out there, looking for you."

"Oh God. What am I going to do? I don't want him to find me. I can't *let* him find me. I'm not going to prison, I'll promise you that. No matter what happens, I won't rot in some stinking jail cell. I told you I'll kill myself first, and I meant it."

"That's no answer, Philip. I don't want to hear any more talk of you killing yourself. You have too much to live for. You're a young man, with your whole life ahead of you. Think about how happy you've become, how you've changed since you began treatment."

"I know, but Jesus. The thought of that cocksucker, creeping around, looking for me. How did he escape? Didn't the poison work?"

"Philip, such things happen. It was dark and you were moving and so was he. It's not hard to miss under circumstances like those."

"You don't really think that, do you? You think I'm nothing but a dumb fuckup who can't do anything right. Not even when my life depends on it."

"That's not so, Philip. The fact is, I admire you. I admire your courage and your intelligence, just as I admire your artistic talent and the way you've used it to make a successful career for yourself."

"Hmph."

"Did you hear me, Philip? I admire you."

"You mean that?"

"Of course I mean it. What you tried to do the other night took a tremendous amount of courage, whether it paid off or not."

"I guess it did, didn't it?"

"Absolutely. You should be proud of yourself, even if you didn't succeed that time."

"I appreciate your saying that, Doctor. It means a lot to me . . . to have your respect."

"Respect and admiration, too, Philip. Don't ever forget that."

"A second ago, you said even if I didn't succeed *that time*. Are you telling me I could get another chance?"

"I think so, yes."

"Jesus, would that be great. I wouldn't miss again, you can bet on that. Next time, I'll stick the gun in his ear and blow his fucking head off."

"I'm sure you would. But there's a better way."

"Better how?"

"Less risk. No danger to you whatever, and no opportunity for anything to go wrong."

"Tell me about it."

"I will. But first, I want to give you your booster."

"Yes, sure. Whatever you say, Doctor. Whatever you say."

50

The cop in charge of property storage reminded Tolliver of somebody you'd run into in a Motor Vehicles office, or maybe in one of the city's innumerable licensing bureaus. Or anyplace else where a clerk could sit on his fat ass and act annoyed when asked to do what he was there for.

This one was right out of the mold. He was bald and grumpy and had a heavy gut that hung out over his belt. His nameplate said he was R. Murphy. Probably he'd been a patrol cop until he either screwed up or became partially disabled, and now here he was with a rubber-gun job, doing as little work as possible while he counted the days to retirement.

"What's the case number?" Murphy wanted to know. His tone indicated he wasn't much impressed by lieutenants.

When Ben told him, the clerk shuffled away from the opening in the chain-link screen that stretched from the counter to the ceiling, moving down the rows of shelves and looking at tags on the objects stored there. He took his time, not going to any great trouble and certainly not moving as if Tolliver might be in a hurry.

As he waited, Ben thought about what he'd seen in his notes. He hoped coming down here wouldn't turn out to be more wasted effort, a wild-goose chase he'd contrived for himself. Both the ideas he'd come up with could very well turn out to be worthless, based on nothing better than hope. For that matter, Beth's possessions might have been returned to her parents, and the things he was looking for already disposed of.

Murphy was back, carrying a metal basket. He set it down on his side of the counter and shoved a clipboard and a ballpoint through the opening. "Sign here to look at the stuff," he said. "But you can't take any of it without an order."

Tolliver put down today's date and the case and evidence numbers, followed by his name and rank. Then the clerk pushed the basket across the counter to him.

Moving a short distance away from the window, Ben took the articles out of the basket and laid them on the counter one at a time. There were the oversized sunglasses, the black leather shoulder bag, the pair of black gloves. The only thing missing was the pistol; Ballistics still had the heavy revolver.

The contents of the leather bag were what he wanted. He opened the bag and took them out. These were the things he'd looked at in Serenbetz's jewelry store the day of the shootings. But Beth Whitacre's wallet and hairbrush and lipstick and compact and pen and the half a roll of mints weren't what he was after.

In the bottom of the bag lay two items. One was the knitted cap. He took that out first and examined it.

There was nothing remarkable about the cap. It too was black, made of soft wool, the edges rolled up—no different from thousands like it, maybe millions. Called a watch cap because it was worn by sailors standing watch, and often worn by civilians in all walks of life. Whitacre had it with her the day of the shootings but wasn't wearing it, perhaps because the weather was warm and sunny.

Tolliver held the cap in both hands and rolled the edges down. What he saw then was something he'd half-expected to see. There was a slot in the front, and when the edges were completely rolled out, they were long enough to cover the wearer's entire face, down to the neck.

Great for keeping your head warm in a cold snap, or a gale. Great for skiing, great for protecting yourself against the weather in a snowstorm.

And great for hiding your face if you were committing a robbery.

He hadn't thought to roll out the cap when he and Detective Novotny were going through the bag that day, hadn't even considered the possibility that it might have been there for such a purpose.

And what did it mean, anyway? Whitacre hadn't been wearing the cap when she went into that store, regardless of whether the edges were rolled up or down. And what if she had been? Would that have made anything different, when she killed three people and then blew the top of her head off?

No, it wouldn't. The cap offered no more proof of what had been in her mind than anything else he'd uncovered in this case. Yet somehow he sensed it was significant. Just how, he wasn't sure. But it was. He knew it.

The second item was the one he had the highest hopes for. Reaching into the shoulder bag, he took that one out as well: a small leather-bound book of telephone numbers.

Ben hadn't gone through it that day in the store; at the time, the little book was just one more object in the list he'd made. Nothing special then, nothing he'd even remembered, until he'd spotted it on the list today when he went back over his notes.

He opened the book now and glanced quickly at the pages. Like the ones in Beth's appointment book, the entries were all in blue ink, and written in her own brand of shorthand. There were dozens of them.

He looked across the counter. Lard-ass was leaning back in a chair, tottering on the rear legs as he read a copy of the *Post*. Ben quietly slipped the book into a pocket of his blazer.

Each of the remaining items, he returned to the shoulder bag, placing the cap in last. Then he put the bag and the other things back into the basket. He pushed the basket back through the opening, but the clerk didn't so much as look up from his paper.

"Thanks," Ben said.

"Uh-huh."

"And say, Murphy?"

The fat cop put his paper down and looked at Tolliver. "Yeah?"

"You ought to take some time off. You've been working too hard." He turned and left the room.

51

At first, the only number Tolliver was able to identify with any degree of certainty was that of Beth Whitacre's parents. After some pondering, he then figured out that "S. WBD" had to represent her brother, Scott, who according to Ben's notes worked for Webley, Blake and Dinsmore, in Boston. Also that number was preceded by area code 617, which was eastern Massachusetts.

In addition, he spotted entries for "Judy," her boss at the Met, and "Ken." The pages in the book ran alphabetically, and under *R* he found two that had *Dr.* in front of them. One such listing was "SR," and he'd already learned that was Susan Roth, Beth's gynecologist. The other was "MR," and seeing the reference to Rainsford produced a bad taste in Ben's mouth.

There was one other doctor entry in the book. That one's name was Ang, but when Ben called the number, he got a recording of a heavily accented woman's voice that said, "Doctor's office is closed. Please call during daytime hours, ten to three, Monday through Friday."

He then checked his directory, but he found no listing for a doctor by that name in Manhattan. A doctor with an unlisted number? Be great, he thought, if one of the guy's patients had an emergency. He made a note of the number, resolving to call it again in the morning.

Over the next half hour, he went through the book page by page, trying to decipher the names and initials, calling many of the numbers in an effort to learn whom they belonged to. "Chase" turned out to be the bank, predictably, and the person who answered his call to the number for "CAA" told him he'd reached the Cornell Alumni Association.

Many of the numbers put him in touch with answering machines that didn't identify their owners except by first names, and he could only guess that they belonged to Beth's friends and acquaintances. Undaunted, Ben went on calling until his arm ached from holding the phone to his ear. But he kept at it, not quitting until he'd called an entry under Z and found himself talking to Zaroff Shoe Repair, on Lexington Avenue.

Curiously, he'd found no number for a drugstore. How had Beth been getting prescriptions filled for the antidepressants she'd been taking? Or had the medicine always been injected? As with so many other questions, he had no answers.

And what about Serenbetz Jewelers? He flipped back to the S's, but he found neither a listing nor a number that would fit.

So the hell with it, he thought. For the time being, anyway. He was bleary-eyed from poring over the blue-ink scribbles. Tossing the little book down onto his desk, he leaned back and stretched.

Now what? Go get a drink, something to eat? Check in with Ed Flynn, see if he'd come up with anything new? No, if Flynn had latched onto something, Tolliver would have heard about it.

He stood up and rubbed his back. The drink and some food sounded like the best course. Then maybe he'd make a few more calls. Some of the numbers hadn't answered at all, and he wanted to try them again. At the moment, the book was all he had. He picked it up and dropped it into his pocket, then left his office and headed for the elevator.

When he reached the ground floor, he thought about his visit to the property clerk. Seeing the shoulder bag and the other things that Beth Whitacre had taken with her to the store on that fateful afternoon had brought a number of mental pictures back into sharp focus.

That reminded him: there was one other point he'd wanted to check out and never had. He'd intended to, but then Terry McGrath had thwarted him.

He glanced at his watch. This was a Thursday, and the stores would still be open if he hurried. And that made this as good a time as any. He left the building and went to the lot where he'd left his car. Pulling out, he turned east and headed for the FDR Drive.

He never noticed the black Toyota following him, two cars behind.

52

Where was the schmuck going? Harkness wondered. Following him through the narrow downtown streets had been easy, with the thick traffic forcing vehicles to move at a snail's pace. But here on the FDR Drive, Tolliver was practically flying.

No matter, Harkness wouldn't lose him. He goosed the Toyota along, hating its sluggishness, wishing he'd rented something faster, more powerful. Too late now; he'd have to do the best he could with it. At least there weren't as many cars on the FDR as on the city's interior streets. So this was one stretch where he could maneuver, even if the Toyota was a shitbox.

Harkness was still stung by having failed in his first attempt, regardless of what Dr. Drang had said. He felt stupid, inadequate. The goddamn cop had been right in front of him, and what had he done? He'd missed completely. Not once, but twice—first with the car, and then with the gun.

You fucking idiot, he berated himself. There never was a time in your whole dumb life that you did anything right. Going all the way back to when you were a snot-nosed kid and you saw your old man die.

Only he didn't just die, did he? What actually happened was that your mother held a pillow over his face until he stopped breathing.

That had been easy to do. At the time, Phil Harkness, Sr., was a paraplegic, a city fireman who'd broken his neck in a fall when Hook and Ladder 7 was fighting a blaze in a warehouse on 29th Street. He'd spent a year after that in a hospital and then six months more in the family's crappy little apartment in Queens, with his loud, filthy mouth the only part of him that was still operable. He'd cursed his wife and cursed his son and cursed his luck and cursed his God for what life had done to him—until Philip had prayed that God would get mad enough to take that life away.

And God did. Using Philip's mother as His agent. One night, she drank most of a bottle of vodka and then applied the pillow. When she was sure her husband was dead, she called 911, and after the medics arrived, she told them he'd simply passed away, poor soul. Philip had pretended to be asleep, but he saw what happened. Later, when investigators came to ask questions, he kept his mouth shut.

The money settled on her by the city kept the old lady in booze until she died, and when she did, it was the second time God had answered Philip's prayers. An undersized, moody child, he spent very little time in this world, preferring instead to live in the one he created with his crayons and later his watercolors. He'd been raised by an aunt afterward, and his talent had gotten him admitted to Pratt. Then had come the involvement with drugs, when whole periods of his memory had disappeared, like chalk erased from a blackboard.

Even when he was hired by the design studio and become recognized as one of its best talents, the terrible feeling of worthlessness had stayed with him, draining him, choking him, causing him to sweat like a pig when he was asked to present his concepts, reminding him, over and over, that underneath his cheap little success, he basically was nothing.

Until Dr. Drang. Starting treatment with the psychiatrist was the true miracle, the wonderful opening of an opportunity to change himself completely, to start over again. In fact, Drang was the only person who'd ever understood him. The doctor had gone deep under the surface to get to know and communicate with the real Philip Harkness.

And he had supplied the medicine that had changed Philip's life.

The same medicine that the rotten fucking detective in the blue Ford up ahead was trying to take away from him. Dr. Drang had explained how it was part of a conspiracy concocted by the government to deny people like him the medication they needed to improve their lives, to overcome the problems that plagued them. Tolliver was only one of them, the doctor had said.

But he was the one Harkness had to deal with now.

The Ford turned off the FDR, and Harkness followed it across town, still with no idea what Tolliver's destination might be. At Fifth Avenue, the cop went south, and then west on 47th. At that point, only a few yards in from the corner, he suddenly stopped.

As Harkness drew closer, he saw that the detective had double-parked and was getting out of his car. Typical arrogance, he thought. Fucking cops thought they owned the city.

The street was clogged with traffic, and as cars jockeyed around the Ford, he saw one driver shake his fist at it. So Harkness wasn't the only one who was pissed off. He crawled by, and as he did, he saw Tolliver go into a jewelry store on the right-hand side of the street.

Harkness felt a surge of excitement course through him. This could be exactly the chance he was looking for. But he'd have to hurry; he had no idea how long the man might be inside that store.

Farther down the street was a sign for a parking garage. Harkness pulled into it and got out of the Toyota, taking the package with him. The attendant gave him a ticket, and he shoved that into his pocket as he hurried back along the sidewalk.

This is it, he thought.

And for once, he wouldn't fuck up.

53

There were several customers in the store when Tolliver walked in, two couples and a woman who appeared to be by herself. The place looked nothing like the way it had the last time he was here. It was immaculate now, overhead lights reflecting brightly from glass cases filled with jewelry, the terrazzo tile floor scrubbed and shining. A guard was standing near the door, wearing a crisp gray uniform.

Two women were behind the counter. One was round-faced and

motherly, wearing glasses. The other was the clerk Ben had spoken with the day of the shootings, Marcia Geller. There was a vague resemblance between them. The older one glanced up at him and smiled, saying, "I'll be right with you, sir."

He nodded and stepped over to one of the glass cases, looking down at its contents. There was a display of rings and bracelets, all very expensive. The stones mounted in them varied: diamonds, sapphires, rubies, emeralds, and some others he didn't recognize. Many of them cost more than he made in a year—which was a good thing not to think about. It might lead him to question why he was spending his life as a cop, and to resent the characters who would walk into a place like this and think nothing of plunking down a wad for one of these baubles.

The guy Marcia Geller was waiting on now, for instance. He had silver hair and a florid face, and he was smiling indulgently at the woman he was with. She was a giggly redhead who looked to be less than half his age, snuggled into a mink stole despite the warm weather. A diamond bracelet was dangling from her wrist, and she was trying to make up her mind about whether she liked that one or one of the others that were laid out on the black velvet pad in front of her.

To a guy like the silver-haired customer, the price of the bracelet was probably pocket change.

But what of it, Ben told himself. Nobody forced you to go on the job, and nobody's forcing you to stay with it. Besides, the only way you'd leave would be if they carried you out.

A few more minutes went by, and the customer traffic thinned. The older of the two women behind the counter asked if she could help him. Tolliver identified himself, then said hello to Marcia Geller, who was eyeing him apprehensively.

"I'm Ethel Serenbetz," the first woman said.

Ben nodded. "Yes, ma'am. I'm sorry for what happened, and for all the trouble you've had. But I'd like you to help me with something I'm looking for, in connection with the case."

Her face sagged a little. She must have been through hell during recent weeks. "What is that, Lieutenant?"

"I want to see your customer records."

"My records? What for?"

"Just some details that need to be checked out. Can you show me how they're kept?"

She hesitated, then said, "Yes, I can. You'll have to come into the office with me."

"Okay, fine."

After telling her niece to take over, she led Tolliver into the back room. Ben noted that the door had been patched and painted; the bullet hole Beth Whitacre had put there was no longer visible. The room had been put in order, as well; everything in here seemed neatly organized.

Ethel Serenbetz closed the door behind them. "It was a terrible thing, what happened here."

"Yes, it was."

Her voice hardened, and she looked at him accusingly. "Nobody's safe in this city. Nobody."

It was a reaction Ben had encountered before. People became furious because of a criminal act that had affected them or someone close to them, and then they took out their anger on the cops for not preventing it.

"Everybody liked Paul," she said. "There was nobody who didn't. Okay, so he had a customer complaint from time to time, but everybody in retail has those. He always handled them well."

"What about his suppliers?"

"Even less problems with them. He never dragged bills—always paid sixty days or less. People were talking about that at the funeral. He was always very fair."

"You said your records are in here?"

"Yes." She indicated the IBM sitting on a table next to the desk. "Everything's in the computer, filed by customer name."

"So each name is an account?"

"That's right." She pointed to a large gray filing cabinet standing against the wall. "Also, we keep copies of the sales slips."

"For how long?"

"Here in the office, for a year. After that, they go in dead storage. We have them going back to when the store opened."

Tolliver returned his attention to the computer. "I want you to call up a customer's account. The name is Whitacre. First name, Beth."

She looked at him. "That's the woman who—"

"Yes."

"That miserable bitch."

"Had you ever heard the name before?"

"No. I heard of her father, of course. But I didn't even know he had a daughter."

"Okay. I know this is hard for you, but it's important. Let's see if her name's in the files."

She sat down at the table and turned on the machine. When it booted up, she retrieved a directory labeled CSTMRS and keyed in the name.

The legend that appeared on the screen read: *ERROR: File not found.*

Ben felt a twinge of disappointment. "See if there's any other customer named Whitacre."

She tapped the keys. The result was the same.

"Would it be in another directory?"

"No. If they bought anything here, this is where the name would be."

"Could it have been erased by mistake?"

"No, the files are too valuable. Nobody touches this except me. And Paul did, of course. But nobody else, not even our accountant."

"Okay, another name. Patterson. First name, Kenneth."

"Who's he, and what does he have to do with this?"

"Just somebody I want to check on."

She went through the same process. There was one Patterson: a Mrs. Martin R. in Great Neck. But that was all.

"How about a Dr. Mark Rainsford?"

Again she hit the keys. There was no such name in the file.

She glanced up at him. "Anybody else?"

He thought about it. "One more. Another doctor. This one's name is Ang. That's A-N-G."

The machine gave the same negative response.

Had he spelled it correctly? Reaching into his pocket, he got out Beth's telephone book and looked under *A*. There was no Ang there, either.

What the hell, he thought. I know it was here—I saw it.

He thumbed through the pages, and there was the listing, under *D*.

The name he'd thought was Dr. Ang was actually Drang. So the person wasn't a doctor after all; Ben had simply misread the letters.

Mrs. Serenbetz was watching him expectantly. He put the book away, saying "Okay, thanks. That'll about do it."

She turned back to the computer and began storing the files.

On a sudden impulse, he said, "Hold on a second. Before you shut it down, try this one. Drang. D-R-A-N-G."

She keyed in the name. An instant later, it popped on: DRANG, DR. JONAS.

Seeing it gave Tolliver a jolt. He stepped closer, peering at the name and the data. *Dr.* Drang?

Under the name was the customer's address and telephone number, and under that was a series of symbols that apparently referred to a transaction. The entry was dated six months earlier.

It read: PR GLD CF LNX CM PS 550 + CSH PU XXXX.

Ben turned to Mrs Serenbetz. "What's it mean?"

"He bought a pair of gold cuff links," she translated. "Custommade by my husband. Paul charged five hundred fifty dollars plus tax, and the customer paid cash. They weren't sent; Dr. Drang picked them up. And there was a dispute."

"A dispute?"

"Some problem with the customer. A double *X* would mean a complaint of some kind. There are four of them there, so there must have been big trouble. But I don't know what went on, or what the problem was."

"Whatever it was, you're saying Drang paid for the cuff links and took them with him. So your husband must have gotten it straightened out."

"Probably."

"He never mentioned the incident to you, whatever it was?"

"No. I was only here part of the time, and he didn't say anything to me about it."

"You have a code for when there's a problem with a customer. That mean you have trouble often?"

"No, it's very unusual. And when it does happen, it's because the customer doesn't pay, or changes his mind or something. Ordinarily, if a customer is dissatisfied, we take the item back, no questions asked. But if the item was something custom-made, like this one, then obviously that's a problem for us."

"But couldn't this mean Dr. Drang was unhappy with the cuff links because they didn't come up to his expectations?"

She bristled. "My husband did beautiful work. When he made something custom, the piece was always special. If anything, he took too much time on things like that. I always told him he should have charged more."

"Okay, I understand. But you don't remember ever hearing anything about this order."

"No, nothing. He never mentioned it." Her eyes took on a faraway look. "Maybe he was embarrassed that this man made trouble. He was always so proud, Paul was."

Tolliver thanked her and wished her well. On the way out, he waved good-bye to Marcia Geller, who was busy with another customer.

54

As Harkness approached the store he glanced over at the cop's car, which was double-parked out front. The vehicle's windows were down, and that was good; it meant he wouldn't have to open a door.

He stepped to the show window and pretended to look at the jewelry that was on display. What he actually watched was the detective, who was standing inside, with his back to him.

Apparently Tolliver was waiting while the two women behind the counter finished serving their customers. Finally the older one spoke to him, and after a moment she led him into the back room.

What was this? Certainly the man wasn't here to buy something. So what was his interest in this place?

At that point, the name of the store caught Harkness's attention. It seemed familiar, but he couldn't quite—

Wait a minute. Wasn't this the jeweler's where the young woman had gone mad and shot a bunch of people and then herself? Of course it was. Harkness had seen stories on television about the incident. He couldn't remember the young woman's name, but he did recall hearing that her family had something to do with politics.

So what was Tolliver doing here? Had he given up on tracking Harkness and now he was on the other case? Was that what he was up to?

Possibly. But so what if he was? That didn't mean Harkness was in the clear, not by any means. Dr. Drang had told him the major danger was due to a plot much larger than a single detective. There was a conspiracy going on, and Tolliver was only one part of it.

Therefore, whatever had drawn the detective here, Harkness had to succeed in knocking him out of the picture. He had to destroy the bastard, before Tolliver destroyed *him.*

And this time, he had to do it right. No misses, no letting rage run away with him, regardless of how satisfying it would be to shoot the cop or to ram a knife into his chest.

No, what was called for now was the simple move that Dr. Drang had laid out for him. It was a fail-safe action that would solve the problem neatly and effectively. And above all, would solve it *permanently.*

There was only one aspect of it that required special care, and that was timing. Harkness had to get that exactly right. He had to wait until he was sure the detective was about to get back into the car before he delivered the package.

Otherwise, there would be another fuckup, and once again, Harkness would be responsible for it. He couldn't bear the prospect of facing Dr. Drang if that happened.

The wait was agonizing. Tolliver seemed to be inside that room in the back of the store forever. Harkness stood on one foot and then the other, aware that his body was trembling slightly—just the way it had the other times, when the stakes weren't nearly as high as they were now.

Reaching into his pocket, he took out the vial of capsules and pried off the top. Shaking out two of the gleaming yellow cylinders, he popped them into his mouth. He had nothing to wash them down with, and that made swallowing not only difficult but painful as the lumps moved slowly down his throat.

A moment later, however, he felt the rush, and then the effect of the medicine took hold. He'd already taken more of the capsules than his daily allotment, but he wasn't worried about that. The important thing was to carry this out correctly, and if the extra medicine helped him to achieve that, so be it. Anyway, Dr. Drang wouldn't know, so there'd be no harm done.

More minutes went by, and despite having taken the capsules, Harkness could barely contain himself. He held the package under his arm, continuing to feign ogling the junk in the show window. Sweat oozed from his armpits and made his sides wet. This was like the night he'd waited in front of that restaurant, only worse. Jesus, would the man never come out of there?

At last the door of the back room opened and the detective reappeared.

Harkness knew there would be only a split second in which to act. He turned on his heel and walked briskly to the curb, stepping off into the street between two of the cars that were parked parallel to the sidewalk.

Pausing, he opened the flap of the package, twisted the knob of the timer a quarter turn to the right, and closed the flap. Then he walked past the cop's Ford, and as he did, he reached in through the open window and dropped the package onto the floor behind the driver's seat.

Cars were crawling past, and Harkness skipped around them. When he reached the far side of the street, he again pretended to look into the show window of one of the stores there, but this time he watched Tolliver's reflection as the cop got into his car and pulled away.

Only then did Harkness relax. He glanced down the street at the disappearing Ford, and his mouth curved in a smile.

55

Tolliver was elated. After all the gut-grinding work and the endless frustration, the running down blind alleys until he'd been on the edge of losing his own mind, he'd finally hit one. Praise God—it was about time.

The question was, what exactly did he have? This Dr. Jonas Drang, whoever he was, had shown up first in Beth Whitacre's phone book, which meant his was a number she'd wanted to have on hand. That, in turn, meant it was possible that he'd been treating her.

But for what? Was he a shrink, the one she'd been going to? Had she been referred to him by Mark Rainsford? Was Drang the doctor who'd prescribed the antidepressant that had been in Beth's blood when she went into Serenbetz's jewelry store with a pistol in her bag?

Or was Drang some other kind of specialist? Or maybe a GP? Or was it also possible that he wasn't the one who'd prescribed the drugs at all?

Whatever, the fact that the same Drang had also been a customer of Serenbetz's was a momentous discovery. Ben didn't know how it was or what it meant, but it was. He knew that as well as he knew he was sitting here stuck in traffic. Not only did that establish a link between the doctor and Beth Whitacre; it also tied Drang to the store where she'd committed a triple murder and then suicide. And on top of being a customer there, Drang had gotten himself into a wrangle with the owner.

But what did the connections mean? Why had Beth gone to that particular store to carry out her attack? Did it somehow involve Drang's dispute with Paul Serenbetz? What was the implication of the watch cap he'd found in her handbag—did that indicate she'd intended to rob the place after all? If that was true, had Drang known of it beforehand? Had he known any of it?

Ben turned right onto Sixth Avenue and then swung east again on 48th, trying one scenario after another and rejecting all of them. As usual, the midtown traffic was maddeningly slow, and the worst part was going across town. Nevertheless, that was the direct route back to the FDR Drive, and the FDR was the fastest way down to the Criminal Justice Building.

The time of day wasn't helping any. The traffic wouldn't ease up in this part of Manhattan until well after midnight. First, you had the people who commuted by car and who now were on their way home. Then there were the other drivers who were coming in for a night on the town. They'd jam up the city for hours, and from around eleven on they too would be trying to leave. Adding to the snarl would be the usual taxis and delivery trucks. The only time the streets would be truly deserted was much later, toward dawn.

Out of habit, he turned on the radio and listened to the chatter of police dispatchers and the responses from patrol cars. It had been years since he'd ridden in a blue-and-white himself, and that was one aspect of the job he didn't miss: long stretches of boredom, interspersed with sudden spurts of adrenaline.

Turning down the volume, he thought again about what his next move should be. The first thing he'd do would be to confront this Dr. Drang. And if Drang refused to open up, Tolliver just might have enough to convince a magistrate there was good reason to look into the doctor's practice.

Somehow, he had to get a prosecutor to help. If they could persuade a judge to sign an order, Ben could get into the doctor's records, and that could provide the break he'd been hoping for.

At long last, he made the southbound entrance to the FDR. When he pulled into the stream of vehicles, he opened the Ford up, whizzing past the UN exit and weaving in and out of the lanes. The traffic along here was heavy as well, but at least it was moving fast.

He had no warning for what happened next.

There was a loud *whump* just behind him and the front seat of the Ford was lifted upward, slamming Tolliver's head against the ceiling. At the same instant, he was enveloped by intense heat, and the interior of the car filled with thick smoke.

His eyes streaming tears, he looked back and saw that the rear of the vehicle was an inferno, burning with brilliant white flames. Instinctively, he opened the door and pulled himself halfway out of the car, his left hand holding the door as he continued to steer with his right.

On either side of him, cars were blowing their horns and maneuvering to get past the stricken Ford. Tolliver eased off the accelerator and the vehicle directly in back of him rammed into his rear end, shoving the Taurus forward and nearly jolting him out of the car altogether.

The fire was throwing off clouds of caustic smoke. Choking and gagging, he fought to control the blazing Ford. Exposed areas of his skin were blistering, and sparks and flaming bits of debris were flying out the open door. Only the fresh air rushing past enabled him to breathe at all. Half-blind, he weaved from side to side, the Taurus hurtling along like a flaming rocket.

There was no turnoff along the stretch he was on now, and no shoulder where he could pull off. If he tried it with the traffic roaring by, it was likely other cars would smash into him and cause a chain-reaction pileup. But if he didn't do something in a hurry, he'd be burned to ashes.

By now, the interior of the Ford was a ball of fire. Jumping was out of the question; the on-rushing vehicles would grind him into the pavement.

He held on for a few more seconds, and then just ahead he made out the 34th Street exit. If he could get off there, he could pull to a stop. He flipped the wheel and the Ford skidded to the right, into the exit lane leading off the FDR. Hanging on to the open door, he flew down the lane and slammed on the brakes.

To his horror he saw a figure appear in front of him. During the split second he could make it out, the figure seemed to be that of a man, some poor bastard of a pedestrian.

Tolliver pumped the brakes, but he was going too fast. The flaming car careened sideways and turned over.

56

The scene on television was surrealistic. Firemen had set up flares in the street, spots of red incandescence that sparked and sputtered at ground level, warning traffic away. The crews directed arching jets from hoses that looked like huge snakes uncoiling from the trucks. On the perimeter, cops were holding back a crowd of gawkers, while overhead an NYPD helicopter hovered, its rotors flailing the air.

But the object of all this attention was what fascinated Drang. It was the molten remains of what had once been a car. Although you wouldn't know what it had been to look at it now. In fact, the only way you could tell it was a car was because the TV reporter was excitedly informing viewers of the fact.

The reporter was a nuisance, Drang thought. He wished the fool would get out of the way so that the wreck would be more visible.

The thing was beautiful. So intense had the heat become that the car had actually liquified. Metal would do that, of course, given sufficiently high temperatures. Drang estimated that at its peak, the fire must have reached something better than 3,000°F. One of the wonders of white phosphorus, especially when it was helped along with generous amounts of gasoline from the car's fuel tank.

Now what was left was a smoking, misshapen blob that reminded him of a painting by Salvador Dali. Nothing could have lived through that. Nothing. And in fact, nothing had, according to what the reporter was babbling. The driver had burned to death, the reporter said. He pointed to where attendants were loading a body bag into a waiting ambulance.

They hadn't needed much of a bag, Drang thought. An envelope would have served just as well. In fact, this had been rather an efficient way to get rid of the body. Saved the cost of cremation. He smiled, thinking about that.

In all, it was a satisfying resolution of the problem. Harkness had sounded downright giddy when he'd telephoned afterward, enraptured that he'd accomplished his task, and accomplished it well. Drang had found it necessary to calm him, speaking soothingly, telling the young man to relax, now that the detective was out of the way at last. "He won't trouble you further," Drang had said.

"But what about the others?" Harkness had asked then. "Won't they come after me, too? How can I tell who they are? Are they following me now?"

"No, they're not," Drang assured him. "And don't worry, we'll handle them just as easily, when the time comes. You've proved that you can take on a tough job under pressure and carry it out brilliantly. You should be proud of yourself."

"I am," Harkness said. "The minute I saw him come out of that jewelry store, I knew I had him."

Drang froze. "Jewelry store? What jewelry store?"

"The one where the woman shot those people and then killed herself," Harkness said. "I don't know what Tolliver was doing there, but that's where he went."

At that point, it had been Drang who'd needed calming. With an effort, he'd told Harkness to get some rest, that he'd see him tomorrow.

The next hour or so had been agony, with Drang up here in the study, switching channels as if he himself was deranged, shuttling from one news program to another, his heart in his mouth.

And then had come this marvelous report on the fire just off the FDR Drive, where the car had turned into a flaming hearse.

How satisfying. How thrilling. And for Drang, how fortunate. If the detective had gotten as far as that store, God only knew where his poking about might have taken him next.

But now such speculation was academic. Harkness had delivered the package, and the package had done its work. Again Drang's brilliance had prevailed, his amazing ability to think through a problem and come up with the perfect solution.

The reporter finished his piece, and a commercial came on. What a shame, Drang thought. The scene of the fire had made such a lovely picture. He turned off the TV and poured himself another dollop of cognac.

Crossing his legs as he relaxed in the leather chair, he thought about what was to come next. Harkness had indeed carried out his task properly, although Drang had taken quite a chance in assigning it to him, especially after the way Harkness had butchered the first attempt.

But today he'd succeeded, and results were what counted. Now would come the real test. What Harkness was to do next would be the crowning achievement of the young man's not terribly distinguished life. And that would be one he absolutely could not botch. It was the one Drang had created him for. Or re-created him, as it were. The final reckoning with the esteemed Dr. Arthur McKenzie.

At the mere thought of McKenzie's smug face, its features twisted in the characteristic snotty smile, Drang felt a bright flash of anger. Even after all these years, his hatred had not abated. If anything, it was stronger than ever.

But now the day of retribution would soon be here. Could Harkness carry out the assignment properly? Could he follow orders one more time, and follow them precisely as instructed? He'd simply have to.

And yet Drang wasn't as confident as he'd like to be. If only Harkness wasn't so unpredictable. If only he was one hundred percent reliable, instead of so often flighty and unstable. If only he was more like Flo Dallure, who had turned out perfectly.

But it was too late now even to consider a change in plans. For better or for worse, Harkness was what he had, and what he must go with. He would try one more adjustment of the drugs he was administering, but he couldn't be sure of the effect that would have, either. He'd simply have to hope for the best. And to a scientist of Drang's skills, hoping was a poor substitute for knowing precisely how a project would conclude.

Stop worrying, he told himself. You're as bad as the patient. It will go just as you want it to, so long as Harkness is prepared properly. He'll do as instructed, and that will put an end not just to one scourge but to two.

Drang swallowed more brandy, envisioning it.

57

You were lucky," Logan said.

Tolliver was in a ward at Bellevue, propped up in bed. The skin was seared on the back of his neck and across his shoulders and his right hand and his hair had been singed. Bandages covered his elbows and knees and he had a fair-sized mouse under his right eye. There were purple bruises on his butt and one hip had been scraped raw. It hurt to flex his joints.

Ben squinted at his visitor. "If I was lucky, it wouldn't have happened."

"Bomb squad said it was a powerful incendiary device."

"No shit."

"You remember any of it?"

"I remember the fire and trying to get the car off the FDR, and that's about it."

"But not the guy in the street?"

"What guy in the— Oh Christ." It came flooding back into his consciousness then, a mental picture of the man who'd been crossing in front of the car, just as it began its long, teetering skid.

"Yeah," Ben said. "I remember. What happened to him?"

"The car went over right on top of him. Fried him."

"Poor bastard. Who was he?"

"Not identified. A bus driver saw it happen, went to the cops afterward. He said the guy looked to him like a derelict, one of the homeless who hang out in St. Vartan Park. No way to be sure, though. Wasn't enough left of him to bury."

Tolliver exhaled, envisioning it.

"They said the car melted," Logan went on. "It burned and the gas tank blew and then all that was left was a puddle of metal. Must have been one hell of a blaze."

"Yeah, I'm sure it was."

"They said usually a car fire burns out everything but leaves a shell and the engine block. In this one, the whole thing just kind of liquified. Somebody wanted you dead real bad."

"I guess they did."

"You got any idea who it was?"

Ben shrugged, and even that hurt. "Offhand, no. But it could've been plenty of people. You know how it is. In this business, you make a lot of friends."

"What about how they got it in your car?"

"No idea of that, either," Tolliver said. "It was just there. It went off and there were flames, and then I was trying to get out while the car was burning. When I woke up, I was here."

"Maybe you'll come up with something . . . when you're feeling better."

"I doubt it, but I'll try." He hadn't reported the earlier attempt, when someone had tried to blow him away with poisoned bullets. Not filing on that had been a breach of NYPD regulations, but he hadn't wanted the hassle. That would only have given Galupo another reason to come down on him. Might even have resulted in his drawing restricted duty.

But there would be no way to duck this one, not after cops and firemen had swarmed over the scene. Logan had said TV reporters had covered it as well. That meant everybody in New York would have been made aware of it. Restriction was a sure thing, this time.

"Media find out it was my car?" Ben asked.

"No. They never knew you were at the scene. A fireman found you wandering around, half out of it. He got the medics to bring you over here. Least you picked a good spot. Half a block from Bellevue."

"Uh-huh."

"You took a real beating—doctors say you left a lot of skin on the road. On the other hand, you could have burned up with the car."

"I realize that. But listen, I think I got a break in the Whitacre case."

Logan leaned forward. "Like what?"

Tolliver described his trip to the property clerk and the visit to the Serenbetz jewelry shop. He recounted what the computer records had disclosed.

The captain listened intently, saying nothing until Ben finished. Then he said, "So there was a connection between the store and this Dr. Drang?"

"Apparently. I'll go see him as soon as I get out of here."

"Good. We need some action. The DA is pissed because he hasn't heard from you, and he wants to know why he hasn't been kept up-to-date."

"Why does he think? If I'd had anything before this, I sure wouldn't have let it sit."

"Yeah, but those homicides made everybody nervous as hell. The papers and TV were screaming about people getting killed on the street for no reason. You can't blame Oppenheimer."

"Okay, I'm going as fast as I can. Or I was, anyway."

"Take it easy, Lieutenant. I'll talk to him. I'll also talk to Galupo, tell him what you told me. See if I can't avoid having you restricted. Meantime, get some rest. Okay?"

"No, it's not okay."

"What?"

"Look, Cap. You want to do something for me?"

"Sure. What is it?"

"Bring me my clothes, so I can get out of here."

"Hey, you don't want to take chances. You need to give yourself time to heal. You could've been killed, either from the fire or from jumping out of that car."

"Thought you just said we needed action on the case."

"Yeah, well. A day or two won't make any difference."

"Maybe it won't. But I'm not staying here."

"Then at least take a little time off."

"I might do that." Tolliver swung his legs over the side of the bed. He had on one of the hospital's shorty nightgowns, and he felt ridiculous wearing it. He also felt sharp pains throughout his body when he moved, but he was damned if he'd let Logan see that.

"You sure you're all right?"

"Just get me the clothes, will you, Captain?"

"I . . . yeah. Be right back."

58

"What the hell is this?" Ben asked. He was again propped up in bed, but this time in his own apartment.

"Chicken soup," Shelley said.

"You're kidding."

"No, I'm not kidding. It's good for you. It'll help you regain your strength."

"I would prefer bourbon, if you don't mind. There's a bottle in the kitchen."

"Maybe tomorrow. Open wide." She lifted a steaming spoonful from the bowl she was holding and put it into his mouth.

The stuff was hot, but he had to admit it tasted good. And come to think of it, he hadn't had anything to eat since the slop they'd fed him at Bellevue. No wonder he was hungry.

Shelley went on ladling soup into him. "You scared the hell out of me, you know that?"

"I wasn't exactly calm myself."

"You gonna tell me what happened?"

"Car caught fire."

"God, I know that much. Why did it?"

"Overheated, I guess."

"Ben, will you be serious? You could have been killed."

"That so?"

"When I saw the tape of the scene, I got sick. It was awful. I don't know how you survived, if you want to know the truth."

"How'd you find out it was me?"

"One of our reporters picked it up from a police report. He wanted to put it on the air, but our news editor turned it down. You know why?"

Tolliver's mouth was full of soup. He shook his head.

"He said you were yesterday's news."

Ben swallowed the mouthful and looked at her. "What are you trying to tell me, I'm over the hill?"

"I didn't say that, did I?"

"It's a good thing."

"Why, you gonna arrest me?"

"No, I had something else in mind."

"Maybe I spoke too soon. I wouldn't want to miss anything."

"Too late. You had your chance."

"Then maybe it's true after all."

"What is?"

"That you're over the hill."

"Let me ask you something, okay?"

"Sure, go ahead."

"What've you got on under that dress?"

"Why, you want to see?"

"It crossed my mind."

She grinned and put the bowl down on the bedside table. Then she stood up and whipped the dress over her head.

As Ben had suspected, what she had on under it was nothing. He studied her body, admiring the full pink-tipped breasts, the well-turned legs, and the blond tuft where they joined her body. And he felt himself respond rapidly. "You planned this, didn't you?"

The grin stayed in place. "It crossed my mind."

"Come here."

He threw off the covers, which revealed him to be just as naked as she was. Now it was her turn to look. "Wow."

"Still think I'm over the hill?"

"More like over the rainbow. I'm impressed."

"You should be."

"Don't go away." She tugged the pillows from behind him and tossed them onto the floor.

Slowly and carefully, he eased himself down flat on the bed.

She was watching him. "Hurts, huh?"

"I hadn't noticed."

"Not much. So just don't move."

"Maybe just a little?"

"Maybe. We'll see how it goes." She got onto the bed and straddled him. Then, reaching down, she guided him into her.

"Ahhh!" she exclaimed. "Lovely."

"Got my strength back, huh?"

"Chicken soup. Works every time."

59

The house was handsome, an imposing five-story structure with a stone facade and black shutters. Its steep roof was tiled with gray slate, and there was a tall chimney at each end. The buildings that abutted the place were equally impressive.

Tolliver was parked across the street, in the green Lincoln he'd borrowed from the NYPD's Motor Transport Unit. The car was a flashy sedan that had been seized in a drug raid, but he was grateful that they'd let him use it.

Looking over at the house, he estimated it was probably worth around $5 million, maybe more—especially in light of its location here in the East 80s. As he sat there, a good-looking blond woman walked out the front entrance, descended the steps, and headed west toward Park Avenue.

Ben got out of the Lincoln and crossed the street, moving slowly. The cuts and bruises made it hard for him to walk, and his joints were still stiff. Also the cloth of his shirt felt like sandpaper on the burns.

He went up the steps to the front door, holding on to the handrail.

The door was painted black and mounted with heavy brass fixtures. A small plaque beside it read J. DRANG, M.D., PH.D.

He pressed the button and waited. Several moments passed, and then the speaker came to life. A heavily accented female voice said, "Who is it?"

"Police," he replied.

"What do you want?"

As if he might be selling raffle tickets. But he kept his patience. "I'm here on official business. Open the door, please."

More moments went by, and then he heard the sound of a lock being undone. The heavy door swung open, and a stocky dark-haired woman peered out at him. She had on a white nurse's uniform with a brown sweater over it, and the corners of her mouth were turned down disapprovingly. "Yes, what is it?"

He displayed his shield and ID, and she glanced at them briefly.

"I want to see Dr. Drang," Ben said.

"Doctor's appointments are finished for the day." As far as she was concerned, that put an end to it. She began closing the door.

Tolliver raised his hand. "Just a minute. I'm conducting a homicide investigation, and it's important that I speak with the doctor. Now go tell him I'm here."

She added a frown to her expression of disapproval. "I'll ask if he can see you."

The door closed in his face.

It was interesting, he thought. This was the type of neighborhood whose residents yelled the loudest about the need for more and better police protection. But until they were in an emergency situation themselves, a cop was a subspecies about on a par with a garbage collector. Necessary, but you wouldn't want to have one in your house.

He was about to hit the button again when the nurse opened the door once more. Her expression hadn't improved any, however. "Doctor will see you. Come this way."

He followed her into a foyer with abstract oil paintings hanging on the walls, then into a small waiting room with a sofa and two chairs, along with a coffee table and a rack of magazines. A potted ficus tree stood in one corner.

"Doctor will be with you shortly," she said, and left him alone in the room.

The sound of music was coming from somewhere in here— strings, rendering one of the vapid melodies Muzak pumped into such places. He remembered Alan Stein once telling him that shrinks often used the sound as a cover, so that people in the waiting room couldn't make out anything that was being said between patient and doctor in the office.

The door opened again, and a man stepped into the room. When he saw Tolliver, he stopped abruptly. His jaw dropped and his eyes popped.

Ben thought, why does this guy seem so surprised to see me? Or is he just annoyed at having a cop come here?

But the man recovered quickly as Tolliver looked him over. He was solidly built, and there was an air of physical power about him. His thick black hair was brushed back from well-proportioned features, and above a prominent nose, his eyes were dark and piercing. Although it was a warm spring day, he was wearing a black suit and a black tie that would have been appropriate on a funeral director.

"Hello, Officer," he said. "I'm Dr. Drang."

His voice was deep, with a trace of an accent that was different from the woman's, but Tolliver couldn't place this one, either. It might have been German, or Viennese perhaps. Then again, it might have been bullshit. Drang didn't ask his visitor to sit down, or did he offer to take him into his office.

Ben flashed his shield once more. "I'm Lieutenant Tolliver. There are some questions I want to ask you, Doctor."

"You said to my nurse that this was a homicide investigation?"

"That's correct. Involving a former patient of yours. Her name was Beth Whitacre."

The dark eyes narrowed. "Ah, of course. Miss Whitacre. A great tragedy."

"You were treating her, correct?"

"I had seen her a few times."

"And it was Dr. Rainsford who referred her to you. That's also cor- rect, isn't it?"

"So?"

"Why didn't you come forward after her death?"

"I didn't want to add to the family's anguish. And anyway, there was nothing more that could be done for her."

"I'd like to discuss that further. Is there somewhere we can talk?"

"What is there to say?"

So the shrink was trying to stiff him. Ben had anticipated that. "This is strictly routine; I'm just finishing my report. But your name came up, in an interesting way."

He went for it, as Tolliver had hoped. "I suppose we could talk for a moment. Come along." He turned and went through a door, Ben following him.

This appeared to be a sitting room, larger but no less blandly furnished than the one they'd just left. The decor was prosaic to the point of dullness, all flat, insipid colors and unremarkable pieces of furniture. Abstract paintings were hanging in here, as well.

The one distinctive feature was a leather couch on the far side of the room, which suggested that this was where Drang treated his patients. A pair of chairs and a wooden cabinet stood near the couch, and there were bookcases beyond it.

The doctor indicated one of the chairs, and Ben sat. Drang took the one opposite, and they looked at each other. Like a pair of pit bulls, Tolliver thought, each sizing up the opponent.

"You said my name was mentioned?" Drang asked.

"Yes, it was," Ben said. "I spoke to several of Miss Whitacre's family and friends."

"And what did they tell you?"

"I learned that you'd been treating her for a period of several months before she died."

That was little more than a shot in the dark. There was no change, however, in the expression on the carefully composed features. Only the eyes seemed alive in Drang's face. "I was greatly saddened," he said, "by her death."

"Did she give you any advance warning?"

"Of what she was going to do?"

"Yes. Did you know she was capable of violence?"

"Lieutenant, I'm sure you realize that I'm not at liberty to reveal details of my treatment of Miss Whitacre. Not to you or to anyone else. Not only would it be unethical for me even to consider it, but there are rules governing my professional conduct that would prevent me from doing so."

"I understand what you're saying, Doctor. But since Miss Whitacre is dead, and since she also killed three other people before killing herself, I thought you'd be willing to shed some light on what happened."

"Why is that anyone's business now?"

Ben struggled to keep his temper in check. "Look, I'm not asking you to do anything unethical. I'm hoping you'll give us information that would prevent anything like this from happening again."

"I see. But that's hardly a practical idea, if you'll think about it. How could I, or any other therapist, for that matter, treat a patient and at the same time keep the police informed? Would you really expect that of a responsible psychiatrist?"

This is nothing but fencing, Ben thought. In fact, not even that. More like dancing around the mulberry bush. It was hard to sit here and listen to this guy toy with him.

Nevertheless, he persisted. "I would expect you to help us learn why she did it, Doctor."

"And I've explained to you my problem with that. I will tell you this much, however. I was totally amazed when I learned what had happened. Miss Whitacre was a quiet, gentle person, and her problems did not appear to be serious."

"While you were treating her, could there have been signs you missed?"

"I doubt that very much."

"Are you sure?"

"Quite sure, Lieutenant. What laymen don't understand is that there are sometimes external factors impacting on a patient's emotional health that are quite unpredictable."

"What does that mean? Are you saying something unexpected might have happened to her? Something that caused her to crack up?"

"It's not feasible to determine that with the information now available to me. It is a possibility, although I must impress on you that that's all it is. I wouldn't want you to draw inferences from anything I tell you and then assume they apply to her."

"You said her problems didn't appear to be serious."

"No, they didn't."

"Is that why you prescribed an antidepressant?"

That caught him off guard. Almost no reaction was visible on the doctor's face, but his eyes shifted a fraction and Ben caught it.

Drang cleared his throat. "I must tell you, Lieutenant, I find your methods quite distasteful. It should be obvious to you that I've been attempting to help you without overstepping the bounds of proper professional conduct. But if you're going to try to trick me into talking about the procedures I followed with Miss Whitacre, I'll have to end our discussion. Is that clear?"

"Quite clear, Doctor. But I'm not here to trick you into anything. I asked a simple, direct question. A couple of them, in fact. So let me ask again. Why did she go on a shooting rampage after you'd treated her for some time and when she'd given you no indication she was capable of doing such a thing? Or if you *did* know she might commit an act of violence, why did you give her medicine, instead of putting her in a hospital?"

The deep voice took on a hard edge. "I think I've allowed this to go on quite long enough. The answer to your first question is that no one knows. As to the second, it's outrageous of you to question my treatment of a patient, especially when antidepressants are in daily use by millions of people and are no more harmful than aspirin."

"But why would you—"

Drang stood up. The dark eyes were snapping now. "Good day, Lieutenant. If you'll follow me, please, I'll show you out."

"Sure. But just one more question. The store where Miss Whitacre went berserk was Serenbetz Jewelers. You've done business in the same store, haven't you? You were a customer there, right?"

"I—that is, it's possible, but I don't recall. I don't remember every store I shop in. This way, Lieutenant."

Tolliver trailed him back through the waiting room and to the front entrance, and then left the building.

After hearing the door being slammed and bolted behind him, Ben crossed the street and threaded his way through the slow-moving traffic to the Lincoln. He climbed into the car and sat there for a moment, looking back at the house.

There were a number of things he'd picked up, despite Drang's protests.

First, the doctor had tried to find out what the police knew and what they didn't.

Second, Drang had deliberately downplayed the seriousness of Beth Whitacre's emotional disturbances.

Third, he was upset to hear the cops knew he'd prescribed an antidepressant.

And lastly, he'd been shocked that Ben had found out he'd been a customer of Serenbetz's. Then he'd tried to sweep that aside, as well.

Tolliver started the engine and pulled away. There was one other thing he'd noticed. Toward the end, when the shrink had gotten pissed off, his accent had disappeared.

60

Drang slammed the door and shoved the dead bolt home. His face felt hot and his hands were shaking. He told Anna to cancel his remaining appointments and went down into his laboratory, where he paced back and forth, wrestling with this stunning new problem.

He'd been surprised when Anna said that a police officer was demanding to speak with him. But when he saw Tolliver, he was thunderstruck. It was like seeing a ghost.

How could the cop still be alive? Drang had been sure the man was dead; he'd seen the pictures of the wreck on television, had heard the reporter say that the driver had been killed. The scene had been an inferno; no one could have lived through such a fire.

Yet suddenly, here Tolliver was, appearing at the house with no warning. Somehow, obviously, the man had escaped the blaze. Then whose body was it that had been picked up at the site? Had someone else been in the car?

It didn't matter, Drang told himself. The cop was alive, and he'd come here, and he'd revealed that he knew far more than Drang would have imagined.

But how had Tolliver traced him? Drang didn't believe for a minute that it was by talking to Beth Whitacre's family and friends. He must have stumbled across Drang's name somewhere in his investigation. Then he'd tried to bluff the doctor into revealing further information.

At first, Drang had been tempted not to speak to him at all, but that wouldn't have been wise. At least he'd handled the situation well, divulging nothing while finding out what the detective had learned and what he hadn't.

But that had also been an unpleasant surprise. Tolliver had discovered that Drang had been a patron of the Serenbetz store. He must have gone through customer records and found that out.

But hold on, Drang thought. What did it prove? So he'd once shopped there, long before the Whitacre incident. That didn't mean a thing.

More troubling had been the cop learning that Whitacre was on antidepressants. How had he gleaned that?

Probably the pathologist who performed the autopsy had ordered tests done on her blood. And so what if he had? There was no way to tie the drugs to the doctor who had supplied them, no matter what Tolliver might have suspected.

In fact, now that Drang thought about it objectively, the detective's suspicion was laughable. Doctor-patient confidentiality was a closely guarded institution in every state in the country, a bastion unassailable by the police, the media, or any other group of busybodies. It was protected by no less an authority than the Supreme Court.

And anyway, when it came right down to it, he'd had no trouble coping with the detective. The bottom line was that Tolliver had no idea what had caused Whitacre to do what she did. Nor would he ever know. Neither he nor anyone else.

Unless Drang chose to reveal the truth, of course. Which he might do someday, after he'd struck the bonanza that would soon be his. When you had enough money, you could do anything you pleased. Some of the greatest pirates on earth had proven that.

Then what Drang revealed about his early struggles would be regarded merely as interesting. They'd be thought of as the kind of difficulties overcome by every one of the great men who had lighted the way toward greater understanding of the human mind and its workings.

Men like Josef Breuer, the brilliant Austrian physician who devised the cathartic method of therapy and whose theory of hysteria became the basis of Freud's approach to psychoanalysis. Or Richard von Krafft-Ebing, the German psychiatrist who was the first authority on deviant sexual behavior and its medicolegal aspects. Or Alfred Adler, discoverer of how the need for self-assertion could cause an inferiority complex.

All of them had been forced to overcome early adversity. They'd had to beat back the doubters, whose attacks were fueled by jealousy and the inability to see beyond the status quo. People were always afraid of innovation, because new ideas would destroy their foolish sense of security. Arthur McKenzie was living proof of the rule.

But all that aside, as long as the detective was alive, the threat he posed was simply unacceptable. The man was like a virus that you stamped out in one place, only to see him pop up in another. Moreover, Drang's plans were at a critical stage; he couldn't allow them to be disrupted now—not when he was at last about to see everything come to final fruition.

Flo Dallure, for example, was unquestionably his best subject ever. Whatever he asked of her, she delivered precisely. It was as if he'd taken up residence in her brain, touching buttons that caused her to carry out his orders exactly as he wished.

And what a pleasure she was to work with. In his mind's eye, he saw her full, ripe mouth, her lush body. Just thinking of her could cause him to produce an erection, even though it had been only little more than an hour since he'd last been with her on the couch.

So how to cope with Tolliver? How to eliminate the problem, once and for all? That was what he had to concentrate on now.

Harkness wouldn't be given another chance; Drang couldn't risk having him repeat his failures. Although the young man's reaction to the drugs was often what the doctor wanted, there were other times when he was like a caged animal, quite unpredictable. The unfocused anxiety, the persecutorial delusions—all were symptoms of acute paranoia, and they were to be expected. Nevertheless, Drang was disappointed that he hadn't been able to exert more effective controls.

But whether he'd succeeded or not, Drang had something more important for Harkness to do than to waste him on yet another attack on the detective.

No, for resolution of the Tolliver problem, Drang had a better idea. The earlier attempts had failed; therefore going after him was clearly not going to work.

Instead, Drang would devise a trap. Which would be an ingenious solution, the doctor thought, and quite fitting. That way, the detective would self-destruct.

Meantime, the moment of truth was at hand. The American Psychiatric Association convention was in full swing, and the banquet was scheduled for tomorrow night.

Opening the drawer in his lab table, Drang got out the yellowing clip from the *Los Angeles Times* and studied the face of Arthur McKenzie in the photograph. Even after all these years, seeing it caused acid bile to rise from his stomach, burning its way into his throat.

Now at last, his patient planning would pay off, and revenge would soon be his. Drang could hardly wait.

61

Norman Krantz was the assistant district attorney Tolliver had been working with on the Rafella case, before being pulled off to go on Whitacre. One of DA Henry Oppenheimer's top prosecutors, Krantz had built an outstanding record in the Rackets Bureau, winning an impressive string of convictions.

When Ben limped into the ADA's office, Krantz was on the phone. He was in shirtsleeves, his pants held up by a pair of gaudy red suspenders. His collar was open, his tie askew. He was mopping his high forehead with a handkerchief as he barked into the instrument.

Tolliver eased himself into a visitor's chair. This was one of the more luxurious offices in the bureau. The desk and chairs were all standard-issue gray metal, bolted to the floor, and the cramped space was crowded with filing cabinets and bookcases and a table holding a PC. Nevertheless, the room boasted two windows, and that made it upscale, especially when you compared it with some of the other rabbit warrens along here.

The windows also indicated that Krantz was a senior ADA. He'd held his job for nearly a dozen years, more than twice as long as the average span for a prosecutor. He was tireless, street-smart, and dedicated to the proposition that members of the mob should do as much time as it was possible to put them away for. All of which made him Oppenheimer's kind of attorney.

Krantz hung up and glanced appraisingly at his visitor. "How you feeling?"

"Wonderful."

"I'll bet. I hear we almost lost you."

"Pay no attention to rumors."

"You have any idea—"

"No."

"Department must've assigned investigators, right?"

"Yeah, from the bomb squad."

"What'd you tell them?"

"That I didn't know what that device was, or how it got in the car. I was going down the FDR, and all of a sudden it went off."

"I saw the pictures on TV of what it looked like afterward. Must've been a bitch."

"I've had better times."

"Bomb guys making any progress?"

"You'd have to ask them. I told them all I could, which wasn't much."

"You think somebody was trying to get back at you because of a case you worked on?"

"Probably. But anyhow, I'm fine."

"Yeah, you look it. Now what about Whitacre—you finished with that?"

"Not yet."

"What do you mean, 'not yet'? You got your victims; you got your perpetrator. The lady went nuts and killed those people and then herself. You even have a motive—she was crazy. What more do you want?"

"I don't know, but I'm working on it. I'm told the boss would like to have a better idea as to why she did it."

Krantz's tone changed. "Mr. Oppenheimer?"

"That's different, huh?"

"I'm sure he has his reasons."

"Yeah, and we both know what they are. Anyway, I'm sticking with it until I come up with something solid."

The ADA sighed. "We could use twice the investigators we've got on Rafella."

"How're you doing with it, by the way?"

"At the moment, not great. We had a witness, but she disappeared."

"Who was that?"

"A dancer named Amanda Mullens. She was Augie Rafella's girl-friend."

"Figures. Testifying against him hasn't been good for people's health."

"Anyway, it's like I told you—we need manpower. Which is why I want you back."

"I'll be back. Whenever I get what I'm after. I thought maybe you could help."

"Me? How?"

"I need a court order for some records."

"Jesus, I don't have enough trouble of my own?"

"Just hear me out, will you?"

The ADA folded his arms resignedly. "Okay, okay. Shoot."

Tolliver gave him a rundown of what he'd been doing on the Whitacre case, including his visit to Dr. Jonas Drang and his suspicions that Drang had been deliberately misleading him. He told Krantz about the postmortem revealing that Whitacre had been heavily dosed with an unidentified antidepressant at the time of the killings, and how he didn't believe her being medicated with such a drug squared with her psychotic actions.

He also told the ADA about finding the knitted watch cap in Beth

Whitacre's handbag, and about his return to Serenbetz's jewelry shop, where he'd discovered that Drang had been a disgruntled customer of the store.

When Ben finished, the prosecutor wiped his face once more and stuffed the handkerchief into his pocket. "You know what it sounds like to me?"

"Tell me."

"Like you've got a large pile of zero. You think some kind of mal-practice charge could be brought against this doctor? Forget it."

"Like hell I will—I want those records. All I'm asking you to do is figure out how to get a judge to issue a warrant."

"Is that all? Listen to me, Lieutenant. You don't have one shred of evidence. So what if the shrink did have her taking an antidepressant? Christ, it seems like half the people in New York are on Prozac, or Zoloft or something. And eventually the other half will be. Besides, couldn't she have been just a little depressed, up until the time she went off her rocker? That's happened, you know. How can you blame the shrink?"

"I'll tell you when I get the records."

Krantz ignored that. "And this thing with the jeweler's. You say the shrink was a customer of the same store some time back, and he got into a hassle over a five-hundred-fifty-dollar pair of cuff links? What does that prove? It's a coincidence, and that's all it is."

"How do you know?"

"I don't. What I'm telling you is, that's how it would be seen in the eyes of the law. When it comes to real evidence, you don't have any. So you write up an affidavit based on nothing but a hunch, and I'm sup-posed to get a judge to sign an order? Not a chance."

"Thanks. Any other friendly suggestions?"

Krantz got out the handkerchief again. "How much do you know about this shrink?"

"Not a lot. I called the Office of Professional Medical Conduct and they said there were no complaints against him. I also checked with them earlier on the guy who referred Whitacre to him. There were none against him, either."

"But they told you there were no problems with Dr. Drang? Noth-ing on him in the past?"

"He was never disciplined, no."

"Huh. Did I say the case looks like nothing? Now it looks like less than that. What you have to realize is that more than any other professional group, psychiatrists have ways of protecting themselves."

"You're telling *me* that?"

"Even when a patient signs a complaint against one of them, it's hard to make it stick. Unfortunately, Miss Whitacre is not here to sign a complaint."

"Then you won't help me."

Krantz looked at him. "The only way anybody can help is to get you off this thing before it drives you nuts, too."

"We've already discussed that. You want to tell it to Oppenheimer?"

The ADA sidestepped the question. "He knows we need investigators on Rafella—especially people with your experience."

"Thanks, counselor. I appreciate your advice."

"You don't have to get sarcastic. I really am trying to help you."

Ben got up from his chair. "Then come up with an idea. When you've got one, let me know." He left the office, knowing that behind him, Norman Krantz would be shaking his head.

62

On Park Avenue, the evening air was balmy. Outside the Waldorf, red-uniformed doormen were busy greeting guests as they stepped from taxis and limousines in front of the stately old hotel. Bellmen were collecting luggage, and another red-coated man was standing in the street, blowing a whistle, signaling cabs to move up as other guests waited to depart.

The scene was typical; the Waldorf had been the leader among luxury hotels in New York for more than a century, first in its original location, where the Empire State Building now stood, and for the past sixty years, here at its present address.

Tonight many of the arrivals were wearing formal attire, the men in tuxedos, the women in chic dresses. They walked on a wide swath of red carpet as they crossed the sidewalk and went up the steps to the main entrance, going on into the marble-columned lobby. As always, there was an air of festivity in the public areas.

Philip Harkness also arrived by cab. He paid the driver and mingled with the crowd, feeling slightly awkward in the tux he'd rented for the occasion; this was the first time in his life he'd worn one. In the lobby, he looked at the directory for the location of the dinner he would attend and then stepped to the bank of elevators.

There was always at least one major business or institutional meeting taking place here, and sometimes several. This was the last night of the annual convention of the American Psychiatric Association, and the banquet would feature speeches by a number of the organization's most esteemed members. In the lobby and then in the elevator car, Harkness was aware that he was much younger than most of the other people whose formal dress identified them as fellow attendees.

The room in which the dinner was to be held was the Starlight Roof, on the eighteenth floor. An attendant was standing at the door. Harkness presented the engraved invitation that had been given him by Dr. Drang, and then he moved inside.

There were dozens of tables in here, each covered in crisp white napery and decorated with a vase of spring flowers. At one end of the room was a raised dais where the notables and the featured speakers would sit. Light from huge crystal chandeliers sparkled on the china and silver.

Only a few guests were at the tables; most of the others were standing in the adjoining Palm Room, where cocktails were being served. There was a bar at either end of that area, with crowds around each of them. Harkness joined the people at the bar on the left, blending in among them as he waited to order a drink.

It was exciting to be here, he thought. He was on a mission of enormous importance and he was confident he wouldn't fail. In fact, failure was impossible; his life depended on it, just as it had when he'd finally succeeded in destroying that shithead of a detective.

He'd done a fine job with that. The man had burned to death, and afterward Dr. Drang had praised him at length. He was proud of his success.

When his turn came, he asked for a scotch and soda. The white-jacketed bartender mixed the drink and served it to him, and Harkness took the glass and moved away. Standing by himself at the side of the room, he sipped the whiskey and looked out over the gathering.

In all this vast horde of people, he didn't know a single soul. Nor did any of them know him. Being aware of that was thrilling, as well. It made him invisible. Philip Harkness, the invisible man.

The truth was that there was only one person here he wanted to know, and then only to identify him. That would be easy; thanks to Dr. Drang, his features had been engraved on Philip's memory as if cast in bronze. Moreover, the man had no more idea of who Harkness was than did any of the others. And he never would. Which was another engrossing thought: Dr. Arthur McKenzie would go to his grave not knowing who had killed him.

Looking at the glittering assembly, Philip wondered where McKenzie was. He looked hopefully from face to face, but he failed to spot him among the handsomely dressed guests, all of them flushed with pleasure at being part of the evening's activities.

No matter. McKenzie would be at the dinner; he was one of the featured speakers. When the time came, the doctor would literally be in the spotlight. Harkness would have no trouble finding him.

"Hello," someone said.

He turned to see a man standing close by, smiling and holding a glass in one hand, extending the other for Philip to shake. "I'm Jesse Linderman," the man said. He was a foot shorter than Harkness and considerably older, his jaw adorned by a white Vandyke. The hair on top of his head was also white, what little there was of it.

Harkness shook the hand and muttered something unintelligible. He hadn't wanted to be approached, but now that he had been, he'd be as polite as possible. With so many people here tonight, this bearded jerk wouldn't remember him.

"Where are you from?" Linderman asked.

"New Mexico," Harkness said.

"That so? Whereabouts?"

Christ—what was a city in that state? "Albuquerque."

"I have a friend who practices in Santa Fe. Mark Kurash. Do you know him?"

"No, I don't think so." Philip sipped his drink.

"Mark couldn't make the meeting this year."

Good, Harkness thought. I'm glad your asshole friend couldn't make it, and I wish you would get the fuck away from me.

"Bring your wife with you?" Linderman asked.

"What? Oh, no, I didn't."

The bearded man laughed. "Neither did I. Never do, in fact, to one of these. Who was the British prime minister who said, Why bring a sandwich to a banquet? Lloyd George, wasn't it?"

Philip tried to smile, but his face felt stiff.

"Been an excellent program thus far," Linderman went on. "Don't you think?"

"Yes, it has."

"Did you hear Banhoffer speak on somatoform disorders?"

"No, missed it."

"Too bad. It was a wonderful lecture. He talked about psychogenic pain and the factors that can induce it, how it's not attributable to any other mental or physical disorder."

"Sorry I didn't hear it," Philip said. His head felt as if it was caught in a pair of giant pincers, squeezing his temples.

"Rang a bell with me," Linderman said. "I had a patient last year who'd been treated for gastrointestinal problems. Turned out the complaints were a classic example of somatization."

Harkness stared at the man.

"Say, are you feeling all right?" Linderman asked. "You look a little pale."

"I'm fine," Philip said. The pressure in his head was getting worse. "Excuse me, there are some people I want to say hello to."

"Oh, sure. Enjoy the evening."

"You, too." Carrying his glass, Harkness moved away, slipping through the crowd. A waiter passed him, bearing a tray, and he put his glass down on it.

Jesus, another couple of minutes there and he could have lost it. What the hell was the matter with him? He'd been careful to take his medicine, and he'd been feeling perfectly all right until that idiot cornered him. Now he was light-headed and slightly nauseous. He'd have to be careful, stay by himself and keep out of people's way.

The lights in the room went down for a split second, and then up again, signaling that dinner was about to be served. The crowds began moving back into the banquet room, men and women smiling and chattering. Harkness stepped along with them, but instead of going to the table that had Dr. Drang's place card on it, he went to the front of the room, toward the raised dais where the speakers would sit.

Some of the speakers were already in their places. The cards in front of them were larger than the ones on the tables. Philip moved past the seated men, his eyes on the cards. There was a podium in the center of the dais, and two places away from that was a card with McKenzie's name on it.

Sitting there was the man he'd been looking for.

The face was remarkably familiar, as if its owner was someone Harkness had known for years. Small, bright eyes, a weak chin. Dr. Arthur McKenzie, distinguished professional, here tonight to be venerated by his peers. Harkness had studied his photo until he would have recognized him anywhere, even at a distance.

Seeing the psychiatrist, Philip's headache immediately disappeared. McKenzie was only a few feet away, gabbing amiably with one of his colleagues, totally unaware that retribution was staring at him.

Harkness slowed his pace, noting the man's air of confidence, his obvious enjoyment in being here tonight. He was totally self-centered, just as Dr. Drang had said.

As he looked at McKenzie, Harkness felt anger seize him, bitter and fierce. This was another of the bastards who wanted to kill him. Who would deny him the medicine that was his lifeblood. Who would leave him dead without ever having known him, without ever caring one whit about who he was, what his needs were.

Philip forced himself to walk steadily by. He went to the end of the dais and kept going, until he reached the side of the room. There were heavy dark red draperies there, and he stepped past them.

This was all part of the plan that had been developed by Dr. Drang, after the doctor had come to the room several days ago to look it over.

The plan called for Harkness to wait in this spot until the moment arrived. Then afterward, he'd come back this way to make his escape.

Just around the corner from where he was standing was the door that led to a stairway. In all the confusion, it would be a simple matter to slip through it and make his way to the floor below, then take an elevator down to the lobby. He'd be gone before anyone clearly understood what had happened.

Just to make sure, Harkness turned the corner and measured the distance to the door. It was only a dozen paces away. He returned to the draperies and stopped just on the other side of them, where he stood stock-still, hidden in the shadows.

He could see perfectly from here. It was an ideal place to watch and wait.

Until the time came to save his life.

63

The wait seemed interminable. Dinner was a multicourse affair, beginning with a shrimp cocktail, followed by soup and then salad and at last the entrée. There were long periods between each serving, and waiters kept the wineglasses topped up as the guests drank and chatted convivially. A string ensemble entertained them as the meal droned on, the music struggling to rise above the roar of voices in the vast room.

During all that time, Harkness rarely took his eyes off Arthur McKenzie, and then not for more than a few seconds as his gaze roved the area.

He was much more at ease now. Everything was going just as Dr. Drang had told him it would, and he knew exactly what he had to do. That was reassuring; he was sharp and alert and ready to act.

In fact, the only question left was one of timing. He'd been instructed to wait until precisely the right instant, and Philip knew when that would be; he'd been drilled on it more than on any other aspect of the assignment. Until then, he had only to stand here and wait, and to remain as calm as possible.

The headache, however, wouldn't leave him alone. Just when he'd all but forgotten about it, the anguish returned, violent and remorseless, like a sudden thunderstorm. One minute, he was fine, and the next, he was afraid his head would split open from the pressure. It was hard to keep his eyes focused when that happened; the images shimmered, as if he were looking out at the crowd through heat waves.

He gritted his teeth and refused to give in to the pain, and as suddenly as it had appeared, the headache was gone again. When it left him, he felt like crying out in relief.

But he couldn't do that, of course. He couldn't do anything except concentrate on the man who was sitting on the dais sipping wine and making witty remarks to the people on either side of him.

When the main course finally did arrive, Philip couldn't tell what the meat was; from what he could see, it might have been roast beef or perhaps veal, smothered in some kind of greasy sauce. Whatever it was, he felt his stomach turn over as the waiters put plates of it in front of the diners. And then he stood in his hiding place for another endless stretch while the guests stuffed their gullets.

McKenzie was obviously enjoying himself. The psychiatrist went on chatting and laughing with his neighbors as he ate, drinking frequently from his wine goblet. Harkness had never seen him in person before tonight, knew him only from the photo Drang had displayed.

Looking at him, Harkness again felt a surge of hatred. Here McKenzie sat, obviously having a wonderful time as he waited to address his fellow psychiatrists on the subject of his glorious achievements. While Philip knew the man was nothing but a vicious fake who had to be stopped before he could do any more harm.

When the guests at last finished their entrées, the waiters took almost as long to clear the tables as it had for the diners to eat the mess on their plates. Harkness groaned at the thought that there'd still be dessert to get through, and then coffee. It could be another hour before the moment finally arrived.

But then the toastmaster surprised him by getting up from his chair beside McKenzie and going to the podium. He was tall and thin and looked cadaverous in his tuxedo, a scarecrow grinning foolishly as he spoke into the microphone.

"Ladies and gentlemen," he said, "my esteemed colleagues, honored guests. I'm Dr. Christopher Brocklin, and it's my privilege this evening to introduce our featured speaker, Dr. Arthur McKenzie. I'm sure all of you here are aware of the great contributions Dr. McKenzie has made in the areas of neurobiology. During his years at Columbia, he has published many important works based on his studies of mental disorders and their causes, and his book *Pharmacology and the Human Mind* has long been recognized as a classic in our field of medicine."

Jesus, get to it, Harkness thought. Stop the palaver and get him on. Let McKenzie give his speech, so that I can do what I came here to do.

"In the interests of time," Brocklin continued, "and also because I'm sure you'll find what Dr. McKenzie has to say more interesting than my dull remarks"—Brocklin was bobbing his head in an absurd acknowledgment of the murmurs of amusement—"we're going to ask him to speak now, as dessert and coffee are being served."

Perfect, Philip told himself. The waiters moving around and these people cramming their faces will add to the confusion. By the time anyone realizes what's happened, I'll be gone.

"And so," Brocklin said, "it is my pleasure as well as my great honor to introduce to you one of the true giants of modern-day psychotherapy, Dr. Arthur McKenzie."

Loud clapping greeted McKenzie as he got to his feet. The doctor took Brocklin's place before the microphone and smiled as he waited for the applause to subside.

Harkness was ready now, poised to attack. He reached inside his jacket with his right hand, fingers closing around the handle of the knife as his gaze fixed on the smiling man at the podium.

When the room was again quiet, McKenzie cleared his throat. "Thank you, Chris. I must say, with an introduction like that one, even I was impressed."

Another round of polite laughter sounded, and the doctor again waited for the noise to fade away before he continued. "Joining all of you at our annual convention is always a source of great satisfaction to me. It's a wonderful opportunity to learn of new techniques in therapy, to see old friends, and to catch up on the latest gossip."

More chuckles.

"But the subject I want to speak to you about tonight is not a pleasant one. It's a problem that affects every one of us, and affects the patients who turn to us in times of emotional and mental crisis. What is that problem?" He paused dramatically. "It is the abuses we are seeing in the prescription of mind-altering drugs."

A low buzzing sounded, as if a wave of insects had invaded the room. Apparently, McKenzie had touched a nerve.

"Sadly," the doctor went on, "these abuses were predictable. During recent years, we've made breakthroughs in the development of compounds that enable us to treat depression, paranoia, and schizophrenia more effectively than ever before. We have truly entered a new era of psychopharmacology. Today, the dangerous antidepressants of the past have either been outlawed or are no longer prescribed. The tertiary amines, for example, such as doxepin or butriptyline. Or the tetracycline maprotiline. These drugs often caused brain damage and sometimes death."

Harkness listened closely to this. He'd known of a number of drug deaths, some of them even occurring among his friends. One guy, a fellow student at Pratt, had ODed on Limbitrol. And a girl had melted her brain with LSD.

"So at that time," McKenzie continued, "we were prescribing drugs that often did more harm than good. Now, however, that is a thing of the past. The compounds of today are much safer, and at the same time so sophisticated, and so effective, they are being hailed as nothing less than miraculous."

Harkness focused even more sharply on what McKenzie was saying. What lies would the devious shit be spinning now?

"Is someone feeling dejected?" the doctor said. "Let them take Prozac or Zoloft or Paxil, and they become cheerful and buoyant, happy about themselves and with a positive outlook. Another astonishing breakthrough is Ritalin, with its ability to help a patient increase the power of concentration. Still another is the use of beta-blockers, which can help to prevent stage fright, because they impede the receptors for norepinephrine. Then there is Dilantin, so effective in reducing stress. And so on. But at the same time, these new drugs, as helpful as they are in the hands of prudent psychiatrists, have also opened the way for what I can only describe as quackery."

There was a burst of applause, and Harkness looked out at the crowd. Apparently they were buying this garbage, swallowing it as enthusiastically as they were the cake the waiters had served them.

"The unfortunate fact," McKenzie said, "is that many unqualified physicians have taken it upon themselves to become psychotherapists overnight. Instead of putting in the years of study qualifying them to treat the complex problems of the mind, they believe they can deal with any emotional complaint simply by prescribing one of the new drugs. That is unconscionable abuse. And perhaps no drugs are more widely abused in this manner than the new antidepressants."

This remark hit Harkness the hardest. Antidepressants were the type of drugs he needed to go on living. The statements he was hearing proved that what Dr. Drang had said was true: McKenzie wasn't only a member of the conspiracy; *he was its leader!*

McKenzie went on: "What happens is that the patient goes to a general practitioner, suffering anything from depression to various stages of psychosis. What any responsible doctor should do in such circumstances, of course, is to refer the patient to a psychiatrist."

And that, Harkness thought, is what really underlies all this bullshit. What McKenzie and the rest of these thieves are after is more business. It's as simple as that. These people aren't just doctors; they're businessmen. They're no different from the pigs at General Brands, or at any other company. And what McKenzie is telling them is that the rest of the pigs should be kept out of the trough.

"But instead," McKenzie said, "the doctor simply prescribes an antidepressant. So what happens? In some instances, his actions lead to catastrophe. Ladies and gentlemen, I submit to you that such conduct on the part of a physician is not only unethical, not only unprofessional"— he raised his voice dramatically—"it is intolerable."

There was another swelling of applause, and McKenzie waited until the room once more quieted down before he went on.

"What can be done?" he asked. "I think the Food and Drug Administration should introduce new rules that prohibit anyone but a licensed psychiatrist from prescribing any drug affecting brain chemistry."

At this, the applause was even louder, and as the audience clapped vigorously, Philip Harkness's mouth twisted in a sneer.

Of course, he thought. You want to keep all the gravy to yourselves, and you want the government to see that you get it. Millions of people screaming for the drugs, and only you could prescribe them. You'd all be even richer than you already are—so fucking rich, you couldn't count the money.

"And I intend," McKenzie was saying, "to recommend such regulations be put in place."

You son of a bitch, Harkness thought. Dr. Drang was absolutely right. What you're proposing is all part of your stinking scheme. It really isn't licensed psychiatrists you want to have this power; it's members of a small club, with you at the head. That's your real objective. So you can keep someone like me from getting the medicine I can't live without. Goddamn you.

McKenzie was winding up now. "I thank you all for your interest and your courteous attention, and I look forward eagerly to joining you again soon. In the meantime—"

"In the meantime, you'll be dead," Harkness muttered under his breath. Gripping the knife concealed under his tuxedo jacket, he stepped out of his hiding place and strode toward the dais.

Suddenly, his headache returned, with greater fury than before. For a moment, he thought he might pass out. He hesitated.

Breathe, he told himself. Take a deep breath, and the hell with the pain. Don't stop, whatever you do. Suck it up and *keep going.*

Somehow, he continued to move forward, forcing himself to ignore the remorseless hammering inside his skull. The members of the audience were all on their feet, applauding McKenzie. None of them paid any attention to the young man whose face was flushed with anger as he made his way through the tables and went up the steps onto the dais.

McKenzie was turning away from the podium, a smile of satisfaction wreathing his small pink face. As he saw Harkness approach, he evidently thought the young man was coming to offer congratulations, and he extended his right hand.

Philip grabbed the hand with his left, and with his right, he drew the knife from under his jacket. He raised it high and paused for a second, making sure of his target. As the psychiatrist caught sight of the gleaming blade, his mouth dropped open. He cried out, instinctively raising his other hand to defend himself.

The effort was useless. Harkness plunged the knife into the side of McKenzie's neck, severing the artery, and then raked the keenly honed edge through the man's larynx and his jugular. He pulled the blade free and stabbed him again and again, as great gouts of McKenzie's blood splattered Philip's face and the front of his shirt and his jacket.

Harkness knew he'd killed him. Knew it without waiting to see him fall. Turning on his heel and holding the bloody knife, he ran back along the dais, retracing his steps.

McKenzie had been stabbed in full view of hundreds of onlookers, and yet for an instant, the guests couldn't believe what they'd seen. They stood gaping and gasping, trying to understand what had happened, and then as realization dawned, shouts went up, and women screamed.

Harkness jumped down from the end of the dais and dashed back to where the draperies were. In the moment of stunned confusion and disbelief, he knew no one would have the presence of mind to stop him. Before an alarm could be sounded, he'd make his way down into the main lobby, where he'd melt into the crowd. By the time anyone realized what had occurred, he'd be out of the hotel and away.

Heart pounding, he brushed past the heavy panels of dark red cloth and rounded the corner. The door was directly ahead of him. He ran to it, grabbed the handle, and shoved.

The door didn't budge.

He shoved again, harder, but with no result. He looked at the heavy metal slab uncomprehendingly. Dr. Drang had told him it would be unlocked. What was going on here?

Behind him, he could hear the commotion in the huge room growing louder, and a wave of panic rolled over him. Continuing to hold the knife in one hand, he twisted the handle and slammed into the door. It didn't give a fraction of an inch.

He hit it again with all his strength. The force of the blow numbed his shoulder, but still it had no effect on the door. The thing was locked, locked tight.

Behind him, a voice yelled, "Stop!"

Harkness turned and saw two uniformed policemen hurrying toward him. They were grim-faced, and both had drawn their pistols. One of them called out, "Freeze! Drop the knife!"

For an instant, he hesitated. Then an unearthly howl boiled up in his throat and he ran at them, brandishing the knife.

Both men fired. The noise was deafening and there were bright flashes from the muzzles of the guns as bullets hit him with sledgehammer force, lifting him off his feet. He staggered backward and fell heavily.

Strangely, he felt no pain now. Yet he was unable to move. He lay on his back and could see the policemen bending over him, but he couldn't see them clearly; their faces were merely two pale blurs floating in space. He realized they were saying something, but he couldn't make out the words.

As he looked up at them, the images slowly faded from sight.

Darkness closed in around him.

64

Jonas Drang sipped cognac and tapped his fingers impatiently on the arm of his leather chair, his gaze never leaving the TV screen. For the dozenth time in the last few minutes, he thumbed the remote, going from the networks to the local stations and then back again through all of them.

But there was no report on the event.

Which wasn't surprising, he told himself. Nor was it anything to be concerned about. The gold Rolex on his left wrist read 9:43, so this was an odd hour, long after the early news shows and not yet time for the local updates or the nightly network roundups. The fact that CNN didn't have the story meant nothing, either; the incident probably hadn't taken place until just minutes ago.

Still, the suspense was making his muscles tense, his throat dry. Even the swallows of brandy were providing scant relief.

Ordinarily, tension was a neural reaction Drang could easily control, just as he could control any other emotion that might affect him. He knew too much about the workings of the human brain, about the neurotransmissions resulting from surges in the levels of biogenic amines, to allow external circumstances to distort his thinking.

But tonight was different—perhaps because the stakes were so high. He could feel his pulse picking up speed, was aware that his breathing was shallower and more rapid than normal, which indicated he was producing excessive amounts of epinephrine. He made a concentrated effort to compose himself.

In a few minutes, he thought, there would be a newsbreak telling him it went exactly as planned. And even if it hadn't, he'd installed enough safeguards to ensure that the incident could never be traced back to him. At this moment, all he had to do was relax and enjoy his brandy.

Besides, everything else was going too well for him to worry now, especially since whatever had happened in the Waldorf tonight was out of his hands.

Instead, he should be thinking about the good things he'd accomplished, and the astounding progress he'd made. He'd learned much through his work with Harkness, and if the man had turned out to be another disappointment, what of it? No scientist ever achieved his objectives without experiencing occasional setbacks along the way. That was nature's way of testing you, just as it had tested Roentgen and Fleming and all the other Nobel prize–winning giants.

On the other hand, if Harkness had succeeded tonight, Drang would have achieved his great stroke of revenge. Arthur McKenzie was a bitter, insidious little turd who didn't deserve to live. And who perhaps, at this very moment, no longer did.

So however it might have gone, Harkness had served his purpose. And in the end, exactly like the rats down in the laboratory, he was expendable.

Therefore, Drang told himself, he should be concentrating now on Flo Dallure. Whereas Harkness had fallen short, Flo was a triumph. With her, he'd taken raw material and reshaped it, had given it new life and meaning. He'd transformed her from a blubbering, self-pitying simpleton into a beautifully formed work of art.

What an achievement. Michelangelo must have felt like this when he sculpted his *David*. Although the tiny Italian had worked with nothing more exciting than cold, inanimate marble, while Drang had molded his masterpiece from warm, living flesh.

Suddenly, he snapped to attention. An announcer appeared on the tube, saying, "We interrupt this program for an important news flash. We have just received word of a shocking crime that took place only minutes ago in the Waldorf-Astoria Hotel in New York. Dr. Arthur McKenzie, a noted psychiatrist, was stabbed to death by an apparently demented man. The assault occurred while Dr. McKenzie was addressing members of the American Psychiatric Association at the organization's annual convention. The assailant was himself then shot and killed by police while trying to escape. His identity is not known at this point, nor have the police established a motive. That is all we have at this time, but we'll bring you further details as we receive them. We return you now to our regularly scheduled program. Stay tuned for updates on the murder of Dr. McKenzie."

The announcer disappeared, and his bland face was replaced by the movie that had been on earlier.

For the next several minutes, Drang sat completely still. Then he got up from his chair and stepped to the dry sink, where he poured more brandy into his snifter.

When he returned, he flipped channels until he got another newscast that reported McKenzie's death. He wanted to be sure that what he'd heard was accurate, that this wasn't another misrepresentation. The escape of the detective from the burning car wreck had made Drang question the reliability of TV news. He'd been fooled once, and he didn't intend for that to happen again.

But this report was essentially the same as the first one he'd heard. Only then did he accept the announcement. When it was over, he turned off the set and sipped his brandy.

Could anything have been sweeter? Was there any way he could have improved on what had happened tonight?

Well, yes. There was one way, come to think of it. If only McKenzie had known who was behind the attack. If only he'd realized, at the last instant, who had killed him. Then it would have been perfect.

But still, Drang had had his revenge, and that was what counted. Now there was only one more problem to contend with: getting rid of that meddling cop.

There was no room for further errors there. And Drang would not make any.

After that, he would put the last phase of his plan into action.

65

Tolliver didn't learn of the McKenzie homicide until the next morning, when he caught the news on WPIC-TV. Watching the report on the tiny Sony in his kitchen, he was flabbergasted.

Another mindless, inexplicable murder, again the result of an assault by a lunatic? And not only that, but the victim in this one was a nationally known psychiatrist?

By this time, the story contained full details of what had happened in the Waldorf, including an eyewitness account of how Dr. McKenzie had been stabbed to death after making a speech before his colleagues. A file photograph of the victim portrayed a slightly built man with soft, unremarkable features.

The reporter said the killer had also been slain; the police had shot him when he attacked them while trying to escape. No ID had been found on his body; as yet, police had not ascertained who he was. They said he appeared to be in his late twenties and, like the guests at the APA dinner, had been wearing a tuxedo. A witness said he'd spoken with the man and that he'd claimed to be a psychiatrist from Albuquerque.

The remainder of the story detailed the high points of Dr. McKenzie's career, giving an impressive resumé of the degrees he'd earned, the colleges where he'd taught, the hospitals and clinics he'd worked in, the honors that had been bestowed on him.

Maybe the killer was McKenzie's patient, Ben thought. Or a former patient. There had been a number of cases like that. Some loony would be treated by a psychiatrist, and eventually the patient would blame the doctor for whatever was wrong with him. Then he'd kill the psychiatrist.

Or maybe this one was something else. There was a case a few years ago where a woman in Manhattan was seeing a therapist and the doctor began an affair with her. When the woman's husband found out about it, he went into the shrink's office and shot him. Then the husband went home and blew away his wife. He later beat the charge on an insanity plea, but that wasn't surprising. Sometimes the verdicts juries handed down were crazier than the defendants.

For that matter, there was a whole range of possibilities as to what had inspired the killing of McKenzie, and ordinarily Tolliver would have had no more than passing professional interest. The Waldorf was on Park between 49th and 50th streets, which meant the Seventeenth Precinct detective squad had jurisdiction.

Yet this was an event he couldn't stop thinking about. A mad killer attacking a psychiatrist? For no apparent reason?

Okay, so Ben didn't have grounds for associating this case with Whitacre. Like the homicides in the Sixth Precinct, there was no evidence there could be any connection.

And yet—

Moving slowly on his sore legs, he left the apartment and drove to his office in the borrowed Lincoln. When he got in, he went looking for Fred Logan, but he was told the captain was in a meeting at police headquarters.

Tolliver spent the rest of the morning running over his notes, trying to pick up a lead, find a new direction. But he got nowhere. The more he thought about it, the more curious he became about the murder at the Waldorf.

On top of everything else, the killer had used a *knife*.

He put in a call to Ed Flynn, but Flynn wasn't in, either. Ben left word and hung up.

By noon, he could stand it no longer. He left the office and got back into the big green sedan, heading uptown for the Seventeenth's headquarters, on East 51st Street.

66

The precinct house was between Lexington and Third, across from the side entrance to the Loew's Hotel.

As he got out of the Lincoln, Tolliver was startled by the sound of sirens. He turned to see a bright red NYFD sedan come flying out of the firehouse, which was next door to the police station. Close on the heels of the car was a hook and ladder, and behind that was a pumper with firemen hanging on to the stern. The three machines roared to the corner and turned south on Lex, passing the hotel with sirens screaming.

Ben watched them go. What with the commotion put up at all hours by the fire-fighting equipment and the cops' cars, he thought it was a wonder anybody in the hotel ever got any sleep. Probably they didn't. He went on into the station house.

Upstairs in the squad room, two detectives were working the day tour. He didn't recognize either of them. That shouldn't have surprised him; the NYPD now numbered more than 35,000 cops, with the commissioner claiming there weren't enough.

A small plate beside the door said the occupant of the squad commander's office was Lt. Dennis Calligan, and this time Ben was looking at a name he knew well. He knocked once on the door, opened it, and stuck his head inside. "Pardon me," he said. "I was looking for the men's room."

The man sitting at the desk looked up and grinned. He seemed much too large for the confined space, his bulky shoulders threatening to burst the seams of his suit jacket. "Ben! Come on in."

Tolliver stepped inside and closed the door behind him. He thrust out his hand, and Calligan's oversized paw enveloped it.

"Good to see you," the big man said. His head was bullet-shaped and shiny, with only a dark fringe around the edges. "I understand you burned up your car. You okay?"

"A little singed, that's all."

"Sit down, sit down. How about a nice cup of tea?"

"Sure, why not?" Tolliver sank onto one of the straight-backed chairs across from the desk. He watched as the squad commander opened a drawer and came up with a bottle of vodka and two Styrofoam cups.

Calligan had been in Ben's class at the Academy, several eons ago. Since then, they'd run into each other only occasionally but had remained friends, even though their personal lives had gone in different directions. Dennis was married and had six kids; they lived in a small house on Long Island.

He filled the cups and handed one across the desk. "Here's luck."

"Salut."

Both men drank.

At room temperature the vodka was rough on Ben's throat, but by the time it hit bottom it had been magically transformed into gentle warmth.

"They tell me you're running the DA's Office these days," Calligan said.

"Not quite. Fred Logan heads up our unit."

"Ah yes, Captain Logan. The department's leading politician."

"One of them," Tolliver acknowledged.

"So tell me, what brings you up this way?"

"I heard about the homicide at the Waldorf last night. But don't worry, Logan didn't send me. I'm working on other things; I was just curious."

"Something, wasn't it? Out of the blue, this guy runs up to the psychiatrist and starts slicing him up like he's salami. Almost cut his head off."

"You identify the killer?"

"Yeah, thanks to our friends in the media. There was the piece in the *News*. Did you see it?"

"No, what was it?"

"After the cops shot him, some reporter who was covering the banquet got a good look at the body. He wrote a description that was in this morning's edition. The killer's boss read the piece and called to ask about him. He was worried about the guy not coming to work, especially because he'd been acting weird lately. We had the boss come in, and then we took him to the morgue and showed him the body. He gave us a positive ID."

"Who was the perpetrator?"

"Name was Philip Harkness. Single, lived in Chelsea. Worked for a design studio, Raymond Mercer Associates. It was Mercer who identified him. Mercer told us the guy had been with the studio five years and was their best talent. But he was also a very strange character."

"Why haven't you released Harkness's name?"

"There's an angle, and we don't want it to get out. At least not yet. We've had reporters all over us, like fucking locusts."

"So what's the angle?"

"Mercer thought he might've been on some kind of drugs. That figured, because the one thing that was on the body was a vial full of capsules."

"Capsules? What was in them?"

"We're waiting to hear from the lab."

"How soon will they let you know?"

Calligan shrugged. "Who can say? You ask, they hold their balls and holler. Same shit you get everywhere—we're swamped, we're backed up, we're doing the best we can. Their attitude is, hey—you got the guy who did it, so what's the hurry? Fucking people, I'd like to bust some heads."

"What else did Mercer tell you?"

"Said he thought Harkness had a girlfriend living with him. Gave us the address, but two of my men went there and so far all they've turned up is more pills. They just called in about fifteen minutes ago."

"No sign of the girlfriend?"

"Nothing that would say who she is, but they'll canvass the neighbors. We should get a line on her."

Calligan topped off their cups. "Now do me a favor, okay?"

"Sure, what is it?"

"Stop the shit and tell me what's going on."

Ben smiled. "Not much gets by you, huh?"

"Very little. In fact, I'm such a great detective, that's why I'm still a fucking lieutenant."

"I have the same problem."

"So I noticed. But at least you got a cushy spot, down there with Logan's commandos. Now come on, tell me. You're working on the

Whitacre case, right? You think maybe that has something to do with this one?"

Tolliver drank more of his vodka. "A tox test showed Whitacre was on drugs, too. The lab thought it was some kind of antidepressant, but they weren't sure just what it was."

"So?"

"So that's why I think there might be a connection between the two cases."

Calligan looked at him. "On the basis of what? Because your killer was on an antidepressant? You gotta be kidding me. Seems like everybody's popping that shit. There was a piece on TV about it the other night. Talked about Prozac, said Merck couldn't make it fast enough."

"Eli Lilly."

"Whoever. But anyway, we don't even know what Harkness was using. And besides the drugs, what else would connect them—that they were both crazy? That really narrows it down, huh? To about five million of our citizens. Listen, Ben. If we get anything I think could help you, I'll let you know. But it seems to me like what you're thinking is a stretch."

"Maybe you're right."

"If I'm not, I'd be damn surprised."

"Just the same, when you locate Harkness's girlfriend, I'd like to talk to her."

"Okay, fine."

Tolliver drained his cup and stood up. "Thanks for the hospitality."

The big man rose as well. "Hey, it was great to see you. You married yet, by the way?"

"Not that I'm aware of."

"You really ought to settle down, you know? How about coming out to our place soon, have a home-cooked meal. Alice'd love to see you."

"I might do that." Ben thought of Calligan's swarm of kids and decided that then again, he might not.

"Good luck with your case," Dennis said.

"Good luck with yours. If you don't mind, I'd like to stop by Harkness's apartment while your men are still there."

Calligan pursed thick lips. "Yeah, I guess I don't have any problem with that. Just don't forget the case belongs to us." He looked through the pile of notes on his desk and scribbled an address on a piece of paper, handing it to Ben.

"Thanks again, Dennis. See you later."

Tolliver left the office and the station house, walking slowly back down to where he'd parked the Lincoln.

67

The neighborhood was a sprawl of small shops, nineteenth-century town houses, and large old commercial buildings. There was also a hotel that had been considered luxurious, back in its heyday. This was the Chelsea, on 23rd Street, where celebrities such as Mark Twain and O. Henry had lived long ago.

More recently, the raunchy old barn had become a favorite of rock stars, who considered it a kind of upscale shooting gallery. Janis Joplin and Sid Vicious had preferred to stay there when in New York, and at present such bands as Total Freakout and the Fuggers were frequently in residence.

The address Calligan had given Tolliver was two blocks from the hotel. When he reached it, Ben saw that the building apparently had once been an elegant one-family home. He parked the car and went inside. The apartment where Philip Harkness had lived was a third-floor walk-up.

As Tolliver reached the top of the stairs, he saw people standing in the hallway, ogling the door to Harkness's apartment and talking among themselves in low voices. A uniformed cop was guarding the entrance. Ben clipped his shield to the breast pocket of his blazer and stepped past him.

Inside, two detectives were peering into cabinets, poking around on shelves, examining the contents of closets. One of them crouched beside a bookcase in the living room, looking through a cardboard box filled with photographs.

Seeing Tolliver, the man got to his feet. He was short and dark-haired and wore a mustard-colored suit. The laminated ID attached to his jacket said his name was George Pappas.

Ben told the detective he was from the DA's Office and that he'd touched base with Lieutenant Calligan before coming here. He asked what the men had turned up.

"For one thing, more pills," Pappas said. "They look the same as what was on the perp's body, in the hotel."

"Where are they?"

"Right here, Lieutenant." The detective took a plastic vial from his pocket and handed it to Tolliver.

Ben opened the container and peered inside. The vial was half-filled with yellow capsules.

At a glance, they resembled the ones Ed Flynn's squad had collected at the homicide scene on Hudson Street. But until they were analyzed, there was no telling what in them. He put the cap back on the vial and returned it.

"What else?"

Pappas shrugged. "Nothing that says this guy Harkness knew the doctor he killed. Some of his personal papers were in a desk in the other room, and there's no mention of McKenzie in any of them."

Tolliver glanced about. The apartment consisted of four spacious rooms, the high ceilings covered in old-fashioned tin paneling. The furniture was starkly modern, running to white leather slings on welded metal supports, and the walls were also white. Paintings without frames were hanging everywhere, their subjects dreamlike street scenes and blurred human figures, from what he could see.

"That other room," Pappas said. "Where the desk is? He must've used that for a studio. There's a lot more of his paintings in there. You oughta take a look."

Tolliver stepped into the room Pappas indicated, the detective following him.

The room was a mess. Open tubes of pigment and containers of paint and dried brushes lay on every surface. Besides the desk, there was a chest and a swivel chair, along with an easel illuminated by a goosenecked lamp. Drips and driblets of various hues streaked the fur-

niture and the bare wooden floor, and there were smudges and spatters
on the walls and on the venetian blinds covering the windows. More
tubes and paint pots sat on the floor. Some of the tubes had been crushed
underfoot and the pots tipped over, leaving dried blotches of vivid color.

Ben saw that the desk was scarred and battered. Like everything
else in the room, paint had been slopped over it. The drawers were
hanging open and were empty.

Strewn about the room were the paintings Pappas had referred to.
There were dozens of them, some lying on the floor, others propped
against the walls. All had an aura of violence about them he hadn't seen
in the ones in the living room. Tolliver picked one up and looked at it.

At first glance, the painting put him in mind of a Rorschach
inkblot, done in tones of gray and black. Then as he studied the lines
and swirls, he realized they portrayed a gnarled tree with dead bodies
hanging from the limbs.

He put the painting down and looked at another. This one was the
portrait of a woman, the subject staring intensely as her hand clawed the
skin from the side of her face, laying bare the bones of her cheek and
jaw. Blood was streaming from her fingers down over her wrist.

Christ, was the stuff in here all like this? He looked further and
saw that it was. Each of the paintings depicted torture and debauchery,
scenes of bestiality and human suffering. Together with the haphazard
spills, they made it look as though someone had gone mad in the room.
Which, Ben thought, was probably just what had happened.

"Some gallery, huh?" Pappas said.

Tolliver made no reply. He went on looking at the bizarre artwork.

A second detective stepped into the room. He glanced at Tolliver's
shield and ID and stopped.

"This here is my partner," Pappas said. "Art Shanahan."

The detective nodded, a wary expression on his face. He was the
opposite of Pappas physically, tall and skinny and with pale skin and
red hair, wearing a gray sport jacket.

"The lieutenant is from the DA's Office," Pappas explained. "Calligan knew he was coming by."

"How about the neighbors," Ben asked. "They give you anything?"

"We talked to an old lady who lives down the hall," Shanahan said.

"She told us Harkness's girlfriend moved out a few weeks back. They had a big fight and she took off. The old lady said the girl's name was Cathy, but she didn't know her last name or where she went."

Tolliver turned to Pappas. "What was in that box of pictures you were looking at?"

"Bunch of snapshots," Pappas said.

"I want to see them."

The three men went into the living room, where the box was resting atop the bookcase.

The photographs were three-by-five color prints, the kind any camera store or supermarket would process. They depicted a variety of young people, posing singly and in groups. In some, the subjects were indoors, but more often they were outside, on city sidewalks, or on beaches, or in the country.

The photos were normal enough, no different from millions of others that were taken by amateur photographers every day, showing people smiling and sometimes mugging for the camera. That put them in sharp contrast to the other graphics in the apartment.

Ben flipped the prints over, checking to see if any of them had dates printed on the back. Many did, running from roughly two years earlier to about eight weeks before today.

He glanced up at Pappas. "You recognize Harkness in any of these?"

"Yeah," Pappas said. "He's in a lot of them." The detective selected a number of the photos and laid them out on the top surface of the bookcase. "That's our boy," he said, pointing.

In each shot, Tolliver saw a casually dressed young man looking calmly into the lens. He was slimly built and of medium height, a lock of his brown hair hanging down on his forehead. Ben noticed that of all the people in the collection of snapshots, Harkness was the only one who wasn't smiling. The boyish face that stared back at him seemed incongruous with the paintings its owner had created, and even more at odds with the violence that had ended the young man's life and that of his victim.

"I showed these to the neighbor," Pappas said. He picked out another photo. "She said this is the girlfriend."

Ben looked at the print. It showed an attractive young woman with an oval face and straight brown hair. There were several shots of her in the box.

"I want to borrow a couple of these photos," Tolliver said. "One of Harkness and one of the girlfriend."

The detective hesitated.

"I know it's evidence," Ben said. "But you'll get them back. You can check with Lieutenant Calligan, if you want to."

"No, it's okay. Go ahead."

Tolliver chose two of the snapshots and put them into the inside pocket of his blazer.

"Where are the papers that were in the desk?" he asked.

"On the kitchen table," Shanahan said.

Ben went in there. Compared with the rest of the apartment, this room was fairly clean. A few dirty dishes were standing in the sink, and a layer of dust was visible everywhere, but otherwise the kitchen was tidy. It featured a large old-fashioned white enamel stove, a modern refrigerator, and a table with four chairs around it. As in the other rooms, everything in here was white, including the counters and the cabinets and the wooden floors.

As Shanahan had told him, the papers the detectives had found in Harkness's desk were lying on the table, arranged in piles. Tolliver sat in one of the chairs, and as he began going through the papers, he saw that many of these also were spotted with drops of paint.

The items he examined were pretty much routine—old receipts, a booklet describing the benefits of a group insurance plan, a list of art supplies, bits of trivia ranging from stamps to a map of Manhattan. It was a little curious, he thought, that there were no pieces of personal correspondence, such as letters or postcards from friends or acquaintances. Nor was there a diary or a journal, but somehow he hadn't been expecting to find one. That would have been too much to hope for.

He did find a few notes in what he assumed was Harkness's handwriting, but these also seemed innocuous. One of the jottings apparently concerned impressions of an exhibit of Joan Miró's paintings at MoMA. Another was a formula for making gesso.

Pappas had followed Tolliver into the room. "See what I mean, Lieu? There's nothing in any of this that'd put him with the doctor."

There was still one thing, Ben thought, that might. "Let me see those drugs again, will you?"

Pappas handed him the vial and Tolliver opened it once more, shaking one of the yellow capsules out into the palm of his hand.

The color meant nothing, he reminded himself. In this age of substance abuse, he'd run across pills in a rainbow of shades, as well as in all shapes and sizes.

Nevertheless, the shiny cylinder looked exactly like the ones that Ed Flynn's men had found beside the body on Hudson Street. The question was, what did it contain?

Placing the capsule on the table, he cut it open with a knife from one of the kitchen drawers and then dumped out the contents, a granular white powder. He picked up a pinch between thumb and forefinger and sniffed at it, but that told him nothing either; the faintly bitter smell was not familiar. He wasn't about to taste the stuff; God only knew what it might consist of.

This time, he didn't ask permission. He took another capsule from the vial and put it in his pocket, then gave the vial back to Pappas. After that, he resumed going through Harkness's papers. The other detectives left the kitchen and went on with their search of the apartment.

Next, Ben dug into the pile of items relating to the designer's finances, and there he found two items of interest. The first was the crumpled record portion of a biweekly paycheck from Raymond Mercer Associates, made out to Philip Harkness. It was dated three months earlier, and the gross amount, before withholding and all the other deductions, was $6,300.00.

Ben did a quick mental calculation that told him the young man had been making a little over 150 grand a year before police bullets had terminated his career. That was a fairly hefty income. And almost surely, there would have been bonuses on top of it, as well as other perks.

Tolliver looked thoughtfully at his surroundings. This apartment was okay, but nothing special. With the salary Harkness had been making, he certainly could have afforded something better. So why had he gone on living here—because material things weren't important to him? Or had he been spending his money on something else?

The second item answered Ben's questions. It was a packet of envelopes from a Chase bank, each containing a statement and a bundle of canceled checks. Once again telling himself not to get his hopes too high, he began reviewing the checks.

They covered a period of four months, according to the dates. Harkness's loopy handwriting was hard to figure out, and random blobs of paint hadn't improved its legibility. But what the checks showed was clear enough. The designer had paid his rent and his phone bill and electric bill and various other mundane charges. And every seven days, he'd drawn a check for twelve hundred dollars, made out to himself.

Why had Harkness wanted over a thousand bucks a week in cash? Everybody needed walking-around money, but in that amount? What had he been doing with it?

Possibly, Ben thought, the same thing Beth Whitacre had been doing: paying a shrink. And the cash would make the payments untraceable—which meant the shrink would be untraceable, as well.

Tolliver slipped one of the checks into the pocket of his blazer, alongside the capsule and the photos of Harkness and his girlfriend. Then he left the apartment. On his way out, he saw that Pappas and Shanahan were in the bedroom. They'd taken the mattress off the bed and slit it open, and now they were examining its contents.

Nothing like being thorough, he thought, even though the horse was not only out of the barn but also dead.

68

The rat was strapped down on the table, glaring at Drang with malice. It was a female, big-boned and husky, the result of a diet consisting mainly of rotting fish. Amino acids in the putrefying flesh had given its coat a glossy sheen.

"You're a real beauty, aren't you?" the doctor said. "You have more muscle mass than most males, and you're also more intelligent.

That makes you formidable, doesn't it? As in any other species, you're by far the more dangerous sex."

He held up the hypodermic syringe to the light and tested it, then deftly inserted the needle into the saphenous vein in the rat's left hind leg. Slowly and carefully, he injected the drugs into the animal's bloodstream.

When the process was completed, he put the syringe aside and smiled down at his patient. "Now then, we'll give that time to take effect. With your pulse rate, shouldn't be more than a minute or two. After that, we'll see what impact it's had on your brain."

As he waited, he sat at the table and made notes. Drang loved being down here at night, loved the sense of solitude, the feeling that he was far removed from the outside world. Except for the shuffling of the rats in their cages, the cellar was as quiet as death. Here there was only his work, and nothing else.

He was sure he had the answers now to questions that had been debated vigorously for more than a century, by men who occupied hallowed places in the pantheon of psychiatry and whose crude hypotheses had been irrelevant.

Freud, with his theories of dynamism, arguing that undischarged sexual energy determined all human conduct, and that emotional problems were traceable to forgotten psychic traumas in early life. How primitive. And how pointless.

Jung, claiming the difference in personality types was biological, and that evolutionary adaptation would benefit the human species. Obviously a bald attempt to curry favor with his Nazi masters. But useless when it came to application in treatment.

Klein, with his contempt for female patients who were subject to extreme mood disorders, calling them hysteroid dysphorics.

And so many others.

What none of them understood was that they'd been mistaking symptoms for causes. They'd looked at the mysteries and shouted, Eureka! like a bunch of witless children, never admitting that their metaphysical explanations were so much balderdash.

While the truth was that the brain, for all its mysteries, was nothing more than a marvelously complex electrochemical machine. Once you understood how to manage its chemical components, you could regulate it as you would any other mechanism.

That was what distinguished Drang from all the others. His discovery of how to *control* the human mind towered above the work of any who'd come before him. It would ensure his place in history. And in the process, it would make him rich and powerful beyond measure.

He glanced at his watch, then bent over the rat on the table. Its breathing had slowed and its eyes were not as bright as they had been earlier.

"Ah, very good," Drang said. "Rest comfortably there for just a bit longer, and then we'll open your skull and have a look."

Sitting back, he thought about the next phase of his plan. He'd already terminated his relationships with all his patients except Flo Dallure, telling them he was giving up his practice for health reasons. Soon he'd be ready to leave New York forever.

Operating in Switzerland would be ideal because the laws there were all in his favor. There was no FDA to snoop and pry, and the banking and tax regulations would enable him to conduct his business in secrecy and maximize his profits. He could produce his drugs in quantity with no interference from the government, and from what his lawyer in Zurich had reported, there would be no shortage of eager buyers. Now his work here was nearly completed; soon he'd be ready to go.

Except for one concern: the cop.

Drang had already devised an ingenious plan for resolving that dilemma. Typical of his thinking, the solution employed an ironic twist that would at last put an end to Tolliver and his prying. One final stroke of revenge, and well deserved.

The telephone buzzed.

Drang's assistant was still in the house, cleaning up his accounts. He picked up the instrument. "Yes, Anna, what is it?"

"Phone for you, Doctor. Cathy Fennel calling."

There were times when he was convinced that Anna was a complete idiot. "I don't know any Cathy Fennel. Tell him I'm not here, and don't disturb me again."

"She said to tell you she's a friend of Philip Harkness."

That stopped him. He realized now who she was: the girlfriend

Harkness had once been living with. He was about to order Anna to question her further, but then he thought better of it. As it was, Anna knew too much of his business.

"All right," he said, "I'll talk to her. Put the call through to me here."

A moment later, a soft voice came on the line. "Is this Dr. Drang?"

"Yes, it is. And you're Miss Fennel?"

She sounded shy and apologetic. "Yes. I'm sorry to bother you, Doctor. I realize it's late."

"Perfectly all right," Drang said. He wanted to probe, to find out what she knew. "How may I help you?"

"I'm concerned about Philip Harkness. He's one of your patients, isn't he?"

Drang parried the question. "What is this about?"

"Phil and I were more or less engaged. But then we broke up a while back, and I haven't heard from him. I don't want you to think I'm being silly, but I just wanted to be sure he's okay."

"Why wouldn't he be?"

She blurted it out: "I read in the paper about something awful that happened, and there was a description of somebody. It sounded just like Philip. I've been trying to locate him, but I haven't been able to."

"But why call me?"

"I knew you'd been treating him, so I thought maybe I should check with you. I hope you don't mind."

With an effort, Drang kept his manner calm and deliberate. "Of course not. I don't mind at all. Have you tried his office?"

"Yes, I called there this morning, and again this afternoon. He didn't come in, and they sounded kind of evasive."

"I see."

"I didn't tell them who I was, of course. You know Philip—he's very touchy, and I wouldn't want to embarrass him. It's just that I've been so worried. I hope you don't think this is nonsense."

"No, I don't think that at all."

"Then can you tell me if he's okay?"

Thoughts were racing through Drang's mind. "Under the circumstances, it would be better if we spoke in person."

Her voice rose in alarm. "Then is there something—"

"I assure you, Philip has been well taken care of."

"Oh, thank God."

"Nevertheless, it would be better if we could talk about it. You might be able to help."

"I'll be glad to do anything I can."

"Good. Could you come to my office?"

"Of course. When?"

"It would be best if you came tonight. I don't want to upset you any further, but it's a matter of some urgency."

"Then I will. Right away, if you want me to."

"Fine, I think you should." He gave her the address and hung up.

Damn it, he thought, why did this have to happen now?

He removed the straps from the comatose rat. Lifting the animal by the tail, he dumped it back into its cage. Then he took off his lab coat and hung it on a wall hook.

Watching his movements, the other rats had begun squeaking. The ones that weren't immersed in a drug-induced stupor themselves eyed him fiercely from behind the wire walls of their cages, as if offended that he was leaving.

Drang adjusted the jacket of his black worsted suit and then climbed the stairway leading up to the first floor. He wanted to get Anna out of here, before his visitor arrived.

69

Drang was alone in the house when the young woman rang the bell. He let her in, smiling pleasantly. "Good evening. I'm Dr. Drang. You must be Miss Fennel."

"Yes. I know I must have sounded foolish when I called you, but I've just been so worried about Philip."

"Of course. I understand just how you feel."

"You said there's something urgent, and that I could help?"

"I believe so, yes. Come along, and we'll have a chat." He led her into his office and she sat on one of the straight-backed chairs, her legs pressed primly together, her fingers nervously twisting a handkerchief in her lap.

She was quite attractive, he thought. Although rather slender, for his taste. Usually he preferred women to be more generously built— more *saftig,* to use the German word for "juicy."

This one, in contrast, was on the slim side. Her straight brown hair framed an oval face, and the expression in her brown eyes struck him as intelligent, if a bit ingenuous. But slender or not, her body was beautiful, from what he could see of it. Good ripe breasts, well-turned legs. She was wearing a gabardine skirt and a tweed jacket, as if she'd fashioned herself after an ad in *Town & Country.*

He sat across from her. "First of all, before we discuss Philip's current situation, what was this incident you referred to?"

"It was something terrible that happened at the Waldorf last night. I'm sure you heard about it—a psychiatrist was stabbed to death. And then the man who did it was killed, too. The police shot him."

"Yes, I did hear something about that. But what made you think it had anything to do with Philip?"

"Like I told you, there was a description of the killer in the paper. It sounded exactly like him, and I guess I got carried away. All kinds of crazy ideas went through my head."

"I see. You and Philip were quite close, I gather. You said you were more or less engaged?"

"Yes. We were living together . . . for almost two years. But then we had a fight and I moved out. Did he tell you that?"

"I believe he mentioned it."

"Lately he's been acting very strange. And I know you've had him on medication."

Drang had always prided himself on his self-control. He waited, stone-faced.

"But instead of getting better," she went on, "he seemed to get worse. He'd have these terrible dreams, and sometimes he'd disappear for hours in the middle of the night. If I said anything about it, he'd fly into a rage. Before we broke up, he hit me. If I hadn't gotten out of there, I don't know what he might have done."

"I'm sorry to hear that."

The words tumbled out of her. "I just couldn't believe it was the same person. When he was asleep, he said a lot of, like, wild things. He talked about killing people, and things like that. So this morning when I read the story in the *News,* I was shocked. I kept telling myself it couldn't be true, that it couldn't have been Philip, but when I called his office, they didn't know where he was. Then I just kept getting more and more upset. So finally, I called the police."

Drang stared at her. "You called the police?"

"Yes. They kept telling me to come in and talk to them, but I wouldn't. I thought, What if I'm wrong? I could cause a lot of trouble, and that would really do it—Philip would never speak to me again. So instead—"

"Instead, you decided you'd better speak with me."

"I . . . yes. I'm sure you think I was acting like a fool, jumping to conclusions."

"I don't think that at all. Tell me, did you give the police your name?"

"No. They wanted me to, but I was afraid." Her eyes were wide, her voice pleading. "Doctor, is Philip really okay?"

"I'd say his condition is excellent."

"That's such a relief. But if you don't mind, I'd appreciate it if you didn't mention this to him, about my coming here tonight."

"Cathy, I can guarantee he'll never know about it. And I hope you didn't tell anyone you were coming here, either."

"No, I didn't. But you said I could help. What's wrong, and what is it I can do?"

Drang rose from his chair. "Perhaps it would be better if I were to show you. Come over here, please." He stepped over to the far end of the room, and she followed him.

"Look up there," he said, "at the bookcase. What do you see?"

"A lot of books. Is there one in particular?"

"Look at the ones on the top shelf. Can you read the titles?"

She moved closer, craning her neck and straining to read the inscriptions on the spines of the volumes.

Quietly, Drang took a position directly behind her.

"I can barely make them out," she said.

"Keep trying." She was shorter than he, the top of her head about on a level with his shoulders. And as he'd noted when she was sitting down, she was quite slender.

That would make it easier.

"They're medical books," she said. "Right?"

He brought his right arm up and clamped it over her breasts, his hand pinching her mouth and her nose shut. At the same time, his left hand gripped her neck, cutting off the flow of blood to her brain. Then he lifted her off her feet, continuing to hold her in a steely grasp. She stiffened and struggled and kicked, but it was like the fluttering of a bird.

Within seconds her resistance slackened, and a few moments after that, it ceased altogether. Drang turned and, holding her unconscious form in his arms, carried her over to the couch and laid her down on it. Then he opened the drawer in the cabinet and took out the hypodermic syringe.

The barrel was full; he'd loaded it just before she arrived. After testing the instrument, he pushed back the sleeve of her jacket. Her arm was thin and finding a vein was a problem.

He fumbled with the task, telling himself to stop acting like some goddamn medical student. When at last he found a vessel, he slipped the needle into it and depressed the plunger.

He waited for a time, watching her chest rise and fall. She was well under now, and going deeper. Lifting her in his arms once more, he slung her over his shoulder and carried her to the door that led to the cellar stairway. She felt even lighter than the first time he'd picked her up. He opened the door and snapped on the lights, then made his way down the stairs.

The rats were excited to see him again. They chirped and squeaked, some of them pressing their pink snouts against the wire of the cages. The animals seemed particularly aroused, he thought, but perhaps that was because he had something with him.

He stepped toward them, carrying his burden.

70

Tolliver's injuries were healing, and he was able to move about much better than he had been earlier. He drove to the Sixth Precinct station house and dropped off the photos of Harkness and his girlfriend with Ed Flynn. He filled Flynn in on his suspicions that the man who stabbed Dr. McKenzie to death might also be the perpetrator in the meat market and Hudson Street homicides. Ed said he'd get the witnesses back in and have them look at the pictures.

Ben then showed him the capsule he'd taken from Philip Harkness's apartment. The squad commander agreed that the yellow shell resembled the ones that had been recovered at the Hudson Street scene, but he also allowed that he had no more idea than Tolliver did as to what might be inside.

Flynn said he'd let Ben know about the witnesses' reactions to the photographs.

From there, Tolliver went to Alan Stein's house and gave the psychiatrist the capsule, asking Stein to have his contacts at St. Elizabeth's check out the contents as quickly as possible. Stein promised he'd get them to rush an analysis.

Ben then spent the next couple of days following up on the papers he'd seen in Philip Harkness's apartment, trying to get a better line on what the killer had been doing with all that cash.

He began by going to the Chase Manhattan offices in the World Trade Center, but they flat-out refused to divulge information to him. He couldn't really blame them; banks were required by federal law to keep their records private. Only a court order would cause their release, and he had no authorization from a prosecutor to apply for one.

Next, Tolliver paid a visit to Raymond Mercer, the head of the studio Harkness had worked for. Mercer tried to be helpful, but he didn't know much about Harkness's private life. As far as what the designer might have been doing with his money was concerned, Mercer had no idea.

Any evidence, Ben asked, that Harkness had been an addict? Mercer claimed to have no knowledge of that, either, although he thought it

might have been possible. What about psychotherapy? That brought
only a shrug. Did Mercer know the name of Harkness's girlfriend, or
how she could be reached? Sorry, no.

Tolliver then returned to the Seventeenth and explained the problem to Dennis Calligan. But Calligan was not eager to permit any further probing by an investigator from the DA's Office, friend or no
friend. His attitude was that the McKenzie homicide was open and shut.
The victim and the perpetrator were both dead, and his detectives had
discovered nothing to suggest a connection with any other case, including Whitacre.

When Ben reached his desk late on a warm afternoon, he found it
awash in paper. Most of the stuff he just pushed aside, glancing only at
his phone messages. Two were of interest to him: one from Lincoln
Whitacre, the other from Dr. Stein.

He called Whitacre first. That would be the more difficult of the
two; better to face up to it.

As Tolliver had expected, Whitacre was hoping to learn of some
progress. When he came on the line he was contrite, explaining that he
didn't want to interrupt Ben's work. But he said that not knowing was
deeply disturbing to him and Enid.

"It's as if we're unable to have her rest in peace," he said. "Even
after the funeral, we don't feel it's really over."

"I understand," Tolliver said. "But at the moment, I have nothing
to report. You know I'm doing everything I can, Linc. I can only ask you
to be patient."

"Yes, of course."

Actually a lot had been happening since the last time they'd
talked, but Ben wasn't about to go into it. There was no point in doing
so until he had something solid, and he didn't feel he was anywhere
near that. He told Whitacre to give his best to Enid and hung up.

Then he called Stein.

"I've got some news for you," the psychiatrist said. "I FedExed the
capsule you gave me down to my friends at St. Elizabeth's, and they did
an analysis. They also gave me a report on the Whitacre woman's blood
serology."

"What did they find?"

"One of the drugs in Whitacre's blood and the substance in the capsule were the same compound. It was an antidepressant, just as your police lab told you. This one was similar in chemical structure to Prozac, although it was much more powerful. In fact, it was capable of blocking the reuptake not only of serotonin but also of two other neurotransmitters at the same time: norepinephrine and dopamine. It was also combined with another type of antidepressant, which your lab didn't pick up."

"What was the second one?"

"At first, they were unable to identify it. They ran tests for a long list of drugs currently in use, and none of the results were positive. So then they began looking for something more esoteric. They finally got a hit, and what they found was a TCA."

"Which is what?"

"A TCA is a tricyclic. Neuroscientists call such compounds 'dirty drugs,' because they can produce very damaging side effects, including brain hemorrhage. Any responsible psychopharmacologist would tell you such a drug shouldn't be used at all. The term *tricyclic* comes from their having three carbon rings in their chemical structure. Amitriptyline is a TCA; so is desipramine. They're dangerous enough when used alone, but when taken together with a substance like the first one, the combination can be devastating."

"What effect would that have?"

"It would be like setting off a bomb in the neural pathways. It could completely disrupt brain function. The results would have been disastrous."

"Good Lord. And that's the stuff that was prescribed for Whitacre?"

"Apparently, yes. One of these drugs would have acted as a kind of amplifier on the other. The first one could increase the blood concentration of the tricyclic by as much as twenty times. Taking them in combination would short-circuit the brain cells in ways that no one could predict. And along with whatever other terrible effects they might have, the drugs would have been highly addictive."

"Could they make somebody psychotic?"

"Absolutely. The neurons would be damaged beyond repair. It's hard to imagine anything more destructive."

"And what if someone had been psychotic to begin with, before they began taking them?"

"It would have been even worse, if that's possible."

"Then why would a doctor prescribe them? Wouldn't he have known how much harm they could do?"

"In my judgment, he must have. As to why he did, you tell me, Lieutenant."

71

Flo Dallure had a truly wonderful body, Drang thought. That was one aspect of her charms he never failed to appreciate. Even now, when he was lying beside her totally spent, it was pleasant just to be close to the lush breasts, the full hips, and the rounded buttocks. He could feel her warm skin pressing against him, still moist from their exertions.

There had been a time, he thought, when he would have responded once more, when he would have found the energy to take her again, perhaps in some more imaginative way.

But that was a while ago, and his interests and his needs had changed somewhat, now that he'd developed the ultimate power that mind control represented. Now he not only dominated her; he *owned* her. Simply by voicing an order, he could make her do anything he wished.

Perhaps as a result, he'd found himself growing increasingly bored with Flo of late. Her unfailing compliance with his demands was no longer as pleasing to him as it had been. In a sense, it was like having taught a puppy tricks. He could call on her to do anything at any time, and she would perform as commanded. No surprises. Perhaps that was part of the problem.

At the same time, he reminded himself, her new personality had been conceived entirely by him. She was what she was because that was how he'd programmed her. Therefore, if she was beginning to pall on him, he could always rework her in some new fashion, along some different line. He'd give that some thought, because it definitely was true: variety did provide a certain spice. Especially with women.

Of course, like any other contrivance, she was also dispensable. If he wanted to develop a new subject, the range of choices was virtually unlimited. But for the time being, Flo would be useful to him, and not merely for sexual reasons.

Beside him, she moved her position slightly. Her fingertips drifted over him, teasing the hairs on his belly. Her voice was soft and throaty. "What would you like me to do now, Doctor?"

"Nothing," he said. "Lie still."

The stroking ceased, and after that, the only sounds were of her steady breathing.

Drang could think more clearly when his desires had been satisfied. And like a chess master, he was always thinking several moves ahead of his present situation.

"Flo?"

"Yes, Doctor?"

"I'm going away, and I want you to come with me. You'd like that, wouldn't you?"

"Yes, I would."

"How much cash do you have in your bank account?"

"I think it's about twenty-two thousand in checking, and around eighty thousand or so in my money-market account."

"Very good. Tomorrow morning, I want you to withdraw all the money from your money-market account, and twenty thousand of your balance in checking. Have the bank give it all to you in cash. Then tomorrow afternoon, when you come for treatment, bring the money with you. Is that clear?"

"Yes, Doctor. I'm to bring everything that's in the money market and twenty thousand from checking, all in cash."

"That's correct. Also, bring your passport. Is it up-to-date?"

"Yes. I got it two years ago, when my husband and I went to France on vacation."

"Very well."

"Should I pack my bags?"

"No, that won't be necessary. I'm not ready for us to leave just yet. I'll tell you when to pack."

"All right."

"Anyway, I may decide to buy you a complete new wardrobe when we get there. And then you wouldn't need to bring anything, would you?"

"No, I wouldn't need anything."

"You understand everything you're to do?"

"Yes, Doctor. I understand."

"Excellent. Now get up and put your clothes on. I'll see you tomorrow."

He watched her leave the room, thinking about what he had to accomplish next. Then he left his office and went up the winding staircase to his study.

72

The voice in the receiver said, "Ben, it's Ed Flynn."

Tolliver could hear the excitement in Flynn's tone. "Hya, Ed. What's up?"

"We brought in Arturo Sanchez, the witness that saw the Hudson Street stabbing? We showed him the photos, and he says it's the same guy."

"Is he sure?"

"He says he's positive. You remember he got a good look at him. The guy walked under a streetlight after he stuck a knife in the victim. Arturo says there's no way he could forget that face."

"What about the other witnesses—the couple who also saw it?"

"They'll be coming in, too. I wanted to get to you right away with what Sanchez told us."

"Okay, Ed. Thanks, that's great."

"You said the guy in the photos is the same one that did the psychiatrist in the Waldorf?"

"Correct. And maybe he did your other one, too."

"How does he connect to the Whitacre case?"

"Can't tell you that yet. But I'll let you know as soon as I can. Call me after you show the photographs to the other witnesses, will you?"

"Will do."

Ben hung up. Then he rose from his desk and left the room, walking across the open area where other members of the unit were working. He went into Fred Logan's office.

The captain was sitting at his desk, busy with a stack of papers. He looked at Tolliver. "What's doing?"

"You better get Norman Krantz in here right away."

"Why, what've you got?"

"A break in Whitacre. But we're gonna need a prosecutor."

Logan snatched up the phone, and minutes later, Krantz entered the office. He was in shirtsleeves, as usual. And he was wearing his red suspenders and mopping his face with a handkerchief.

When he saw Ben, Krantz said, "Uh-oh. This looks like trouble."

"You mean, this looks like I was right," Tolliver said. "Sit down, counselor. See if you can tell me I don't have probable cause this time."

Krantz dropped into a chair, but Ben remained standing as he quickly summarized what he'd uncovered over the past few days, ending with a recap of his phone conversation with Ed Flynn.

"That's sensational," Logan said. "It's a breakthrough."

Tolliver turned to the prosecutor. "Now do I get my fucking court order?"

Krantz shifted in his seat. "I don't know."

Ben felt heat come up into his face. "What the hell do you mean, you don't know? You telling me we still don't have enough evidence to look at Drang's records?"

"I'm telling you I'm not as confident as you are that a judge would issue a warrant."

"Jesus Christ. Didn't you hear what I've been telling you?"

"Don't get your balls in an uproar," Krantz said. "Look at what's real, and what isn't. Okay, so the drugs in the Whitacre woman's blood were the same as in a capsule that was in Harkness's apartment. However, that information comes from a source other than your own department's lab, which means it's not an official finding. And by the way, have you checked on whether Harkness's body had been autopsied yet?"

"Yeah, I did check. It hasn't been."

"Okay, so we have no evidence that he actually took the stuff, right?"

"Yeah, but—"

Krantz raised a hand, palm up. "Listen to me, will you? That's point one. Point two brings up another problem."

"Which is?"

"Which is, it's fine about the photos. I'll grant you that. Now Flynn's got witnesses who can identify Harkness as the man also responsible for this other homicide, the one on Hudson Street. If all the witnesses agree, that is."

Logan spoke up. "Good for our unit, too. We'd get some of the credit."

"Okay," Krantz went on, "but as far as your key issue there is concerned—that this Dr. Drang was treating both Whitacre and Harkness—where's the proof?"

"You got a point," Logan said.

"Bullshit," Ben spat. "It's one of the reasons I want those records."

Krantz again waved a hand. "I realize that. But what you don't have is grounds for ordering Drang to turn them over. New York State law is very specific about probable cause for issuing a warrant. It says you have to show that the material sought is directly related to criminal activity. You have no evidence of that, Lieutenant. Even if it's proven beyond question that both Whitacre and Harkness were taking the same drugs, you can't prove they were prescribed by Drang. Keep in mind, you're dealing with the Fourth Amendment here."

"Holy God."

"Then there's your theory on why Harkness wanted all that cash you say he was spending. How can you be sure he was paying a psychiatrist with it—and especially the same one Whitacre was seeing? Maybe the answer is that he was sucking the money up his nose. The capsules already indicate he was a druggie, so why isn't that a possibility?"

Tolliver slammed his fist down on Logan's desk. "Because I know that fucking shrink is behind this, that's why. I'm telling you, Harkness and Whitacre were both his patients. He was feeding them that shit, and that's why they went crazy and killed people."

Krantz was wiping his face with the handkerchief again. "And that's what you're gonna put in your affidavit? What you've got, Lieutenant, is mostly a theory. On that basis, a magistrate is gonna say, sure, here's your order? Think about it."

"I have thought about it."

"All right, then think about this. Suppose somehow we do get an order and it turns out you're wrong. And suppose the media gets hold of it. Imagine what they'd do with the story. You know what would happen then? I'm sure you do, but let me say it. Your Dr. Drang would sue the hell out of the city, and you know what? He'd win. How do we look then?"

There was a moment's silence in the room. Then Logan said, "He's right, Ben. The DA would have your ass for breakfast."

Tolliver didn't bother to answer that. Apparently the captain had already decided where to put the blame if anything went wrong.

Nevertheless, Ben gave Krantz one more shot. "Okay, look. I'll admit a lot of this is supposition on my part. But even so, there are just too many things here that point to Drang, including that beef he had in the same jewelry shop where Whitacre did the shootings."

"We've been over that," Krantz said.

"So what you're saying is that you can't get an order. Is that right?"

"No, it's not right. I said I'm not as confident as you are. But I'll tell you what, Lieutenant. You write your affidavit, and I'll take the request to a judge. I'll do my level best to get a signed warrant ordering the doctor to turn over his records."

Again there was silence. Then Tolliver said, "You know, counselor, you're not a bad guy after all."

"Tell that to my mother," Krantz said. He got up from his chair and left the office, wiping his face with the handkerchief.

73

Jonas Drang went into his study and closed the door. Spring was really here at last, and the outside air had become almost pleasant. Too bad the weather wasn't always like this. Summer would arrive soon, bringing with it the oppressive heat and humidity that settled over Manhattan like a damp shroud. Not that it mattered; he'd be gone by then. He opened the window and breathed deeply.

What he inhaled bore the unmistakable stench of the city: mixed odors of cooking food and exhaust fumes and overripe garbage, overlaid with the stink of hydrogen sulfide wafting off the river. He slammed the window shut and went to his desk, rubbing his nose in disgust.

Once he left here, he doubted very much that he'd ever return—especially in light of recent events. He'd solved his problems in brilliant fashion, but it made no sense to push his luck. The sudden appearance of Harkness's girlfriend had been out of the blue. He didn't need any more surprises like that one.

Of course, he still had to settle with the officious cop. That was a top priority. But handling it would be a pleasure. Amusing, even.

After that, he'd say good-bye to New York forever. Opening a drawer to the desk, he got out a folder containing the papers pertaining to his move and began reviewing them.

First off, there was the latest fax from his banker in Zurich concerning the villa he was buying. The villa was in Kreuzlingen, on the shore of Lake Constance. The closing was to take place immediately; that was one of the stipulations in the purchase agreement and it had been accepted by the seller.

It would be pleasant to experience life there, wouldn't it? He pictured himself sitting on his lakeside terrace on a spring evening, sipping brandy and enjoying the view. The air would be pristine and sharp, as clear as the crystal of his snifter. Nothing like the reeking fumes you were forced to breathe in New York.

Next he looked at another fax, this one from Chemical Bank, confirming that his funds had been wire-transferred to Zurich. Only a few thousand remained, and once he was in Switzerland, the account here would be closed. His securities had been sent as well, to a Swiss broker who would be handling his investments. Things were moving along nicely.

Rising from his chair, he went to the dry sink and poured himself several ounces of cognac, sniffing the fragrance and then rolling a mouthful over his tongue before swallowing it. The villa in Kreuzlingen had a fine wine cellar, with temperature and humidity controls, and a capacity of more than a hundred cases, over a thousand bottles. Stocking it would be a pleasure; he'd go to the Rhone Valley to buy his Burgundies, and then to Bordeaux. But he'd have nothing from the Loire; the wines made there were for peasants.

He returned to his desk, and as he sat down, a knock sounded at the door. That would be Anna, telling him she was finished with her task of settling his household accounts and taking care of the last few petty details. "Come in."

She opened the door and stepped into the room, looking as dour as ever, he thought. And as ugly. She was wearing her dark hair in her usual fashion, parted in the middle and tied back in a bun, and she had on a brown woolen dress that was much too wintery for this time of year. Also, it fit her like a sack. Which in her case might have been a blessing; she had the body of a bear.

She clasped her hands in front of her, speaking in her heavily accented English. "I'm done, Doctor. Everything is in good order. All the summaries are on my desk, if you want to go over any of them with me."

He flicked a hand dismissively. "No, no. I'm sure they're all fine. There really wasn't much left, but I'm grateful for your diligence. You've been very dependable."

"Thank you."

He'd already let his housekeeper go; now it was time to dismiss Anna, as well. "I hate saying good-bye, so I won't dwell on it." He opened another drawer in the desk and took out an envelope. Handing it to her, he said, "Your salary's in here, and I've added something extra as a gift for you, a gesture of thanks for your good work."

She continued to stand there, her bovine features as sullen as ever.

"Well go on, open it," Drang said.

"All right." She turned back the flap of the envelope and peered inside at the thick sheaf of bills. "It looks like a lot of money."

God, but she was dense. "It is a lot, Anna. But that's because I greatly value all the help you've given me. Aren't you going to count it?"

"Yes." She withdrew the bills and laid the envelope on the desk, then went through the stack with her thick fingers. When she finished, she glanced up at him and one corner of her mouth lifted in a smile. "Thank you," she said.

"You're quite welcome."

She put the money into a pocket in her dress. "But it's not enough."

For an instant, he wasn't sure he'd understood her. "What did you say?"

"I said it's not enough. It isn't enough money."

This was astonishing. She'd never talked back to him before this. In fact, she'd never displayed the slightest hint of discontent, let alone rebelled at anything he'd ordered her to do. What had gotten into the blockhead?

Anna answered his unasked question. "I know all about you— what you've been doing."

"What I've been doing? What are you talking about?"

The cynical smile stayed in place. "You had two patients that never should have been allowed to go out on the street. When you treated them, they got worse. They should have been in a hospital. They went out and they killed people. It was your fault. You knew what they would do."

Drang became conscious of his mouth going dry, of acid churning in his belly. Yet he gave no outward sign that her accusations bothered him. Instead, he acted bemused, as if a pet monkey had suddenly learned to speak. "That's absurd."

"No it's not, Doctor. I know a lot more, too. Mrs. Dallure? Every day when you take her in your office downstairs, you screw her on the couch. She pays you a thousand dollars a week, and for that she gets screwed by you. Just like the other one. And plenty before that."

Jonas Drang certainly would not allow himself to be pushed around by some mutinous servant. His tone grew harsh. "Anna, what you're saying is disgraceful. You could get yourself in a lot of trouble by making these wild charges."

"Not as much trouble as you."

"No? Let me remind you that you're an illegal alien—a Bulgarian who has no lawful right to be in this country. I could report you to the immigration officials."

"So what? You do that, we both lose. But you're the one who loses the most. All they can do is deport me. You would go to jail."

He gaped at her. And thought of the detective who'd been dogging him. The cop would be fascinated to hear her story. God*damn* this oafish sow.

As if reading his mind, she said, "Maybe I should talk to that policeman, the one that came to the house. Lieutenant Tolliver, right?"

Drang felt a surge of anger. There was no question that she could put him in considerable jeopardy. In fact, she could ruin him.

She returned his gaze steadily. "Well, Doctor? You going to give me what I want, or not?"

His brows knitted in a deep frown. He sat back in his chair and glanced away, bringing the tips of his fingers together and tapping them slowly, as if giving her question careful consideration.

At last he said, "Perhaps we can work something out."

74

Anna continued to stand before Drang's desk, wearing the knowing smile. Her expression had become intensely irritating to him, but he gave no indication of that.

Nor did he reveal what he was actually thinking. "What do you want?" he asked.

"I told you what I want. Money. Real money. Not some little piece of shit in an envelope."

He nodded. "How much?"

"I want twenty thousand dollars now, in cash. You got cash, plenty of it. I know, because the patients pay me. And I know why many pay cash, too. So you can cheat the government."

"Twenty thousand dollars."

"Twenty thousand *now*. More later."

"Later?"

"The first of every month, you send me twenty thousand dollars. From your bank in Zurich. I know about that, too."

The filthy bitch, he thought. She must have been reading the faxes. Probably she'd also been listening in on his phone calls, monitoring them on an extension. The stinking, filthy bitch.

She cocked her head. "So come on, Doctor—what about it? We got an agreement here?"

Drang pressed his lips together. His instinct was to beat her face in and then break her neck. But that might not be so easy. She was as burly as a truck driver, and obviously on guard.

A course of action formed in his mind. But he mustn't appear too eager, mustn't give himself away. "Frankly," he said, "I'm amazed by all this. Simply amazed."

"You shouldn't be, somebody who does the things you do."

He shook his head sadly, while with his right hand he carefully opened the bottom drawer of his desk, out of her line of sight. His collection of offbeat drugs was in there, the strange compounds that had caused excitement in the medical community for a time and then had faded as they proved less than effective or, in some cases, deadly.

Tucked in among them was the vial of cyanide capsules.

The problem was to keep her from seeing what he was doing. He couldn't glance down at the labels, as much as he wanted to. Instead, he'd have to go entirely by feel. And he'd better not make a mistake.

"So?" she said. "What's your answer?"

"I don't know. I'm thinking about it." The vial was squat, he remembered, about two inches high. Unfortunately, there were also a number of similar ones in the drawer.

"Tell me now, Doctor. Or I go to the police."

"You win. I'll give you the money."

The crooked smile widened. "Good."

Her confidence had risen, he saw. Now that she'd spit out her tawdry demands and he'd appeared to acquiesce, she was emboldened. What would the pig do now—ask for more?

Of course she would. "There's something else I want, too," she said. "One of the paintings in the foyer. The Braque? I want that."

He pretended to be shocked. "Good Lord, Anna. That's a very valuable piece of art." Stalling her while his hand sought the small plastic cylinder.

"Sure it is. What do you think, I'm stupid? That's why I want it. You won't miss it; you can buy another one. For your fancy villa in Kreuzlingen."

At this, he again felt a rush of anger. How much more did she know?

Again guessing his thoughts, she said slyly, "There's other things I know about, too."

The vial was a tiny bit smaller than the others, and it had a distinctive raised cap. Ah, there it was—he'd found it! He was careful, however, to keep his expression impassive. "Such as what? What other things?"

"Never mind, Doctor. I know them. And that policeman, he would like to know, too."

"Stop threatening me, please. I've already agreed to your, ah, requests."

"Including the Braque?"

Gripping the vial, he pried off the cap with his thumb. He sighed. "Yes, including the Braque."

She bobbed her head once, obviously pleased that she'd prevailed.

"But how can I trust you," Drang asked, "to keep your end of the bargain?"

"Because my word is good. You know that."

He knew no such thing. Wasn't she demonstrating her dishonesty at this very moment? "Yes, that's true. As I said earlier, you've always been most dependable."

"While you took advantage."

Resentment-of-authority syndrome, he thought. Manifesting in envy and bitterness toward the one in charge. Hating him because he was more intelligent and more successful than she, blaming him for her own failings. He should have seen this coming.

She thrust out her chin. "So open the safe and give me my twenty thousand dollars."

Now it was already *her* twenty thousand dollars. "All right, Anna." He plucked one of the small globular capsules out of the vial and cupped it in the palm of his hand, then gently closed the drawer.

Getting to his feet, he stepped past the fireplace and went to the far end of the room. There was a marine painting on the wall, a James Buttersworth of a sloop under sail. He swung the painting back on its hinges, revealing the door of his safe.

With his left hand, he rotated the dial, calling up the combination from memory. When the tumblers had dropped into place, he opened the door and reached inside, withdrawing a packet of cash. Printed on the paper band was the amount, five thousand dollars.

Anna had followed him and was standing nearby. He handed her the packet, and turning back to the safe, he withdrew three more, identical to the first. He handed those to her as well, then closed the door of the safe and swung the painting back into place.

"Well," he said gravely, "I hope you're satisfied."

She stuffed the money into the pockets of her skirt, two bundles on each side. "We got a deal, yes."

"No further trouble?"

"Up to you. You send the money, no further trouble."

"Good, I want to be sure of that. And now that it's settled, I suppose we can part friends, can't we?"

"Friends?" She laughed, taking his entreaty as a further sign of weakness. "Sure, why not?"

"No reason at all. In fact, why don't we have a drink on it? We'll drink to the future, and to our new understanding. I'll pour you some cognac."

"Yeah, okay. But sit down. I'll get it for myself."

Damn it. He returned to his desk and settled into his chair, choking back his disappointment. Although he had to admit that for her to let him prepare the drink would have been too providential even to think about.

When she was seated across from him, she raised her snifter and extended it toward him, making no attempt to disguise the expression of triumph on her unsightly features. She was savoring the moment, he knew, reveling in having beaten him. Taking her revenge, enjoying the reversal of their roles. Now *she* was in charge here, and for her, that would be enjoyable indeed.

He picked up his snifter and touched the rim to hers, the Baccarat crystal ringing musically. They both drank.

"What are your plans?" he asked offhandedly. "Will you take a vacation?"

"I already made a booking on the *Royal Princess,* a ship that's going for a cruise in the Caribbean."

How unspeakably vulgar, he thought. A tub filled with used-car dealers and insurance salesmen, accompanied by their bleached-blond trollops. He would have expected her to go to one of those dumps in the Catskills, or to Atlantic City. The *Royal Princess* would be even worse. "That's wonderful, Anna. I'm sure you'll have fun."

"Oh, yeah. I never been on a cruise before." She was relaxed now, and that was good.

But suddenly, he became aware of a new problem: The heat from his hand had begun to melt the gelatin walls of the capsule. The surface was already sticky. He had to do something, and quickly.

"How long will you be gone?" he asked. With his other hand, he raised his snifter and drank off the rest of his cognac.

"Three weeks. I'm leaving Saturday."

"I see. You should have good weather at this time of year."

"I hope so."

He held out his snifter to her. "Pour me another swallow, would you please?"

"Sure." Without getting up, she turned and reached behind her for the bottle, lifting it from the dry sink.

As she did, Drang leaned forward and dropped the capsule into the few drops of brandy that remained in her glass. When she turned back, he had already assumed his previous position.

While she poured the amber liquid into his snifter, he said, "Please join me, won't you?"

She put the bottle down on the desk. "No, one's enough for me."

He felt sweat trickle from his armpits. "Oh, come now. I'm really trying to show you I have no hard feelings."

"Yeah?"

"I mean it. I've always liked you, Anna."

"Hmph."

"Please?"

"I guess it wouldn't hurt." She picked up the bottle and poured herself a hefty belt.

Drang shifted in his chair. "When you come back, will you be staying on at the same address? I want to be sure the checks reach you."

"Yes, the same."

"I've never seen your place. I gather you're happy with it?" He didn't give a damn whether she was or not; his purpose was to keep her talking, thereby giving the capsule time to dissolve.

"It's all right." She raised her snifter. "Maybe later sometime, I'll move to a better one."

Watching her, he held his breath. He was counting on the strong liquor to cover the cyanide's characteristic bitter almond taste. If it didn't, if she realized what he'd done . . .

She never blinked. Bringing the snifter to her lips, she swallowed the cognac in one determined gulp.

He smiled. "Splendid brandy, isn't it?"

"It's all right. I have to go now."

"What's your rush?" he said. "I'm enjoying our little chat, now that we've reached an understanding."

A look of puzzlement crept over her face, and he knew she was wondering what he was up to. Wondering why this crafty man was being so cordial to her, this crafty man she claimed to know so well.

She studied him, her head again cocked to one side. "Just don't forget what we agreed. You miss once, even one month payment, and I go right to the police."

"I won't forget, I promise you. In fact, I'll always remember just how this was resolved."

"Okay, good." She rose to her feet. "Good-bye, Doctor. I'll take the Braque with me."

Still smiling, Drang said, "I was thinking, it might be nice if I gave you a little going-away party. A send-off, as it were."

"If I want anything more from you," she said, "I'll tell you."

"As you wish."

She turned to leave, and at that moment, the first pangs hit her. She winced, and Drang watched with clinical interest as the symptoms became increasingly evident. Her mouth dropped open and she gasped for air, then began breathing rapidly. Grimacing, she bent over and gripped the back of her chair.

Hyperpnea, he thought. Accompanied by tachycardia and ventricular arrhythmia. That was because cyanide rapidly produced lactic acidosis, inhibiting oxygen extraction from the blood. The substance was wonderfully toxic; could kill in minutes. Even faster if inhaled. But in this instance, ingestion would have to do.

Anna's lips were drawn back and she was panting. Her eyes bulged as her gaze fastened on him in an instant of horrified understanding. She spat out some guttural bit of invective—a curse, he supposed, in Bulgarian—and then she fell to the floor, clutching her belly and groaning. Her legs thrashed and the cries grew louder, as if she was being tortured. The piteous shrieks reached a peak as the poison did its work.

Drang sipped his cognac absently, fascinated to observe the various phases that followed the initial onslaught of agony. As he watched, Anna vomited a brownish stream that dribbled down her chin. She bucked and writhed as the muscle spasms grew steadily deeper, and then she went into convulsions.

Shuddering, her eyes rolling back in her head and her mouth foaming, her body was wracked by violent paroxysms. She kicked and twitched until at last her limbs became rigid and she was still.

Afterward, Drang sat quietly for a long time. There was no sound in the room now except for the ticking of the antique Patek Philippe clock on his desk and the muffled rumble of the city that seeped through the cracks around the windows. Finally he rose and, carrying his glass, stepped over to where Anna's body lay, looking down at it dispassionately.

She'd made quite a mess. He'd have to clean it up himself, and wasn't that repugnant to contemplate?

But all's well that ends well. He gestured toward the inert form. "I told you I'd give you a send-off," he said.

Raising the snifter, he drained the last of the Rémy Martin. "Bon voyage, Anna."

75

Cathy Fennel drifted in and out of consciousness. She was cold and thirsty and her joints were stiff and she had a brutal headache. It felt as if a leather belt had been fastened around her skull, drawing tighter and tighter until she couldn't stand the pressure for another instant. She gritted her teeth and tried to cry out, but no sound came from her parched throat.

Then suddenly the pain abated, leaving her gasping for breath. She lay trembling and fatigued, grateful for the respite. But after a few moments, the belt began to tighten once more and the cycle was repeated.

In between the attacks, she wondered if she was having a nightmare, then decided she probably was. She was held fast in the grip of a hideous dream, and as hard as she tried, she couldn't wake up. She bit her lip until she tasted blood, but still she was unable to rouse herself.

Oddly, the dream seemed very real. She saw herself a prisoner in a dungeon, lying on her back in a tiny cell that had thin steel bars all around her. The dungeon was damp and dark and the walls were crudely built of large blocks of stone held together by mortar. The only illumination came from a lamp that stood on a table some distance from where she lay. With great effort, she managed to turn her head toward the light.

What she saw struck her as equally strange. A man was sitting at the table with his back to her. He was wearing a white coat and he was working at something in the lamplight. She could hear a whirring sound as he operated a tool.

After a time she became aware of another sound, as well. This one was high and squeaky, and for some moments she thought it was the chirping of a flock of birds. But that didn't make sense, either; no birds would be flying in a dungeon. It was hard to think straight, especially when every few moments the awful pain returned.

She moved her head once more, just enough so she could look in the direction the chirping sound was coming from. What she saw then was far stranger than the man at the table. And much more frightening.

There were rats here.

That was what was making the noise. It wasn't coming from birds, but from rats. They had long snouts and red eyes and they were only inches away from her. They were in cells as well, separated from hers only by the slim steel bars.

She cringed and tried to drag herself as far away from them as possible. But she hadn't the strength to do that, and even if she had, there was no room; the steel bars prevented her from making any but minimal movements.

The sounds increased in volume. The rats were making more noise now because they were excited. They were seeing her move and they were responding to that and it was making them frantic.

Some of them were standing up on their hind legs and gripping the bars of their cages with their front paws. They were squealing loudly, their noses twitching, mouths open, revealing the two long yellow teeth in their upper jaws.

As sluggish as her mind was, she could see that they were large muscular creatures, looking powerful in their greenish brown coats, their naked scaly tails waving and flickering behind them. Watching the rats return her gaze with openly savage belligerence sent a wave of terror washing over her.

Again she tried to call out, to yell for help. If only she could make the man at the table hear her, he would come to her aid. He'd rescue her, set her free and take her away from the rats that were straining to get at her with their dreadful teeth.

But still she was unable to make a sound. It was as if her vocal cords were frozen in her throat. Her head was pounding and her mouth was dry and it hurt even to breathe.

She thought then of the time when she was a child and had had a streptococcus infection. They'd taken her to the hospital in an ambulance and stuck needles in her. She'd been delirious, and the pain in her throat had been terrible then, as well. Much like what she was suffering now.

Except that then her mother had been with her and there was a kindly doctor, and the nurses had fussed over her. And there was TV and ice cream. The antibiotics had done their work quickly and she'd gone home after a day or two.

She wished she could go home now. She'd go home and Philip would be there and he wouldn't be angry with her any longer. Instead, he'd hold her in his arms and stroke her hair and tell her he loved her. She'd be warm and safe, and he'd bring her a cool drink and that would make her throat feel better, and the pain in her head would also be gone. She'd curl up in her bed and sleep for hours.

But she couldn't go home. She could hardly move.

Something had changed. She listened, realizing the rats were making a different noise. They were still chirping and squeaking, but they were making other sounds, as well. She looked at them and saw that they were gnawing at the bars and that was what she was hearing.

They were trying to get through the steel, trying to get at her.

Frantic with fear, she rolled her head over once more so that she could see the man at the table. Somehow she had to get his attention, had to let him know she needed help. If she couldn't call to him, perhaps she could move her hands or her feet and strike the bars and he'd become aware that she was here and in danger.

She tried desperately, but she couldn't force any other part of her body to respond. Only her head seemed to work. She could think, and she could move her head. No matter how terrible the pain, she had to make a sound with her voice. If she could do that, the man would rescue her.

She opened her mouth, conscious that her lips were cracked and her tongue was so thick and dry she couldn't free it from her palate. It was stuck there, as if it had been glued to the surrounding tissues.

And the headache was back. She closed her eyes, telling herself that no matter how bad it got, it wouldn't last. It would be fierce and it would get worse and it would threaten to render her unconscious, but then gradually it would recede.

Go on, she told herself, make an effort. Open your mouth wider. And get some air into your lungs—you'll need it.

She managed to force her lips farther apart, and that was when the man at the table shifted his position and she could see that he was working with a small electric saw. She remembered her father using one something like it in his workshop.

As she watched, the man put the saw down on the table, and then he lifted something away from whatever it was he was working on. He placed the part he'd cut away in an enamel dish, then picked up a scalpel. When he returned to the larger object, she saw that it was round in shape and held in place by viselike clamps mounted on the table.

Realization came to her then. The object that the man in the white coat was crouched over was a human head.

There was no torso attached to it; there was only the head, held firmly by the metal jaws. What he was doing now was removing the brain. He cut with the scalpel and then used an instrument that looked something like a ladle to scoop out a portion of the shiny gray cells. She could see them glistening in the lamplight.

She made a sound then, a long, piercing shriek that came boiling up out of her throat. It died in a choking rattle and she pulled more air into her lungs and screamed again. After that she lay sobbing, without the energy to cry out again, but unable to take her gaze away from the horrifying sight.

The man was looking at her. He seemed neither surprised nor upset at having been distracted from his ghoulish task. Instead, he smiled and put down his instruments. He got off the stool and walked toward her, and she could see that he had jet-black hair and dark eyes.

She knew then who he was. This was the doctor who had been treating Philip, the one she'd turned to when she'd been so worried. He was Dr. Drang, and Philip had seen him in his nightmares.

Now she was seeing him in a nightmare of her own.

76

Hold on to your hat," Norman Krantz said. "You're about to see a small miracle."

Tolliver looked up from his desk at the prosecutor, who was standing in the doorway of the tiny glass cubicle. "What is it, counselor?"

Krantz stepped into the office and dropped an envelope onto the desk. "Your court order. It forces Dr. Jonas Drang to turn over his records on Beth Whitacre and Philip Harkness."

Tolliver looked at the envelope and then at Krantz. "Praise the Lord."

"Sure. And while you're at it, you can also praise the Honorable Susan B. Fleischer. She had trepidations about this, too, but she also had the guts to sign the warrant."

"That's really great. I'd about given up on it."

"Yeah, I'll bet you had, Lieutenant. Anyhow, a few days wasn't bad—especially when I didn't think we could get one at all."

"No, I guess not. But listen, I really appreciate your help."

"A word of caution."

"Yes?"

"Everybody's kind of sticking their neck out on this, as you're aware. Therefore, you want to play this strictly by the book. Get the files on Whitacre and Harkness, and that's all. Don't touch anything involving the doctor's other patients, or anything to do with any other part of his professional or personal life. Clear?"

"Clear."

"That's it, then. Bring the records back here and we'll go through them. If there's any evidence of wrongdoing on the doctor's part, we'll take proper action through this office."

"Okay, fine."

"Just don't give the shrink any grounds to claim police harassment or abuse of his rights."

"You know me, counselor."

"That's exactly why I made that little speech. Good luck, Lieutenant." He turned to leave the office.

"Hey, Norman?"

Krantz looked back. "Yeah?"

"Thanks."

77

Tolliver took the warrant out of the envelope and looked at it. Krantz was right; this was a small miracle. But Ben wasn't about to question his good fortune. He didn't know Judge Fleischer, but he did know he owed her a debt of gratitude. For now at least, she'd reaffirmed his faith in the criminal justice system.

It was getting late; otherwise he'd hit Drang with the order tonight. But better to do it first thing in the morning and not give the shrink something else to bitch about. As Krantz had said, this one had to be played strictly by the book.

The telephone rang. He answered it: "Lieutenant Tolliver."

The owner of the voice was female, her tone flat and uninflected. "Hello, Lieutenant. I have a message for you."

"Yeah? What is it?"

"The doctor asked me to tell you good-bye. He said he was sorry he couldn't wait around to see you go on making a fool of yourself."

"What? Who is this?"

But all he heard next was a click and then the dial tone.

He put the phone down.

The first thing that went through his head was that this was a gag of some kind, that the caller was one more nutball who got her kicks taunting the police. Cops got more than their share of freaky phone calls.

But she'd referred to the doctor. And the message was that he was saying good-bye?

Ben felt a growing sense of unease. No one in the general public would know about this aspect of what he was working on. Book or no book, something told him he'd better get up to Drang's tonight, serve the warrant and get those records.

Tucking the envelope into his pocket, he left his office and went out to the elevator. As he rode down to the ground floor, his anxiety grew rapidly. He hurried from the building and jumped into the Lincoln.

On the way up to 80th Street, thunder rumbled, and fat raindrops hit the windshield. He found a parking spot two blocks from his destination, and when he got out of the car, the rain came down in torrents. He turned up the collar of his blazer and ran as fast as he could on legs that were still slightly gimpy, the downpour pelting him and stinging his eyes.

By the time he reached the tall stone house he was soaked to the skin and his shoes were squishing with each step. He went up the steps and rang the bell.

The place was dark, and there was no response. He rang again and again, but no one answered the bell. The house remained silent.

Goddamn it. Could the call have been legitimate—the shrink had skipped? Had the warrant arrived too late?

Whatever, there was no advantage in remaining where he was, standing out here like a dummy with the rain beating on him. He turned to leave, and with a sense of futility, he reached back and grabbed the door handle.

To his surprise, the latch gave and the door swung open. He hesitated only a second, and then he turned and stepped into the dark foyer, closing the door against the driving rain. At least he was out of the storm. Water was running off him in rivulets.

The hallway was pitch-black. There had to be a switch in here somewhere, probably near the door. He groped for one, and after a moment, he found it. But when he flipped the toggle, there was no answering illumination; the foyer remained darker than the inside of a boot.

What was this—had the electricity been turned off? If so, why? The ominous feeling became more intense. It looked as if his suspicion was true; the doctor had gone, and as a parting shot, he had indeed made a fool of him. Tolliver felt like kicking himself.

Nevertheless, he was here now, and he wished he had some light so he could look around. That would be another breach of the rules, because the order gave him no right to conduct a search. But what the hell.

The trouble was, he couldn't see a thing. A flashlight would be a big help, but he had little chance of finding a store open where he could buy one. And besides, he didn't relish the thought of wandering around in the rain. Outside, the storm continued to pelt the slate roof and the face of the building, the thick walls muffling the sound of the downpour.

Then he remembered the minilight attached to his key chain. He got out the tiny gadget and pressed the button. The beam provided only a weak glow, but it was better than nothing.

There was no furniture in the foyer but a settle and two chairs. He seemed to remember seeing paintings when he was here the first time, but now the walls were bare.

There was a door on his left. He opened it and saw that it was a small office, probably that of Drang's assistant. He peered into the cramped space. In the dim light, the furnishings appeared stark and unused.

Stepping inside, he picked up the telephone from the desk and held the receiver to his ear. It was dead. He put the instrument back down and tried the fax. That was out as well, but of course it would be, without electric power.

The conviction that he'd gotten here too late grew deeper. Moving to one of the filing cabinets, he tried the top drawer and found it unlocked. He pulled it open and saw that the drawer was empty. So was the one below and the one below that. A quick check revealed that the drawers in the other cabinets were empty as well; whatever file folders had been in them earlier were gone.

Tolliver felt a sinking sensation in the pit of his stomach. His worst fears were being confirmed; Drang had disappeared and had taken the records with him. Outside New York, the court order would be useless.

Not only that, but tracking the shrink would dredge up more problems. Drang hadn't been charged with a crime, hadn't even been declared a material witness. There would be no way Ben could induce any of the medical boards to help locate him.

And now, just by being here in this house, Tolliver was not only ignoring NYPD procedures; he was violating the law. Christ, what a mess this had turned out to be.

He went into the doctor's office next. His eyes had adjusted to the darkness, and even in the puny beam cast by the penlight, he could make out the shapes of the furnishings clearly. The tables and chairs cast odd shadows in the gloom, and the heavy drapes were drawn tightly across the windows.

This room had the same strangely antiseptic feeling as the last time he'd seen it, bland and unlived in, like a hotel room. But now there were no paintings on the walls in here, either.

Looking about, he noticed a cabinet near the head of the leather couch. He stepped over to it and opened the drawers. There was nothing in any of them, but by this time, he would have been surprised if there had been.

As he stood there, he spotted another detail that was different. The bookcases still held volumes, but not nearly as many as he recalled seeing earlier. As least two-thirds of the books were missing, maybe more.

It wasn't hard to deduce what Drang had considered important when he departed, and what he hadn't. The doctor had taken the records and certain books and some art and personal possessions with him, but he'd left behind just about everything else.

There was a door recessed in the wall holding the bookcases. Ben opened it and found himself looking into a bathroom. It was a small area, with only a sink and a toilet and a stall shower, but strangely, all four of the walls were lined with mirrors. He stepped out and closed the door.

So now what? Outside, the storm continued; he could hear the rain lashing the windows, beating on the roof and the stout walls, and he had no desire to go back into it. Instead, he'd stay in here and go on nosing around.

Leaving the doctor's office, he went through the halls to the back of the house, where he found himself in a large high-ceilinged kitchen. All the appliances were outsized: a black stove flanked by surfaces covered in Dutch tiles, a towering refrigerator and a freezer, both clad in stainless steel and big enough to walk into. A profusion of copper pots and pans hung from racks overhead, and a rack of knives was attached to the wall. The equipment loomed grotesquely, casting long shadows.

Double doors led into a pantry. He pushed them open and poked his tiny light inside, finding nothing on the shelves. And the cupboard was bare, he thought. Like everything else that would tell you somebody was living here. He shut the doors and turned away.

And at that moment, he heard a sound.

He froze, listening.

It might have been the creak and groan characteristic of an old house, or it might have been the wind rattling the shutters. Maybe it was rain pounding on the tiles and gushing through the gutters.

Or maybe it had been a footstep, treading on a wooden floor, somewhere above him.

Instinctively, he shifted the penlight to his left hand, reaching behind him with his right and slipping the Mauser from its holster. He stood stock-still and listened for a full two minutes, gripping the pistol.

But all he heard were the wind and the rain.

Finally, he relaxed, telling himself he was getting jumpy over nothing. Old houses could do that to you, particularly in a rainstorm. He snapped on the safety and put the weapon back into the holster. Then he resumed his search.

There were two small bedrooms back here, probably servants' quarters, each with a tiny bathroom. Closet doors were standing open in the bedrooms, revealing nothing but a few wire hangers on the racks.

Retracing his steps, he went back into the foyer, then through the door at the end of the hallway. Ahead of him, a staircase rose against the wall. Going over to it, he saw that the stairs wound all the way up, giving access to each of the three floors above this one. Cautiously, he went up the treads, hearing them creak in protest under his weight.

On the second floor was a large sitting room, furnished in antiques of mahogany and cherry, with Persian rugs underfoot. This area had a good deal more charm than what he'd seen downstairs, although it appeared to be no more lived in than any of the others. As on the first level, the windows were covered by heavy draperies, and the walls were just as naked as all the others.

There was also a spacious dining room on this floor. The table and chairs were again mahogany, the cushions of the chairs covered in dark green leather. A crystal chandelier was suspended from the ceiling, and there were crystal candle sconces on the walls. A hunt board stood on one side of the room, and on the side opposite was a chest with an ornate mirror above it. Someone sitting at the head of the table would be facing the mirror.

Looking around, he saw that just off the dining room was a serving pantry, equipped with a dumbwaiter that connected the facility to the kitchen. A door in the hallway led into a lavatory, this one containing only one mirror, over the sink. There were no other rooms on the floor.

He climbed the stairs once more, and on the next level he found four bedrooms, each elaborately decorated with Victorian furniture. One, larger than the others, was apparently the master, and he examined its contents carefully. The room held an intricately carved four-poster bed with a lace canopy, along with a bureau and a chest of drawers, all of them massive and remarkably ugly. The closet and the drawers were empty.

The other rooms on the floor were furnished in the same style, but on a smaller scale. He inspected each of them, always with the same result. After that, he made his way to the top floor.

Up here, the noise of the storm was much more discernible, the rain beating a tattoo on the thick slate tiles of the roof. The thunder had died away, however, leaving only the pounding rain in its wake. He turned away from the stairs and opened the first door he came to.

Apparently this space had been used for storage. It was filled with odds and ends: old pieces of furniture, a trunk filled with moldy clothing, boxes of dishes and a dressmaker's dummy, stacks of old newspapers and magazines, and various other bits of junk, all of it covered with a thick layer of dust.

Going back into the hall, he tried the door on the opposite side of the stairway.

The room he entered now ran across the front of the house and featured dormer windows and a stone fireplace. The windows were shuttered tight and he could hear the rain beating against the wood. This might have been used as another sitting room, he thought, or perhaps as a study. Or both.

The furnishings in here weren't merely old but also battered. There was an ancient desk with a leather top, and a well-worn leather swivel chair behind it. Even before he inspected them, he knew the drawers in the desk would contain nothing. The bookcases had been stripped clean; not a single volume remained on the shelves.

There was also a dry sink made of well-worn pine, the wood a deep honey color. It stood against the wall just across from the desk, near the fireplace. Probably had been used as a bar, he thought.

As he was about to leave, he noticed there was one other unusual feature in here. This was the only room he'd seen that had a picture on the wall. The painting hung at the far end of the area; it depicted a sailing ship in a heavy sea. Curious, he walked down to it for a closer look.

As he approached, he saw that the frame was mounted on the wall by a vertical hinge that ran down the left side. He swung the picture back, discovering that it concealed a wall safe. The door of the safe was ajar, and when he opened it, he found the narrow space empty.

And that was it. He'd been through every damn room in the house, and the only thing he'd accomplished was to leave puddles everywhere. His wet clothing had him thoroughly chilled, and his teeth were chattering. He'd hoped the downpour would have let up by now, but it continued its steady drumming, so he might as well sprint back to the car. He left the room and went down the winding staircase.

When he reached the ground floor, it occurred to him that the only area he hadn't seen was the cellar, if there was one. Old houses in Manhattan sometimes had them, sometimes didn't, because excavation often required blasting through solid rock. He looked around, then saw a door in the hallway he hadn't tried previously. He opened it and found himself looking into an empty closet.

So maybe there was no cellar here after all. He turned away, and then he remembered seeing another door, next to the kitchen. He hadn't tried that one, either. Reversing course, he made his way back down the hallway.

The beam from his penlight was growing weaker; in another minute or two, the batteries probably would fail altogether. As it was, he was barely able to make out the door he was looking for.

Feeling his way, taking one cautious step at a time, he finally picked it out. When he reached it, he grasped the knob with his free hand and opened the door. Ahead of him lay a steep flight of stairs leading down into yawning darkness.

The tiny light flickered, and he cursed it silently, thinking this was a hell of a time for it to give out. Groping around down there in the dark wouldn't be a very good idea. In fact, it would be stupid, because he was sure the cellar in this gloomy old building would be as devoid of any sign of Drang's whereabouts as the rest of the place. The thing to do now was to get out of here, run back to the car and drive himself to where dry clothes and hot coffee were available.

Again he heard the noise.

This time, there was no mistaking it; the sound was a footstep, somewhere on the floorboards behind him.

He spun around, at the same time dropping into a crouch and snaking the Mauser out of it holster. Holding the pistol out in front of him, he snapped off the safety and then swung the penlight back and forth, but the feeble beam did little to penetrate the murk. Squinting hard, he saw nothing but shadows.

At that instant, the house was suddenly flooded with brilliant light. Half-blinded by the glare, he blinked, and then his breath caught in his throat as he saw what was coming toward him.

It was an apparition—a nightmare in the form of a woman.

He recognized her at once as the one he'd seen leaving the house the first time he'd come here. Only now, she seemed subhuman. Her blond hair was standing out from her head, and her face was contorted in an expression of rage. Her eyes protruded from her head and her lips were drawn back over clenched teeth. She had on some kind of long white gown that made her seem all the more like a wraith.

As he stared at her in stunned surprise, the woman opened her mouth and let out an unearthly screech. At the same time, she raised her right hand and he saw that she was clutching a black object the size and shape of a soup can. Screaming, she ran toward him.

The first thing that went through Ben's mind was that what she was brandishing was a bomb. The second thing was that he was about to die.

He raised the Mauser and shot her in the chest.

She staggered but kept on coming. He fired again, and this time he hit her in the belly, causing her to double over. She dropped the cylinder and clutched her stomach with both hands, lifting her head and looking up at him with that terrible animallike grimace. Then she toppled to the floor.

A cloud rose from the black object, and immediately an acrid stench bit Tolliver's nostrils. He realized that what she'd been holding wasn't a bomb at all, but something just as deadly. It was a canister filled with gas.

He clamped his mouth shut and pinched his nose with his fingers, but it was already too late. A clawing sensation began somewhere in his chest and rose to his throat; his vision became blurred. He saw double images of the hallway and the woman's body with a pool of blood under it, everything garish in the bright light. Then the scene began to whirl, faster and faster, and he tried to move away, but he had no feeling in his arms or his legs and he was no long able to think clearly.

He was vaguely aware of falling, of tumbling over backward through the open door into the cellar. His head struck the stairs as he went bumping down them, but he couldn't feel that, either.

78

Tolliver's wrists burned and it hurt to breathe. Each time he sucked air into his lungs, it felt as if his ribs would crack. But the pain in his arms and his chest was nothing compared with the anguish in his head.

A low chuckle sounded. He forced his eyes open, and in the dim light, he saw Jonas Drang sitting close by, watching him.

He picked up another sound. On the other side of the room were cages filled with rats. The furry creatures were squealing with excitement.

Ben tried to move, and then realized he was sitting on a wooden chair and his wrists were tied behind him, the bonds so tight they were cutting into his flesh.

"Well, Lieutenant," Drang said. A small smile played at the corners of his mouth. "The game is over, and you've lost. What do you say now?"

Tolliver's voice was a hoarse croak. "I say untie me and give yourself up, fuckhead. I'll tell the judge you were cooperative."

Drang laughed. "At least you still have your sense of humor. My only regret is that I don't have time to use you in one of my experiments. It would be interesting to probe your mind. With a scalpel."

Ben looked around. In addition to the rat cages, there was a long white laboratory table with a single work lamp on it, emitting a narrow cone of light. Scattered pieces of apparatus were visible on the table: a retort and a rack of test tubes, jars and bottles, a small refrigerator. Against the wall beyond the table was a sink with a hose attached to a spigot, and beside that was a large vat of yellowish liquid. Cabinets were nearby, their doors standing open.

He swung his gaze back to the doctor. "If you run, you won't get far. My backup'll be here any second now. It'll go better for you if you cut me loose."

"Don't try to bluff me, Lieutenant. If you had others with you, they would have been here long ago. I thought you might come looking for me. You were acting out of anger and frustration, which always clouds one's judgment. You're even breaking the law by illegally entering a private residence. I find that comical, don't you?"

Ben winced. The hammering inside his head was making his nausea worse. He thought he might puke.

Drang noticed. "What is it—aftereffects of the gas? Trichloroethane will do that to you. But you needn't worry. The compound has no affinity for hemoglobin, and therefore does no lasting damage. It leaves no residue, either. Now that you've awakened from your little nap, you'll soon feel better. For the time being, that is. At least long enough for me to satisfy your curiosity."

"Curiosity about what, asshole?"

"For one thing, I know you're wondering why I didn't destroy you when you were unconscious. The answer is, you'll do that to yourself. In fact, you already have."

"What are you talking about?"

"It's rather simple, actually. Both my first attempts to kill you failed. So this time, I wanted to be sure my strategy would work. And that's what it's doing, perfectly."

Tolliver looked at him. "That wasn't you, was it, shooting at me on Tenth Street?"

"Of course not. It was one of my patients. The poor fellow took a very strong dislike to you."

"Philip Harkness."

"Precisely. It was also he who gave you that little car-warming. With my help, naturally."

"You made up that firebomb, and he put it in my car."

"Very good, Lieutenant. You're rather slow, but you do get there eventually."

"No wonder you were so surprised when I showed up here afterward."

"Yes. I was amazed, frankly, to see you. I still don't know how you lived through that fire. Altogether, you've been quite a nuisance, which is why it'll be a pleasure to dispose of you now. As far as the young lady you shot is concerned, she'd begun to bore me, as well. That's why I decided to get rid of both of you at the same time. I'm becoming an expert at that."

"Who is she?"

"That's not important. What is important is that you killed her. Which makes you a murderer, doesn't it?"

"You crazy bastard."

"Crazy? Hardly that, I assure you. But let me fill you in on what happens next. Before I make my departure, I'm going to arrange another surprise for you. Then after I've gone, I'll telephone the police and tell them I'm a neighbor and that I want to report a break-in at this house. When the police come to investigate, they'll find the lady, and they'll also find you. Or what's left of you. Sort of a *Romeo and Juliet* ending, as it were. And equally poetic, don't you think?"

"Stop playing with yourself. It won't work."

"Oh, but it will. A renegade cop breaks into a home and shoots an unarmed woman, then dies himself. What an embarrassment for your superiors. They'll fall all over themselves to cover it up as quickly as possible. I'll be out of the country by that time, but I may institute a lawsuit against the city anyway. Terrible example of police misusing their authority. Outrageous, in fact. Can't let such a thing go unpunished." The psychiatrist smiled. "Now do you see?"

"What I see is that I was right about you all along."

"Right? There is no right, Lieutenant. And no wrong. Only idiots like you think in such terms. While the fact is that in any form of animal life, including ours, there are only winners and losers. As I pointed out earlier, it's obvious which category you fall into. And which one I do."

"Listen, if you plead insanity, you could go to a hospital instead of prison."

"Now you're the one who's babbling like a madman. Hospital? Prison? You couldn't be more wrong. Where I'm actually going is to a place so beautiful that someone like you couldn't conceive of it. While I'm there, I'll go on with my work, and the rewards will be enormous. What do you think of that, Lieutenant?"

"I think you're a fruitcake."

Drang laughed again. "I must say, the notion that you could outwit me is even more absurd than your clumsy attempts to ransack this house. You see, I was following you as you went banging and bumping your way from one room to another. I was afraid you might fall and break your neck, which would deprive me of the satisfaction I'm enjoying now. Also, it would have prevented you from eliminating our blond friend."

"Why her?"

"I told you why; it was because she'd outlived her usefulness. Women are like brandy, you know. When you first try Courvoisier, for example, you're thrilled with the flavor. So you drink it regularly. But then over time, you become accustomed to it and it loses its appeal. Becomes rather mundane, in fact. So you switch to Hennessey, or Martell's, or whatever. Variety really does do wonders for the taste buds."

"She was one of your patients, wasn't she?"

"Yes, of course."

"Just like Harkness, and Beth Whitacre."

"Not quite. She was like them only to the extent that they were also my patients. But Whitacre and Harkness both had rather major shortcomings, as they demonstrated by their actions."

"Whitacre by killing those people in the jewelry store and then blowing her head off. And Harkness by murdering Dr. McKenzie and several others."

"You're correct, up to a point. But those events were inconsequential when measured against the work I've been doing."

"Just what is this work of yours?" Ben didn't care what it was. What he cared about was staying alive and finding a way to get out of the trap he was in.

The psychiatrist sat straighter in his chair, flushed with his self-importance. "My work, Lieutenant, is the achievement of a goal men have sought for literally thousands of years. What I've perfected is the implementation of mind control—the means by which to gain total mastery over the minds of other human beings. Can you imagine what that's worth in today's world? The military applications alone are staggering to think about. Through my methods, people can be programmed to act and think exactly as ordered. The heads of state in many countries would pay absolutely anything for this. Before long, I'll be incredibly rich. Then for the rest of my life, I'll live in luxury."

"Or in a rubber room."

"Nonsense. What you have to understand is that my procedures are far more productive than such crudities as torture, for example. That was employed in all ancient civilizations, and is to this day in many modern ones. But torture is only moderately effective, and eventually it destroys the subject. Also, I haven't succeeded through what has been called brainwashing, either. Those techniques were first developed by German scientists and later improved upon the Russians and the Chinese. But the methods were extremely primitive, and not very practical."

"You're doing it with drugs, aren't you?"

"Precisely." Drang smirked. "Better living through chemistry."

"What are the rats for?"

"Research. One phase of it, anyway. I was using them to test some of the compounds in vivo, and later I did neurological experiments with their ground-up brains cells. That's no longer necessary, however."

"Why isn't it?"

"Because now I've perfected a method of using human brains for the same tests. The results are much more reliable."

"You use *human* brains?"

"Don't look so shocked, Lieutenant. Even medical students learn anatomy by dissecting cadavers. What's the difference?"

"The cadavers are dead to begin with. Are cadavers what you work with?"

"No, but that's immaterial."

"Where did you get—" A picture suddenly formed in Tolliver's mind, a scene of an office devoid of any sign it had ever been occupied. "What happened to your assistant?"

Drang's eyes gleamed. "You do have *some* powers of detection, don't you? Or was that only a guess? No matter, you're correct. Anna volunteered to make the supreme sacrifice, and I made excellent use of her brain."

He gestured toward the long container of yellow fluid that stood against the far wall. "The rest of her disappeared in that vat of acid, which eliminated what people in your business refer to as the corpus delicti. No body, no evidence. But I was describing my methods and explaining the use of the drugs. Shall I go on, or are you no longer interested?"

"Go ahead."

"Very well. I'll define the steps in basic terms. The drugs inhibit the reuptake of neurotransmitters. Thus they prevent the brain from functioning in its former, normal way. Or abnormal, as the case might be. In a sense, they reorder the circuits, wipe the slate clean. Then I load in new information that I've devised to fit the situation and the patient. Unfortunately, my earlier attempts produced a few glitches."

"Meaning you broiled their brains."

"The drugs are extremely powerful, I'll admit. And dangerous, if not used correctly. For example, by causing the production of too much dopamine in the brain's limbic system, they can induce paranoia and sometimes catatonia. Or by impacting on the norepinephrine receptors in the locus ceruleus, they can produce terrifying delusions. Patients may hallucinate, feel they're being pursued by wild beasts. They may also have convulsions, or slip into a coma and die. And sometimes, as in the case of Whitacre, they commit suicide."

"And you call yourself a doctor?"

"On the other hand, when the compounds are used in proper amounts, the results can be quite satisfactory. Highly effective, in fact, when employed with my techniques and my skills. Unfortunately, my earlier experiments weren't always as successful as I would have liked them to be. But learning through trial and error is still the most effective scientific procedure."

"Whitacre and Harkness again."

"Whitacre was a mess. Did everything wrong. She was supposed to rob the jeweler, whom I personally disliked for reasons I won't go into."

And I know what they were, Tolliver thought. Aloud he said, "That's why she had the watch cap with her, wasn't it?"

"Yes, but she didn't put it on, as she'd been instructed. The whole thing was a kind of test, actually. I wanted to be sure I could direct a patient to perform an extremely risky task under pressure. I'd also programmed her mind so that if she failed, she never would have tied me to any of it. What I didn't foresee was that her brain circuits would send conflicting signals and she'd end up shooting the people in the store."

"Why did she kill herself?"

"I'll never know for sure, but I believe she realized what she'd done, and the enormity of her guilt overwhelmed her emotionally. So she shot herself."

Tolliver thought of the videotape, and the terrible expression of torment on the young woman's face when she shoved the barrel of the gun into her mouth and pulled the trigger. He stared at Drang. "You supplied the pistol, didn't you?"

The psychiatrist waved a hand impatiently. "Lieutenant, don't be tedious. As you're well aware, guns are as easy to buy in this city as drugs. And that is very, very easy. I supplied the pistol Harkness attempted to kill you with as well, of course."

"And the poisoned bullets."

"Certainly. Too bad he couldn't shoot straight. The merest scratch would have made it unnecessary for me to have to deal with you now. But Harkness's lack of dependability was just one more of his shortcomings. I was able to control him better than I had Whitacre, but that was in part because I was perfecting my techniques as I went along. Still, his psychotic episodes were what eventually convinced me he had to be terminated."

"And Dr. McKenzie along with him?"

"Right again. And good riddance."

"What did you have against McKenzie?"

"The man was a menace. Back when I was beginning my work, I wrote a paper on my theories and my experiments. It was early in my career, and I'll admit I made certain errors. At any rate, he went out of his way to ridicule me. Called me a charlatan, if you can imagine."

Ben could imagine.

"I vowed then," Drang continued, "that I'd retaliate. They say revenge is a dish best enjoyed cold, and there is a certain amount of truth in that. I had the pleasure of liquidating him, while he had no knowl-edge of who was behind it. On the other hand, I think it would have been more gratifying if he *had* known."

"And you got rid of Harkness at the same time."

The doctor smiled. "As I said, that's another technique I'm per-fecting, Lieutenant. This time, my opponent will know exactly who de-feated him, and how. Which is another reason why I'm explaining all this. In your case, my revenge will be complete."

"I still say you'll never get away with it."

"And you'll still be quite wrong. But unfortunately, you won't be alive to admit your mistake. And now we're going to put the final phase of my plan into action."

"We?"

"My protégé and I." He turned and spoke over his shoulder. "Come out here, please."

From out of the shadows behind Drang, a woman stepped for-ward. She was slender and well built, and she wore a blouse and a straight-cut skirt that showed off the curves of her body. Her brown hair fell to her shoulders, and her oval face was striking.

Ben recognized her at once. She looked just as she had in the pho-tos that had been in Harkness's apartment, except that instead of the carefree smile she'd been wearing then, her face was solemn. This was the missing Cathy, Harkness's girlfriend.

Her eyes were what struck him as odd. They were totally lacking in expression, as dull and lifeless as the glass orbs in a doll's head.

"Say hello to the lieutenant," Drang said.

Her voice was a monotone. "Hello, Lieutenant."

The psychiatrist turned back to Tolliver. "Lovely, isn't she? My new brand of cognac, fiery and delicious whenever I want her to be. I'll be taking her with me to that beautiful place I was telling you about, the one you'll never get to see. I think she'll be a delightful companion, don't you?"

Ben stared at her. It was like looking at a wax effigy.

Drang rose to his feet. "Now tell him good-bye."

"Good-bye, Lieutenant."

The psychiatrist held up a small device that resembled a TV remote. "This controls the gates to the cages. After we go upstairs, I'll open them. The rats have been highly stimulated by drugs, and they're also very hungry. Starved, in fact. So it won't take them long to decide where their next meal is coming from. By the time your fellow officers arrive, you'll be nothing but a pile of bones, picked clean. Of course, the forensics experts can use them to identify you. Or if that's too difficult, there's always your badge. And your pistol. The one you committed murder with."

"You lousy shit."

"There goes your anger again. Remember how I told you it can affect your judgment? You should learn to restrain yourself. Meantime, enjoy dinner with your friends."

Drang led the young woman to the stairs, sending her up ahead of him. When he neared the top of the steps, he paused and looked down at Tolliver. "Hope you don't mind, but I'm going to turn out the light. Mustn't waste electricity, you know."

He snapped a switch and the cellar instantly became a black pit. There was the sound of a door opening and slamming shut, and then Ben was alone in the darkness. Alone, except for the rats.

He strained against his bonds, but they wouldn't give. Shortly after that, other sounds reached his ears: a sharp *click,* followed by the scraping of metal against metal. Then the chittering and the squealing increased in volume as the animals discovered they were free.

79

Drang surveyed the hallway. The body of Flo Dallure lay facedown where it had fallen, in a pool of blood that had already become a viscous mass. Her blond hair was fanned out on the floor, and her mouth was frozen in an expression of her final agony. One sightless eye was visible, staring at nothing.

It would be interesting, he thought, to dissect her brain, to examine the changes the drugs had effected in the circuitry connecting the prefrontal cortex with the basal ganglia and the thalamus. But there was no time for that now. Nor would his plan permit such a procedure. Instead, it was vital that the investigating police find her exactly as she was, with the detective's bullets lodged in her corpse.

The pistol that had been used to kill her lay nearby, where Tolliver had dropped it. The weapon was a semiautomatic, compact and flat. It was rather small, and Drang thought it was curious that the detective hadn't carried something more powerful. Guns were the most phallic of all symbols, which was why criminals—and cops—preferred the largest and the mightiest they could lay hands on.

The psychiatrist turned to Cathy, who was standing motionless beside him. Again taking her hand, he led her down the hallway to his office, carefully skirting Tolliver's pistol and the body of the dead woman. Once inside, he motioned her to a chair. Leaving her sitting there, he went to the bookcases at the end of the room.

On the underside of one of the shelves was a switch. Drang pressed it, and a section of the bookcase swung around silently, revealing a shallow space that stretched to the ceiling. Inside were a black leather attaché case, a woman's handbag, also of black leather, two lightweight nylon travel bags, and two tan raincoats.

He took the attaché case from the space and carried it to a nearby table, laying the case on the surface and thumbing the combination locks. When they snapped open, he swung back the lid and began checking the contents of the case. He'd already gone over the items inside several times, but a lifetime as a scientist had ingrained in him certain indelible habits, and thoroughness was one of them.

First, the passports. His was in perfect order, of course. He looked through it anyway, then put it down. Cathy's was the one he wanted to be sure of. He picked that one up and opened the dark blue cover, studying each of the pages.

The passport had been issued to Florence Dallure. According to the stampings it had been used by her a number of times, to visit such cities as London, Paris, and Rome, and at the conclusion of each of those trips, she had been readmitted to the United States through the port of New York.

Flipping back to the first page, Drang lingered over the photograph mounted there. It was one he had taken himself, a head shot of Cathy

Fennel. He had removed Flo's photo and pasted on this one in its place. Then he had carefully faked the embossed seal that covered the photo.

If the passport was presented to a U.S. official, it would be spotted instantly as having been altered. But that was not a problem; it need only get past some clerk at check-in, and an officer in Zurich, and Drang knew they would hardly look at it. The passport was for one-way use only.

He returned the passport to the case and then looked through the folder containing the airline tickets. There were two of them, for first-class seats on a Swissair flight leaving from JFK two hours from now, and the tickets were in order. He'd confirmed the reservations by telephone earlier in the day.

Next Drang got out the envelope containing cash and checked the bills. They added up to exactly one thousand U.S. dollars in fifties, twenties, and tens, plus another thousand in Swiss francs. In addition, the case held five thousand in traveler's checks.

The rest of the cash he'd had in the house, including the money Flo had brought him, had been wired to Zurich by his bank here in New York. The reason for the small amount he'd be taking with him now was so that he'd have money in the unlikely event of an emergency, but he didn't anticipate needing more than a fraction of it, and then mostly for tips. A car would be at the airport in Zurich to meet him; his lawyer had arranged for it.

In the case were also two other items, which were of great importance to him. One was a box of diskettes on which his records had been stored. The files that had been in Anna's office, he'd burned. The other thing in the case was the current volume of his hand-written journal.

A few minutes remained before it would be time to leave for the airport. But first, there was something else he wanted to be sure of. He turned and stepped back to where Cathy was sitting.

She seemed not to have moved a muscle since he'd left her there. Face composed, eyes blank, she sat with her hands folded on her lap. Again he thought it would be good to make further slight alterations in her personality; she was too quiet this way. Certainly he wouldn't want her to become voluble, but a touch more animation would be welcome. As it was, she resembled a statue more than a living woman.

There would be plenty of time to make such changes once they arrived at the villa.

"How are you?" he asked.

"Fine, Doctor."

"Are you looking forward to our trip?"

"Yes."

"That's good. What is your name?"

"My name is Florence Dallure."

"Excellent. Sit there for a few more minutes, Flo. And then we'll leave."

"Yes, Doctor."

80

At first, Tolliver thought he was imagining it, that his mind was deceiving him by conjuring up the kind of thoughts that sometimes are exaggerated by darkness.

But then he felt the unmistakable tugging at his pants leg.

Although he couldn't see them, he knew the rats could see him. They were nocturnal animals that hunted and scavenged and fed in the dark. They were testing him now, probing to see whether he would fight back. Instinctively he lashed out with his foot, felt his toe strike and heard the shrieks as the kick flung one or more of them away from him.

But then a moment later he felt the tugging again, more determined this time. Normally rats would run from man, scurrying away to slip silently into their filthy hiding places. But these creatures were hungry.

And that wasn't all. In addition to desperately craving food, the rats were crazy—as crazy as the psychiatrist himself, because of the drugs that had been pumped into them. Tolliver had known that as soon as he'd looked at them, when he'd come to after being knocked out by the gas. The rats had been highly agitated, squeaking and gripping the metal bars of their cages.

And now they were loose. They were running free over the cellar floor, seeking food in the darkness and willing to risk battle even with a man because they were crazy from the drugs and from the hunger that was driving them. The man was their enemy, but he was also something to eat.

For a minute or two, Ben thought his eyes would become accustomed to the dark. He opened them wide, hoping to admit more of whatever light remained down here. But it didn't work, because there was no light. The cellar was black as ink and sealed tight. From what he'd observed earlier, the only door was the one at the head of the stairs.

The rats were at him again. He kicked with both feet, sending several of them flying, yet an instant later they were swarming over his shoes once more, sniffing at him and tearing at his trouser legs with their razor-edged teeth. He went on kicking furiously, his toes colliding with the furry lumps, producing squeaks of anguish and fury.

This time, however, one of the more tenacious animals refused to let go. Ben felt a stinging pain as the rat bit deep into his calf, and it wasn't until he swung his leg wildly that he was able to dislodge the attacker.

After that came more bites. As soon as he succeeded in shaking one rat off him, another would take its place. The wounds were bleeding, and the smell of blood was sending the animals into a frenzy. They screeched and threw themselves onto him, yanking and ripping at him with their long, curved incisors.

He tried to stand, but that didn't work, either. He was bent over, his hands tied behind him, the chair bound to him by the ropes. The best he could do was to jump up and down in his wild efforts to free himself of the rats, and now he could feel blood streaming down his legs.

If this kept up, there would be no escape. Eventually the rats would understand that all they had to do was to avoid his thrashing legs. They'd leap onto his back and his shoulders and his head, aware that he couldn't strike them there.

When that happened, he'd be doomed. They'd shred his flesh, causing the blood to flow faster and faster, until the loss of it caused him to lose consciousness and fall to the cellar floor. Then Drang's prediction would come true: He'd be reduced to nothing but a pile of bones.

What a hell of a way to die.

He kicked and stomped, but already he sensed his attackers were growing bolder, and he felt himself growing weaker. A rat sprang onto his arm, and then he felt it run up onto his shoulder. An instant later, there was a jab of pain as the creature sank its teeth into his ear. He stumbled through the darkness until he ran into the wall, banging his head against the stones until the squealing beast fell away from him.

Do something, he thought. Do some fucking thing, and do it *now.* Or else you're dead.

If only his hands were free, he might at least have a chance. Yet as hard as he tried, he was unable to loosen the bonds. He struggled and wrenched at the ropes, but it was no good. It was as if his hands were encased in cement.

Another rat scampered up his back and bit his neck, and again the only way he succeeded in breaking the grip of its jaws was by crushing it against the wall. He was fighting for breath now, kicking at the rats, his chest heaving as sweat poured down him and mingled with the blood from his wounds.

His hands. How the fuck could he get his hands loose? If only he had something to cut the damn ropes with. If his hand were free, he could—

Glass! There was a glass retort on the lab table. He'd seen it when the light was on. Now where the hell was the table? He shuffled toward where he remembered seeing it, and was rewarded by bumping into the edge. Bending over, he felt with his chin along the surface, but he couldn't locate the retort. He ran his jaw back and forth, finding nothing.

Where was it? He'd seen the goddamn thing—he *knew* he had.

Frustrated to the point of madness himself, he slammed his arm against the edge of the table. And he heard something wobble in the darkness. Stretching himself out in that direction, he touched a smooth object with his face.

This was the retort—he had it! The glass receptacle was on a small stand that had rattled when he banged the table. More rats were clinging to his legs, biting them. He kicked and shook his legs with little effect and moved his face along the retort until he reached the narrow end, the neck. Then he gripped that part of the device in his teeth and dragged it to the edge of the table.

Turning around, he hit the retort with the back of the chair and was rewarded with the sound of breaking glass. He felt with his hands until he located the shattered bowl of the retort, then brought the ropes binding his wrists into contact with the jagged edge of the glass.

The position was torture, especially with a pack of starved rats trying to chew his flesh, but he knew this would be the only chance he'd get. He worked the ropes back and forth over the broken glass, gritting his teeth and kicking with one leg and then the other.

It took several minutes, but at last he felt the rope give way. He strained mightily, and an instant later, his hands came loose. Pulling himself away from the chair, he turned and grabbed it, using it to flail at the rats.

Another idea occurred to him. Dropping the chair, he beat several more of the animals away from him with his hands, then jumped up onto the table and felt around for the hose that was attached to the sink.

Rats hate water and fear it, and they will swim only as a last resort. He remembered learning that when he was a young patrolman and the cops had chased a burglar who used the ancient sewers under lower Manhattan as escape routes. Eventually they'd caught the guy, but Ben would never forget the stench in those reeking tunnels—nor the hordes of rats that scampered alongside the streams of sewage.

One end of the hose lay on the table. When he located it, he followed it by touch to the spigot in the sink and turned on the water full force. Then he played the spout from the hose down onto the floor.

There was an immediate reaction as the rats shrieked and fled from the strong jet of water. He poured gallons of it onto the shrilling creatures, then heard them scuttle away. Reaching down, he grabbed the chair and hauled it up onto the table to keep them from clambering up onto it. After that he let the water run for some minutes, until he was sure the floor was covered to a depth of several inches.

The rats had no choice now; he sprayed the walls of the cellar as well to keep them from climbing. They went on squealing; then Ben heard the clink of metal and he knew they were taking refuge atop their cages.

Again he felt around in the dark, this time until he located the work lamp. It was bolted to the table, and its long arm was mounted on a swivel and hinged so that the beam could be pointed in any direction.

He unscrewed the bulb and then forced the arm downward over the side of the table until the open socket was in the water.

Reaching back, he turned off the water. The cellar was quieter now, the only sound the chittering of the rats. He took a deep breath and tried not to think of the pain from the bloody bites on so many parts of his body. Then he jumped down from the table.

Slogging through the water that covered the floor, he ran to the stairs with hands outstretched, again feeling his way in the darkness. When he got to the steps, he started up them and was startled to find the treads covered with rats. Some of them jumped up onto his legs and bit him. He beat them away with his fists and kicked them into the water.

As soon as the steps were clear, he scrambled up to the top and felt for the light switch. He found it and flipped the switch on. There was a loud *sput!* and a flash of blue light as the water conducted a powerful jolt of electricity throughout the floor of the cellar and sent it flowing through the metal of the rat cages.

Ben turned the switch off and then the only sound in the darkness was that of his own tortured breathing.

81

It was time to go. A glance at his Rolex told Drang he was already cutting their departure for the airport closer than he'd intended.

They'd be going by taxi, because he'd decided taking a limo would be too risky; the companies that ran them kept logs, and he wanted no record of a car being sent to this address tonight for a pickup going to JFK. So instead, they'd walk over to Park and catch a cab—which was another reason to hurry.

He rose to his feet and snapped shut the locks on his case. He and Cathy—or *Flo,* he reminded himself—would put on the raincoats and each would carry one of the nylon travel bags. He'd taken one step toward the space where they were hanging when the lights blinked and he heard the strange sound.

There had been a certain amount of muffled commotion coming from the basement before this, but he'd more or less tuned it out. The noise had been made by that stupid cop as he struggled against the onslaught of the rats and finally succumbed, just as Drang had expected.

But this had been different.

Turning back, he made his way out of the room, on the way passing the young woman, who continued to sit motionless in her chair.

When he reached the end of the hallway, he sensed that something here had changed, as well. He stopped, taking in his surroundings. The blood that had seeped out from under Flo Dallure's body was darker now; as it dried, it had turned almost black. Except for that, however, her body looked exactly the same as it had been after she was shot. The detective's pistol, too, lay where it had fallen.

So then, what could have—

The *lights.*

The lights in the kitchen were out. He was positive they'd been on earlier; he remembered looking into the kitchen when he'd first come up from the cellar. Now the room was dark, and *that* was what was different.

Ah, he had it then. When the lights in his office had blinked a moment ago, it was because a fuse had blown. There were no circuit breakers in this old house, and the ancient wiring caused trouble from time to time.

Intent on checking out the problem, Drang stepped into the kitchen and opened the broom closet. The fuse box was in there, mounted on the wall. Alongside it was the master switch he'd thrown earlier to turn the lights back on. He swung back the door of the box and scanned the two vertical rows of fuses.

Sure enough, one of them had blown. The inscription next to the fuse indicated it had served the lights in the kitchen and also the outlets in the cellar.

What had caused it to blow? What was that meddling fool of a cop up to? There was no way the idiot could break his bonds—the rats would be feeding on what remained of him by now. *Wouldn't they?*

Suddenly, a sensation of angst passed through Drang's chest. It wouldn't do to have his plans go awry at this point, not on this very last day of his years in New York, when his efforts had brought him to such a triumphant climax.

Snatching open a drawer, he took out a carving knife and left the kitchen, stepping to the cellar door to listen.

Suddenly, there was a violent crash. The door gave way, splintering wood flying from it. Tolliver reeled into the hallway, his cheeks streaming blood.

Drang let out a roar of rage and swung the carving knife, aiming the point of the blade at the cop's face.

82

When Ben kicked the door open, the first thing he saw was Jonas Drang coming at him with a long-bladed knife. The doctor was like a rabid dog, eyes wild, teeth bared, a roar coming from deep in his throat. The blade flashed in the air as the point hurtled toward Tolliver's face.

Instinctively, Ben pulled his head back and at the same instant raised his arms in the cross-block cops used in defense against a knife attack. The move interrupted the swipe just enough to make the blade miss his chin by a millimeter. He felt a sharp sting as the point ripped the front of his shirt, leaving a bloody slash on his chest.

Drang's charge had the momentum of a runaway truck. It carried him headlong into Tolliver, and Ben went over backward down the cellar steps, the doctor grabbing at him with one hand and swinging the knife with the other.

The only light in the cellar was coming from the open doorway. As Tolliver bumped and banged his way down the stairs, Drang clung to him fiercely, struggling to stab him with the knife. Ben seized the doctor's knife hand and then drove his knee into Drang's groin, but the blow produced only a grunt.

The man was incredibly strong. Tolliver could never protect himself from the knife with a one-handed grip. He used his other hand as well, knowing that would leave him exposed to the fist Drang had free.

He was right; Drang clubbed him once, twice, three times, the short, powerful blows crashing against Ben's jaw and setting off bright flashes in his head, making him groggy. But as the two men hit the bottom of the steps and rolled into the ankle-deep water, Tolliver managed to shake the knife out of his assailant's hand. It flew off and landed with a splash.

Both men scrambled to their feet, and Drang landed another punch. Partially dazed from the pounding he'd taken, Ben slipped to one knee in the dirty water, and Drang kicked him in the face, catching him on the point of the chin.

The impact snapped Tolliver's head back and he sprawled sideways, twisting his neck to keep his mouth above water and struggling to regain his footing. At that moment, he could only vaguely discern the shadowy figure in front of him, but it was enough to see the doctor make a mistake.

Instead of kicking Ben into unconsciousness when he had the opportunity, Drang turned and grabbed the chair from the surface of the table where Tolliver had left it. He raised the chair high to smash it down onto his enemy's head.

Ben gathered himself and drove headlong into the other man's belly.

The blow knocked the wind out of Drang. He dropped the chair and stumbled backward.

And fell into the vat of acid.

The rank air in the cellar was rent with a long, piercing scream. In the dim light, Tolliver saw the psychiatrist try to drag himself out of the vat, gripping the sides and rising partway. He got as far as pulling himself into a sitting position, and even in the semidarkness, it was apparent that he was hideously burned. The corrosive fluid had blinded him and was eating into his flesh. Wisps of caustic vapor were coming off his skin.

Again Drang cried out, but this time the sound was like a howl from hell. He pawed at what remained of his eyes, and the cry trailed off to a pitiable whimper.

Then he fell back into the vat.

For a full minute, Tolliver stayed where he was, bent over, with his hands on his thighs, gasping for breath. He knew he had to get out of here, call for help. The telephone had been shut off; he'd have to go into the street.

But it was hard to get himself moving. He was exhausted and battered, weakened from the pounding he'd taken and from the bites. Yet he couldn't stay where he was, up to his shins in cold, filthy water with dead rats floating in it.

He'd also need antitetanus and rabies shots and a heavy dose of antibiotics. That realization was what roused him. He turned and, still breathing hard, slopped through the water to the stairs.

It hurt like hell to go up them; there wasn't a single part of his body that didn't ache. He took one step at a time, afraid that if he tried to rush it, he'd pass out. When he got to the top he paused again for a few moments, steadying himself. Then he stepped through the doorway into the hall.

Cathy Fennel was standing there, the same blank expression on her face, the same vacant stare in her eyes.

She was holding Ben's pistol, pointing it at his chest.

83

The young woman was standing perfectly still, the pistol rock-steady in her right hand as she fixed Tolliver with that strange unblinking stare. The only indication that she was a living human being was the pressure her finger was exerting on the trigger. He could see the pressure slowly increasing as he looked at her.

"Cathy," he said gently, "put the gun down."

Something flickered in the dull, expressionless eyes.

He tried again. "Cathy—"

Her voice was flat. "My name is Florence Dallure."

What the hell was this? Whatever it was, it had to have originated with Drang. Ben would sort that out later. If she didn't shoot him first, that is. For now, he had to figure out a way to get the pistol away from her, find a way to stay alive.

He took a half step forward. "Flo, put the gun down."

In answer, she brought her left hand up to join her right, holding the Mauser in a two-handed grip.

"It's all right, Flo," he said hastily, stepping back to where he'd been. "Everything's fine now."

She made no response, nor did she lower the pistol. It was weird, he thought, to be looking into the muzzle of your own gun. Knowing you'd carefully loaded the clip yourself with rounds of hollow-point that could blow a large hole through you. Out of the corner of his eye he could see the body of the dead blonde lying in its black pool of blood, gruesome evidence of the power packed in the compact semiautomatic.

"Flo—"

"Shut up."

His mouth was dry, and he could feel his pulse throbbing in his temples. He wished to Christ he could think of something to say to her that would make her back off.

An idea struck him. "Flo, Dr. Drang said to tell you to put the gun down."

That stopped her. She lowered the Mauser a half-inch. "Dr. Drang?"

"That's right. He said to put the gun down. On the floor."

She frowned. "No, You're trying to trick me." Raising the weapon once more, she pointed it at the dead center of Tolliver's chest.

There had to be some way of reaching her—some way of getting through whatever it was that Drang had implanted in her head. Maybe if he could think of something she cared about . . .

"Philip loved you," he said.

There was no mistaking it this time. Her eyes widened and she blinked twice, rapidly. "Philip?"

"He loved you. He loved you when you were Cathy. Don't you remember that? When you were Cathy, Philip loved you."

She winced, then shook her head as if to clear it, or to resist the struggle that had to be going on in her mind. "Where is he?" There was a tremor in her voice, and her eyes suddenly filled with tears.

"You miss Philip, don't you, Cathy?"

She didn't correct him now. Instead her shoulders slumped and then shook as she began to cry. The hand holding the Mauser fell to her side.

Ben stepped closer and took the pistol from her, returning it to the holster at the small of his back. He put his arms around her and she collapsed, weeping.

84

Ben took Cathy out onto the sidewalk, holding her close to him, knowing if he let go she'd fall. She was babbling now, interspersing her sobs with unintelligible fragments of speech. He stopped the first civilian who came along, waving his shield and telling the guy to call 911 in a hurry.

The pedestrian took one look at the tattered, bloody detective and the ranting woman and scurried off to find a telephone.

When police from the Nineteenth Precinct arrived in a patrol car, Tolliver told them there were bodies inside the house and to call homicide detectives and a crime scene unit. Then the cops put him and Cathy in the car and raced down Second Avenue to Bellevue, where she was admitted to the psychiatric unit and given sedatives. Tolliver told the admitting doctor what little he could about her, but he was close to falling down himself.

The doctor had him taken by wheelchair to the emergency room, ignoring Ben's protests that he could walk. Once there, he was stripped of his foul clothing and bathed, and his wounds were cleaned. After receiving a battery of shots, he was put to bed, where he sank into a deep, benzodiazepine-induced sleep.

By the next morning, the breaking story of the psychiatrist who had used mind-altering drugs to enslave patients inspired a wild scramble among the media. The three broadcast networks vied with one another and with CNN for approaches that ran from the predictable to the bizarre, and the tabloid shows went mad themselves with endless coverage.

In addition to the New York papers, every major metropolitan daily in the United States ran detailed stories, accompanied by heated editorials warning against abuses made possible by the new drugs. All the weekly news magazines ran articles, as did the gossipy monthlies.

Virtually everyone in journalism agreed it was one of the best stories since O.J.

Ben Tolliver and Captain Logan were given commendations by the police commissioner and the mayor in a ceremony at One Police Plaza, where they were flanked by a legion of brass. Tolliver alone credited Dr. Alan Stein with having provided invaluable help in the case.

Lincoln and Enid Whitacre held a second service for their daughter, a small private ceremony at St. Bartholomew's Church. Judy Corelli, Ken Patterson, and Ben Tolliver were the only nonfamily members invited to attend. Afterward, the Whitacres embraced Ben, telling them how grateful they were for what he'd done for them, and for Beth.

Tolliver had promised himself an extended vacation, but because of time pressure imposed by the need for him to return to work on the Rafella case, the trip was reduced to a weekend on Nantucket. He and Shelley stayed at the White Elephant, and although it rained most of the time, they seemed perfectly happy to remain alone together in their room.

Cathy Fennel bore indelible scars from her experience with Dr. Drang. After a lengthy period of psychotherapy at Bellevue, she was committed to Wingdale Hospital, where she remains at the present time. Opinions vary among psychiatrists who have examined and treated her, but all agree it is unlikely she will ever recover to the point where she can rejoin society.

At year's end, the makers of Prozac, Zoloft, Paxil and the other leading antidepressants all announced record growth in sales and earnings. Together, their gross volume exceeded $5 billion, a 25 percent increase over the previous year.